GRUMBY

GRUMBY

A Novel

ANDY KESSLER

RICHARD VIGILANTE BOOKS

PUBLISHED BY RICHARD VIGILANTE BOOKS

Copyright © 2010 by Andy Kessler

All Rights Reserved

www.richardvigilantebooks.com

RVB with the portrayal of a Labrador retriever in profile is a trademark
of Richard Vigilante Books

Book design by Charles Bork

Library of Congress Control Number: 2010930812

Applicable BISAC Codes:

FIC016000FICTION / Humorous

ISBN 9780982716328

PRINTED IN THE UNITED STATES OF AMERICA

10 9 8 7 6 5 4 3 2 1

First Edition

For my Mom, who has endured plenty of my tall tales

CONTENTS

PART V

EPILOGUE

PART I

SEEK and SCAN

6:19 a.m., January 2, on Interstate 15 outside of Barstow, California

The final thing I remember from last night is being lifted up horizontally and used as a device to pull the arms of four or five $1 slot machines at the same time. We had been doing this for a while and one or two of the machines would pay off each time, sparking another round of coin drops and someone else getting hoisted. Stupid pet tricks. It was probably four in the morning at the Tropicana and no one else was around, except the change-making matrons who were laughing more than we were. Nothing like an audience to make a dumb idea seem brilliant.

My head is killing me. It doesn't help that the sun is coming up behind us and reflecting right off the rearview mirror into my eyes. That's probably what woke me up, that and the foul smell of the two clowns passed out in the back seat next to me. My Oakleys are somewhere in the trunk, not that I remember packing or getting in the back of this dumpy rental car. Taurus? I lean forward and sure enough, there's the tacky script of Taurus imprinted right into the passenger side dash. Yep, there's Richie, my old high school hacking buddy, sprawled out in the front seat, with a small stream of spit dotting his more than wrinkled shirt. Reminds me why my head is hurting. I have the vaguest of memories of Richie with a dwindling pile of black $100 chips at a Blackjack table. He must have lost ten grand. I didn't even know he had that kind of money. My Visa card stopped working in the middle of the night, which pissed me off since I pay my bills and had barely used it.

Anyway, we're headed back to LA and some party in Venice Beach for the day and then I have to catch a flight back to the Bay Area. Why I agreed to go to Vegas for the weekend is beyond me. I hate the place, though we did have fun. We wasted $250 on a room we didn't use, and wait—it's coming back to me now, that's right, it was a West Coast bachelor party for one of my college buddies. OK, consciousness is starting to percolate back into the system.

John is driving, ripping through the desert at eighty-five miles an hour—I'm guessing, as all I can see are cars headed the other way out the passenger side windows. John must have heard me— he cranks the radio knob hard to the right, and the whole car begins to shake with the metallic scraping of extremely loud static. Charlie, in the middle back, poor sap, begins to twitch and Russ, on the far side, violently kicks the front seat, sending Richie jolting forward until his seat belt catches and begins to choke him. All worth the price of admission.

"Put something on or turn the damned thing off!" Charlie screams and throws a faint punch toward the driver's seat before leaning back and trying to fall back to sleep.

John hits the SEEK button and some foul pop music from the '70s starts pulsating through the factory-installed, no doubt cheap cardboard speakers on the back dash.

"Not this! Change it," I shout.

"Do it yourself," Richie says, a little too nonchalantly.

"What? You're sitting right there."

"Gloria Gaynor."

"Wha?"

"'(If You Want It), Do It Yourself,'" Gloria Gaynor."

"What the?"

Richie starts singing along with the lyrics.

"*Waitin' around for someone who can help you. Oh, someone who can help you find your way. Then if you think there's no one you can turn to. Well, there's someone just a lookin' glass away. Well, if you want it, go out and get it. You got to do it yourself, do-do-do, do it yourself . . .*"

"You really are a wussbag," Charlie barks, except it comes out "wooz-bage."

"Hey, I just happen to know my music."

"That's not music."

"Maybe not, but I can whip any one of your butts in SEEK and SCAN."

"I don't even know what that is, but you're on." So my power alley is sports trivia not music—but no way I'm caving to some Gloria Gaynor-loving weenie.

Richie leans over and hits the SEEK button on the radio. A few seconds later some smaltzy crooner starts blaring through the speakers.

I'm stumped. I have that Shazam thing on my iPhone that pulls up song names, but we're in the middle of the desert with no cell phone service. Plus, Shazam sucks. Way too slow.

No one else speaks up. Richie looks to the back seat with an evil smile.

"You'll remember."

"Never heard it before," I say.

"'Promise Me You'll Remember'? Harry Connick Jr.? '91? Godfather III? C'mon, what's the matter with you guys?"

"What's the matter with *us*?"

He starts singing again, "*We may not have tomorrow, it's not for us to say . . .*"

John reaches over and hits the SEEK button again. Thank God.

More static, then loud pounding bass and a screeching guitar start shaking the car.

I was in.

"This is about John's girlfriend. 'Whole Lotta Rosie.' AC/DC. *'Forty-two, thirty-nine, fifty-six, you could say she's got it all.'*" A little air guitar to finish it off until John, now pissed off at himself for waking us all up, hits the SEEK button again.

Mariachi.

No matter. Hot off my AC/DC connection, I jump right in.

"Mariachi Brothers. The song is 'Chew Pa Mees Waywos.'"

"What the hell are you saying?" Richie asks.

"Chew Pa Mees Waywos," I confidently repeat. It was a Spanish curse I had learned as a kid from someone I met from the Dominican Republic.

"That's not even Spanish," Richie insists.

"Absolutely, and it's the name of the song. Hit SEEK."

"No way," Richie shouts. "We need a ruling."

"From who?"

"Do you mean Huevos, as in Huevos Rancheros?"

"I might," I bluff.

"My eggs. Hmmm," Richie thinks out loud. "Chew pa. Chew. Are you saying Chupar?"

"Probably."

"Chupar mi huevos. You suck my eggs? That's the title?"

"Well, you suck MY eggs, you drooling, uh, tooling . . ." It's early and my comebacks are a little weak.

"No score," Richie declares. "And the rules are changing. From now on, we hit the SCAN button. That gives you about five seconds to get the song or move on along the dial." Richie is sounding more and more like a cheesy DJ I'd like to throw out the window.

"*Floating, falling, sweet intoxication! Touch me, trust me, savor each sensation!*"

Oh great. Show tunes.

"Anyone?" Richie asks with a big smile.

Several grunts are heard from my right. Then the radio starts scanning again.

"You lose," I declare. "No points."

"Allow me to sing it for you. *'Let the dream begin, let your darker side give in . . .'*"

The radio scans completely around the dial and settles in on the same station. In two-part harmony, Richie and the radio finish the song together: *"'. . . to the power of the music that I write, the power of the music of the night.' Phantom of the Opera.* Andrew Lloyd Webber. 1988. Pointage for me."

"There is something seriously wrong with you for even knowing this. Did you go to band camp as a child?" Charlie jumps in. Snickers all around.

"Plus, you're way too smug for six in the morning."

"It ain't smug if you're winning. Dizzy Dean. 1934," Richie claims.

"That's not even close to what Dizzy Dean said. Maybe Dean Martin," I yell.

Charlie jumps in. "Hey, Richie, remember at the start of the trip you told me to tell you if you were being an asshole?"

"Yeah?" Richie shrugs.

"Well, you're being an asshole."

"Yeah, well, I just know how to win. I'm a natural leader. The rest of you are followers. Next song please." The radio locks in— Christina Aguilera, apparently. Ugh. This goes on for what seems like forever and I get destroyed, although Richie is a touch embarrassed when he got both George Michael and Barry Manilow back to back, especially when Charlie keenly notes Richie's resemblance to both of them.

Still, I feel like an idiot losing to Richie. Not to mention that

I knew a lot of the songs but was usually late to chime in. With others, I had no clue. It's the same with game shows on TV; I know the answer, it's right there on the tip of my tongue, and then DING, some bell or buzzer goes off and I feel like an idiot.

I'm also still bothered by the sight of him losing big time at Blackjack. OK, it's not the losing that bothered me—it's that he had it to lose.

When it looks like everyone else is back asleep and John is focusing on driving, I sneak in a question. "Hey, Richie. You still doing that, uh, stuff we used to do?"

Richie pauses, turns slowly around to look at me. We lock eyes for a quick second, and then he drops his head, turns back to look out the front of the car. "Yeah, well, kinda."

Uh-oh.

• • •

It takes most of the week to recover from the mess known as Vegas. It takes even longer to get over losing to Richie at SEEK and SCAN. I can still picture that smug look on his face as he nailed song after song, from Fergie to Bing Crosby to Kraftwerk. I hate smug. Revenge is in order.

Don't get mad, get even. Was *that* Dizzy Dean? Ivana Trump?

The techie in me won out. Besides, this shouldn't be that hard to code.

I love gadgets. Always have, always will. I buy them when they come out, take them apart, search online for hacks that make them better. Everything is hackable. Phones, cameras, DIRECTV boxes, printers, games—it doesn't matter. For no good reason, the world is filled with programmers with nothing better to do on a Saturday night than to hack every possible device.

I really do love these guys.

Maybe because I saw myself in them. Maybe because I was them. Like every hacker, I have hope that one of my little projects will turn into something big. But even if it doesn't, the thrill comes from doing something no one else has done, no matter how stupid that "something" might be. It's the challenge. Useful isn't always the mother of invention for hackers; more like mother-in-law, perhaps.

I do a lot of digging. Faint memories from dozing off in the back of physics lectures started trickling in, at least what was written on the blackboard.

Music, once you get past the wailing guitars, which I rarely can, is just a bunch of frequencies mushed together. Like voices, it's got to have a unique signature. No two voices are the same, no two songs are the same, well, except all of Bachman Turner Overdrive.

Hmm. I lean back in my chair and stare at the ceiling. This always seems to help. The longer I stare the more thoughts fly through my head. After a few minutes, I start to see shapes dangling from the ceiling. At first it's a large multisided shape, spinning around. That broke into a few smaller shapes still spinning that also broke into more even smaller shapes until there was an army of shapes spinning around by the ceiling. And I could make out a label on each shape.

I sat up in my chair. If I could just break every song ever recorded into a bunch of small, few second clips, maybe break them down to some unique signature, then it's just a simple table lookup—heck, easier than a Google search, then I could spit out a song's title, artist, date, album, sales, whatever. Richie can eat my musical dust, and I could wipe that show-tune-singing-smarty-pants look right off his face.

After a bit of digging around, I find this great piece of code that does discrete Fourier transforms. More or less converts music into a sum of frequencies. I started running my AC/DC songs through it. I let the program run for a few seconds and end up with a ten-megabyte file filled with numbers. I could format the numbers into groups, but it still is a lot of data to do something with. What I really want is a signature, a simple number that I could then look up in a master file that would return a specific song.

The numbers aren't all that hairy. Say a million songs ever recorded. Each three and a half minutes long; let's round that to 200 seconds. The SCAN button jumps in five seconds. So I need a signature for say a series of overlapping three-second clips for each song. Still, that's just 200 or 250 million numbers—no big deal. It was the millions, maybe billions of numbers for all of the different frequencies that make up each second of music of each unique song that was quickly filling my terabyte drive.

The trick is to get the end result, that little signature, to be unique. I start digging through papers on the Web, lots of academic stuff that quickly puts me to sleep, a few commercial products but nothing I can use. Still, each of them talks about the same four things: pitch, brightness, loudness, and harmonicity. In effect, what makes each clip of music unique is its overall frequency, the balance of its highs and lows, and its beat. The American Bandstand indicator: it's got a good beat and you can dance to it; I give it a "95."

Actually, harmonicity is not only the beat. It's also how well, say, the singer or guitar player keeps up with the bass player and drummer. Slightly ahead or behind, it makes a difference and makes each performance unique.

Now I'm onto something. I can come up with a number for each of these characteristics. I try summing them, I try weighting them. Differences. It still ends up a huge load of data and I'm not getting unique numbers.

And then I trip across Burnside's lemma from 1897. At first I almost miss it, something to do with orbit counting used in some obscure group theory to find symmetries. Yeah, whatever. Turns out it's just what I need. Running my numbers through old Bill Burnside's formula (which he supposedly stole from a few other mathematicians—way to go) based on the relationship of all four musical characteristics and voilà, I get what seems like a unique number. In theory, anyway. Those guys back in 1897 didn't have the computer firepower I have, but then again they had a lot more time to think.

The Fourier software is painfully slow, even on my eight-core PC. Fortunately, I'm not the first one to want to run these transforms in real time. Every cell phone in existence has a digital signal processor, or DSP, that is built just to do this stuff. Mostly, it just digitizes your voice to some small packet that can be zipped around the cellular network, but I read that a few folks had hacked the DSP code to get higher quality sound out of their phones, that kind of stuff.

It takes about a week, but I find a hack to the latest Apple iPhone 4G that lets me play with the internal DSP chip. I use most of that code and add a bit of my own to control the DSP and get the right data off of it as inputs to my PC. Within a couple of days, I'm pumping music through the phone and moving tons of numbers into my PC, which run though a modified version of Burnside's lemma to output a unique number for each three-second clip. Slowly but surely, I start building a library of unique codes for all the stolen MP3s in my collection. I run down to Best Buy and buy another eight-core PC and a couple of terabyte drives. I hope that'll be enough.

TuneBuffoon

4:45 p.m., January 10, Palo Alto, California

This music project has become all-consuming—the real world will have to wait.

There will always be jobs out there. One of the benefits of living in Palo Alto is that almost every startup, every company eventually finds itself with a shortage of programmers—this place is the land of opportunity. Software schedules are written on rubber bands and I can usually land an assignment with a phone call or two. I never make all that much, journeyman wages really. It's no secret that the way to make money around here is to work for a hot startup and insist on stock options and cash in when they go public. Not all programmers do, but there is this "try and fail and try again" mentality in the water.

Unfortunately, I never really get the opportunity to work full time at one of these places. My background is a little offbeat—perhaps dicey is a better word. I'm not an engineer or comp sci major, so I usually get turned down even before the background check. So I code for hire on a semi-irregular basis. No biggie, I like the flexibility. Plus it gives me time to think. It's easy to get bogged down in loops and subroutines and remote calls and a lot more fun to think in the abstract, about big systems, servers, networks, routine tunneling, clouds. I think about that stuff a lot. You can't teach it, you have to live it.

Yeah, and I have this dumpy apartment in Palo Alto. I don't care; I don't need much. For the longest time, I only had a futon and some chairs I "borrowed" from the pool at the apartment complex, one fork, two spoons, and a coffee cup. Since landing a few decent gigs, I've slowly expanded my worldly possessions. A dining room table and a seriously fluffy pillowed couch both from IKEA. Broadband. Gadgets galore. That's all one really needs.

It takes forever, well, a couple of days, anyway, because I keep tinkering, but I finally get my 3,000-song collection of mostly heavy metal tunes cataloged, run through my iPhone's DSP, weighting pitch, harmonicity, and all that stuff. And I now have a not very large file with unique numbers for each short clip of each of these songs. I can hold the iPhone up to my speaker and like magic the song name and artist pops up in three seconds.

I write another piece of code that scrapes every Amazon page that sells CDs. It's not that hard to do, and what the heck, they are the world's largest store, or something like that, so I figure they have everything. Plus, they have the album artwork and even short clips, which might come in handy someday.

I set the output of the Amazon page scraping as an input into the BitTorrent file-sharing service and try to download as many songs as I can. I quickly give that up after just two days. My new terabyte drive, which I just added, is full.

Needing to pay the rent again, I take on a short consulting gig. Nothing hard. Fortunately, they all have big fat Internet connections, so I can download all day on my laptop at my client's office. It turns out to be too much of a good thing. One afternoon my client comes looking for me with yet another stupid question, wanders into his office, and overhears Barbra Streisand singing, "*People who need people are the luckiest people in the world.*" It will take a while for me to live that down.

I run the numbers. With the next several centuries of free time and way deep pockets, I can probably catalog any and all show tunes and one-hit wonders and every note Leonard Bernstein coaxed from the New York Philharmonic. Not enough time in the day.

I need help. We all need help. Fortunately we live in the first time in human history when we can all get all the help we want. Maybe there's a shortcut. I look into things like Gracenote and freedb, giant databases that tell you what album you are ripping by the number and length of tracks on the CD, but for what I need, they are basically worthless. Until I figure out how they stock them with data.

I want badly to get something, however crude, up and running to kick Richie's musical butt in SEEK and SCAN next weekend. Powerful motivation. But I sure as hell can't do it myself.

People who need people, indeed. It occurs to me that I'm not the only one who is audio-challenged, and maybe I can tap into that "nothing better to do on a Saturday night" crowd.

So I buy the Web address TuneBuffoon.com off of GoDaddy. com for $9.99 a year—a bargain. It doesn't take long to put up a simple Web page announcing an open source project in musicology.

The top of the page has a download button for my tune lookup program. A simple app for the iPhone that will listen to music and then pull up the song name and artist. Of course it only works with Metallica and UFO and Slayer and AC/DC and the Dead Kennedys, but it's a start.

Farther down the page are instructions on how to add songs from your own collection. First, there's an app to install on your iPhone that hacks the onboard DSP and another that sits on your PC or Mac that pulls the information generated by this code and uploads it back to TuneBuffon.com. Pretty simple.

Never mind that both programs completely take over your iPhone and PC and broadband connection churning and uploading information back to me. I want all the raw data, so I can tweak my algorithms and make sure I get a unique number. What works for Jimmy Page ought to work for Yo-Yo Ma and his violin, you'd think. Heck, Yo-Yo only has four strings—should be easier.

The site's up for a couple of days and I have exactly one download and two songs characterized. This isn't going well, especially since the songs were "I Love You," which threw me for a loop, and then "The Wheels on the Bus Go Round and Round." Yup, Barney the purple frickin' dinosaur. "You love me, we're a happy family, with a great big hug and a kiss from me to you." Yuck.

Not exactly what I had in mind, unless SEEK and SCAN somehow accidentally hits a PBS station. Still, it's a start. Beats doing it myself.

The weekend smackdown with Richie is approaching fast, so it's time to go big time. One night before crashing, I log onto Facebook and dig around until I find a group about music. iLike seems to be the most popular, so I put up a notice about my code and a pointer to TuneBuffon.

I search for cell phone hacks and stumble across one called Howard's Forum, HoFo as the locals like to call it. Under the iPhone forum, I put up a similar notice and then call it a night.

•　　•　　•

I wake up early the next morning and notice I have 250 emails from places like New Zealand, Estonia, Johannesburg, and Trenton. That's odd. I check TuneBuffoon's logs and have something like 6,000 hits, 2,200 downloads, and files from 1,500 unique songs. And it's just six-thirty in the morning.

The song count would have been higher but there was huge overlap—about one in ten of the files uploaded are for Soulja Boy. Jeez.

The emails are almost all requests for my source code and a few oddball remarks—that I am personally responsible for dumbing down music and did I know how to get in touch with Jon Bon Jovi. They must have pulled my email address off of the WHOIS database that lists all Web site owners and their contact info. I quickly pay GoDaddy another $25 to keep my information private.

In the meantime, this thing is spreading like wildfire. By lunchtime I've got 10,000 downloads, almost 25,000 by the end of the day. Thousands and then tens of thousands of songs get characterized. And it keeps growing and growing. I get a note from my Web hosting service that I'd have to pay an additional $25 a month for another ten gigabytes of storage and another five gigabits of bandwidth. Sure.

• • •

What is most remarkable is that this thing even works. I had swagged a guess at the weightings for my algorithm but for the most part it's right, spitting out unique numbers for each three-second clip. Every once in a while, the numbers aren't unique, and I'm not sure why. Two and sometimes three or four song names come up. Based on the number of songs I had so far, it seems like it's 99.44 percent accurate. About as pure as Ivory soap. But all you really have to do is wait another second or two for the next three-second clip to kick in and throw out the erroneous songs and narrow down to the right one. A little coding and I get the display to blink the multiple songs until the algorithm locks onto the right one. It's fun—kinda like a TV game show.

By the end of the week, I have almost 200,000 downloads and something like 150,000 unique songs coded and loaded. Has anyone ever grown anything quite that fast?

Plus it all fits on my phone and unlike Shazam or any of the other song identity apps, TuneBuffoon works without a data connection. Even if I'm stuck in a basement . . . or an elevator. Always wondered about elevator music.

Another weekend, another wedding. Richie's toast.

•   •   •

Before I leave my apartment, I download the latest file with info on those 150,000 songs onto my iPhone.

It's way too early on a Saturday morning and I'm on my way to Portland. Richie, in yet another rented Taurus, picks me up. Great. I get in the backseat and nonchalantly bring up SEEK and SCAN and how much fun it was last time but that I was hung over back then and now I think I'm ready. But this time, let's play for $100. Richie agrees in an instant. Cocky bastard starts going on about this being his power alley and no one can ever beat him at anything and he has been SEEK and SCAN champion since summer camp and I tell him he might not want to tout that last one too loudly.

It isn't even close. I kick his smug ass.

After he pays me with a crisp $100 bill, I tell him about TuneBuffoon and show him my iPhone displaying the songs on the radio. Richie is pissed.

"Ha!" I laugh right in his face.

•   •   •

I'm thinking how to incorporate movies into my app (hear some dialog, instantly know what movie it's from). But I get interrupted a few too many times by emails and then calls from my Web hosting company demanding I upgrade to a still bigger package and do something about all the bandwidth I'm sucking up from them.

They think they have problems? I'm buying huge hard drives,

so I can process all these files and update the song and now movie database. I now own a dozen iPhones and I'm bidding on eBay for another dozen or so. Time and money sucking away. I start digging around for a cheaper host. It seems that Estonia, of all places, has the cheapest rates. I'm about to change everything, move TuneBuffoon.com and all my files when the screen gets stuck. I hit the reload button and get an exclamation point in a yellow triangle and "Address Not Found." A little more digging and I figure out that Estonia's Internet has been taken down. That's weird.

And then it comes. The knock. *Darkness at Noon*. Really just a local police officer with a sheepish look on his face.

"Mr. Buffonte?"

"No."

"Sorry, I have a cease and desist and subpoena letter for a Turner Buffonte."

"Tune Buffoon?"

"Could be."

"Can I refuse it?"

"If you want to come down to the station and talk to my captain you can. But I was told not to leave unless I deliver this. Sorry."

"Any idea what it's about?"

"No clue. Never had to do anything like this. Usually just court hearing stuff."

I take the letter, go back inside—it's a certified letter from the RIAA, the recording industry cops, insisting that they have obtained the log files from my server and that I am involved with pirating music and subject to a $750 fine for each illegal download. If I don't take my service down, I could see my wages garnished, "ignore at your own peril," etc. Not having much wages, the joke is on them. It looks like a form letter, for God's sake. Plus, it's addressed to Mr. Tune Buffoon. I think I can ignore it without much peril.

Still, since I know I'm not actually stealing any music—the whole point of the unique code was to not have to deal with the humongous amount of data in the actual songs—I'm curious. I check and the log files seem to be corrupted. There are names of thousands of songs with the word "copied" next to them. What's that all about? I check my code and there's no way I generated those files.

•   •   •

Next morning I check the usage logs again. They seem legit. But something like 200 million copies of TuneBuffoon have been downloaded and as many song files uploaded to my servers. And this time, it's the master song file that's corrupted. Every song is tagged Harry Connick Jr., "Promise Me You'll Remember." There's an urgent message from my hosting company that I owe them $15,000 for bandwidth and storage fees. I quickly scan the files and every download is coming from the same IP address, the same location. What the?

I don't have that kind of money and plus my stupid Visa card still doesn't work.

I'm almost finished and my phone rings. The Caller ID reads Harry Connick. I pick up. A voice screams "Ha!"

It's Richie.

I'm speechless. Finally, I ask, "What are you doing, Richie?"

"Just screwing with you."

"Not funny, asshole."

"Visa card working?" Richie laughs.

"That was you?" I ask.

"Ha!"

"Turn it back on," I plead.

"Just admit I got the best of you," Richie says and hangs up.

View

Richie and I go way back.

We grew up together in the Bay Area. It had its moments. I wore shorts every day. Ate artichokes. Became a Metallica fan. Grew my hair long. Drove an old but dependable Mustang. And being surrounded by technology companies every day in industrial parks, on billboards, at electro-gasmic stores like Fry's, it was almost impossible not to become a techie.

I've been writing code since I was a teenager—can't remember the exact age. Richie would come over my house, and, being adolescents, we would try to figure out how to cause the most mischief while getting in the least amount of trouble. Richie was smaller than I was, and I was pretty slight, so it's not like we were going to shake down ten-year-olds for lunch money—we had to use our heads. It was always a contest of who could cause the biggest splash.

First, it was prank phone calls, which lasted a good six months. We mostly hit pizza places: "Can I talk to the guy who took my order last time?" "A large steam pizza please," "Could you put the crust on the inside?" that kind of stuff. Richie was king. He could do it with a straight face—I usually started laughing halfway in.

Once that thrill was gone, we moved on to email pranks. The easiest was a fake message from Amazon confirming an order for $1,200 worth of mechanics tools. All our friends got one. They figured out pretty quickly it was from us, so we needed a lot more email addresses. I went to see my high school guidance counselor and complained I wasn't getting announcement emails from the school. As she pulled up my info on the school computer system, I watched her type in her first initial and last name as a login and "pookie" as her password. It took Richie all of five minutes that afternoon to, uh, "harvest" the database of student emails. It was our first taste. Every kid on the football team and his parents got emails confirming they had signed up for a sexually transmitted disease awareness group. Sweet.

Our high school had a course in Web design—probably the easiest class after woodshop. In the back of the room, we set up a bunch of fake businesses online. I think our nationally syndicated pizza delivery service, pizza4u, still exists.

To do cool Web sites you really had to learn how to write code. At first it was pretty easy. We would just download pieces of code from existing Web sites that we liked and then customize them to do what we wanted. Soon we were writing code from scratch. There was no programming class in high school—go figure—so we bought programming guides, those O'Reilly books with funny furry animals on the cover and even a few Programming for Dummies books.

PHP, Python, Ruby on Rails, Java, Perl. Eventually we learned them all, each slightly different and good at one thing or another. I was like a sponge. Of course it was constant competition between us. I pulled an all-nighter once, perfecting a digital cockroach to crawl over Richie's screen and eat his text. He got me back by changing all my passwords to "dickspittle." I still don't know how he did that. So to get him back, I wrote a piece of code to crawl the Web and automatically post Richie's picture on every gay Web site it could find with the tag "pookie" and his email address. I think he still gets funny emails today.

From there I started playing with hardware. I liked to take gadgets apart to see how they worked, to see if I could write some code to make them do something else. Richie got into that for a while too.

Then we moved online to see how far each of us could go.

Eventually, we took the whole competitive thing a little too far.

•   •   •

Now I'm almost thirty, still in the Bay Area, still wear shorts every day, still write code. I'm hooked.

Look, I can't sit here and legitimately expound the virtues of sitting in front of a screen most of the day, muttering to oneself, chugging way too many 5-Hour Energy drinks, and being deficient in many of the most basic social skills.

But there is something about it, some attractor force, maybe even an addiction.

When you code, you get this feeling, a grip, a wicked sense of empowerment. Control. Man over machine. You not only bring the machine to life, you give it commands and it listens. People don't listen. You have to debate, persuade, negotiate, and make your case, and in the absence of that, grovel and beg. Coders don't beg. We command.

Once you figure out methods and objects and classes and procedure calls, you're the master. You want the screen to flash in turquoise spirals? Done. You want to prompt users to tell you their social security number? Done. You want to throw in a few jokes or Easter eggs for your own amusement? Done. Master Blaster.

But that trivializes it, in a way. The jokes are fun. But that's not what keeps us riveted. Does it save you time? It better. Save you from some hassle? Hope so. Does it do something that's impossible to do in real life? Now we're talking.

It wasn't very hard to write code to go out and look up almost everything I needed to pass a Western Civ test in high school. Why read the book when I could write code that would summarize all the trivia for me?

I hacked into a Garmin GPS to gain access to its point of interest database. I had just gotten a ticket, so I wanted Garmin to start reminding me where the red light traffic cameras were in our town. Turns out lots of people wanted that. The hack let thousands of Garmin users enter their own information into a huge national file. It was us against the authorities. We won.

For a while, I was part of a group that was hacking DIRECTV receivers to get them to quit blocking channels. I wanted to watch the *Late Show with David Letterman* at 8:30 p.m. in California when it ran on the East Coast rather than wait until 11:30. OK, my parents wouldn't let me stay up that late. With a bunch of coders I never met, we worked it out and for a few years we got every channel. Most houses had Pay-Per-View. We just had View. My rationalization: they were blasting their signals to my house, so they must want me to watch it. My parents didn't complain.

I hacked into our Wi-Fi router extending its range to work in the whole neighborhood. Did you know it could do that? The manufacturer dials back the capability. We liberated it. Did you know the difference between a $750 hearing aid and a $4,000 hearing aid is a piece of manufacturers' code that artificially cripples the $750 version. Is that right? Is that good? My dad hears real well now. I've hacked digital cameras and printers and toys and anything and everything with code in it. My car as well.

There is no better feeling of accomplishment. Nothing tops writing code that can do something hundreds or thousands of humanoids working together couldn't. You do it for yourself, but the real satisfaction is maybe thousands are using it to beat the system. There are just so many ways the world doesn't work. We . . . make . . . it work. Power to the people, or something.

It's not easy. Lots of trial and even more errors. But when you're done, and all that meticulous, unforgiving code pays off, it's really hard to describe the feeling. You walk on air for days. "I just saved the human race 2.7 billion hours of phone calls and $420 million in traffic tickets." Pretty cool.

Then the feeling wears off and you have to do it again.

So basically I write code that offloads all the annoying garbage I have to do in real life. My goal is to not stop until I've gotten rid of all of the crap. Maybe I'll walk on air for a week.

Then what? My head usually hurts trying to get my arms around it, but every once in a while inspiration hits. It's that sense of empowerment that seems to keep driving me.

•   •   •

In the meantime, I'm a coder for hire. Got to pay for In 'n Out Burgers somehow. Sometimes the jobs are interesting—code to scour the Web looking for the best interest rates for a finance firm or the cheapest parts for some manufacturer. Often they're dull. I can't tell you how many accounting programs I've customized for some screwy new regulation. My reputation is out there, and I've even been approached to write security code to prevent hackers from breaking in. I usually pass on those.

A job usually lasts a week or two and then I'm out scrounging around again.

It's not a bad life, I guess. But every programmer, every coder, every hacker I know harbors a secret hope that some piece of code he writes is going to hit it big, become indispensable, change the world.

Gotta have dreams.

Hack Furby

"Take him. Please. Just for a little bit. I'll owe you big time." It's Maria, my next-door neighbor. I've partied with her husband, Mark, who is some sort of doctor but don't know her quite as well. She's with her son, Mikey.

It's Friday night and I was hoping to tweak my code so no one, especially Richie, can make me look silly again. I decide to change the rules. To prevent freeloaders, you have to send me a music file before I email you the ever-growing master file that has the lookup table for every song characterized so far.

"But, wait. Where are you going?" I ask, as she shoves Mikey into the open door and then heads back down the walkway.

"Mark's working late. Our daughter has a play date and I'm out of here. Just out," she turns around and says in the most exasperated tone I have ever heard from her.

"And who is watching . . ."

"You."

"Isn't he hungry?"

"Fed."

"Dirty?

"Bathed."

"When will you . . . ?"

"Maybe never. Certainly after he's asleep. Bye." And with that, I hear her car fire up and tires squeal down the block. I like little kids, to a degree. But here I am with my neighbor's kid, barely three, and full of life—he seems like a handful.

What to do? *Call of Duty* seems out of the question. But so is sitting him in front of my twenty-two-inch monitor and letting him surf the Web for kiddie stuff. Young pups have already ruined a mouse or two of mine with melted chocolate and Nickelodeon green goo.

"What do you want to do?" I ask him.

"TV."

"No. Your mommy will kill me if I sit you in front of the boob tube. What else?"

"TV."

"Not gonna happen. What else do you do for fun around here?"

"Sing."

"OK, that oughta work." I start hunting around for some sort of player.

"You sing."

"Yeah, not my thing, buddy."

"Sssssiiinnnngggg . . . ," he begs.

"I ain't got no rhythm. I gave up singing long ago, scout." Tears start welling. Jeez. "How about you sing?"

"Raffi."

"What?"

"Raffi."

He pointed to his bag. Maybe it's some kind of toy. I open the bag and he reaches in and pulls out a CD of songs by Raffi, some guy who looks like a bagger at Trader Joe's. *Singable Songs*, it says. Fair enough. I drag out a CD player and pop in Raffi.

"The more we get together, together, together, the more . . ."

I have an immediate urge to run out of the room and stick my head in a bowl of ice water.

Still, Mikey has a huge smile on his face and remarkably sings along with Raffi. He keeps looking over at me and insistently yells, "Sing!"

". . . *down by the bay* . . . ," I sing, moving my head side to side as I plot revenge on this very sick Raffi dude.

I reach into the bag and the kid has got just about every toy ever invented. Jeez, when I was his age I had some Tinkertoys and blocks to hit my sister with. Mikey's like the "clowned" prince of Palo Alto, with a duffle bag filled with dinosaurs and Power Rangers and Godzillas and radio-controlled cars and SpongeBobs.

I have, I am often ashamed to admit, quite the toy collection myself nowadays. I open up my closet to see if I can find something fun. Mostly cool electronic stuff that I like—the Robosapien robot, the Pleo dinosaur, Squawkers McCaw, and FurReal Parrot that talk back to you—even the Furbys I had found on eBay, are all lined up neatly on the shelf of the closet. They all look a little dusty and neglected.

My mind drifts away from Raffi and back to the cop showing up at the door with a cease and desist order and hiring lawyers and I keep getting interrupted by Mikey tugging at my sleeve to sing along.

And then it hits me.

I get up and head toward the door.

"Where?" he asks.

"I'll be right back, I swear," I insist.

I run to my toolbox and grab a screwdriver, a pair of pliers, and wire snips. Never were three more devilish tools invented.

I grab one of the Furbys. Turning my back to the kid, I undo three small screws, pry the Furby open, and peel back the fur. Past the battery holder is a small speaker and a circuit board with three chips that must control a few tiny motors and a microphone and what looks like a light sensor.

I figure it shouldn't be that hard to hijack control of this thing.

The microphone and speaker are first. I construct a simple connector so that I can hook them up to whatever I want. On another trip outside the Raffi-fest room, this time insisting that I had to go potty, I do a quick search and find the Web site hackfurby.com and print out the pin outs of the three chips. From there, it's pretty easy to build a small USB connector that gets me at least electrical control of the chips. I can take over the memory space, meaning I can reprogram it at will.

The DSP on my iPhone can spit out pitch and harmonicity and all that, so I write a small routine for the iPhone that can make the Furby move its eyes and mouth along with the music. It's pretty crude, but, amazingly, it works OK.

Mikey puts on disc 3 of Raffi, who I now have plans to one day hunt down for revenge and inflict similar mental anguish on his soul. But now the Furby is totally into it, blinking its giant eyelids and opening and closing its beaklike mouth, even swaying side to side as Raffi belts out ". . . *and you'll play a tune and I'll play a tune in more and more wintry weather . . .*"

Mikey sings along and doesn't take his eyes off the Furby. The smile? Worth its weight in gold.

With Mikey occupied, I have time to do the final tweaking of TuneBuffoon. Do I feel guilty abandoning a small child to the care of Raffi and an animated bag of fur? Not even a little.

Meeta Shows Up

"Check it out." Richie tells me over an IRC, Internet Relay Chat channel.

"Check what out?" I type.

"Remember those boxes we broke and put rootkits on and datapipe.c?"

"I thought the spooks shut all those down," I say.

"Yeah, well, anyway, I kept operator status on a few. It's how I dumped all that crap on you, and, well, . . . I've been followed around online by someone and I figured out they're a bunch of Estonian hackers and they've been trying to backdoor my bots to shut me down, so I . . ."

"That was you?" Richie took down Estonia's Internet? "Are you crazy?"

"Probably. I still got it, don't I?" Richie seems to need a daily affirmation of his hacking prowess.

The doorbell at the front door of my tiny apartment buzzes. Someday I am going to have a place with a Winchester chime, but a weasely buzz goes with this dump.

"I gotta go," I type. "Richie, you need to lay off. It's not a contest." I close the channel.

It's pretty late for doorbells. The Feds? Another cop delivering a subpoena or here to cuff me and read me my rights?

I tidy up a bit, making sure nothing too incriminating is sitting out on my coffee table and walk slowly to the door. I open up to find a strangely dressed, dark olive-skinned fellow in Wrangler jeans, a Nike "Just Do It" T-shirt, wearing a pair of bright yellow and green-strapped Crocs. It's a very odd look, for a cop anyway, so I start laughing.

"May I be pleased to speak with you?"

"You delivering papers?" I ask.

"Oh no, I came to have tune talk."

"Huh?"

"Huh?" he asks back.

"Who are you?"

"Meeta. I have come to application with you."

"What?"

"I can increase your invention."

"You're not a cop?" I ask with squinted eyes.

"I would love a coppa Joe," he comes back with a big smile containing the brightest teeth I have seen in a while.

I'm still confused but nothing is on TV, and I haven't found a decent book to read in months, so I invite him in. He awkwardly shuffles his way in and sits down on my fluffy IKEA couch, sinking in deep and low, then tries to compensate by bending forward to keep his head level and facing me. I don't get too many visitors.

"OK, start from the beginning. Who are you and what brings you to my luxurious dumpy apartment?"

"I am Meeta. I come from outside near Mumbai," and then he hesitates. "I am nearest, uh, I move next to undergrad at IIT Delhi, you know it?"

"Sure, the MIT of India?"

"M . . . I . . . T?"

"Go on."

"So I write programs. Code. Hack. You know?"

I nod.

"Well, I have come to the U.S. to study silicon valleys and find fortune before returning home as a triumph."

"So why are you bothering me?"

"Well, I am little embarrassed. I have friend who knows how to back hack WHOIS, you know it?"

"Yes."

"And I ask him to back hack TuneBuffoon.com and I received your address, so I came to give you an application for a job. I know Linux, I know DSP, I know network protocol, I know C Plus Plus, I know Ruby on Rails, I know Python, I know . . ."

"OK, OK."

"And what I don't know I have fifty friends who know or they know someone who know and we can create just about anything in several days or two."

"Like what?"

"Well, I try your Tune code and I am amazed both how small and simple and exact it is. I have already written code to show album cover and lyrics. Here, let me show . . ."

Sure enough, on the screen of his iPhone is an album cover of Michael Jackson reclining in a black shirt and white jacket looking all sorts of normal and underneath words were scrolling across, "You know it's thriller, thriller night. You're fighting for your life inside a killer, thriller tonight."

"You did this?"

"Yesterday."

I walk over to the stereo, hit play on the iPod connected to it, crank the stereo up nice and loud, and walk back. I grab the iPhone from Meeta and goddam if a purple image of five lit head candles and the title *Deep Purple Burn* take up most of the screen, and scrolling across the bottom of the image is "the city's ablaze, the town's on fire, the woman's flames are reaching higher, we were fools, we called her a liar . . ."

"I looked through your original music file and made sure so-called Deep Purple was complete."

"Impressive," I say.

"Darth Vader compliment, with thanks to you."

"How . . . ," I start.

"I have already written code to automate image and lyric databases, but I want to write client code for display and interfacing."

"What el—"

"Words, music, script, video, search, dialog, triviation, reality augmentative."

"OK, OK, slow down. You want a Budweiser or something?"

"Uh . . . you have scotch?" Meeta asks sheepishly.

I do, and we end up draining the bottle and then everything else I have in my kitchen.

We talk and talk. I tell Meeta what I'm trying to do, beyond music. I have only a vague notion, so it's helpful to talk it out. Devices, servers in the cloud, a personal tool, video, voice recognition, huge databases of information. I go on and on.

"May I please say to you something?"

"Sure."

"Your code is best I have seen. Sleek, compact, direct, sexy."

"Sexy?"

"Where is your training?"

I hesitate. I don't want to get into it.

"UCLA," I say.

"Ah, yes, very famous."

"Uh-huh. I mostly figure out what I need on the fly. I look up lots of stuff in those O'Reilly coding books, with the . . ."

"With the funny animals, yes, I know them," Meeta nods violently.

"Mostly it's lots of, what's the best way I can put this, hands-on experience."

"Yes," Meeta says loudly. "Hands all over it."

We talk and talk. As Meeta sips his fourth or fifth scotch, he starts to slur. I've never heard someone slur in an Indian accent. I try to experience something new every day and this fills today's quota. "I have much hands-on." It came out "handzzzown." "Sometimes it is too much and I can have regrets."

"I hear you," I say.

"Yes, I must admit to possessing a past." *Pazzzzt.*

"Meeta, we all have a past." *Amen.*

We talk until about four in the morning when I finally stumble off to bed.

Eyes and Ears

I wake up around seven the next morning, I have a lot to get done, yet all I can do is curse myself for babbling all through the night and talking about possibilities with someone I have just met, don't have a clue of his background or capabilities or trustworthiness or even his last name, and I just unloaded everything I thought I would do with this invention. What a dope I am.

I stroll out to the kitchen to get something in my system. I dump whatever is in the fridge into a blender with some ice to make a smoothie. As my blender starts whirring, I hear a moan from the living room and some stirring on the couch. Buried under a pile of cushions of my man-eating couch is Meeta, looking worse for wear.

The words "need coffee" come from under the cushions.

I never could get rid of him. Thank God.

·   ·   ·

TuneBuffoon is running itself and the files keep getting larger and larger, now well into hundreds of thousands of unique songs. But in the cloudy aftermath of last night's conversation spilling my little techie heart out to Meeta, I find myself thinking about Furby.

The interface is simple. That's good.

The problem is that it's pretty basic stuff inside, a tiny microphone, tinny speaker, and a few servomotors. I need a little more horsepower than that. Luckily, there are about a dozen different chips available for low-end robotics and after a little digging around, I find exactly what I'm looking for—this little ARM9 controller chip that sucks up almost no power, can control all sorts of analog lines, and at $10 is about as much as I want to spend. Tons of ports to play with and someone has already ported LINUX onto it, meaning I have an entire operating system I can shove inside a little toy. A single USB cable comes out the back, mostly to download code.

Before long I have the Furby dancing around and singing just fine. But every time I look into its eyes, I have this creepy feeling it's staring back into mine. Maybe because it has those big eyes like Japanese anime characters or maybe I have been spending too much time playing with stupid electronic dolls and am slowly cracking up. No matter. It sparks the greatest idea.

I rummage around the Web until I find what I'm looking for and have two small CCD imagers overnighted to my home. These things are small. Maybe three-quarters of an inch deep cylinder and about as round as the Furby's eyes. I can pop out the eyeball and replace it with the imager. The new eyes are not as dilated as Speed Racer's, which solves the creepiness of being stared at. But now it watches like a Peeping Tom. Through the USB cable, I can download video of everything the Furby can see.

And hear, as it turns out. Built into each imager is a tiny microphone. So the Furby now has two eyes and two ears.

The Furby speaker is lame, cheaper than ones in old AM radios. I try to get the Furby to talk, and he tries, but all I get is this low rumble-mumble. Combine that with the big dilated eyes and the effect is just out and out sad. It's almost as if the Furby is grumpy.

You'd be grumpy, too, if someone had ripped you to shreds, installed cameras in your eyes, and ran wires out your backside.

That night, way later than I should have been playing with it, eyes bleary from coding, as I'm muttering to Meeta—yeah, he's still here—I spill a can of Red Bull on the Furby and it seems to groan, like an old man. It must be the electrolytes somehow firing up the low-power chips. Whatever, it's late, and I immediately christen it "The Grumby."

Meeta likes it and the name sticks.

In the morning at Fry's Electronics store, I shell out another dollar and put in a better speaker, so the Grumby will sound bright and happy and can talk and sing and belch and spit out whatever other sounds I want from it. And trust me, its first words weren't "goo goo" or "Dada."

•　　•　　•

I walk into the back corner of my apartment, what I jokingly refer to as the Manor Dining Room. There's a small table and chairs, but it's quickly turned into a development lab. PCs and iPhones and wires and monitors are everywhere. Somewhere in this mess is Meeta. I know because I can hear a keyboard chattering.

"What the heck are you doing?"

He holds up a finger as if to say, "Hold on a second."

I heard the word "One."

Meeta is sitting in front of his monitor typing away. A hacked and jacked Furby is sitting on top of it—actually it looks like it's attached with a huge loop of Velcro, like a bandage for a head wound.

Between typing, Meeta waves his hands in front of the Furby, waits a few seconds, and then mumbles what must surely be Indian curses and then goes back to typing.

"Really, what are you doing?" I ask.

"If you must know, I have found the most excellent use of the stereovideography."

"Have you been watching *Bill and Ted's Excellent Adventure?*"

"No, does that involve use of CCD imaging sys—"

"Go on . . . sorry I said anything."

"Two video inputs mean that motion is much easier to detect than looking for changes between frames within MPEG streams."

"OK?" I ask slowly.

Where was he going with this?

"So I most often find myself touching my twenty-inch monitor's screen as if it's the iPhone over there." Meeta points to the iPhone sitting on his desk and I think I hear a grunt. "I am always attempting to do the zoom or change pane with finger swipe."

I chuckle. That happens to me all the time. It's tough to move back to a mouse after using the iPhone Multi-Touch for a while. Unlike the old click and grab and menus of PCs years back, Multi-Touch lets you slide your fingers around the screen to do the same things: zoom in, flick through, zoom out. It's addicting and hard to go back to lousy mousing around.

"So I texted a classmate from IIT who wrote several algorithms on stereovideography and got testing code on motion sensing which, as said, can be real-time usable and I am just about to . . ."

Meeta holds his hand up to the Grumby with his thumb and index finger wide apart and then squeezes them together until they touch. I do this every day with my own iPhone, the pinch-to-expand move. Zoom out. Sure enough, a photo in an open window on the screen zooms out. Meeta repeats the pinch several times and keeps zooming out. Then he pauses and starts with his thumb and index finger touching and then spreading them out and the image zooms in.

I'm blown away. It's an air version of Multi-Touch. Executed by the Grumby.

Meeta does a quick swipe in the air with his index finger from left to right and the window switches photos. He flicks his finger from up to down and a browser window scrolls down. This was the coolest thing I'd ever seen.

"I can select and tap and double tap too. Those are quite easy. By later today I would mostly have the iPhone set complete."

"And how . . . ," I start.

Sensing my question, which Meeta does with alarming frequency, he interrupts and answers, "A very minimal meta-language. You describe the motion and then train the code with a repetitive example process. I have been working on numbers. Two is easy, thirty-three, not so much."

I immediately think of a few dozen gestures I'd like to train this thing on.

"Can you set me up on another machine to play around with this?" I ask.

"Sure. My classmate has lent me his application code. Should I suggest to him this could be open sourceable for him?"

"Don't you dare! You think we could buy the code?"

"Yes, no, I don't know. I will inquire."

"Offer him shares."

"Shares of our code?"

"No. Shares in our company."

"What company?"

"Just offer him 10,000 shares in our company in exchange for exclusive rights to his code and set me up to play with this. Put it on my laptop. And tell him we are going to hire him."

• • •

It takes me no time at all to come up with a demo. I have a few ideas of what every warm-blooded American male would insist on in a gesture interface. And a few things I just know they will try.

Because I try them myself.

"Meeta, check this out."

"Yes, boss."

"Please don't call me that," I plead.

"OK, boss. Sorry."

I move the cursor arrow on the screen by moving my finger around in the air. I place it over the "close window" icon of Firefox, the one with the red "x." I tap and an annoying box pops on the screen, like it does every damned time I close Firefox windows, reading: "You are about to close three tabs. Are you sure you want to continue?"

Two boxes underneath say, "Close tabs" and "Cancel."

I give the Grumby the thumbs-down sign and it appears that "Cancel" gets clicked and the box disappears. I move the cursor over the red "x" again, the same box shows up, but this time I give it the thumbs-up sign and sure enough the tabs all close and the box disappears.

"Very cold."

"You mean cool?"

"Better than cool, much lower temperature. Very cold," Meeta says matter of factly. I take it as a sign of approval.

I open iTunes and click on "I Love It Loud" by Kiss. The Grumby begins dancing around and mouthing the words, ". . . *loud, I want to hear it loud, right between the eyes . . .*"

I hold out my hand, thumbs, and fingers in the shape of a cylinder, like I was gripping the volume knob of a stereo, and then I turn my hand clockwise. The music gets louder and louder as I twist my hand.

"Frigid." Meeta says with a completely straight face.

"Uh, . . . thanks."

I twist my hand back the other way, counterclockwise and the volume drops.

I do a few more. Thumb and pinky out. In a Bart Simpson-voice, Grumby says, *"Cowabunga, dude."* Index finger and pinky out, other two fingers touching thumb. "Hook 'em horns," and a short clip of "The Eyes of Texas." And then a silly one: fingers spread wide, bottom of both hands together, thumbs interlocked, and then wave all fingers, just like every one of us does when standing between a projector and a screen—evoke the sound of birds chirping. OK, more stupid than silly, but I still catch myself doing it more than the others just to get the birds to chirp.

I save the best for last.

"And now for the *pièce de résistance*," I announce.

"Is that Spanish?"

"Sort of."

Coming up from underneath, I flip the Grumby the bird—the one-finger salute. I give it the finger. And it feels good, actually.

"*Ten hut*," it screams. Right out of an old World War II movie clip.

Meeta loves it. "Kelvin."

It's perfect. The ultimate Easter egg. I'm betting that after five minutes playing with gestures nine out of ten people will flip Grumby the bird. And we'll be ready.

I leave Meeta and walk down the hall on my way home and all I can hear is "*Ten hut. Ten hut. Tehhhhhnnnn hut.*"

Visa Financing

I'm buying computers and iPhones like they are going out of style. Ripping, number crunching, testing, tweaking. I'm updating the TuneBuffon player almost daily. That isn't really a problem since I have a legion of testers who will put up with bugs and tell me what works or doesn't. But I still need raw horsepower to crunch the deluge of tunes and movies and everything else that is showing up in the database.

iPhones are cool, but I can't tell you how many requests come in on the site begging for other players. So I also start buying those new Motorola PHZRs, Palm Pres, Nexus Ones, and a bunch of others. Money, money, money.

Then my stupid hosting service keeps asking for more money. I quickly blow through my monthly bandwidth allocation, and the bills tick up from $20 a month to $100 to $500–$600–$700 a month. A little crazy. Plus, Richie messing with my regular Visa card cut into my credit limit. Asshole.

Paying the host beats buying and hooking up servers on my own, but I am quickly draining my checking account. There's a business somewhere in all this, I hope, anyway, but I'm way too busy to think it through. Every other startup just sells ads. I suppose I will too. But I hate ads. I don't think I've ever clicked on an ad. Not on purpose, anyway. Stupid.

So for now, I just charge it. Easy. I have a United Visa card and an American Airlines MasterCard, each with a $10,000 credit limit. I gladly pay the $135 minimum monthly payment and put off the rest for another day.

"Boss . . ."

"What Meeta?"

"We just received an extremely urgent call from the wonderful hosting service and they have made a friendly request for new credit card information as the previous, how they say, "overstretched credit facility" is refusing financial restitution."

"I'm over the limit?"

"Yes, it appears so."

"Do you have a credit card, Meeta?"

"Yes, but I have been warned about over-exuberant American behavior regarding debt and promised my mother it would be for emergency situations only."

"Don't you think this is an emergency?"

"Well, it appears that funds are not forthcoming and . . ."

"And?"

"And they will shut down our operations without payment and . . ."

"And?"

"And this constitutes an emergency?"

"Do you need to hear sirens, Meeta?"

"I do have a Diners Club."

"Use it. I'll pay you back, in spades."

"I would prefer dollars."

"You'll get those too."

I watch Meeta type away on a Web site, turning over his card looking for the expiration date. I figure that buys us a few weeks at most.

I think of driving over to the local Wells Fargo and applying for a loan, but somehow explaining to them that I have a Web site that allows people to win at SEEK and SCAN, for free, and the fact that I am dumping ten grand a month and might someday come up with a business for all this isn't going to turn on their cash spigots.

Fortunately, just about everywhere I turn I get offered yet another credit card. Amazon practically begs me to put my growing purchases on an Amazon card. Buy.com pops up an ad for its own credit card every time I try to check out. So I click "Yes" . . . wait, no, I don't . . . I give the camera a thumbs up and it pushes the "Yes" button for me. It's REALLY easy to forget how to click.

And with that, I begin my very own collection of credit cards.

I sign up for a couple of different Capital One cards. A Gold and a Platinum. I hope like hell Richie doesn't find those. I get an email congratulating me on the acceptance of my application almost instantaneously after I air click "Submit." American Express seems happy to send me a Gold Card, for $50 a year, with no credit limit at all. How do they do that?

And then I hit pay dirt. I get a Chase Home Improvement Rewards Visa card at 0 percent APR financing for twelve months on all purchases and balance transfers. I'm pretty sure that means I don't have to pay them back for a while, at least I hope so, which is good news since it's unclear how I would even if I wanted to.

In the meantime, real life is getting in the way.

DMV

The place is packed. A complete zoo. I'm stuck in Department of Motor Vehicle hell. It looks like I'm at a United Nations Security Council meeting. Every nationality one can imagine is in line with me.

I just need to change one letter in my VIN number. Some moron data entry person, in Sacramento or more likely in Mumbai, transposed two digits. Mixed 'em up. Idiots. Now I can't get insurance.

"Here's jour numba. G428. Wait ta be called," the woman behind the information counter that I just waited through ten minutes of shuffling to talk to says to me.

"Is this a bakery?" I mutter.

"What was zat?"

"I just need to fix a mistake in my registration so I can get insurance. I can do it myself if you just let me at the computer and . . ."

People behind me in line are starting to "tsk" and shuffle papers and mutter to themselves.

"Seet down and wait jour turn please. And don leave. We close at five sharp."

"How long?"

"Jou should have made a reservation."

"Now you're a restaurant?" I mutter again.

"There mo seats in the room in the back."

Ugh. Every single seat is taken. I can't find the spillover room. I could die here and no one would know. A woman in a chair across from me looks like she has. Days ago.

A computerized voice comes over the loudspeaker: "*F125, please go to counter 6.*"

F? I hold my head. It's throbbing. I surf the Web on my phone to kill time.

After an hour or so, "*G365, please go to counter 3.*" I can't stand it anymore.

I pick up my phone and dial.

I hear, "Yo."

"Richie?" I ask.

"Hey."

"Hey. How's it going?"

"You still cheating at SEEK and SCAN?"

"I'm at DMV."

I hear a loud laugh on the other end of the phone.

"Richie? I need a favor. You owe me."

"What are you an idiot?"

"Do you still have the code to . . ."

"You do too."

"I can't do it."

"Because of a silly indictment?"

"Well, yeah, if I can't write code, I'm out of work, so you gotta help me and . . ."

"It's the virtual packet trick. We've done it a million times."

"Can you . . .?"

"Man, what's your problem?"

"Just do it. I'm running out of time and . . ."

I hear clicking. I shut up. And wait.

"OK, I'm in. What do you need?" Richie asks.

"Just change the S8 to 8S."

"That's it? Transposed? How appropriate."

"Yup." I'm humiliated even asking Richie for help.

"Really?" he asks.

"Really, Richie," I sigh.

He pauses. I hear more clicks.

"You need it printed, don't you?"

"Yes."

More clicks.

"G428, please go to counter 4."

There are grunts from all around the room.

I jump up. Why we had to break in to fix something that I could have done myself from the comfort of my own home. Stupid. It's why I hate the system so much. I just have to change it.

"You're the best," I say, as I hurry to counter 4.

"Say it again." Richie insists.

"You're the best, Richie."

"I know."

In a moment of weakness, I say, "Richie, you gotta come check out my new toy sometime. Eyes and ears and gestures and voice recognition. It's pretty cool."

Silence.

And then I hear him hang up.

Things We Need

"**M**eeta?"

"Yes, sir."

"Can I ask you a question?"

"Is that the question?"

"No."

"Then yes."

Meeta is turning into a real wiseass. Maybe it's from hanging out with me, who knows. I'm both annoyed and proud.

"All right, just listen. You mentioned your friend, your classmate, who was doing research on stereovideography and . . ."

"Yes, he is now our employee."

"Yeah, OK, good. We'll have to get around to setting up a company one of these days . . ."

"I would also very much like 10,000 shares."

"You got it. Make it 20,000 shares."

"Very charitable, thank you."

"Anyway, I was wondering if you know anyone else?"

"Why yes, I have many acquaintances that you speak of," Meeta beams.

"Do you know anyone that does speech recognition?"

"Many."

"How many?"

"Many, many."

"With code?"

"I will inquire promptly. Anything else?"

"Probably."

I wonder how deep a well Meeta is able to tap. I'll just have to keep asking.

In the meantime, I go to Amazon and order a copy of Andy Kessler's book *Eat People: Unapologetic Rules for Entrepreneurial Success*. I've been searching around for a book on how to create markets and companies with huge lasting value, and everyone is buying this one. I read one review that said the chapter describing intelligence at the edge of the network is worth the price alone. That is what we're doing, isn't it? Intelligence at the edge of the network. I like that!

• • •

The next morning Meeta declares, "Well, I have been IMing all last night and I have built a coalition of the willing for you."

"Meeta. That's great," I say distractedly, "but what the heck are you talking about?"

"You asked me to find speech recognizers and algorithmically inclined classmates and . . ."

"Oh, yes. Of course. And what did you find?"

"I have about a quarter centennium of programmers at the ready to write subroutines and patches of code as you need them."

"Quarter of a centi—?"

"Twenty-five."

"Oh."

"They will work for no money for maybe six months, but it will cost you 250,000 shares. I offered them stock in you and they were most appreciated and now are loyal to your effort."

"OK, let's get going," I say.

"Let's get down with it," Meeta exclaims a bit too loudly.

"Let's figure out what we have and what we need and then farm it out to the Meeta Coalition," I say.

"All good things start with an inventory," Meeta says.

Who am I to argue?

"OK. We have a silly looking creature with eyes and ears and a speaker and motors," I start.

"Yes."

"And a kick-ass microprocessor."

"The best ass for kicking," Meeta agrees.

"In many ways. It's got a USB cable and we just found that chip to do Wi-Fi and Bluetooth."

"And GPS. I found a better chip that does all of these using simple to program pipelined DSP devices and .. ."

"OK and GPS. Let's not get too deep here."

"I can be very shallow if need be."

I throw him an "are you that English-challenged or just screwing with me look." He just smiles back.

"OK. We have this proprietary algorithm to index and look up recorded music."

"And movies and TV shows."

"OK. And now we have gestures."

"Watch this," Meeta says. He turns to the Grumby and raises both hands and flips it two birds.

The Grumby shakes back and forth and the voice of Bruce Willis says, "*Yippee kiyay, motherfu—*" interrupted by the sound of a gunshot.

I can't help but laugh.

"*Die Hardest*? OK, but we're missing all sorts of stuff. We need voice recognition. We need some way to store all this audio and index it, so we can search it later."

"Yes, I have one of my classmates who has algorithms for . . ."

"We'll get to that. Let's focus on what we need."

"OK, yes, boss."

"If we break it down to words, that's still an infinite number of combinations. We need something contextual. Some way so we can know what is being said. Not just a few commands like our gestures. I want to know who is saying what, in sentences.

"We can . . ."

"And then we have to do something with the cameras. They're eating up all the cycles and bandwidth. There's gotta be some way to shrink it down to its elements on the device and then just move information about the important stuff. Maybe it's that same context thing."

"Yes, I think the . . ."

"And if we know what's being said we ought to be able to crawl the Web and find everything that relates to it. Google and Yahoo and Microsoft do that in their sleep. Why can't we?"

"Because of the scale of the . . ."

"And at some point I want this thing to know what I'm interested in before I say it or flip it the bird." I stop and look at Meeta and he's furiously writing this all down on a pad.

"Yes, we can get all of these. If I can beg for your indulgence and a bottle of scotch I will go into accumulate mode with the coalition. If they don't have it, they'll know where to get it."

Lawyer Lorita

8:55 a.m., January 28, Page Mill Road, Palo Alto

I drive up to Wilson Sonsini's law offices—it's a short hop from the road to their building but then a beautiful entrance leads to their lobby. I drive right up and stare into the building, with its light wood paneling and austere postmodern look. I don't know why but I'm enchanted. By a law office. Go figure.

Unfortunately, I have to park my car and walk what seems like a half a mile back to the lobby through the dredges of the parking lot. I guess the entrance is set up for limo drop-offs. Someday.

I walk into the lobby, check in, and sit down in a wonderfully comfortable chair to wait.

I have my buddy Mark to thank for the introduction. When Mikey wouldn't stop crying and kept yelling "Burby" and pointing to my apartment, Mark marched over. I showed him the singing and dancing routine and even how Meeta got gestures working. Mark had it saying "ten hut" within a few minutes and I remembered why we get along. Mark's a doc but he doesn't really practice anymore. He works with medical startups. When I asked him about setting up a company, he called me back about an hour later with the name of a lawyer at Wilson Sonsini and told me to ask for the equity plan. So here I am.

After no more than ten minutes, a slightly nerdy looking

woman, with shoulder length hair that seems to be cropped in the form of a wedge, walks into the lobby. She says her name is Lorita, shakes my hand, and invites me back to her office. We chitchat on the walk through the labyrinth of halls and offices and light wood-paneled walls.

"Is that beechwood?" I ask.

"Is what, what?" Lorita asks back.

"The walls."

"Oh. You know, I never really noticed. I can have an associate check on that."

"No, please don't. Just curious."

"Well, now so am I."

We finally arrive at her office and I'm offered another really comfortable chair, like the one in the lobby. I suspect these lawyers like people sticking around for hours and hours, billing away.

"So what can I do for you?" Lorita asks.

"I was told that you were the best at setting up a company."

"It's one of my specialties. I started as an M&A lawyer but got tired of the grind, you know what I mean?"

I don't, but nod anyway. She babbles on for another fifteen minutes on her background and the ability to pull in other lawyers in a virtual team or something like that. I mostly focus on a spot above her head and stare out the window behind her.

". . . and you have a startup idea?"

Now she has my attention.

"No, I'm up and running," I say.

"Oh. What's the name?"

"I don't have one."

"No problem. We can just go with Newco. I'll have to fig-ure out how many Newcos we have and get the proper numeric extension. Revenues?"

"No."

"No problem. They can be a distraction. Employees?"

"No, well, actually, yes. I've got this guy and he's got this other guy or guys and . . ."

"OK. You'll need an ISO and ESOP and probably a 401K . . ."

"And a BMF besides?"

"Uh," she grunts, ignoring my Cheech and Chong reference, "simple structure, maybe an LLC for now that we can flip to a C-corp when you do a funding. You know what I mean?"

Again, I nod stupidly.

"Anyone else doing what you're doing?"

I pause. "Not that I know of," I say meekly.

"No matter. But, I'd be in a hurry. Nothing sits for long around here."

I nod. Point taken.

"Have you done a financing?" Lorita asks.

"Visa," I deadpan.

"Oh, wonderful. That's quite a coup. Is that Visa International or one of the member banks? Chase, First USA, . . ."

"No, no. Not Visa. Visa cards. About a dozen of them."

"Oh. That's different. No matter. We'll set it up so that you can do a venture round quickly, by establishing the structure they'd just come in *pari passu*, you know what I mean?"

I give up on the nod and just smile. She hasn't even asked me what my startup does and already I have a bullet-proof structure with Latin phrases and everything.

She writes down some notes on a yellow legal pad, naturally, and asks a few more questions about how many board seats I envision and if piggyback rights on an IPO is something I have thought about. Jeez.

"We can have something by next week."

"Thank you so much for taking the time. We haven't discussed your fees and I am deep into Visa and . . ."

"We like to think of this as the first steps on a long journey and what modest fees we . . ."

"I was thinking about the equity pay plan."

"Oh, I was just about to suggest that, you know what I mean?"

I do.

"Ten thousand shares?" I offer.

"Oh, well. Of course that depends on the number of shares you have outstanding. We like to own between 20 and 100 basis points at inception and then participate in future financing. I'll take it up with the investment committee, but it shouldn't be a problem. You should see some of the crap we've gotten involved with, you know what I mean?"

She finally looks up from her yellow legal and number two pencil and smiles. Even more than expert advice, I'm a big fan of honesty.

"Do you have anything patentable?" Lorita asks.

"Do I?"

"Do you?"

"I might."

Lorita gets up and gestures me to follow her out of her office. As we walk down the hall—is it beechwood-lined? I still don't know. Lorita says, "Let me set you up with our patent partner before you leave. He's terrific. Just describe what you're doing and he'll set up generic patents with broad claims and over-reaching importance. He's so good—he practically does this stuff in his sleep. It will probably come in handy someday."

She walks into an office that looks just like hers. I follow her in and sit down in yet another incredibly comfortable chair. As she leaves, I hear her whisper "equity plan" to the patent partner. Figuring this isn't going to cost me anything, I unload on him everything Meeta and I have thought about, and then some.

Know-It-All

8:12 p.m., January 29, Palo Alto

The party is outside in the backyard of some fitness freak's home. Supposedly the couple has just redecorated and is afraid that someone might steal its expensive audio equipment, so they move the party outside, pumping really bad songs from the '70s through speaker rocks that look really stupid because they are the only rocks in sight. A marble walk runs around the entire length of a lap pool, and a fountain sits at the top spitting water in random shapes and directions. The house is not all that big and neither is the property, so it's pretty jammed. The house is mostly dark, except for bright lights glaring from a spotless workout room complete with weights and a punching bag.

I spot Mark, my doctor friend, at the other end of the pool standing dutifully next to his wife Maria and stuck in a conversation with another couple. He looks ready to chew his arm off to escape.

As I bob and weave in Mark's direction, I catch snippets of conversation, avoiding eye contact. Then one snip catches my attention that doesn't sound right.

"There has never been a presidential election when a candidate won Delaware and lost the election."

Can that be true? I sneak a glance at the group, a fat Asian guy with a plate full of Nachos, a slight Indian guy with a comb-over who lives a few doors down from me, and then the oddest-look-ing fellow with what appears to be a mullet. I haven't seen one of those, well, since I drove through Pittsburgh a decade ago and stopped for breakfast.

I must have been staring too long. Uh, oh.

"You know Roger?" It's Comb-over grabbing my arm and introducing me to Mullet. Damn. He's executing his own exit strategy.

"No, I'm afraid . . ."

"We were just talking about oil and energy and somehow got to Delaware," Roger says. He likes to talk, I gather.

"I was just . . ." I try the old "would love to stay and chat" thing to no avail.

"Delaware is probably more important a state for this country right now than any other."

"That's quite fascinating, but . . ."

"Oh sure. Dupont is a national treasure. Notice, the Duponts put their company about halfway between New York and Wash-ington for a reason."

"So they could control Amtrak?" I ask.

"That's a possibility. But their original strategy of creating a chemical giant started in the eighteenth century, and Delaware is the perfect bridge between political markets and capital markets and . . ."

I quickly flick my eyes across the marble patio looking for a lifeline. Mark is still stuck in couple hell. My other friends are nowhere to be found and my drink is full. Damn. I'm stuck. Note to self: start chugging.

". . . with biofuels, the efficiency goes up. But it's really nano-polymers for solar panels they have in the labs, which will lower the cost per watt into microcents within a few years and at that point you shut the ports and the solar age begins . . ."

Microcents? That doesn't sound right, but Roger barely takes a breath.

I'm feeling stupider by the sentence. This guy has facts by the barrel and makes such convincing arguments. I'm almost queasy, questioning my own intelligence. I thought I knew a lot of things, but Roger is either smarter or sounds smarter or pretends to be smarter. It doesn't matter. I stand there confused, feeling somehow inadequate. The defensive side of me tells me to run away fast. The offensive side tells me to fight back, with words if possible.

". . . in square footage, the U.S. would be energy independent if you just covered the equivalent of the state of Iowa with solar panels."

"Wouldn't that piss off people living in Iowa?" I ask.

"We already have that much in parking lots. Look, these are silicon-based panels," Roger goes on, ignoring me. "Chips get faster every year. The same thing is going to happen once we have these nano-polymers from Dupont. My guess is that efficiency can go up by three or four orders of magnitude, and that's just a start . . ."

I hate guys like this, Mr. Know-it-alls. They love the sound of their own voices and swirl in the feedback loop of their own logic and self-adoration that quickly turns into delusions of brilliance. There's just one way to stop them, their silver bullet, stake through the heart: the magic factoid. That one tiny bit of truth that knocks down the pedestal of cards they prop themselves up on.

Unfortunately I'm drawing a blank even though I can smell the bullshit piling high. I just don't have any facts coming to mind. Mercifully, my beer runs dry, and I'm practically chewing on my plastic cup to make the point. I notice Mark frantically signaling, thumb and pinky out tipping toward his mouth. Like smoke signals. Need. Beverages. Go. To. Keg.

". . . and you could transmit most of that energy with fiber optics that AT&T has already been putting in."

I give Roger a two-finger salute and duck out, with Nachos and Comb-over giving me the saddest eyes, like I'm abandoning them on a rooftop in Saigon.

About halfway to the keg it hits me. I stop, look up to the sky, and let out a bit-too-loud moan. Solar panels are about 10–12 percent efficient right now. The best they can be is 100 percent efficient, and even that breaks a few too many laws of physics. Three or four orders of magnitude means 1,000 or 10,000 times. I fell for it. I could have shut Roger the frickin' know-it-all down in an instant but I missed it. Better if I knew what percentage of the United States was covered with parking lots. Actually, all I needed was a quick way to look this stuff up and call his bluff. It got me thinking about that intelligence-at-the-edge thing.

Say What?

"What is the capital of Azerbaijan?" Meeta asks. The Grumby sits for a few seconds and then starts shaking and twitching and says, "*Baku.*"

"Is that right?" I ask.

"I would not be in doubt," Meeta shrugs.

"OK, that was pretty easy. You could type that question into Google and it would spit out the answer."

Meeta nods his head in a sort of "watch this" nod. He then asks, "What is Google's market cap?"

Pause.

"*One hundred sixty-one point one four billion dollars, down two point six four billion dollars in today's trading.*"

"OK, now that's pretty cool," I say.

"*Kelvin,*" says the Grumby, in Meeta's voice.

"How did you do that?"

"*How?*" the Grumby says.

"It is quite simple to the first order. We run the speech through a simple open source voice recognition system. The benefit is it has been trained by thousands or millions of people using it and teaching it words. Quite spectacular."

I nod.

"Then it is quite simple to key off the question words. You know—who, what, when, where, why, and how."

As he says those six words, the Grumby responds.

"*Who?*"

"*What?*"

"*When?*"

"*Where?*"

"*Why?*"

"*How now?*"

"Huh?" I ask.

Meeta shrugs. "Well, I didn't ask a question. He is easy to confuse."

"And when you do ask a question?" I ask.

"*When, when?*" the Grumby says.

"One of my classmates has a very intriguing parsing algorithm. It takes the words and groups them into the most likely phraseology for search optimization."

I squint my eyes and turn down my eyebrows. Meeta recognizes that as the international sign of confusion.

"Well, we toss the "ofs" and "ands" and "thes" and group the question into a series of phrases. Then we launch several parallel searches to Google, Microsoft Bing, Yahoo, and Ask. Almost always Google comes back first. We then parse their search results for key phrases and compare it with what the others come back with and almost always an answer is formed."

"And getting it to say kelvin?"

"Oh, I listen for the word cool."

"*Kelvin,*" the Grumby adds.

"May I?" I ask.

"Well," Meeta swallows. "I am not sure that the settings are yet optimized for random non-demonstration invocations."

"In other words, you've rigged it in demo mode."

"No, well, maybe. We've only been at it since this morning. Try it anyway."

"When was the war of 1812?" I ask with a smirk.

Pause.

"June eighteen, one thousand eight hundred and twelve until February eighteen, one thousand eight hundred and fifteen," the Grumby answers.

"Is that right?" I ask no one in particular. "I guess it is."

Meeta says, "Whew."

"OK, let me give it another. Who is buried in Grant's Tomb?"

Pause.

Another pause.

"No one," the Grumby spits out.

Meeta shakes his head, looking upset. "That does not sound correct. There must be some parsing error and . . ."

I laugh. "Nope, he's right. One more."

"What . . . is the air-speed velocity of an unladen swallow?"

Pause.

"What?" the Grumby asks.

"What?" I repeat.

"What, what?"

"What?"

This goes on for a while, seeing if I could break the Grumby's parrot mode. Still, just being able to launch search requests from questions asked is quite amazing.

"What do you think?" Meeta asks.

"What?" the Grumby asks.

"Can you turn that off?"

"I'd rather not. Let's go to another room."

•　　•　　•

"Yes, it is quite rudimentary, but already we have thought of several ways to improve results."

"How's that?" I ask.

"Well, so far it has been human intervention. If we know what questions are to be asked, then we can better break down the question into its proper phrase segments for parsing optimization."

"And how many people do you have?"

"Well, there is me and there is a classmate of mine who has studied . . ."

"OK, OK. Let me think about this." I beg.

I stare at Meeta. Something he said before sounded familiar.

"Tell me again about the voice recognition."

"Well, as you know, you can buy voice software like Dragon or ViaVoice, and they are OK in a limited way. But I have a classmate who has taken the college Sphinx and CAVS and optimized the input selection . . ."

"Whoa. Whoa. Slow down. Sphinx, CAVS?"

"Yes, of course. You must know them. The famous Carnegie Mellon Sphinx voice system allows for Kolmogorov entropy estimation from acoustic attractors and . . ."

My eyes must have squinted.

"It's free and it runs on Linux."

"Bingo."

"But quite more importantly, we have been playing with another open source project named VoxForge that collects transcribed speech to build acoustic models for Sphinx and others and . . ."

". . . and the more people that send in speech the better the recognition," I finish.

"But, of course. The many beats the few," Meeta exclaims to me as much as to himself.

He's right. It's not so much the individual—it's the collection of all those connected individuals. It's why no one has ever done this before.

"Well put. So what we really need to do is figure out a way for lots of people to submit their questions—it almost doesn't matter what—so that we can figure out how to break it up into the right phrases to blast to search engines, or maybe we even create our own database and this thing will optimize itself over time."

"Quite right," Meeta says like I had just stated the obvious.

"It's TuneBuffoon for questions. TuneBuffoon on steroids."

"Isn't that illegal?" Meeta asks.

"Asking people to help for free?" I ask.

"No, the steroids."

"It's just a figure of speech. Never mind. Let's see if we can rig up a system that works with TuneBuffoon to get everyone to start talking."

"Asking questions."

"Say what?" I say.

"Asking questions," Meeta repeats.

"No, maybe that's what we'll call it. 'Say What?'"

"Brilliant."

"We need something we can download to iPhones and every other phone. You think this code on the Grumby can port?"

"Tomorrow."

"Tomorrow what?" I ask.

"The code is all portable. The team will have it done by tomorrow," Meeta insists. "I found this Russian guy. He wrote some code for the 'foon . . ."

"'foon?"

Meeta smiled. He is Americanizing before my very eyes.

". . . and has some ideas and wants to write other stuff. He wants to do the port, so he can learn the internals and says tomorrow, so . . ."

"You da man," I say proudly.

"I like the sound of that."

"You da man," I repeat.

The GC

I'm all for doing good. Work hard, spend little, and find your calling and all that. But even though I hate to admit it, especially here in California, I can't stand the really extreme granola-munching types. The ones that smugly insist they are saving the planet by building huts in Costa Rica even though they could have just donated the airfare and the Costa Ricans would have been better off. Or biking everywhere. Or not using plastic bottles. Or bathing only once a week.

I guess I'm just jealous. They seem to have some inner peace because of some self-reinforced impression that what they're doing is making a difference. Hey, whatever. To each his own.

But I want to make a difference too. I'm just not sure how. Self-deprivation is not my style. I'm looking to do good—it's do well, isn't it? (whatever)—rather than just feel good about myself.

But all I really know how to do is code.

Watching this whole thing unfold has got me thinking. I write some code, set up a simple feedback loop, and it harnesses the smarts of lots of other people. The more people the better, and the end result is they're all better off.

I'm not all that good with people. They're annoying. But it's really all about people, isn't it? If I can just get some code that uses people to help other people, then maybe that's my "do good." If I can get enough code in people's hands, then it can outdo the whole smugly thing about building huts one by one or saving the planet.

If I ever get some spare time . . .

Stump the Machine

"Say What" is taken. Instead, we call it "Stump the Machine."

The application is pretty easy to set up. First, Meeta, or someone in his Indian mafia, defeated the limits to multi-tasking on the iPhone, so now we can run more than one program at the same time. Pretty elegant. I doubt anyone at Apple will ever figure out how we do it, which is good, because I hear their new general counsel is a tough son of a —.

Anyway, using the DSP on the iPhone, we capture all the sounds spoken and run it through a modified voice recognition system. We just listen for who, what, when, where, why, or how (we add will and can too) and then capture the next set of words. Almost everyone pauses after asking a question, so the last word is easy to figure out.

We then upload these words and fire them off to search engines, including a rudimentary open source search engine that we set up on our own server. This turns out to be a smart move, since after a while there are lots of repeat questions. Spelling doesn't matter that much as the search engines will fix words that are close.

The trick is to put the words in the right groupings before firing off the search. Context matters. We don't have any particular insight into how to do this, so instead we just blast all combinations of words and then compare results until we got some repeat answer.

For questions with simple yes or no answers, I steal the responses from the Magic 8 Ball: "As I see it, yes" and "It is decidedly so," as well as "My sources say no" and "Outlook not so good."

If we can't get any results that match, we'd have the app ask, "Could you please rephrase the question?" Often, we could gain context just from the rephrasing and learn something about how to categorize that question, which we file on our own server. I quickly change it to the Magic 8 Ball theme, "Reply hazy, try again" and "Better not tell you now."

We return the result to the iPhone and using another open source piece of code that does text to speech, give the answer, and then ask, "Is that correct?" In other words, we have real humans tell us if we're right or wrong as we build up our knowledge base. If we do it right, like TuneBuffoon, there will be millions of humans helping us.

There are four different answers, "Yes," "No," silence, or any other words spoken.

Any answer besides "Yes" will produce one of a rolling list of prompts, from "Answer, please" to "So, what is the answer, smarty pants?"

We download the answer, although I'm not yet sure what we are going to do with it. I'm sure Meeta has an old classmate who will think of something.

•   •   •

I put the Stump the Machine code up on TuneBuffoon the next morning with a request for help in debugging a new iPhone application. Meanwhile, Meeta and friends are quickly porting it to the Nexus One, because they all own one. A DSP is a DSP; the only hassle is we need a decent amount of processing power and memory on the phone to do the recognition. Smartphones are needed, although I already figure out we can just transmit the raw voice data and do the recognition on our server. Someone can even call in with a question, but that will cost us money, putting in phone lines, so we quickly squelch that idea. As it is, we're getting killed on server costs.

Why? Because it took all of about two seconds for Stump the Machine to start circulating and get downloaded. Lots of people read about the announcement and start twittering about it. News spreads like wildfire. The server immediately starts filling up with questions and answers and rebuttals and curse words. Within an hour, we have 5,000 downloads and by the end of the day we have close to 50,000, plus hundreds of thousands of questions logged. I haven't seen anything like it.

I send Meeta to run out and get another couple of servers and hard drives.

"My Best Buy card is overprescribed," Meeta complains.

"They won't let you charge on it anymore?"

"The man retrieved a pair of scissors and cut it in half in front of my eyes."

"Ouch. Here. Use my Home Depot Visa card. We'll see how long that lasts."

. . .

After a while, scanning through the list of questions becomes more fun than writing code. "What is the square root of 2?" "What is the time?" and "Who was the MVP of Super Bowl XXXVII?"

A few ask who is going to win the next Super Bowl. Even more ask about *Star Trek* trivia.

So I decide to have some fun with this.

It is my turn to do a demo for Meeta.

"Check this out."

He turns around and faces me across the table in the Manor Dining Room. His hair points in a dozen different directions, his eyes are bloodshot, and I think I notice a small tick, an increasingly perceptible shaking of his head.

"When was the last time you slept?"

"*Could you please rephrase your question,*" the Grumby states.

"About an hour ago," Meeta answers.

"For more than five minutes?" I ask a little more sternly.

"Friday."

"Today is Tuesday."

"Yes. Who has time?"

"*It's four-oh-three-p.m.,*" the Grumby states, pauses, and then adds, "*Does anyone really know what time it is?*"

"You wanted to show me something?" Meeta asks.

"That was it," I said, shaking my head.

"What?" Meeta asks.

"*What?*" asks the Grumby.

"I mean is that the "check this out" matter?" Meeta asks. There was a developing art to asking a question without triggering the Grumby.

"Yup. I sorted the questions we've received so far by frequency and word choice and you can really learn a lot about human psyche. Or maybe human psycho."

"In a particular manner?"

"Everyone eventually asks the time."

"But I don't get it. You tell the time and then say no one knows it? Very confusing."

"Chicago?"

"Chicago time?"

"Transit Authority. Never mind. Check this one out. Who's on first?" I ask.

"*What's on second?*" Grumby Abbott shoots back. And then the entire Abbott and Costello routine starts playing until I say "Stop."

"I just watched that on cable." Meeta says, his smile widening and his head shaking a bit more violently than before.

"Sleep!" I insist.

"Soon. More?" Meeta asks.

"Why a duck?" I ask.

"*Whya no chicken?*" Chico Marx asks back through the Grumby.

.　　.　　.

Gag answers are fun and I probably spend a little too much time and laughs playing with it. More seriously, though, I notice two disturbing trends. First, we are getting a lot of incorrect answers. After the first few simple questions are asked, the questions get harder and often 25 percent or less are labeled correct. And second, I notice that people stop playing after about three or four wrong answers. Often, after asking a hard question, which would return a wrong answer, instead of saying "yes" or "no," the questioner would just say "idiot" or "asshole" and stop playing. Either the answers are wrong or the person who asks the question has no clue what the right answer is. Can we trust these folks?

.　　.　　.

Meeta walks over and seeing I look perplexed says, "I think I know how to solve the answer problem."

"I don't care. You need to get some sleep. I don't want to be responsible if you go into a rage and murder my neighbors because you haven't had deep REM for a week."

"You will provide thanks for feedback."

"I'm happy to give you feedback—get your back horizontal and get SLEEP!" I shout.

"Get the feedback and you get the correct answers," Meeta says as he stumbles off looking for couch cushions to hide under.

I look at him and follow his path to the couch. That's it. Pure Meeta genius.

We need a feedback loop.

As I sift through the questions coming in, looking to apply some gag answers, I can't help but notice how many of them are the same—the *Star Trek* trivia, math questions, geography, that kind of stuff. Our algorithm and parsing are pretty simple, but it's the search engines that can't get things in the right context. But by asking for the correct answer, we have context and feedback.

I can't assume everyone is honest or smart enough to know the right answer. So we accumulate answers to a specific question. After we get ten of them I start to look for matches. Then it's as simple as taking a vote—if 70 or 80 percent agree—I can play with that percentage. Then we can assume with reasonable assurance that this is the right answer.

Meeta sets it up so we can know who everyone is. We ask for an email address before we let folks download our code, but we also capture the IMEI code, a number that's unique to each cell phone. In effect, we know who everyone is. As a fallback, we can identify people with the IP address of the device it comes in on, but it reminds me that for the next version it would be nice to have a truly unique identifier for each device and maybe for each speaker.

The feedback turns out to be one of our most useful features. From watching Ohio State football games, I learned that the greatest reward system is to slap stars on the helmets of players for outstanding plays.

So we do the same thing. It isn't even hard. Each time someone submits the correct answer for something that stumps the machine, we send a star—an asterisk if you must know—to their phone's screen. And we keep track on our servers. If you go to our Web site, you can see your ranking. Meeta is working on a Facebook app that ranks you against your friends—who is smarter or at least provides more questions correctly. It's amazing what people will do for free. And it's a lot more fun than stupid Farmville.

OK, after all that, we file the correct answer, we hope, in our own database, so when it's asked again the answer will come up right away as well as be checked against search results. I'll figure out how to weigh it all later, but done right we end up with all the correct answers to commonly asked questions. Of course, the more questions we get the less common they become.

So now we have both a learning system for correct answers and a way to reward those who consistently give correct answers.

I wonder for a second what would happen if the majority were wrong. Are there any absolute truths? My head hurts thinking about it, or anything too weighty, but God help us if the challenged become the majority.

The downloads continue. We hit a hundred thousand quickly and it keeps going up. After the TuneBuffoon rocket ship, I should have known. Still, it amazes me.

This thing takes on a life of its own. Hundreds of thousands of downloads mean millions of questions. Folks appear to be sitting around all day collecting stars on their screens, trying as hard as they can to stump the machine and then get rewards for providing the right answer. I feel like I'm giving out doggie treats. Maybe I am. But people are smarter than dogs, right?

·   ·   ·

With the feedback loop in place and our database growing, the percentage of correct answers keeps going up. Not just because someone says "yes" when asked if it's right but because it's in our database and we know it's right. My goal is 50 percent. We hit 75 percent within a few days and 90 percent within a week or so. And then slowly but surely the number keeps ticking up.

The more correct answers we spit out the stranger the questions get. If our database and the search results just return chicken-scratch nonsense, we have a deep-voiced Darth Vader say, "most unknowable."

No surprise, but I keep running out of storage space and server cycles. I can't run this from home anymore, but I've been having so much fun focusing on the exceptions and funny lines that I keep blowing it off.

"Meeta, here it is."

"It is so?" On the one hand Meeta's English keeps improving, but on the other hand he has completely eliminated who, what, when, where, why, and how from his vocabulary to shut the Grumby up, so it's a mixed bag.

"Watch this: What . . . is the air-speed velocity of an unladen swallow?" I ask my Grumby.

"*What do you mean? An African or European swallow?*" the Grumby asks.

"Holy Grail, . . . I just watched that on cable. I love cable," Meeta screams.

"Ask again."

"What . . . is the air-speed velocity of an unladen swallow?" Meeta asks.

"*In order to maintain air-speed velocity, a swallow needs to beat its wings forty-three times every second.*"

We are on our way. I'm not sure, 100 percent sure, where we are going, but we are picking up speed. And running out of money at about the same clip.

"Meeta, you think anyone might pay us money for this stuff?

The gesture thing has got to be worth something? Maybe Apple or Google or someone?"

"I can inquire. My network extends through the electronic landscape."

"You mean you know people in a lot of these companies?"

"That is so . . . I just said."

My phone rings.

"Excuse me," I say to Meeta.

"*Al Travis,*" my Grumby says. Announcing Caller ID was about the easiest thing I ever implemented. I vaguely remember the name.

"Hello."

"Al Travis, Langley. Remember me?"

Uh-oh. Those guys.

"Yes?" I ask.

"You shouldn't have done that."

"Done what?"

"DMV." Damn. These guys know everything.

"I . . ."

"You promised no more stunts like that. It's part of your agreement. Technically, I can ban you again from . . ."

"I couldn't take it. You ever been in a DMV? You're part of the government. Do you have any idea how lame that place is?" I ask.

"Irrelevant," he says firmly. "You and your pal Richie had best be careful."

"But . . ." I wonder if he knows it was Richie who did the hack. As mad as I am at Richie, I already screwed him once. I can't do it again.

"Hey, listen," Al Travis continues, "We're interested in what you're working on. You really should work for . . ."

"TuneBuffoon?" I interrupt. I want to probe for what he knows.

"It's more than that, isn't it? We could hire you and Richie."

Richie?

"What you see is what you get," I interrupt again. They tried to get me to work for them before. No way.

"Look, we're going to do this anyway, end up in the same place. Richie is pretty good. You might as well use our systems and . . ."

Richie again. Is that where he got the money to drop at the Blackjack table?

"Hey, we do need money. Can you write a check for—I don't know—twenty million bucks?"

"Funny. Anyway, keep us in mind. And no more shenanigans. OK?" and he hangs up.

Jack

I'm in the middle of a deep, deep sleep, dreaming of weird gestures to implement—don't ask—when my cell phone rings. More like gongs. I have long ago set my ringtone to "Hells Bells." I don't get many calls. There's no Caller ID on this one for some reason.

"Hello?"

"He-chh-chh-llo. This is Ja-chh-chh-chh-tures."

"Who?"

"*Who?*" my Grumby asks. I reach over and unplug it, a bit violently, actually.

"You the chh-chh foon?"

"Who?"

"Chh-Buffoon?"

"Who's this?"

"Sorry, bad connection. Better?"

"A little."

"I'm in Kenya. Big game."

"I'm in Palo Alto," I say.

"Are you chh . . . uneBuffoon?"

"In a matter of speaking. How did you get my number? My mother doesn't even have this number."

"My associate has everyone's number. Listen, I'm back ch-ch.

We want to invest. We backed most of the current wave of Web ch-ch-ch companies and ch-ch them pretty quickly and . . ."

"Who is this?"

". . . I'm on a trip and heard about you from this guy in Moscow with kid's books and we've done due diligence and we think you are the next big thing and would like to offer you 5 million at 7 post chh-chhhhhhh . . ."

Moscow? Kid's books. What the?

"Who is this?"

"Ack . . ."

"Who?"

"Jack ch-chh. Red ch-ch Ventures."

And then the line goes dead.

PART II

Personalities

1:38 a.m., February 10, Palo Alto

I'm tired. But we have to push on.

"*Are you in or out?*" a Grumby says. That's weird. It sounds so familiar.

"What the heck is that?" I ask.

"*Rosemary's Baby*," Meeta answers.

"What?" Where does he come up with this stuff?

"George Clooney. Danny Ocean. *Ocean's Eleven*," Meeta tells me.

"OK, I get it. What are you doing?"

"Well, we have all these movies that are showing up encoded in TuneBuffoon. I matched them up against the Internet movie database.

"IMDb?" I ask.

"Yes, and I can get information of interest. Release date, director, actors, everything. It was just some coding to go through the movie audio and pull out all the dialog and match it up with actors and create a database of movie lines across films.

"*The truth can be adjusted,*" comes from the speaker.

"That's from *Michael Clayton*, I think. I saw it on cable," Meeta explains.

"And you've done this for how many movies?"

"I'm not sure. I'm only limited by how many BitTorrent lets me download and then I match them up against our database, and

IMDb and Netflix scrape other sites for movie lines. It takes some crunching. I think I'm at a couple of thousand."

"*Things are never so bad they can't be made worse.*"

"Clooney?"

"Bogart."

"Oh."

"Oh, and check this out."

Meeta clicks around until I hear, "*That's hot.*"

"Paris Hilton," Meeta informs me.

"What are you going to do with all this?"

"Isn't that what you do?"

"I suppose. Keep going, I'm intrigued," I tell him.

About five minutes later, I walk over to Meeta's work place.

"Do me a favor. Pull up every Marx Brothers movie and TV show as well as every Don Rickles concert, Johnny Carson appearance, whatever."

"No problem. I have to warn you, it is a lot of snippets."

"Can you sort them?" I ask.

"By what?" Meeta asks back.

"Well, how did you come up with the Clooney and Bogart lines?"

"They're the most popular."

"How do you know?" I ask.

"You just search against the quote and see how often it is cited and then . . ."

"Do that for all the quotes you have, for every celebrity you can find," I tell Meeta.

"What are you thinking?"

"We're getting into the personality business," I say, thinking out loud.

•   •   •

I start thinking about conversations I've had, with Meeta, with friends, at cocktail parties, with know-it-alls, with cashiers. I look up conversation components and get a bunch of hogwash about turn constructional units and things like lexical, clausal, phrasal, and sentential. Not knowing what any of that means, I write up a list of all the little snippets I might need to fake a conversation, which on a personal level, I have been perfecting for years.

Conversation starter—hey, yo, wassup, hello, what's happenin'?

Affirmative—Yes, yup, you got that right.

Negative—no, nope, no way, not, you're kidding right? fuggetaboutit!

Query—what do you think? any clue?

Funny anecdote—I was hanging out at the bar and in walks a priest, a rabbi, and an IRS agent . . .

Something about the weather—feels like rain.

Current events—did Pashtun fall again last night?

Sports score/fashion statement—how 'bout dem Yankees; love your shoes.

Complain about something—why can't they fill these potholes faster?

Self-deprecating comment—I'm just a good old boy; what do I know?

Insult—for a fat guy, you don't sweat much . . .

Deep thinking—I think prices are down because of the jet stream.

Opinion—I'm pro-choice except when it comes to children.

Catch phrase—That's what *I'm* talking about!

Random saying—We really are a nation of shopkeepers. Can you get me a bucket of prop wash?

I set up a simple screen interface that creates buckets that I can drag and drop quotes into. Meeta passes along about 300 chunks of dialog from George Clooney, from various movies, and from TV interviews. I don't even have to listen to all of them; Meeta includes the speech-to-text translation along with it. After about thirty minutes moving word chunks to the right buckets, I realize I can only move about half of them, so I end up creating ten more conversation buckets for things like anger and surprise and apologizing and negotiating. But I don't want to go higher than twenty-five buckets; I think it would get too complicated beyond that. I have no desire to personally drag and drop dialog into these stupid buckets, but like TuneBuffoon and Stump the Machine, I know hundreds of thousands of faceless volunteers who will.

Still, I have another hundred Clooney-isms that are uncharacterized. What to do?

I think about it for a while. What happens when you don't understand what was just said? It takes a while, but I realize the answer is so simple. When in doubt, do nothing.

Nothing. Let the technology drive the conversation, at first, anyway. If a conversation turns toward the truth or any of its synonyms, perhaps "fact" or "accuracy" or "verity" or antonyms like "lie" or "falsehood"—thank you dictionary.com—and the same for anything about adjusting, and sure enough, I have the newly suave George Clooney Grumby belt out, *"The truth can be adjusted."*

It's a start. I keep thinking that I really can create intelligence at the edge. I play around for a while, but I can't get a decent conversation with George Grumby Clooney to make much sense. Maybe the whole middle of the night thing is getting to me. It needs a lot of work—I'll play with this some other time. I should probably stick to music for now, anyway, because I'm still going broke rather quickly.

Visit with VC

10:07 a.m., February 11, Atherton, California

Trying to buy another terabyte drive at Best Buy, I watch in horror as my Home Depot Visa card is denied and cut in half in front of me. I think that's a new low.

Money, money, money. The better we do the less money I have to do more.

If only Visa would send just one more credit card. I've read so many horror stories about venture capitalists—greedy, empty suits, boring value subtractors, low-handicap golfers—that I have no real desire to work with any of them.

Instead I find myself in my Jeep, gas gauge pushing E, looking for a house on Park Lane in Atherton, the town next to Palo Alto. Acre-plus lots vs. fifth of an acre lots in our town. And I doubt there are any apartments.

I was told to look for the house with the gate. They all have gates. The whole place smells like money.

I finally find the right house and pull up to a box that hangs out over the edge of the entryway. It has a button and a telephone keypad. I type in my telephone number to see what will happen and the box starts beeping loudly. I wonder if I can get alarms to go off. I push the button and it seems to dial its own number and after a very long minute a voice comes out of the box.

"Que?"

"I've got an appointment to see Jack?" I half ask and half plead.

The gate opens up. I feel I'm being admitted into the Land of Oz.

• • •

Venture capitalists call themselves VCs. Scary, like Vietcong. I wonder if that's deliberate.

Jack—yes, the same Jack that called me from Kenya or wherever—had insisted we meet at his house in Atherton rather than at his office on Sand Hill Road. I couldn't decide whether he was trying to impress me (working so far) or was embarrassed to have me meet his partners before he could filter me.

I have plenty of time to think about all this because the driveway just keeps going and going. It's paved with tiny white stones, no doubt from an exclusive Italian quarry, and each seems set perfectly in place. Lemon trees and flowers galore line the driveway. I slow down and think about picking some fruit. Maybe that's the approach. He has money. I need money. It should be as easy as picking fruit off his trees. Or maybe I should play hard to get. Of course this never worked in high school and maybe VCs aren't like emotional sixteen-year-olds. Then again . . .

I end up on a circular driveway—man, I love circular driveways—that runs past the front door. It's beautiful, which instantly pisses me off. Off to the side is a shorter driveway leading to a detached garage. A drop-dead gorgeous red Ferrari Spider is parked at an angle in front of the garage like the owner is worried that someone is going to drive up and park next to him and ding the door. The garage doors are open and it looks like a car show of classics inside.

I already hate this guy.

I ring the doorbell, which plays the theme from *Chariots of Fire*. A Mexican woman in a French maid's outfit opens the door and motions me in. Weird. I walk through two massive front doors into an entryway with a ceiling at least two stories high sporting a massive chandelier that looks like a giant squid.

Between two staircases that wind their way to the upper floors, like out of a Hitchcock movie, is, and I've got to describe this right because I still can't believe it, either a painting or a photo or a photorealistic painting. The image is more than odd, and I stare for a few seconds until I recognize it—staring back at me is a very young and very naked Brooke Shields. Ew.

I have to look away. I think I hear the Franco-Mexican American maid snicker.

She leads me through the house. Brooke Shields is nothing. The walls are littered with the most amazingly Ugly art. Yes, Ugly with a capital "U." Like it was painted at the isolation wing of a mental hospital. One piece of, uh, art, has several giant heads with hands that stretch out and hold themselves up over a vat of boiling purple oil. Another seems to be a rat gnawing on a decomposed foot in a formal dining room. Tasty.

There is junk strewn everywhere; it's the most unkempt place I have ever seen. We pass shelves with books lying every which way, a tennis racket, a toilet plunger, empty candy wrappers, and half-eaten yogurt containers with white plastic spoons sticking out. I don't know, maybe it's art too.

Finally, I'm seated in a room with a giant flat-screen TV, probably a hundred-inches wide.

The art here is even scarier: a giant egg with a baby riding a scorpion inside, a mother that is shown giving birth a bit too graphically to a toaster.

Jack finally enters, talking on his phone, holding up his finger to say hold on. I catch snippets of the conversation; it seems that he is booking a big game hunting trip in Namibia or somewhere. He snaps his phone shut and without apologizing jumps right in.

"So, we have the top IRR in the Valley," Jack starts.

I must have looked confused.

"IRR? Internal rate of return?" He pauses. "We are the best at what we do."

"OK."

"Look, I don't do all this investing for my own personal gain," Jack says. I look around the room at all the art and wonder if he is about to tell me he is supporting a colony of deranged artists in the woods of Eastern Washington State. "It's for the kids. We choose our limited partners very carefully. They're all endowments and foundations and that kind of stuff. Every time we make money it's another fifty scholarships at Stanford and Yale and all."

I bet if he sold half of the dreck hanging on his walls he could probably just buy Harvard and let in whoever he wants.

"So I'm interested. I've done some work on TuneBuffer. My associate, actually. He thinks it's Web 2.5, but we can easily turn it into a Web 3.0 charmer."

"Well," I respond, "we do turn things around and have our users rip all the music, run it through our algorithms, and compile the database, so if that's what you define as Web 3.0 . . ."

"Yeah, whatever. Just be careful letting others do the work. In my experience, people are stupid. Ever been to a 7-Eleven?"

"Not recently," I admit.

"No matter. You're definitely onto something. You do it right and we can make this thing deal-bait for Google or Viacom or even Microsoft. We like to dress things up for five or ten baggers . . . you interested?" Jack asks and finally pauses himself.

I focus on just one word—what does he mean by "thing"?

"Look," I say, "I'm a little new at this game. I've spent lots of time and lots of Visa's money building out this service, which took off much faster and much bigger . . ."

Jack's phone rings. His ringtone is the theme from *Jaws*. *Dum-dum. Dum-da-dum-da-dum-dum.* He holds up his finger.

"OK. All right. Uh-huh. Call a board meeting and we'll get the votes together to get rid of him. Uh-huh. Just do it." He snaps his phone shut.

"So how much?" Jack blurts out.

"Excuse me?" I ask.

"What will it take?"

"To build out more servers and get a few folks to coordinate the coding that we do in . . ."

"Bottom line." Jack states about as matter of factly as you can state anything.

"I'm not sure. I was hoping to talk to you about getting help in building out a company. I think we can do a platform that expands on the basic . . ."

"OK. I get it. Here we go. We'll do one point two for sixty, that's two post, usual terms, two times liquidation preference, participating preferred, three board seats. We can close this by Monday."

Dum-dum. Dum-da . . .

He answers the phone and again I get the held-up finger.

"A. G.? What's shakin'? Uh-huh? Really? I hear biz is in the tank. Jeez, you frickin' hedge fund guys want to know everything," Jack yells into the phone. "I'll make some calls, but what do I get out of it?"

I tune out and think back to what Jack just said. I may be wrong, but I think he just offered to buy 60 percent of my company for $1.2 million. That's either really good or a huge sham of an offer. I have no clue.

I stand up and start checking out his bookshelf. One section seems to be all Oprah book selections. And then there's what seems like an altar to some guy named Eckhart Tolle. Displayed prominently is the book *A New Earth: Awakening to Your Life's Purpose* and right next to it is *The Power of Now: A Guide to Spiritual Enlightenment.* All right then.

There was a red button in the middle of the Tolle shrine. I look around. Jack is still on the phone. What the heck. I push the button.

"To be conscious of Being, you need to reclaim consciousness from the mind, an essential task on your spiritual journey."

Weird.

The phone snaps shut. I'm sure my face is several shades of red darker.

"So?"

"So." I'm not sure what else to say.

"Deal?"

"Or no deal," I deadpan.

"Valuation?" Jack asks.

"Seems so."

"We can sharpen our pencils."

"And dot the "t's" while the ink dries," I say.

"Yes, I see. So you are flexible?" Jack asks.

"Sprightly."

I'm not sure what he's trying to say, but I get a raised eyebrow and an ever so slight nod that seems to imply he appreciates my negotiating skills.

Dum-dum . . .

I don't wait for the held-up finger. I leave the TV room and wind my way back to the front door, no hired help in sight. I can't help myself and pause to stare at Brooke Shields's birthday suit for just a little longer than is socially acceptable. I then get the shivers, run out the door, jump into my Jeep, and spin my back wheels on his driveway.

From the road I call Lorita and fire questions rapid fire, demanding an education in high finance. I get back an earful on post-money valuations, ratchets, liquidation preference, piggy-back-registration rights, participating preferreds. Some of it sinks in, though not much. I think they make this complicated so you need lawyers. Brilliant. Lorita and I agree that Jack's offer sucks.

Sand Hill

1:14 p.m., February 15, Menlo Park, California

I get my Jeep up to about ninety-three miles per hour, a personal record. I'm way late and driving on Interstate 280, which as far as I can tell doesn't have any speed limits. So far, I've been passed by two black Porsches and a red Ferrari. The sign reads "Sand Hill Road 1 mile." My lawyer Lorita pulled in some favors, so I could meet with a bunch of venture capitalists to see if we can get a better deal than the one Jack laid on me. And I've been whipping through Fred Wilson's avc.com to see if I can learn the venture business by osmosis.

I turn left at the first light, following signs for 3000 Sand Hill Road, and start winding around left and right before coming upon a mini-village of three-story buildings and what looks like a used car lot for late-model German sedans. I park way too close to someone's 7 Series, setting off the alarm. I jump out and squint in the sunlight looking for building 4. Finding it, I take the stairs three at a time, figure suite 215 is on the second floor, and scramble in.

The "bit too stunning" receptionist doesn't look up. I try to get her attention. She's clearly busy, but it's not until I walk closer that I realize she is furiously filing her nails.

"I'm here for a one o'clock with Roger," I blurt out.

She casually looks up, smiles brightly, and lightly whispers,

"Roger's not here right now, but we expect him soon. Please have a seat. Can I get you something? Green Tea? Yerba Mate? Kombucha mushroom drink? Renée Zellweger swears by them and we're an investor."

I don't want to offend anyone, so I gently shake my head "no." I check the lobby for incense and am relieved not to smell any.

I expected the walls to be filled with bad modern art—like the ugly stuff in Jack's house—but the walls are blank. Except for a framed horizontal poster of block letters that spells out "Knowledge is Good." I stare at it for a while. It rings familiar. Isn't knowledge great? Or maybe knowledge is power? Or was it a little knowledge is dangerous?

OK, time to move on.

Wanting to know everything about these folks, I read the firm's bland brochure about five times. Seems the firm was hot in the late '90s and then went cold until they discovered biofuels, iPhone apps, and nano-particulates.

After thirty minutes of filing and buffing, the receptionist waves and says, "Roger just twittered that he'll be right there."

"No problem," I lie. So I wait. And wait.

I look through picture books on the end table. Each of them is a Shutterfly make-your-own-book thing filled with amateur photos and cheesy captions. One of the partners likes to build huts in Costa Rica. Or so it seems. The "photo journey" begins and ends on a Citation X jet.

I sneak glances at the receptionist. She spends precisely twelve and a half minutes per nail. This could go on for a while.

I pick up another book called *Virtue and Vice*. How appropriate. No pictures. Just sayings, page after page after page—on temperance and prudence and fortitude and justice and perseverance and tenacity, let alone all seven deadly sins and then some.

There were a few chapters of prose toward the end of the

book, discussing Greek tragedies, ripped by Shakespeare, about people with huge ambitions and inflated vanities whose virtues are also their vices, so they inevitably blow up, restoring order to themselves and the world around them. It's amazing the crap you'll read when bored to tears.

At nail number five, at the fifty-seven-minute mark, the receptionist says, "Let me walk you to our conference room."

As I walk through the door, I spot Roger, Mullet and all. Ugh. The know-it-all from the cocktail party! He jumps out of his seat to shake my hand.

"I've been playing with TuneBuffoon all morning and I'm a huge fan. I've been looking for a platform like this to build for a while, and you are 100 percent right in the sweet spot."

"Well, I appreciate that. I have a short presentation that goes through what we're trying to do and . . ."

"Brilliant. This socialized networking thing is just so great. You get people to work for free and do all your stuff and the market is hungry for these kinds of deals."

"What makes us unique is dividing the task between DSPs and servers and . . ."

"Have you talked to Jack at RedMark yet?"

How did he know? It was a short, crackly conversation but what the heck. "Yeah, he called me and has been playing with it and . . ."

"We can get a term sheet together pretty quickly. I've got a designer startup in mind, nineteen engineers and a biz-dev guy. You'll be merger-bait for Google or Yahoo in no time, probably already getting feelers, I bet."

I nod.

"We can scale this thing, turn it into both an ad network and a subscription music service and try to value it at $500 to $1,000 per sub." Roger's eyes turn up toward the ceiling and start moving his fingers as if an imaginary calculator sits in front of him. Very weird.

"I have a ten-slide presenta—."

"I'll talk to my partners. My guess is we can go three or four for two-thirds, maybe syndicate it out. You've got to promise to stop returning Jack's calls. First startup for you?" I nod "yes." "Yeah sure, we'll get you liquid quickly. My guess is eight figures and you'll end up running a division at . . ."

Roger stops mid-sentence. The receptionist sticks her head in the door. "Your one-thirty is here."

"Got it. We're done, right? I'll have an associate draw up paperwork. I look forward to working closely with you."

And with that he's gone. Flash, bang.

I spend the rest of the day running from meeting to meeting on Sand Hill Road. Everyone smiles, treats me like I'm his friend, makes all the noises that they'll fund me right on the spot. But no one does.

Visa to VC

11:51 a.m., February 21, Palo Alto

I t's been almost a week.

Nothing. Nada.

I've lobbed a dozen calls into Roger and all the other VCs I met. Not a single returned call. Jag-offs.

And it eventually hits me. "Knowledge is Good" is the motto of Faber College. As in *Animal House*. Words to live by.

My phone rings. No Caller ID announcement by my Grumby. Maybe it's Roger.

I'll let it go to voice mail in case it's . . .

"Hu-llo," Meeta says, picking up the phone.

"Don't, no, let it . . . damn." Too late, Meeta is already chatting.

"It is a nice woman from Visa. She's in Hyderabad. I can tell from her accent. Something about credit constriction," Meeta smiles.

"Give me the phone, wiseguy."

I grab it from Meeta. This can't be good.

"Yes?"

"You are the owner of the account ending in 3141?" Miss India asks.

"Could be."

"Do you have it in your possession?"

"Yes. I'm sitting on it."

"Could you please . . ."

"How do I know you are from Visa?"

"Was your last purchase for $13,427 from an Internet service provider?"

"Yeah, OK. What's the problem?"

"Despite communications attempts on our part, you appear to continue to be in arrears on this account. Actually, from our records, you are in arrears on several different Visa accounts. We can no longer extend you credit."

"But I have been a terrific customer. I pay my bills on time. Surely you can cut me a break."

"Your history has been appropriately discounted, and this blemish on your record can be removed with a payment right now to make your account current. If you have a check, we can do a cash transfer over the phone.

"Yeah, the check's in the mail."

"I'm sorry, sir. Either it's now or . . ."

"Or what?"

"Or your account will been terminated and passed along to a collection agency and . . ."

"I've got other ones: MasterCard, Diners Club, and a Shell gas card. Ha. I don't need you."

"Sir, I must also inform you that your credit history will also be transferred to other credit services over the next twenty-four hours."

I hang up.

"Meeta."

"That didn't end well?" he asks.

"Meeta. As quickly as you can, pay our hosting bill on that last American Express card that works and then get down to Fry's and buy as many phones and drives as you can—and hit the snack aisle hard as well."

I've been broke before. Beyond beer and pretzel money, I've never had much use for cash. And I don't need any more blocky

Scandinavian furniture. But now we have this tiger by the tail, some weird business that's growing like a radioactively mutating weed and we're burning probably $20,000 a month and the old credit card financed startup thing is imploding in my face.

I need to raise some serious money fast.

·   ·   ·

"May I speak with Jack, please?"

"I'm sorry, he's in a meeting. Let me transfer you to his voice mail."

"Jack. It was great to meet . . ."

"Yeah."

"Jack?"

"Yeah."

"I was just trying to leave you a voice mail about TuneBuffoon."

"Oh, I was just dialing out. Trying to call you actually." I hear a muffled chuckle. "What's up?"

"I thought about what we talked about and have done some due diligence," Lorita taught me that expression, sounds official, "and I think we're ready to move on our end."

"Great, great. Any thoughts on a business model yet?"

"I've been doing some thinking and . . ."

"Don't think too hard. These things come over time. You commit to a business too early and it'll probably be wrong. Don't sweat it."

"Uh, OK. Anyway, I'd like to raise $2 million, which probably takes us out three years and then we ought to have profits and the like."

"Yeah, well, we need to do five mil minimum."

"Oh." I try not to sound disappointed.

"You sound disappointed. Take the five. Accelerate the plan. Works every time."

"Sure, yeah. Anyway, I was hoping to get a term sheet and . . ."

"You sound like you're in a hurry."

"No, yeah, but . . ."

"No worries, we're all in a hurry. I'm thinking big things for you. You scale this sucker and the sky's the limit."

"I agree and . . ."

"So I figure seven post."

"That means?"

"Two pre, seven post. We get something like 70 percent for our five mil."

"Well, I was thinking something more like . . ."

"We can probably go three pre. I'll have to run some numbers."

"I've got a lot of employees who own a bunch of shares, and I want to make sure they're taken care of."

"We can create an option pool. No problem. My guess is the lowest we'll go is maybe 55 percent. That should work."

"I was hoping to control the process and was told that valuation of options was important."

"Control? Yeah, figured. OK, yeah sure. You're pretty far along. My guess is you'll hit breakeven pretty quick once you figure out a model and we won't get diluted. So, yeah, sure, you're right. Fifty-fifty. Five pre, ten post. And we get two board seats. Have your lawyer draw up papers and we can get this done by the end of the week."

"It's Thursday."

"So, some lawyer pulls an all-nighter. My guess is you're paying them equity anyway. Make 'em work for it."

I'm not sure what just happened, but I think I just negotiated the deal of my life.

•   •   •

"May I speak to Lorita, please?"

"I'm sorry, she's in a meeting. Let me see if I can get her to pick up."

Now, that's a change.

"Lorita speaking."

"I just got an offer for $5 million for half the company from Jack at RedMark Ventures. He says he'll sign final papers tomorrow and I could use the money. Can you get it done that quickly?"

"Sure, it's all boilerplate stuff. Letting us write it means we can do it on our terms. The only thing that bothers me is that you said half the company."

"I got him down from 70 something percent."

"You should never sell more than half, or even half. It's messy governance. I'll do the share count so that it's 50.1 percent–49.9 percent. Economically, they'll be close to half, but it gives you some wiggle room."

"For what?"

"You never know. You know what I mean?"

•   •   •

And sure enough, I have a signed purchase agreement and articles of incorporation by three in the afternoon the next day. Jack signs it, I sign it, and just like that Jack hands me a check for five million bucks. Wow.

I stop at a Wells Fargo Bank in Palo Alto to set up a corporate account. They seemed happy to have me. I deposit a check for $5 million and walk away with a set of checks emblazoned with a stagecoach and the coolest set of horses galloping away. My money was clearly going somewhere. I just have no idea where.

Yuren

I t's nice to have money in the bank. Heck, it's great. Orgasmic. We pay off all the credit cards, rip up most of them, and make a shopping list of what we need.

In addition to fast computers and hard drives, my main expense now is Furbys. They are increasingly hard to get. Even though we've got tons in the bank, I'm spending way too much time on eBay, bidding on these little fur balls, and dropping $50 or more on each one.

I haven't quite told Jack and the folks at RedMark Ventures about all this Furby stuff. Better they think we are focusing on TuneBuffoon and then spring all this on them once it works. I figure it would all help with the rollout of TuneBuffoon, a platform of sorts, so I'm not worried about it.

Meeta and I become experts at ripping off the fur and soldering in the cameras, microphones, and better speaker. The real hassle is getting the processor chip and USB connector in just right. We have to unsolder and then bend the pins of one of the chips inside the Furby and it takes much too long and the pins keep breaking. I am almost at the point of ripping all the electronics out and re-engineering them myself. But the GPS and Bluetooth parts I have my eye on are too damned expensive and I'm hoping they'll get cheaper, so I can design them in.

Meeta and I make a short video on how to build a Grumby, which we post on YouTube. On our site we put up detailed plans on how to hack into Furbys and which pin to bend and how to put the cameras in the eyes, along with the latest version of our code and the most rudimentary of an SDK, a software development kit, so anyone can both play and program one. I put a PayPal contribution button on the page, too, asking anyone who downloads our code and likes it to make a donation. We get some money but not much.

A few days later, *MAKE Magazine*, this really cool hacker and project magazine, discovers us and puts up a blog entry pointing to our site and the YouTube video. It's our coming-out party. Unfortunately, we aren't quite ready.

In the next twenty-four hours, the video is watched over half a million times. There is no way to contact us. I refuse to even put up an email on our own Web site, so the comments section on YouTube quickly fills up.

"First, does a Furby scream when you skin it?"

"Can I do this to my blowup doll?"

"If a Furby's derby is absurdly Burberry . . ."

Who thinks this stuff up? The rest are something like "where can I buy one of these?"

And just like that, a redesign becomes a priority. That stupid video has sparked a worldwide Furby shortage. To do the hack, you need the old "classic" version of a Furby. The world is running out of old Furbys, and nobody's making more.

One of the comments on YouTube is intriguing. It's from a guy in Shanghai who claims to have a toy company and he has some ideas for the creator of the Grumby and please email him at yuren@toys4us.cn.

Just about everything in this comment is intriguing. China. Shanghai. A company named Toys 4 Us instead of Toys R Us.

And of course, someone whose name would have meant years of verbal torture on American playgrounds.

I compose a note saying I'm the creator of the Grumby and what does he have in mind.

I get back a file with detailed drawings and photos of something that kinda, sorta but not quite looks like a Furby, but isn't. Yuren claims to have a series of factories and over 10,000 workers and he can turn around anything we want in less than twenty-four hours.

It's not until I get to the bottom of the message that I get the punch line. He will sell me the outside shell as a finished product at $2.25 each. If I want my own electronics inside, he will mark up our bill of materials, our costs, by 10 percent.

After a series of emails that stretch over a couple of days, I get more and more excited. We finally set up a time to do a Skype video conference call.

"Hell. O."

"Nee-Ha-OW," I respond.

"OK. Very good. Your Chinese is fluent."

"Yeah, well, I am out of Chinese words."

"I spent four years at the University of Michigan studying industrial engineering and human psychology."

I laugh.

"Can I ask you a question?" I ask.

"Of course."

"It's caused a bit of a stir around here. How do you pronounce your name?" I asked sheepishly.

"In Chinese it's no different than the word "urine." In America I figured that out pretty quickly and went by Yuri. People thought I was Russian."

"Urine it is," I say.

"OK, first things first. If I am going to manufacture these things for you, you must take down the plans from your Web site."

"But there are lots of hackers who . . . ," I start.

"I understand. But they can buy them cheaper from us."

"OK, that's fair."

"And I can buy pretty good quality imagers and microphones in China," Yuren explains.

"The trick is the placement. The code needs to know the exact distance between them, so we can run motion algorithms." I explain.

"We can get a knockoff of the ARM9 controller for pretty cheap. What else do you need?"

"I have my eye on this Bluetooth chip with . . ."

"Yeah, we can get that with integrated GPS and Wi-Fi along with an accelerometer sensor on the same chip. In case someone wants to shake it."

"For?"

"Five bucks."

"That's it?"

"That's it. In volume," Yuren answers.

"Man, oh, man." I pause to think. "So all in?"

"Imagers aren't cheaper. We can get decent microphones and speakers but with a controller and Bluetooth and—my guess is we're talking $30 or $33. Add the shell and our markup and maybe $35—let's say $40 on the outside."

"Wow."

"That's my business. If I were you, I would just preload it with TuneBuffoon code and then sell upgrades. The cheaper the base unit the more likely that . . ."

"Wow."

"I'm doing this because my guess is you are going to sell millions of these things."

That's the first time I've heard that number. I'm stunned into silence.

"Too much?" Yuren asks.

I just stare at the screen.

"Tell you what I'll do. I'll get a prototype together tonight. You email me the latest code for the ARM9 and I'll show you what we can do this time tomorrow."

"We gotta deal," I say, falling behind a few sentences. I probably would have bought them for twice as much—it beat leaning over my dining room table and sniffing solder smoke.

•　　•　　•

I play back the video with Yuren about three or four times until it sinks in. Yuren is going to manufacture a fully loaded Grumby for under $35. We load our software on it and sell it for probably $80–$100 to all the folks that watch the YouTube video.

"Meeta."

"Yes, my taskmister."

"You mean taskmaster?"

"You asked me not to call you boss."

"Meeta. Do any of our esteemed equity workers know anything about manufacturing?"

"I don't think so."

"Marketing?"

"Not as of yet. IIT is very engineering dependent and . . ."

"Business development? Contract law? End-user licenses?"

"These are very American jobs. Why are you asking me?" Meeta looks confused.

"Because I think we are now really in business," I say without much emotion.

"As opposed to what we were doing before?" Meeta asks and for the first time I think I hear a hint of a sarcastic tone.

"*What, what?*" the Grumby on my desk says.

"Well put. We've got a lot to do. Somehow I gotta believe we're not the only ones that can do this."

· · ·

Meeta and I do a joint Skype video call with Yuren, who, as promised, shows off a prototype of his Grumby. We know it is real when we see Yuren gesture and hear *"ten hut!"*

Yuren says he would get a line going and make a thousand Grumbys. They are all of a basic design, though Yuren suggests that someone could create a skin business, swapping out Yuren's basic fur for another. Not us, I insist.

Yuren suggests we ship the Grumby with TuneBuffon and a limited set of gestures as well as the listen and respond code. Meeta has already figured out a way, so as soon as a Grumby gets plugged into a PC via USB or a Bluetooth connection, a browser window opens up to our Web site and we'll sell upgrade modules. He's not sure what that means quite yet. Neither do I. First things first.

Real Offices

"Where do you want the servers?" Meeta asks.

"Put them in the network operations center. Duh," I answer.

Meeta just stands there and looks at me, straight-faced, no emotion.

"OK," I finally say, trying not to laugh. "Where should we put the network operations center?"

Meeta drops the rack of servers he was holding in the middle of the place and says, "Right here?"

"Yeah, how about in that back corner. I have the feeling we are going to have to air condition that space or we are all going to sweat like pigs when this thing runs hot."

"OK, but I get first dibs on offices."

"You go right ahead."

I spin around in a complete circle. Meeta just rented 20,000 square feet of almost completely open office space in the bowels of Milpitas. Thirty cents a square foot, services included. So six grand a month, not too bad, and we've already paid for six months. Plus, there's lots of room to grow.

The place is a dump, but it beats working out of my home. The steel gray carpeting is about a millimeter thick, and that's in the good spots that aren't worn down. Whoever was here before us had left in a hurry; there are tons of desks and chairs and cubicle dividers scattered around the place. We'll need all of those.

"This is mine," Meeta says, dragging a desk over to the side of the office, about ten feet from the window. It looks out into an empty parking lot—scenic.

I pull another table a few feet from Meeta's and declare my office space. I sit down, pull out a laptop, position it in the middle of my new desk, and . . . I'm immediately bored.

"Let's see what else this place has got," I say.

"I'm in," Meeta agrees.

So we stroll. The kitchen is barren but reasonably clean. A few closets have some paper and pens and another has several sealed boxes. Meeta rips one open and pulls out what looks like a user's manual for some weird contraption.

We both flip through it.

"Some kind of network equipment?" Meeta asks.

"I don't think so. This thing has some oddball settings and warnings about a laser. What is iris heterochromia?" I ask. I keep flipping.

"Isn't that laser wavelength multiplexing?"

"Coloboma? Micro-invasive intraocular implants? What the? Some sort of eyeball factory? Ick."

I read on. Laser eye improvement?

"Check this out and give me some hand help," Meeta says. I look over and he's inside another closet pulling out the weird-est-looking contraption. It looks like a dentist chair but there's an attachment that looks like it wraps around your head and then clamps to your face with hooks for your eye sockets.

"Man, that's gross. I think I saw this in *A Clockwork Orange*," I say.

"This is the most hugely coolest thing I've ever seen, the world beyond kelvin," Meeta practically screams.

So we slide the chair toward the front door. "This absolutely must be the chair for the waiting room," Meeta insists.

"We have a reception area?" I ask.

"We do now!"

It looks pretty cool by the front door. I suspect it will scare most people away. Meeta sits in the chair and pulls the containment mask to his head. I get a little queasy.

"Enough. We've got tons to do. First off, getting those servers hooked up. And a T-3 line set up. We are going to suck bandwidth like a tennis ball through a garden hose."

"Huh?" Meeta asks.

I ignore him. "More desks. Find some surplus Aeron chairs. And most important, an espresso maker and some serious munchies for the kitchen. No one in their right mind will work here without all that."

"Yes sir. We can fit many people in here."

"Not just anybody, Meeta. We need surgeon-class programmers."

"Eye surgeons?" Meeta says. I still can't tell if he's kidding.

"Just the best. Those that can outcode anybody. If not, they don't belong here. We can't afford to train anybody. We need DSP coders and database junkies and some algorithm folks and speech and Bluetooth and who the heck knows what."

"I'll get the word out. Usual deal?"

"Yeah, but now we have money! Hey, we can pay a salary. Try to cap it at eighty grand. It would be nice if the money lasts for a little while. And, of course, 10,000 shares. With more shares as a bonus for milestones and hitting shipping dates and success and . . ."

"This is going to be fun, no?" Meeta asks.

"No. Yes. If it doesn't kill us first," I say.

Dumplings

Around 11 p.m. PST, February 27, Somewhere over the Pacific Ocean

This seat is so uncomfortable and my knees are sore from rubbing against the magazine pouch. I wake up every three hours and pop another four Excedrin PM. After the third time, they stop working. I'm stuck in a middle seat on an aging steel tube hurtling across the Pacific, stuck as always between a chatty gray-haired woman and a drooling fat guy.

I brought my laptop to do some coding but the batteries are long gone, so I stare at the movie screen ten or fifteen rows in front of me and play "guess the dialog." My brain is too fried to plug in the headset, so I just sit there, rehashing all the things that have gone wrong in my life and all the things that can still go wrong. Boredom brooding. Man, I hate flying.

We finally touch down and I can't wait to get off the plane and breathe some fresh air. The terminal is modern and stretches forever, finally ending in a huge maze of lines leading to an immigration checkpoint. My phone doesn't seem to work in here, I wonder if they are jamming. Thirty minutes later I stumble up to a seventy-year-old man in a shabby uniform and crooked glasses.

"You visit?"

"Yes."

"Visit?"

"Yes."

"Visit person, visit beeness."

"I'm sorry."

"Beeness, beeness. Money, money."

"Oh, yes, I am on beeness."

"Visa say personal."

"Well, I am visiting a person. Old friend."

"Uhhhh." More of a growl than a statement. He stamps my passport and waves me through.

I walk through a set of double doors and am immediately hit with the sounds, smells, and utter chaos of Shanghai. And I'm still in the airport. It takes another fifteen minutes of wandering around until I spot a sign in the distance bobbing up and down with the picture of a Grumby on it. That's got to be Yuren.

"Welcome."

"Thanks. It's great to meet."

"Let's get out of here. My car is in the garage."

Three elevators and a few long hikes through a packed garage and we come upon a steel gray Yugo.

"They still make these?" I ask.

Yuren laughs. "It's not really a Yugo. We took one apart and are trying to manufacture them. No one claims the rights to the Yugo anymore, so I figure I could own it by default. We're trying to bring up an assembly line; it's not so easy." On cue, the Chinese Yugo backfires.

It's also the smallest car I've sat in for a very long time. My knees rest on the passenger side of the dashboard. There is no backseat, just a small space for my duffle bag.

We race through the parking lot. Yuren pays the fee and practically spins his wheels getting out of the airport and onto the entrance ramp to the highway. And then we stop. The ramp is packed and as we inch closer, the highway is jam-packed as well. It's five in the evening.

"Rush hour?"

"Always" is all Yuren can say.

We crawl in silence for a while.

Living in the Bay Area, I am used to fog, driving over the Golden Gate Bridge without seeing the actual bridge or where I am going. This is worse. The smog is engulfing. The fuzzy outlines of buildings become visible in the distance and as we pass them, they don't get any clearer. It's like driving through a crowded bar of cigar smokers.

"I've got something for you," Yuren says as he reaches behind his seat and pulls up one of his Grumbys. I recognize it from the Skype call.

"Awesome" is about all I can say.

I immediately start playing with it and get it to sing as I try to run it through its paces.

"Do you like the model?" Yuren finally asks.

"I think it's terrific. The eyes are softer and the motion a lot smoother. I'm not sure where you got the speaker from, but it's crystal clear, better than anything I've used and . . ."

"It could be better," Yuren says.

"The sound?" I ask.

"The whole thing. Once we get to volume, I can squeeze some parts suppliers for better quality. We are gearing up a line with three shifts to make these things and . . ."

"You can make money at $35?"

"Yeah, sure. With volume. I want to understand your plans for selling and distribution."

"Well we are still working that out. It really becomes a game of shipping free software that works on generic platforms and then we . . ."

"Save it for dinner. We're almost there."

It's been at least ninety minutes since we left the airport, but I notice the fuzzy buildings are getting closer together and a funny looking building with several ball shapes across a river.

"That's our TV Tower."

"Unique," I say.

"We are here. It's the Bund. I figured you might enjoy a meal. I have reservations at M on the Bund. I heard it's excellent, Euro-fusion or some such thing. Shopping in the building and a view of the TV Tower and the Pudong skyline. Sound good?"

"Do they have dumplings?"

"More like goat cheese salad."

"Can we go somewhere for dumplings? And a beer? I've been dreaming about that all flight."

Yuren smiles. "Of course, there is one right around the corner behind the Bund. No foreigners."

"Even better."

We park in an alley that's barely wide enough for pedestrians or bicyclists—I guess that's the advantage of a tiny Chinese Yugo—and walk to a small, uh, the only words I can use to describe it is "rat hole," down the block.

We walk up to an opening in a wall to order. The signs are completely in Chinese. I peer through the opening and see three women hunched over boiling pots and woks. This is the right place to be.

Yuren orders an assortment of who knows what and six Tsing Taos, which they hand him in a cardboard carrying case and we take over to a table in the back.

"As I told you on Skype, you are going to sell many, many of these," Yuren says.

"I hope so."

"I know so. I know every device selling in the U.S. because they are all made here by friends of mine."

"Does everyone manufacture around here?"

"More or less. Lots of electronics, but we make toys and shoes and barbeque grills. I even manufactured Visa cards for a while by the tens of millions. My guess is that everyone in America has at least five credit cards."

"Probably."

"I sold that business to a friend. Your Grumby is going to be big. I needed the space," Yuren explains.

"Why do you think so?" I ask.

"I've downloaded your applications and they are addicting. TuneBuffoon, Stump the Machine. I'm sure you can do others— Sing-Along? Stump the Teacher?"

"I hope you're right. We made some calls to stores and they all require long sales cycles. There was a toy show in New York last month and we were told to wait until next year's show, that all the holiday selections have already been made," I say.

Yuren looks disappointed.

"But we set up shop on Amazon. You can sell anything you want on Amazon. They'll even do inventory for you; some algorithm determines how many units to order. Fulfillment, billing. It's amazing."

"So online only?"

"We found a buyer at Wal-Mart who loves the idea but can't commit."

"Why not?"

"No history. She says she'll track the Amazon sales numbers and we should be ready for an order if it works."

Now Yuren smiles. "You get Wal-Mart and then you'll get Costco five minutes later. Guaranteed. Amazon, Wal-Mart, and Costco and you're done! Everybody knows that."

The dumplings keep coming. So does the Tsing Tao. We talk and talk.

"Need sleep. Excedrin PM stopped working," I finally say.

"Let's go. Where are you staying?"

"The Feng Ye Super Lucky Hotel," I answer.

Yuren's eyebrows shoot up. "How did you pick that?"

"Priceline. It was cheap."

"It sure is. Lock the door."

"Is it not safe?" I ask.

"From crime? Yes. From rats? Not so much," Yuren chuckles.

"Should I?"

"Don't worry. You'll live. I'll pick you up at your hotel tomorrow morning at six thirty. I'll give you a tour of the factory and get you back to the airport in time for your flight," Yuren says.

•   •   •

Yuren is prompt. We're on our way by 6:32 a.m. The smog hasn't lifted. Shanghai is still visible only if you squint real hard and half imagine what the buildings might look like. But even through the smog you can tell that there are huge buildings, say the Houston skyline, replicated at each point of the compass no matter how far you drive in any direction. After a fifteen-minute drive, we pull up in front of one of the faceless fifty-story buildings. Yuren declares, "Here we are."

"I thought we were going to the factory," I say.

"This is it. In Shanghai we build up, not out."

We take the elevator to the forty-second floor. The doors open to a loud, teeming assembly operation. Boxes are piled up along the windows and tables, and tables are filled with parts and nuts and bolts. Looking closer, I can make out Grumby skins waiting to be attached. Yuren doesn't waste any time.

We walk around for a while, visiting about six of the floors. Yuren says he has eleven floors in total but rights to the whole building if he wants it. Yuren hints that like perhaps half or more of the new buildings in Shanghai, this one is mostly empty.

"Let's go to my office," Yuren shouts.

We step inside a corner office and when Yuren closes the door a complete silence envelopes us.

"Look, I am very excited about this product, as I hope you can tell," Yuren starts.

"I am too."

"You're OK with the $35 cost?" he asks.

"That will work. It's cheaper than me assembling them myself," I explain.

"We'll build in a price declinator as we ramp up and figure out our costs and negotiate better discounts."

"Great."

"But I want you to pass it along with your own price declines."

"Uh, I think we can do that," I say.

"I've watched others, like Apple, keep cost declines for themselves. I benefit from high volume not high prices."

"I get it."

"I hope so. Our model is to build more and more factories to handle volume and then automate, so we can produce anything cheaper than anyone, worldwide."

"Like Yugos?" I kid.

"We may get that to work but I'd rather sell electronics. Much cleaner," Yuren admits.

"OK, I'm in."

"Your lawyers can draw up papers?" Yuren asks.

"I'll email them on the way to the airport. Let's keep it simple. I got a feeling this is going to be a fun ride."

We shake hands. And that's that.

•   •   •

On the way back to the airport, Yuren hands me a small bottle. In big letters it says "Imovane Aventis." Underneath is the word "Zopiclone." I rattle the bottle and then open the top. Inside are maybe twenty pills.

"You want me to smuggle these into the U.S.?" I ask.

"No way. You can't have them all. Take two and put them in your pocket. When they board your row, swallow both of them. You'll thank me when you get back."

He hands me a bag and I do as he tells me, walk back to another middle seat in the two-five-two configuration, sit down, and the next thing I remember is being jolted awake by the wheels touching down at SFO.

Listen

11:16 a.m., March 1, Milpitas

I drive straight to the office—I hate wasting even one day. At first, I think I may have walked into the wrong building. I recognize the eyeball torture chair in the lobby—wait, we have a lobby—but not much else. Yellow dividers separate the entryway from the rest of the space. I walk through an opening and stop in my tracks.

All at once, about thirty pairs of eyes look up at me from monitors sitting on about a dozen tables. It looks like a hub and spoke emanating from a central point. Two half-round horseshoe-shaped tables fill the middle. It could just have easily been a war room at the Pentagon. Well, except everyone's wearing a black T-shirt and sneakers and has hair pointing in all directions of the compass and . . .

I turn around and face the other side of the space away from the windows. A conference room with seating for twenty is set up, cordoned off with dividers. In the back near the kitchen are a pool table and a ping-pong table. Just to the side sits a *Star Trek The Next Generation* pinball machine with Picard's voice beckoning someone to play. Along the wall sits a fifty-inch flat screen with scattered cables hooked up to both a Wii and an Xbox 360. A plastic guitar is leaning against the wall.

And how did I miss this in my first look around? Painted on

the wall is a mural of Brad Pitt and Edward Norton from *Fight Club* with the words: "Mischief. Mayhem. Code."

"Meeta!"

Meeta comes running from the back of the office.

"Welcome back. We have made much progress but we have a million questions for you. You had better sit down."

Meeta led me to one of the horseshoe desks and pulls out the chair for me.

"OK, you can introduce me to everyone in a little bit, but I have a surprise for you."

I reach into the snazzy duffle bag I bought on the streets of Shanghai and produce one, then two, and then all five Grumby beta units and pop them on the table. I hear ooohs and grunts and oh, yeahs from around the room.

The questions come rapid fire.

"How many I/O channels should we enable in the processor?"

"What is the longest sentence we can expect?"

"Can I hire my cousin?"

"Do we capture GPS coordinates every second?"

"Can we capture other trained gestures?"

"Can I use MySQL or should I write my own database?"

"Can we get softer toilet paper for the bathroom?"

Meanwhile, I watch as all five Grumby models get passed around, plugged into USB ports, and coding starts fast and furious. After a few minutes I hear "*ten hut*" and a round of applause and I know we are on an extremely fast track.

Over the next twelve hours, I meet each of our new employees. Thirty-two of them. One is forty-two years old; the rest are all under thirty. Maybe ten are from India, the rest a United Nations of Chinese, Serbians, Koreans, Romanians, one each from Macau, Estonia, and Zimbabwe—oh, yeah—and three guys from Cleveland. And five women, who ought to keep the place somewhat civil. Or maybe not.

I hear each of their backgrounds, projects they've worked on, and what expertise they are bringing to the party. And party it is. *Star Wars* toys are everywhere. So are Nerf guns, Slinkies, Jack Skellington figurines, and a three-foot-high *Alien vs. Predator* battle re-enactment in sculpted plastic.

Even with thirty-four of us arranged like a bicycle wheel to one side of the office, the place still feels empty—there's a ton of room to expand and at Meeta's hiring clip, I suspect it won't take long.

The place is humming—well, not so much humming but instead an odd sound I haven't quite heard before. It's a mixture of key clicks, mouse clicks, grunts, chuckles, and more clicks. A modern factory of sorts. An idea factory.

• • •

Around midnight—I think it's midnight, it's dark outside, anyway—I dig out the personality code from a week ago. I think I've got a new tweak to keep the conversation more realistic.

George Clooney Grumby, as he is wont to do in real life, I suppose, keeps saying totally inappropriate things. If the subject of money comes up, I'd hear, "*There's a Chinese man with a hundred sixty million dollars behind that door. Let's get him out.*"

And for no good reason, I keep hearing, "*We need a grease man not an acrobat.*"

I keep thinking about real-world conversations and what happens if something stupid is said. Usually silence or just a long "uhhhhhh" or a sarcastic "yeah" and the other person walks away.

And then it hits me. All you have to do is listen. Create an instant feedback loop.

I set up an appropriateness index for each piece of dialog and initially set it at zero.

If there's a long pause, or if the conversation doesn't flow, or the subject is immediately changed to something else, then the too-cool-for-school *"the truth can be adjusted"* line probably isn't the best choice, and I decrease the counter. The more negative the index the less likely we should use that set of words. On the flip side, a positive index means the comment is worthwhile.

It's what a dorky teenage boy does. Learns how to hold a conversation by updating his appropriateness index through painful trial and error. Except I'd have thousands of dorky Grumbys updating each other. Way cool.

"See what I mean?" I ask.

"Some people just lack vision."

"Something I want to ask you . . . ," I start.

"I stole things."

"Uh, thanks for that," I say.

"Thanks for the game, fellas."

"Hey, George, will you ever get married?" I ask.

"My wife left me. I was upset. I got into a self-destructive pattern."

"Sorry."

"You lose focus for one second in this game and someone gets hurt."

"If you say so." I start laughing.

"What I'm about to propose to you happens to be both highly lucrative and highly dangerous. If that doesn't sound like your particular brand of vodka, help yourself to as much food as you like and safe journey. No hard feelings."

"Uh, what are you talking about?" I ask. I don't know how it came up with that.

"No, but you're sweet to ask." Well, this is rev 1.0. Once lots of people use this it will train a lot better.

"Well, nice talking to you," I finish.

"You don't know how many times I played this conversation out in my head the last two years."

It's starting to make sense, but I have to admit it's a little spooky.

•　　•　　•

I take a break. It's 2:00 a.m. Meeta is still here. No surprise.

I look around. There are maybe ten or twelve others still around, still coding away. Two guys are playing Guitar Hero on the Xbox with headphones on. I hear snoring and look around until I notice someone sleeping under the pool table. Man, I gotta go home. "Meeta, we need a better SDK."

"Recording tape?"

"A software development kit. We have a chintzy one up, but we really need some better way to describe all our functions, speech recognition, image processing, communications, and put it all out there so everybody can use it."

"Isn't that the crowned jewels?" Meeta asks.

"In a way. But someone else is going to come up with something we didn't think of."

"But I have hired the surgeon-class programmers you asked for."

"Joy's law," I explain.

"I am not familiar."

"Bill Joy, Sun Microsystems." I throw up some air quotes and need to remember to add that to the gesture database. "Most of the smartest people work for someone else." I pause. "Look, I'd rather run the risk that someone copies everything and tries to create their own Grumby than misses the next coolest feature. Put it all out there. I have Lorita writing a foolproof license agreement."

"Nothing's foolproof," Meeta says, mimicking me.

"It is if it's yours. If we can control what gets used, or at least get paid for everything that's used, we might even make some money. What I have no clue about is the whole back-end thing, when we go beyond a few thousand real users," I say. "I'm over my head."

Meeta looks tired. "Yes, I know," he says.

"Know what?"

"UCLA and all." He pauses. "I snooped."

"It's late. Some other day," I sigh.

"We all have a past, right?"

Meeta looks like he swallowed a cat.

Tutor

12:37 p.m., March 6, Palo Alto

Ouch. Almost a week of burning the midnight oil. Yuren sent a box with a dozen of the first set of Grumbys off his manufacturing line. Everyone now has access to one to test out, and the whole office has been in burn-the-wick programming mode.

I haven't crawled into bed before three or four in the morning in a while. But we released the software development kit into the wild. Being first has to count for something. I have Meeta track downloads but haven't seen any new applications. I hope someone is playing with our stuff.

Then again, I'm so damned tired I'm not sure how much I really care anymore. I'm enjoying a morning at home—oops, it's already afternoon—and my phone rings. It's my buddy Mark. I have his son Mikey (and Raffi) to thank for creating Grumby in the first place, so I gave him one of the early Yuren units to play with.

"You gotta see this?"

"See what?" I'm in serious veggie mode.

"Some guy in Russia has come up with the neatest thing."

"The neatest what?"

"It's too amazing to describe. You've got to download it and try it. You'll need a four- or five-year-old."

"Can I rent one?"

"Illegal in most states. I'll bring mine over tonight."

•   •   •

At about seven Mark shows up at the door holding hands with his daughter Pamela, Mikey's older sister. How cute. He's got a stack of kids' books tucked under his other arm. I recognize the top one, *Goodnight Moon*, but have no idea what this is all about.

Mark sets up his Grumby on the coffee table and sits on the floor next to Pamela. He picks up *Goodnight Moon* and waves it in front of the Grumby.

I hear a woman's voice come out of the Grumby with "*Thank you, we are all set to read*" in a nice pleasant and vaguely recognizable British accent.

Pamela giggles.

Mark states, "Pamela has never read this before."

I raise my eyebrows. If I remember correctly she's barely four years old.

"*What's your name?*" the Grumby asks.

"Pamela," she giggles. And then she starts to read.

"In. The . . . ," she starts slowly.

Then she pauses, struggling with the next word.

The Grumby starts helping, "*Guh-guh-guh.*"

Pamela follows, "Guh."

Another pause.

"*Gur, gur, gur,*" Grumby prompts.

Pamela continues, "Gur, gray, great!" with a big smile.

Then she pauses again.

"*Gur-gur—*"

"Gray, gree, green room." Another big smile.

"*Yes?*" Grumby asks. "*In the great green room . . .*"

"There was a t-t-t—"

"*Tell, tella*—"

"Tele-p-p—"

"*No, telef-f-f*—"

"Ah," Pamela squeals. "Telephone. And. A. Red. Balloon. And. A. Pic-too-ree."

"*Picture, Pamela, picture.*"

"Hey, wait a second. I know that voice. That's Mary Poppins." I'm shocked.

"Shhhhhh," both Mark and Pamela shush me with fingers to their lips. Fun family.

"Picture. Of. A. Cow. J-J-J—," Pamela is stuck again.

"*Jummmm*—"

"Jumping. A picture of a cow jumping over the moon," she finishes.

I can't believe it. Mary Frickin' Poppins teaching kids how to read. A doll imparting its intelligence, which it got from us. We taught. Now it teaches. Absolutely amazing. Why hadn't we thought of that? I think my Polish babysitter taught me how to read when I was five or six, which is why I still hear words with an Eastern European accent.

Bored with silly cows, precious and quickly turning precocious, Pamela grabs another. "How about this one?"

"Well, if you think you are ready?" Mark patronizes or maybe it was just classic doting, as all fathers do.

Mark holds up another book.

"*Thank you. We are all set to read.*"

"We went to the beach, just gr—"

"*Grandma . . .*"

"Just Grandma and me."

And so it goes on. Little Pamela pours through the stack of books like she's an eighth grader.

Around the fourth book Mark says something to the Grumby and the voice changes to Sylvester Stallone's. Not quite as soothing as Julie Andrews, but Pamela sits up straight, pays closer attention, and makes a lot fewer mistakes.

Mark walks up to me with a smile on his face, leans over, and says very softly in my left ear, "You hiring?"

"You're a doctor." I remind him.

"I can learn to code," Mark sighs.

Sued and Screwed

10:42 a.m., March 7, Milpitas

B ack in the office the next morning I can't wait to show
Meeta Mary Poppins in a can. When Meeta sees that I'm
in, he comes running to my desk.

I'm about to launch on him when he blurts out, "This doesn't
sound good."

"What?"

"*What, what?*" a chorus of Grumbys lets loose.

"Might you describe the dilemma?" I ask, without triggering
Stump the Machine. Note to self: we need to implement a code
word to turn Stump the Machine off.

"Ree-ah-ah?"

"Huh?"

"You know this R-I-A-A? I am now reading a press release
from some such Recording Industry Association of America.
There is still a recording industry in this country?" Meeta asks.

"And it says?"

"It says the Ree-ah-ah has filed an injunction for a cease and
desist order for TuneBuffoon for copyright violation and is asking
for damages of $750 per copyright infringement."

"But we don't violate any copyrights," I shout.

"It doesn't say that," Meeta deadpans.

"No kidding." I pause and think. "How do they even know

about us? Someone must have turned us in. This is not good. How many copyright violations do they say we have infringed?"

"They claim that based on the number of downloaded copies of TuneBuffoon at 50,000—hey, didn't we already pass one million?"

"Over the weekend."

"And the number of songs in our database—they are also a little low at 200,000—and assumed usage patterns, they calculate that we owe them . . . wait for it . . ."

"C'mon."

"There are a lot of zeros. I think that says one and $5 billion."

"WHAT?"

"*What, what?*" the Grumbys grumble, almost sounding annoyed.

"Let me see that—Meeta—you've got it wrong. That's $15 billion."

"Didn't we just raise money from RedMark?" Meeta asks me.

"We're still a little short."

"Well then this email is probably not welcome."

"From?"

"From our ISP."

"I paid them several days ago. Everything we owe. Even paid for a few months in advance."

"Yes, they are quite happy with our finances. But they received a cease and desist notice from this RIAA and an invoice for $15 billion and are quite sad to inform us that they have unplugged our servers from the network."

"Jeez. Not good." I think for a second. "Can we just put it up on our own servers here?" I ask Meeta.

"Sure, we can do that rather quickly, but we barely have a ten-megabit connection, and I don't think we can handle much downloads."

I look at Meeta's Nike T-shirt. "Just do it," I tell him.

• • •

A few minutes later I get an email.

"Well that didn't take long. RedMark has called an emergency board meeting conference call in five minutes," I sigh.

"We can disconnect our phones claiming the RIAA has shut off service," Meeta offers. I'm starting to be able to tell when he is kidding and when he is not.

"I'll deal with it. Get Lorita on the line and see if she has any ideas."

My cell phone rings. "Well, here we go."

I shake my head, take a deep breath, and click and hold the green button on my phone, which puts it into speakerphone mode.

"Jack, how are you?" I ask.

"Did you know about this before we invested?" Jack asks me.

"Know about what?"

"This blatant copyright violation. I had no idea. That's a pre-existing condition and we can sue you for just about everything."

"I'm not sure what you are talking about."

Meeta starts laughing and I hold up my finger to my mouth for him to be quiet.

"*Shhh,*" the Grumby chorus shushes in unison.

"New gesture," I hear Meeta whisper.

"We just received notice that the service has been shut down by the RIAA and . . ."

"Actually, TuneBuffoon is up and running just fine." Meeta holds two thumbs up. "Pull it up on your Web browser and you'll see . . ."

"Whatever. There has been a material change in business conditions. I want to call a board meeting to order. I've got my partner Jeff on the line as well." Jack starts abruptly.

"OK, I like board meetings," I say.

"Great. Old business, none. Finances, none. New business?" Jack takes over the meeting.

"I propose a motion . . . ," Jeff starts.

"Aren't we missing someone?" I interrupt.

"No, we're all present." Jack snaps.

"Uh, I get two board seats."

"Well, you haven't nominated anyone and we'll have to take that up at the regular board meeting next month."

"But I . . ."

Meeta's phone rings.

"I propose a motion . . . ," Jeff starts again.

"Just a second." I say. I want to see who is calling Meeta.

"We don't have time," Jack says tersely.

"I propose a motion that the board vote on termination procedures for the chief executive officer," Jeff finishes.

"I second." Jack adds. "To be replaced by Richie . . ."

"Wait," I interrupt. "You're firing me?" And what does Richie have to do with any of this?

"All in favor?" Jack asks.

"Aye," Jeff says.

"Aye," Jack says.

"FAIL," Meeta yells.

"FAIL," his Grumby repeats.

I'm stunned. I just sit and look at my phone.

Meeta's phone rings.

"Hang up," I hear softly from Meeta.

"Huh?" I ask.

"Lorita says, "Hang up," Meeta says a little louder.

"All against?" Jack asks.

"HANG UP!" Meeta screams.

In a daze, I reach over and hit the red button on my phone and cut off the call.

"What just happened?"

"Lorita was listening in. She called from her cell phone to tell you to hang up." Meeta says.

"Is she still on the line?" I ask.

"She had to look something up and said she would get right back to us."

"I think I just got fired. I've never been fired in my life. Arrested, yes. Fired, no."

"I think they wished to fire you but did not complete the task," Meeta says with a smile on his face.

His phone rings.

"It's Lorita again."

I grab the phone.

"Hi."

"Hi. Do you copy any music when you run it through TuneBuffoon?" Lorita asked.

"No."

"Does any music ship in the code?"

"No," I say.

"Do users copy any music? Even a note?"

"No. We just run it through a filter and classify it. We don't even keep the MP3 files."

"I figured. I've got our copyright guy drafting a countersuit and press release accusing the RIAA of techno-terrorism and harassment and we'll treble damages unless they immediately withdraw their cease and desist and put out a press release stating that our code is clean."

"We're suing the RIAA for $45 billion?" Man, I like how they think.

"Sure sounds like it. And, uh, since you took a venture investment, the clock is ticking around here. You know what I mean?" Lorita asks.

I think I actually do. "You're charging me?"

"Yes."

"No problem, you deserve it. And the board meeting?"

"Don't agree to any board meetings without me present?"

"Got it. And somehow they tried to put in an old friend of mine as CEO."

"Did you ever vote?" she asks.

"No, I hung up."

"Good. That means you're still CEO. And get a new friend. I'll send out a notice that we are taking their vote proposal to a shareholder vote."

"So the shareholders get to decide if I'm fired?"

"Sure, that's the way it works with corporate governance."

"But won't they . . ."

"You're still the majority shareholder, remember? At 50.1 percent."

"Oh."

"I assume you will vote to keep your job?"

"Got it. So I still have a job?"

"And your company."

"Cool."

"OK, let me get on this."

"Uh, can I ask you a question?"

"Sure."

"I can't trust those guys again, can I?" I ask.

"I wouldn't." she answers.

"But they're still on the board. They still own shares. They're still around to annoy me?" I argue.

"Just wait. These things usually work out," Lorita says with a calming voice.

Recap

"There's someone here to see you," Meeta says.

"Who?" I ask.

"He won't say. He looks pissied off," Meeta tells me.

"It's pissed off." I correct.

"Yes, hissied and pissied."

"Send him back," I say. I think I know who it is. It was only a matter of time.

Jack walks in briskly and stands over my table.

"Jack, nice to see you. Would you like a tour?" I ask.

"OK, Mr. CEO by shareholder vote. We need to restructure our deal."

"I thought we have an agreement that we both signed," I reply calmly.

"Look, if you've been in the venture business as long as I have, you would know that all of these agreements are subject to changing conditions and changing terms. That's just how it's done. We can work this out in a friendly manner or we can sue you for breach of contract and making false statements during our due diligence process and . . ."

"You want the whole company?" I ask, waving my arms around our office space, for some reason ending up pointing at the *Alien vs.*

Predator battle sculpture. "You can have my old pal Richie run it."

Jack grimaces. "No. We want out. We can't have a lawsuit hanging over our heads. We've built our reputation over decades and can't be seen as party to an infringement suit, let alone a deal that went sour this quickly."

"So you think we're worthless?"

"Probably. Getting sued for billions is not something that happens to small companies."

"But we don't infringe on any . . . ," I start.

"When we invested you had a service up and running and now it has ceased and ISPs won't touch you and your burn rate is going to accelerate and . . . and . . ."

"And?

"We want out?"

"Just like that?"

"Just give us our 5 million back," Jack demands.

I start coughing uncontrollably, slipping in the word "bullshit" between coughs.

"We've done this before. Just transfer the capital back, a reverse wire, and we'll sign an agreement that the previous agreement is null and void."

"I can't do that?"

"Why not? It's the right thing to do. Material change. Force majeure."

"What is force majeure?" I ask.

Jack was about to answer when my Grumby cuts him off.

"*French for major force, events beyond our control, releasing our obligation . . .*"

"Who is that?" Jack starts.

Oops. I haven't quite told Jack about this stuff.

"*. . . war, strike, riot, earthquake, flooding, volcano . . .*"

"The RIAA is a frickin' tsunami," Jack says.

"It didn't say tsunami."

"Just give us our money back," Jack says, ignoring the odd voice coming from a toy.

"Like I said, I can't do that," I say.

"Why not?"

"Because I don't have it. It's gone."

"Gone?"

"Well, some of it."

"How much?"

"Maybe half."

"On what?"

"Credit cards, ISPs, offices, legal, machines, iPhones, travel."
I neglect to mention the trip to China.

"That's it?"

"And we prepaid some expenses so we won't get cut off."

"We'll take back the rest," Jack insists.

"But I'm running a company."

"Not for long. You're shut down," Jack says rather sternly.

"Actually, the service is still running from servers over there and . . ."

"You have twenty-four hours," Jack snaps like he's done this before.

"Before what?" I ask.

"Before WE shut you down. Three phone calls and no one will do business with you again. We do a lot of work with your counsel—they won't like losing our account. And a lawsuit from us on top of the RIAA's and no one in his right mind would come work here. And you'll never raise another penny of venture capital."

"Are you threatening me?"

"No. I'm just telling you that you have twenty-four hours or else."

"Yeah, well, pissy off," I shout.

. . .

"So how much is left?" Lorita asks.

"Probably four and a half million. We really haven't spent that much."

"OK, keep prepaying. Rent, electric, uh, legal. I'll negotiate a recap."

"A what?" I ask.

"A recapitalization. Kinda like a do-over. We'll retain enough to keep the company running for a month or two and send the rest back."

"Just like that?"

"Well there's always a tail."

"A tail?" I ask. "A rat's tail?"

"They get to keep something. Probably 5 or 10 percent of the company."

"For what?"

"Look, you did spend five hundred grand of someone else's money. They won't just forget that happened."

"I don't want to see or hear from Jack again," I insist.

"Yeah, well, these things are like a divorce. Everyone hates everyone else, but you still have to meet to hand over the kids on weekends."

"Can you keep them under 10 percent?"

"I think so."

"And no board seats. Getting fired by Jack once was plenty."

"I think we can do that. But you better go raise some more money because you've probably got about a two-month clock ticking away."

"I think I still have another credit card I haven't completely abused."

All Bro

I finally have a real job and almost instantly get fired. Jeez. Is that some sort of sign?

But Lorita is good. RedMark Ventures ends up with just 9.9 percent. And no board seats. And no Richie.

And one pissied-off entrepreneur fired up to succeed, driven by a clear vision marred only by streaks of the crimson blood of revenge. I saw that in a movie once. What's that old saying? What doesn't kill you makes you, uh, bitter, vengeful. It's always nice to have motivation.

I don't know what it is about me. I get near authority and I freak. I have to rebel against it. Take it down. Show it that my way works better.

I like being on my own. Yeah, yeah, I still have Meeta and crew, but I look at them as an extension of me. It really is about the power of the individual. Against the system. With something to prove. A machine is just a tool, a powerful tool, in the hands of individuals.

But not just my hands anymore.

Maybe that's the end game for all this. Used to be it was only as good as what I could type in or display on my screen. Now it has sensors, its own inputs. It learns and not just from me. I didn't teach it to teach kids to read. It has eyes and ears but people don't learn through just eyes and ears. They learn psychically. People take the pulse of others around them and learn how to be human. How much can Grumby learn? To be human? No, probably not. But to be human for us? We fake being human a lot. Can Grumby do some of the faking for us?

Like you, I had to read George Orwell's *1984* in high school. Cool story. Big Brother watching you. What a joke that turned out to be. I prefer to watch Big Brother. A faster machine and quicker Internet access and we all become Big Brothers, not so much watching each other but spitting out enough data that we can vibe off each other. What's hot, what's not? Learn from each other's experiences, mistakes, maybe even moods.

Late night TV. Way high up in the cable channels. A happy-looking priest with a German accent. "To be human is to be in relation."

My Grumby in is relation to more people than I could ever know and certainly more than I ever want to know. Grumby doesn't even think it's hard.

If we do this right, our Grumbys can be the ultimate extension of the individual, which paradoxically means the ultimate network. I've heard of Metcalfe's law: the power of a network varies as the square of the nodes. I wonder if Metcalfe knows the priest. Hell, maybe he converted.

It's the individual on the edge of the network, webbing out to billions of others that drives society, not the nameless, faceless solitary authority system blindly churning away at the center shouting orders no one can hear.

Big companies, at least the ones I've done contract work for, seem incredibly dysfunctional. They're good at one thing and do it day in and day out until some other company comes along with something better. It's rare that good ideas work their way back to the top. Big government seems even worse. All top down.

I can think of twenty ways to improve DMV, but who would I even talk to? And why bother? The rest of government just seems like a giant ball of red tape wound in knots and impossible to unwind.

But if we can get enough sensors out there, and I can measure what each person is doing, thinking, what his or her interests are, we can remake society around the individual.

Yeah, right! Nice challenge, anyway.

At least maybe I can keep tabs on Richie, maybe even set up an early warning system on his hacks. Hmmm.

Bada Bing

A snappily dressed UPS dude, brown socks and all, shows up with twenty-eight huge boxes labeled "office supplies." Meeta signs for the shipment and rips open one of the boxes, which contains thirty-six individually boxed Grumbys. Yuren has come through.

Before I can even pass one out to everyone in the pit, Meeta has Grumbys up for auction on eBay with a $79.99 "Buy It Now" price—PayPal payments only.

He also quickly edits our TuneBuffon home page to announce availability of Grumbys on eBay and on Amazon. And that's it. We're in bizness.

I'm not too keen on eBay since we have to ship them to individuals, while our Amazon Advantage account lets us ship Grumbys en masse to a warehouse in Kentucky, and they handle all the details, paying us twenty days after the end of the month. Amazon has some super-secret algorithm that calculates, based on its prediction of forward sales, order quantities and then emails you an order for units to ship to Kentucky.

Our first order is for two units. Ouch. Some algorithm.

I shouldn't have worried. Within an hour our Amazon page is saying we are sold out and it will take two to three weeks for orders to be fulfilled. In succession, we receive emails from

Amazon with orders for two more Grumbys, then eight, then twelve, then fifty, then a hundred.

eBay is selling them as fast as Meeta can restart the auction.

One of our servers crashes. Then another.

"Meeta, what the heck is going on?" I ask.

"Slashdot."

"What about it?"

"Someone posted a review of the Grumby on Slashdot around the same time we turned on sales, and now the traffic to our site is going through the roof."

"Who even has one to rev—?"

I stop and look around and thirty-two happy faces are playing with their new Grumbys, gesturing, talking to them, and I hear lots of strange voices responding.

"Well, it's getting out there," Meeta says sheepishly.

"Did you . . . ?"

"I thought it would be useful to have a firsthand experience documented for future users and . . ."

"Well, we're not ready."

"Too late, eh, mate?" Meeta says with a funny accent, even for him.

"What?"

"Sorry, I've been getting Mel Gibson up and running."

"You better contact Yuren and tell him to ship thousands of these to Amazon's old Kentucky home directly, as fast as he can."

"*Bada bing*," says the Grumby sitting on Meeta's desk. Wait a second. Was that Tony Soprano?

"Sale," Meeta explains.

"*Bada bing, bada bing.*"

"I hacked into Amazon's inventory system, so we can know every time when one is sold and know how many more units we need to ship," Meeta explains.

"Nice," I compliment Meeta.

"*Bada bing . . . bada bing . . .*"

• • •

"OK, Meeta, we need to think this out quickly before these Grumbys get delivered."

"Think out what?"

"What will they run?"

"Buffoon, Stump, gestures, everything." Meeta says quickly.

"Not so fast. We should make money on our software."

"You think?"

"I dunno. This is the Internet. Everything is free. It would be nice to pay for all these people and flat screens and pinball machines you were nice enough to load us up with."

"So how?"

"I don't know," I say slowly and deliberately. "But we have probably twelve hours to figure this out."

"TuneBuffoon is already free."

"Yeah, sure. I don't want to mess with that. It runs on the iPhone already, so running on the Grumby is a no-brainer."

"And it's better to have Stump the Machine in everyone's hands to train the system."

"Sure, but not the results."

"We should charge."

"For what?"

"For the full package. A little knowledge is dangerous . . . and free, but a lot of knowledge will cost you."

"I will cook up an unlock scheme. PayPal?"

"Yup. No credit cards. Too expensive."

"And gestures?" Meeta asks.

"Yeah, same thing. You get the first ten or twenty, but if you want more it will cost you."

"Everyone will want more," Meeta smiles.

"Of course, I don't use a mouse anymore. No one around here does."

"The Clooney thing isn't ready but it will be soon."

"Can we do it like ringtones?" I ask Meeta. He looks confused. "You know, you get Clooney for free and pay up for others."

"Don't we have copyright issues with Cloo—?"

"It's nice to have friends in strange places," Meeta explains. "Our great Estonian contingent, Ivanov something or other, has a few friends back home who will host all the personalities."

"They don't care about copyrights."

"It's a little—how might you put it—loosie goosie," Meeta explains.

"So you just . . ."

"You upload what you want and point to what clips you need. We don't touch them. When Grumbys power up they pull down what they need from Estonia, not from us."

"But won't people using all this do the coding of all the per-sonalities for us? We can still charge?"

"Ah ha."

"What?"

"I don't know. Something you just said. Either we get this right or this is all just for fun."

I pick up my phone and dial Lorita.

"Wilson Sonsini Goodrich and Rosati."

"Rosati, please," I say.

"Ha, ha," Lorita's secretary says, "I'll get Lorita for you."

"Hey."

"Hey."

"I love this thing. George Clooney talks to me all day. You know what I mean?"

I did. "I got a question."

"Shoot."

"Can I set up a license arrangement so that others do all the work but we are the only ones that can sell what they do?"

"I can arrange it."

"That we are the only ones that can run code on our own machine."

"That's tougher. Someone can always write assembly code. And they can certainly run it on their own machine. But if they use your libraries, your interface, then you can claim that any code written is really an upgrade to your own and needs to go through your license before they can sell it for anyone else to use."

"So if someone writes the greatest application ever for the Grumby then we own it?"

"No, you don't own it, but you can demand exclusive rights to its use, paying a fair and reasonable remuneration for their effort."

"Meaning?"

"Meaning you pay them whatever you like."

"A penny?"

"Well, if it's too little they'll just pull the code, won't they?" she asks.

"OK, so there is legal fair and market fair."

"Something like that."

"I want to put all that in our software development kit."

"Smart."

"Can you put together a licensing agreement based on what we talked about?"

"Sure, I'll have an associate draft something up and . . ."

"I need it in the next two hours," I say. Might as well get everyone on our pace. Wasn't Lorita the one who told me that nothing sits around here?

"Oh."

"Oh, you can't do it?"

"I can do it, but a little more notice next time please!"

"Sure, sure," I laugh. Fat chance of that.

•　　•　　•

"Got it." Meeta says.

"Got what?" I ask. It's always something bizarre with Meeta.

"The unlock. It's foolproof."

"Nothing is foolproof." I counter.

In the background I hear, "*Bada bing . . . bada bing.*"

"It is when it's your system. Here it goes. You pay via PayPal. As soon as we get the money we send an unlock code allowing you full use of that feature for a year."

"One year. I like that."

"You can't buy beer—you can only rent it," Meeta says.

"Uh, huh. And what stops those unlock codes from floating around the Web?" I ask. "I haven't paid for software in years and I'm sure you haven't either."

"Because we GPS it. People have thirty seconds and the Grumby needs to be within thirty feet from where the unlock was paid for or the unlock code expires."

"So no unlocking in a moving car?" I ask.

"Wouldn't that be dangerous?"

"And if it expires?" I ask.

"We send your money back. And remember, Grumbys check in all the time. We find duplicates, we shut them all down."

"And we can do this easily?"

"I already have the code done."

Damn, he's good.

"Just a snag," Meeta continues. "Before we can get any of the money out of PayPal, they need to do a background check. To avoid identity theft, they have been doing tighter security around accounts. Can you fill out the application?" Meeta asks.

"No, why don't you fill it out? You're in charge of this stuff; I trust your judgment," I say.

"And?" Meeta waits.

Well, now is as good a time as any.

"And . . . ?" I pause. "I'd never pass it."

"It's that UCLA thing, isn't it?" Meeta asks while nodding knowingly.

"Uh-huh." I pause, close my eyes, open them, and then launch. "If anyone ever asks where I went to school, I tell them UCLA."

Meeta just stares.

"Inside joke. University Closest to the Lompoc Area."

"Lompoc, as in . . ."

"Yeah. Not very flattering."

"I'm OK with it." Meeta says.

I knew we would have this conversation at some point. I'm about to launch my story when Meeta asks, "Look, can I admit something to you?"

"Uh, sure. Unless it's some repressed childhood sexual fantasy." I smile, "I'm all ears."

"Yeah, well, I didn't go to IIT Delhi either."

"Either?"

"I moved to Delhi to fool my parents but I taught myself. To program. I would spend time at an Internet café and read manuals and sample programs and got good enough to hack into its computers to send grades to my parents twice a year."

"Brilliant."

"Thank you. And?"

"And . . . you're too qualified to work here." I laugh.

Meeta laughs too.

I swallow, take a deep breath, and say, "OK, here it goes. I started programming back in high school. PCs were pretty lame, so I tried to get, uh, bigger machines. Me and another kid, my best friend, well, you know him now, Richie, would have a contest who could get deeper."

"Deeper?" Meeta asks.

"It wasn't hard. We started with DMV. Piece of cake. I had a driver's license at fourteen. Then anything. The harder the better. The mayor's office, the governor. These were big prizes. Then I figured out how to get into the local U.S. Air Force base network. That was cool. From that, Colorado Springs and then, believe it or not, the Pentagon. Not anything too secret, mostly personnel stuff. Then Richie figured out how to give himself one of those ultra-top-secret SCI security clearances. I made him give me one too. With that, I got into the Fort Detrick systems in Maryland and started reading NATO satellite transmissions. The troop stuff is all cryptoed and I wasn't all that interested, anyway. I liked the personal stuff. You wouldn't believe how much time NATO spends on menus and what type of wine was needed for the generals."

Meeta's mouth is wide open and he appears to be in a trance. I don't blame him.

"Anyway, once I'm inside I could read almost anyone's emails and at one point I got into Al Gore's Blackberry; yeah, I knew about he and Tipper separating years ago, and . . . ," I pause.

"And?"

"And, well, we were kids. And stupid kids at that. The Feds brought a bunch of huge hard drives to my Internet service provider and were reading everything I was reading and showed up with warrants and rummaged through the house and confiscated every computer and printer and notebooks, everything. To say the least, my parents were pissed off. Still are, actually."

"Yeah?"

"So the Federales threatened to send me to Lompoc prison, and I . . . I, well, kinda ratted out Richie."

"Is that what's pissying him off?" Meeta asks.

"Probably. Well, anyway, I was just a kid, so some judge in New York agreed that I should just be banned from touching a computer for five years."

"And?"

"And so let's just say I have a lot of repressed coding to get out of my system."

Neither of us says anything for a few minutes.

"We're birds of a feather." Meeta says.

"Indeed."

"With something to prove?" Meeta asks.

"World domination."

"I'd settle for less." Meeta says.

"Yeah, me too. I've got a few ideas." Not settling for much less, actually.

BS

It's Friday. The recap was Tuesday. Seems like a year ago so much has happened. Time is moving fast.

As I walk by on my way back to my desk from a fierce game of *Star Trek* pinball, Meeta adjusts the Grumby in front of him and motions his head as if to say "check this out." I stop to watch.

"The capital of California is Sacramento," Meeta speaks slowly.

The Grumby's eyes widen and it emits the sound of a soft bell—from a hotel front desk?—and utters, "*Correct.*"

"The capital of Illinois is Chicago," Meeta speaks again.

The Grumby's eyes narrow and a loud buzzer sounds like at the end of a basketball game. After a moment, in a quiet whisper, the Grumby says, "*It's Springfield.*"

"What's going on?" I ask.

"I've assigned one of my friends as a project manager on Stump the Machine," Meeta tells me.

"Very good. That almost sounds like we're a real company. Project managers, assignments. Pretty soon we'll have an org chart. And retirement benefits."

"He says Stump the Machine needs to be turned around."

"Something wrong?"

"No. It's gotten too big and harder to stump."

"That's a bad thing?"

"Well it could be. It's still growing but the second derivative has rolled over."

"Growth is decelerating?"

"That's one way to put it. According to the stat files, minutes spent peaked approximately two weeks ago. We still get new users every day, but they aren't using it as much. It appears that we know everything there is to know."

"I doubt that."

"The stats say differently. You can see it in mean-time-to-completion."

"Meaning?" I ask.

"Meaning people ask three questions and then go do something else."

"So we've become a know-it-all?"

"It would appear as such," Meeta laughs.

"So how do we turn it around? Should we forget stuff?"

"Oh, no. Turn around means a backwards-forwards implementation."

"I don't get it."

"There is nothing to get. We stop asking to be stumped, but we do the stumping."

"By asking harder questions?"

"By listening," Meeta offers, "to our users."

"Poll them for ideas?"

"No, we just listen and stump the know-it-alls."

"When they . . ."

"Yes, when they are not doing truth," Meeta says.

I break out into a huge smile.

"Are you telling me that we have a . . ."

"Yes, how would you say? We have the world's first detector of stumpiness."

"A Bullshit Detector," I declare.

"Yes, if I understand your use of a farming analogy," Meeta says.

"Because we know everything. That's brilliant."

"Well, we have a parsing engine and from that a rather extensive knowledge base, but we don't know everything. What we don't know we can quickly query."

"So when someone lies, we can call bullshit on them."

"Again, the reference is beyond my colloquial depth. But if you are saying that we can tell when someone is not telling the truth, well, that's the truth."

"And we know the right answer?"

"Well, of course. That's the only way to know that it was not the truth."

"This is way too cool. I may want to keep this for myself."

"We'll have a better demo in the next day cycle."

"Tomorrow?"

"Later tonight," Meeta corrects.

"Email it to me. I'll try it on my iPhone at home."

"No horsepower."

"What?"

"Stump the Machine could afford the lag of connection speeds and search queries. It almost helped to have a waiting time to implement the illusion of thinking."

"And?"

"And this so-called detector only works on the Grumby. We need to load the parser and knowledge file locally or we just bog down the connection and the detection would take too long. After three to five seconds, at least from the first uses, the illusion of detection has passed."

"It's too slow."

"No horsepower on the iPhone. The Grumby, as you have

designed it, is many horses. It is a beast. A beast of a detector. Ultra-kelvin."

"This is the ultimate, isn't it?" I ask.

Meeta's eyes widen. I thought I could hear a hotel bell and Meeta utter, "Correct."

Ramp

6:10 p.m.

Now we've really been discovered. Grumby is the top story on Digg.com.

2,092 diggs.

Sales keep moving.

"*Bada bing.*"

My Skype client pops on the screen.

I click to answer. It's Yuren.

"Meeta sent me a beta of the BS Detector. I would buy a Grumby just for that. We need to do a Chinese translation."

"Shouldn't be too hard. Actually, it may train itself in Chinese once we load a dictionary of English to Chinese. I'll ask Meeta. He knows someone who can do it, I guarantee."

"Grumbys are selling well?" Yuren asks.

I pause and turn around. "Meeta, turn up your volume."

I turn back to my Grumby, which defaults as a Web cam out of the right eye, I think, though I'm always staring at the wrong one.

"Wait for it," I tell Yuren.

"Wait for wha?"

"*Bada bing, bada bing, bada bing.*"

"Enough Meeta."

"Those are sales?" Yuren asks.

"It's moving. Can you ramp faster?" I ask Yuren.

"Yeah, that's why I'm calling."

"What?"

"Tell me about your financing."

"Well we have a first-tier venture capital firm, RedMark Ventures, that owns a stake in the company."

"Well put. I read on TechCrunch that they walked and got their money back after the RIAA suit."

"Well, yeah. I was getting to that. Basically, we've prepaid a lot of things and have enough cash for sixty, maybe ninety days of operation. So we are actively raising capital. What startup isn't?"

"And your Amazon terms?"

"Terms?"

"When do they pay you?"

"Oh, something like twenty days after the end of the month."

"So, thirty- to fifty-day terms."

"I guess so."

"You talking to stores?"

"We've had some inquiries. Wal-Mart. Costco. Best Buy."

"You can't afford them. I think they have ninety-day terms."

"Someday."

"You can't afford me. You owe me $150,000."

"Uh, yeah, I know. We'll wire some money as soon as we get paid. Things are tight. The more we sell the more we owe!" I complain.

"OK, here's the deal. I'm going to front you $250,000."

"That would be awesome."

"I want warrants."

"What are those?"

"Warrants to buy shares? C'mon."

"Oh, yeah sure, I knew that." Note to self: call Lorita and get further up to speed. The coding is hard enough; the finance stuff is just one funky thing after another.

"Well, 250 is about all I can front you. If you keep growing at this pace, and I am gearing up hoping that you do, you're going to need a lot more working capital. It would be a shame to fail succeeding."

I swallow hard and have trouble speaking. Yuren is right. I need to get some more money on board.

"Yuren, you're a lifesaver. I do appreciate it. I'll make sure you get some shares. I'll get more money." Somehow.

Spying

"There is a gentleman in the lobby wishing to speak with you. He looks like a wrestler. Small head, giant chest. And I think he cuts his own hair."

"Meeta, how do they keep finding us? Does he have any money?"

"I didn't ask."

"Ask everyone you meet," I say, and shake my head. I'm now scheming with Lorita to figure out if there is anyone we can tap.

"Do you have any money?" Meeta asks me snidely.

"Who is this guy?"

"Something about Nielsen."

"Leslie Nielsen?"

"I don't think so."

"Harry Neilsen Schmeilson?" I ask.

"Is that a real name? He has a funny accent. And seems to be in a hurry."

"I can't be bothered. I need to find money to keep this thing floating."

"He claims to have a market for measurement or something like that. Listening to users. Sounds like spying on users if you ask me. Should I go ask him for more details?" Meeta asks.

"No. Don't bother. Write down the Web address and tell him

to download the SDK and come back when he has something that works."

"He said something about wanting a roadmap and where we are going."

"We can't even afford to stock jelly beans, let alone afford to give out maps. Meeta, c'mon. Turn on your charm and tell him in the nicest of ways that unless he's got a check for $20 million to get lost and come back with a demo."

"Your wish is my . . ."

"Stop. And quit watching reruns. *I Dream of Jeannie* won't get you up to speed on American culture."

"Yes, Master."

Jeannie

Money. Why is it that we always need some quick? Yuren is floating us, but our $250,000 extension is quickly running dry. Grumbys are selling, but we're not getting paid fast enough to pay for the next shipments from Yuren. Plus the airfreight is killing us. I can't lose this race to get lots of Grumbys out there before anyone else for the lack of money.

Lorita gives us a few more names, but only one returns my calls. And he is in the South of France. So I fly all night to Paris where I miss a connection due to a French mechanics strike, so it takes me all of the next day to get to Nice. I'm now in the South of France. Lucky me.

I stumble through the airport and come upon a sign with my name on it.

I walk over and ask the person holding it, "Are you Johnny?"

"It's Jeannie. As in funny," he answers as he grabs my bags and walks me to the parking lot.

"I'm sorry. I had no idea. Been flying for the last two days it seems. It's nice to meet you, Jeannie."

"No, no. I'm Raphael. Jeannie asked me to pick you up. He will *rendezvous* with you for breakfast *dans le matin*."

We climb into a Jeep-looking thing.

"Mini Moke," Raphael explains.

We wind our way onto a two-lane road and some beautiful

countryside—as far as I can tell, anyway, because it's now dark, which depresses me, as I have completely lost a day of my life and I don't have much time to waste. A loud clicking sound pounds from the dashboard, making me nervous until I realize we're turning left. A sign lights up that says "Hotel du Cap."

I point to the hotel and start to speak, but Raphael interrupts, "*Oui*, celebrity hangout, as you say. We are in Cap d'Antibes, which is usually quiet except when your Hollywood arrivistes come visit."

"I have yet to arrivé," I tell Raphael.

Raphael let out a laugh. "Not yet from what I am told."

We turn into what appears to be a huge compound, dirt driveway, overgrown brush, a building or two scattered about. We turn right into a courtyard of two buildings.

"*Ici.*"

Raphael hands me a key and says, "I'll pick you up at seven for breakfast, *le matin*, yes?"

"*Oui et merci*," I say in my high school French accent.

My guest quarters are huge. Giant bed. Several couches and four different coffee tables filled with antique mechanical toys. I want to play with all of them—soldiers with rifles that shoot, wind-up panel trucks, a two-foot-tall bear—but think better of it. I'm here for money, not to play games.

· · ·

At seven sharp, I hear the bad unmuffled exhaust of the Mini Moke pull up to the door. I'm ready.

Raphael drives me to the main house, which seems to sprawl over acres of the massive waterfront property—that's the Mediterranean, right? We go inside and Raphael walks me through a maze of rooms until we come to a patio out back that looks over the water.

At the table sits a large fellow with a mop of dark, unruly hair. He can't be more than thirty-five.

"Jeannie." He introduces himself and shakes my hand.

"A pleasure. I have a gift for your toy collection," I say.

"Good. Great. First let me show you around." He gets up and motions me to follow. The place is spectacular. Well, that's an understatement. The sun is shining off the water, soaking in the lush gardens. I've never seen so many different-colored flowers. We pass several pools and every once in a while come up to little sanctuaries, private sitting areas surrounded by taller hedges. I could get a lot of coding done here.

"So," Jeannie starts, "you seem to have a quite interesting business. You must have venture capitalists crawling all over you."

"I do, we did, I had a bad experience, so I'm here," I say.

"Yes, yes, not to worry. We all have our stories."

A short, perky blonde appears out of nowhere and gives Jeannie a huge hug.

"Thanks," she says with a British accent. "Must catch my plane. Toodles." And with that she plants a big wet kiss on Jeannie. He couldn't have planned it better for me wanting to be him.

"So, you were saying?" Jeannie motions.

"You've seen some of the things we are doing?" I ask.

"My iPhone is quite happy with you."

"OK, but have you seen our Grumby?"

"I have been trying to order one, but Amazon will only ship in the U.S. And there is a two- to three-week wait."

"I brought you one. But there is more to it than what it does out of the box. We have developers around the world who are in love with this thing, writing code for education, for business, for games. I can't quite believe how fast this has taken off and . . ."

I stop as Jeannie points to a giant freighter anchored off the coast.

"Second largest personal watercraft in the world. Paul Allen's is about twenty feet longer."

I assume it belongs to Jeannie.

"I don't get paid fast enough by Amazon. And Wal-Mart will be worse. My Chinese supplier is strapped, and . . . ," I continue.

"So this isn't a seed deal?"

"No. We make huge markups on these things, and we are just starting to sell applications. We're just growing too damned fast."

"Well maybe you can't tell, but I live on a fixed income. Asset-rich, cash-poor. Like many in Europe."

"Oh."

I must sound disappointed, as Jeannie quickly says, "That doesn't mean no."

"Oh?"

"I did a lot of work doing diligence on you. I know lots about your Grumby toy and a lot about you." Jeannie looks me straight in the eyes.

"Oh." I think I sound disappointed again.

"A quite impressive portfolio of accomplishments. You know your way around networks. I can overlook your past discretions, or is it indiscretions. Perhaps that is what is driving you. I hope so because I very much want to be involved. We just have to be creative. My accountants will figure it out."

"Yeah, no, that would be great." I break out into a smile.

"You can stay for breakfast. Or you can run and catch my jet back to London with, uh, with her. I'll arrange for your connection back to SFO. And I'll have an answer within forty-eight hours."

"I, uh, are you sure? It would be better if I were back and . . ."

"Go. Run. Don't stop until you make it."

It's not quite Humphrey Bogart on a tarmac, but they are inspiring words.

Takeoff

4:24 p.m., March 19, Milpitas

No more travel. Not ever. Not if the world ends. I'm done with that. Jeannie's private jet from Nice to London, a Falcon 200EX, with the hot blonde as carry-on baggage was something quite special. The takeoff felt like a rocket ship. Sadly, seat 45F on the United flight back to SFO put an end to my traveling days. Not a chance. Not going to do that again. Well not without my friend Imovane along for the ride. Plus I can't afford the time away.

"Good trip?" Meeta asks.

"Grrrr." I look around at a quite bustling office. There seems like fifty more bodies from a few days ago. "And who are all these people?" I ask.

"More programmers—10,000 shares each. Most found us. We all take turns grilling them in the conference room. As you most eloquently requested, we only take the surgeons."

"Surgeon class."

"I have many interesting things to show you. A game developer in Seoul has figured out a way to do gestures to control the . . ."

The ringing sound and pop-up of my Skype connection interrupts Meeta. He knows by now to continue the conversation later.

"So it's a go?" It's Yuren.

"I just got back."

"I have the China Industrial Bank telling me about a line of credit from some guy named Julius Baer in Zurich, contingent on a signature from a nice cape in France. Does any of that make sense?"

An email pops on my screen from Jeannie. "I have arranged a $10 million line of credit. My bank, Julius Baer, will lend it against some of my assets. In exchange, I would like a 10 percent stake in your company. Quite simple. What say you?"

"Yuren, is $10 million enough?"

He starts coughing. "It should be," then he pauses and continues, "for now, anyway."

I type back to Jeannie. "Deal. But what if we need more?" I hit "send."

Ninety seconds later, I have my reply. "I will sign the papers right away. I can probably arrange a $20 million line of credit but would need to sell a few things that I would rather not, like some of my waterfront or a share in my small ocean liner. So let's agree that my stake goes to 20 percent if you have taken down more than $10 million. Please just give me some notice. And tell Yuren that he has a very good reputation on Bahnhofstrasse in Zurich."

"Yuren, it's a go. Crank them out as fast as you can."

"Ay-ay."

"What? Is that Chinese?" I ask Yuren.

"*Star Trek.*"

"Engage," I say, doing my best Picard.

•   •   •

Walt Mossberg at the *Wall Street Journal* likes it, kind of. He writes, "Not as easy to use as an iPhone or a Mac but a promising entertaining tool for the nonprofessional." Still, we'll take it.

David Pogue at the *New York Times*—not so much. "There are so many missing features that it really is just a bad case of Ship-at-All-Costs-itis. The interface is half-baked and navigating through Grumby apps makes the 1040 tax form seem like a breeze—the Grumby is a mess."

As they say, never trust a man who buys his ink by the barrel. On the other hand, no press is bad press as long as they spell your name right. I hope that's right.

Whatever. Sales keep ramping.

"*Bada bing.*"

•　　•　　•

I finally tell Meeta to kill the stupid bada-bing sound. It's been driving all of us crazy. It's exciting that sales are going through the roof, so in its place Meeta puts up a counter on the fifty-inch plasma screen mounted on the wall. It now reads 12,878 and is ticking up quickly. Kinda looks like the national debt clock in Times Square.

Still, our office is anything but quiet. There's a crowd around the Xbox and all sorts of music blaring. Rock band is my guess. "*Slow ride, take it easy . . .*" Yup. Foghat. I liked it the first ninety-nine times.

"So let me finish what I was telling you. A programmer in South Korea has taken our API and written some new gestures for our library."

"Excellent. Are there some weird secret Korean high signs we don't know about?"

"You mean the famous Little Rascals? I saw Alfalfa and Spanky on cable last night. I have so much to learn."

"Yes," I say.

"No, he has written music gestures."

"A conductor?"

"No, but I hadn't thought of that. More like a rock star."

"You mean . . ." I look over at the crowd around the Xbox.

"Precisely. We found an open source program for the PC called Audio Surf that . . ."

". . . encodes any song in your collection. I've heard of it," I say impatiently.

"So we got the gestures from Korea and it turns out it was only a little bit tricky to train the imagers to look for moving fingers. You no longer need a guitar. Each of the four fingers moving represents a different button and . . ."

"Wait a second—let me guess—you've invented Air Guitar Hero?"

"Basically. That's what they've been playing over there," he says, pointing toward the Xbox. "And that is a great name for it. Do you think we can use it?" Meeta asks.

"I doubt it, but who cares. We can call it anything we want; this is a great add-on module. We can give it away with "Slow Ride," but I guarantee you can only listen to "Slow Ride" for twenty-four hours before you go bonkers and will pay anything to play another song. Ten bucks seems a small price to pay to unlock the code."

"I would pay double."

"OK, twenty bucks it is. Meeta, you are a one-man pricing department."

"Do I get a raise?"

"Sure, take another 10,000 shares."

"I already did."

"Someday we are really going to need a finance department. And Meeta?"

"Yes."

"Keep this stuff comin'."

"To kelvin and beyond," Meeta says.

. . .

"So much for George Clooney," Meeta blurts out.

"What do you mean?" I ask, as I turn away from reading about conversational dynamics. I notice the plasma counter reads 26,442. Wasn't it just 15,000? I stop doing the math but that's something like $2 million in sales.

It's weird. I spend way too much time checking the counter on the plasma. A proxy for success. My mood swings up and down based on how a stupid counter is doing.

Moods again. Taking the pulse. Not just someone's mood, the desires, wants, needs, emotions that flow from it. Or what's needed to change it, restore harmony. Am I slowly turning into Eckhart Tolle?

Can I somehow turn that into a number, so I can measure it and display it, satisfy it, put a price on it?

Meeta interrupts my thoughts with, "It's the Anchor."

"Anchor? What?"

"The Anchorman."

"The movie?" I ask.

"The voice."

"What ARE you talking about?"

"Since we put out the engine, I have written a monitor to track personalities."

"And?"

"And the geeks rule. There are a few Miley Cyruses and Jennifer Anistons but for the most part the personalities registered and in most use are Adam Sandler, Bart Simpson, and Will Ferrell, the . . ."

"The Anchorman."

"Yes, it is so. We can pull up frequency and phrase usage.

Though it doesn't make any sense, *"You stay classy, San Diego"* scores high on the appropriate scale. Is that a bug?"

"Maybe a feature."

"It also flags words I am afraid I do not understand," Meeta complains. "Can you please explain what 'Son of a bee sting' means? And 'Sweet Lincoln's mullet'?"

I start laughing. "It's just funny. Will Ferrell is just funny. Like Bill Murray, he can say anything and I'll just laugh."

I pause. Funny. The conversation thing is hard to pull off. We have all these snippets, hosted in Estonia, of course. Some are appropriate—some are not. I've got the ultimate feedback engine with my appropriateness index: if people pause for too long, a pregnant pause in the conversation, then we learn something and most likely the previous line was not the best at that point in the conversation. Grumby was basically going to learn to talk like an adolescent, try enough lines until it learns what's appropriate. But what if the line is funny? I hadn't thought of that.

"Can we scan for laughter? I'll bet there's a dozen different types of laughter: ha ha, guffaw, whatever. Just pull it from laugh tracks off of sitcoms. Then we can listen for people laughing and know which lines work. Like a standup comedian in a night-club."

"I love it. Standup training?" Meeta asks. "Of course, I have learned the hard way in this country that many people prefer to laugh at me."

"It's still a laugh. And people love to laugh."

"I'll get one of my friends on it," Meeta declares.

"Aren't you out of friends?"

"I get new ones every day. All seem to want to work here."

Meeta clicks on something and his Grumby speaks, *"Aren't you out of friends?"*

That isn't quite my voice but pretty close.

"You're recording our conversations?" I ask.

"Not really, well, sort of. Not your voice but your words. We record everything. Time and GPS tag it and store it on our servers. One of my friends in Mumbai has been working on a scheme that uniquely identifies voices. He started with your TuneBuffoon algorithm . . ."

"Our algorithm."

"OK, yes, our algorithm and altered it for voice. Since we have a digital signal processor working away we can come up with unique codes for pitch and resonance—something he calls polyphony auditory segregation. I'm not quite sure what that means."

"So?"

"So he thinks each person is unique—each voice is unique—and we can both flag it and use the attributes to mimic it on playback."

"We ought to sell that code. Every credit card purchase could be verified with the owner's unique voice signature. Then again, I hate credit card companies," I say.

"They were our early stage venture capitalists," Meeta reminds me.

Ignoring him, I ask, "But wait, don't we have to store huge audio files?"

"No, no, just words that kind of get inverse encoded, so they come out sounding just like the person that said it. It's their signature. Of course, we tag it for where and when."

"Does it work?"

"I think. Like all of our code, we need to train it. Stump the Machine was stupid until we had lots of people feeding it information. Same here. The more words, the more voices, the better our algorithm weighting. So far it just works on the iPhone, but we'll have it on the Grumby by morning. The storage part shouldn't be too much of a problem; we have enough servers for now."

"So we can record meetings?" I ask.

"Of course." He clicks a few times on his screen.

An email notification pops on my screen, from Meeta.

It says, "So we can record meetings?" I click on the attached file and it says, in something pretty close to my voice, "*So, we can record meetings?*"

From the Air Guitar Hero crowd I hear someone let loose a "Bitchin'."

I look at Meeta and just shake my head and smile. Over his shoulder, the unit counter keeps ticking up and up. This whole thing has a mind of its own, in many ways.

"I've been meaning to ask you something of import," Meeta says.

"Such as?"

"Well, how do we know?"

"How do we know what?"

"How do we know what apps to do next? We seem to just come up with things. Do we ask people what they want?"

"*If I had asked people what they wanted, they would have said faster horses,*" Meeta's Grumby blurts out.

"Huh?" I'm sure I look startled. "How the . . ."

"Oh, I've been playing with sentence deconstruction and then do a lookup to a quote to make Grumby seem smart."

"Who said 'If I had asked people what they wanted, they would have said faster horses'"? I ask the Grumby.

"*Henry Ford, circa 1919.*"

I stand their shaking my head. "He's right. We can't ask. We just have to come up with neat stuff, like this quote thing, that no one would even know they want. We just have to scratch and claw until we find things that work."

"*Business is never so healthy as when, like a chicken, it must do a certain amount of scratching around for what it gets.*"

Henry Ford, I'll bet.

•   •   •

"Thanks for working up our financing stuff," I tell Lorita.

"The hardest part was getting the cap table together, figuring out who owns what," Lorita complains.

"RedMark has 9.9 percent and Jeannie has 10 percent and I own the rest."

"The math is a little more complex than that."

"Why?"

"Jeannie gets 10 percent of Jack's 9.9 percent."

"Oooh, I like that."

"Well, and 10 percent of your stake too."

"Yeah, OK, I get it."

"No, no, that was the easy part."

"Then what?"

"Do you know how many 10,000 share grants have been made?"

"No idea. Thirty-five? Fifty?" I ask.

"Well, Meeta has forty-two of them for himself."

I just laugh.

"Fifty-seven others were given out in the U.S., twenty-nine in India, and about a dozen others around the world."

"I'm OK with all those."

"Yeah, that may be, but we did percentage math with your investors and share math with your employees and they don't yet connect."

"So?"

"So how much do you think you own?"

"I don't get what you're asking."

"I add up 140 share grants or 1.4 million shares. If you only have 2 million shares, then these folks own most of the company. If you have a billion shares, then they own .14 percent."

"Then I declare we have a trillion shares," I laugh.

"Seriously. Pick a real number. Just make sure you own over half, so no board fights come back to haunt you."

"No, you're right. All these ten thousand shareowners ARE the company. They do all the hard stuff. Employees should own 20 percent and I want Jack to own less than 5 percent. With the credit line, Jeannie gets 10 percent and then I get the rest. No, check that. Add another 10 percent for Meeta, which leaves me 55 . . ."

"No, 54 percent. Wilson owns 1 percent," Lorita reminds me.

"How could I forget? That's perfect," I agree.

"We'll create an option pool for future employee grants. It's tax-advantaged over pure stock grants . . ."

"No one is going to care what you give them." I say. "Ten thousand shares sounds like a lot even if it isn't."

"Someday they will. I've been through enough of these."

· · ·

We release Air Guitar Hero on our Web site, only usable with three songs, and within twenty-four hours sales of Grumbys top 50,000 units. Yuren skypes us every day with updates. He can handle the surge. He had a shortage of eyeballs, of all things, but found another supplier and continues to ramp factory space to make Grumbys.

Our base unit comes with TuneBuffoon, Stump the Machine, Bull Detector, a George Clooney and a Will Ferrell personality, and a three-song version of Air Guitar Hero as well as instructions on how to unlock using PayPal.

The API, the programming interface we released on our Web site for developers, has been downloaded 20,000 times. Since the API uses our servers, we can pretty easily track what is being developed, or at least tested.

One that we should have thought of was developed in Romania, a Facebook application that filters Facebook's newsfeeds and alerts people to what's going on with their friends. After lots of vampire and Transylvania jokes, we got in touch with the Romanians and offered to share our unique voice code stuff so that Facebook updates come out in your friends' voices. I think that might be a little creepy but most everyone else loves the idea.

But this also gets me thinking. The cool thing about Facebook or Twitter that lets people send 140-character messages about what they're doing is that you get this sort of awareness of what your friends and passing acquaintances are up to. Somehow, via all these updates, they are part of your life. I've tried all these apps and even though I'm in front of a stupid screen most of the day, the biggest hassle is changing my status or typing the updates in all the time. What if you can automatically update your Facebook profile based on a set of questions we ask? Even better would be a learning system that listens to conversations and automatically updates the profile. Capture someone's mood via sighs or off-handed comments or even—what the heck, we have two cameras—their body language, if they roll their eyes, are tired . . .

A Little Action

9:12 p.m., March 23, Sunnyvale

"**Y**ou *are* taking this weekend off, aren't you, Meeta?" I ask.

"It's only Tuesday. And I am not so sure. What is so important?"

"It is a weekend of utmost importance," I tease. "It's the Sweet Sixteen round of the NCAA college hoops tournament. Whoever is left standing at the end of the weekend goes to the Final Four," I explain.

"My Final is to get this next release done so that I may go to relax. And yes, this college basketball is very curious. Giant indoor stadiums, colored clothing, beautiful girls jumping around in excitement, and the strange goal of getting an orange ball though a metal hole. Yes, you must count me in for this yearly tradition." Meeta rarely does sarcasm but when he does it, he does it well.

"You'll get it eventually. It's the pureness of the game, the finesse of a crossover dribble, and then driving to the basket. Or a three-point shot for a buzzer beater. I live for March Madness."

"Seems pointless," Meeta says sharply.

I just look at him like he's not from here. How can I explain? "Look, if you really want to learn about this most American of traditions, you've got to learn how to bet."

"Bet?"

"Wager, check the spread, see how many points the underdog is getting, over/under, that sort of stuff."

Meeta glances over with a quizzical look on his face.

"Listen, it's a long weekend. You gotta have a little action on these games in order to get through it."

Meeta seems to like the word action, even though I'm pretty sure he has no idea what it really means. He leaves my desk shaking his head.

•   •   •

"How was your weekend, Meeta?"

"Lots of action," he says with the widest grin I've ever seen. "I have performed substantially."

"What happened, c'mon, let's hear it."

"Well, you told me about the wager system and under spreads and it sounded quite intriguing."

I thought of correcting him, but he's on a roll.

"It didn't take me long to figure out that your American March Madness consists of teams from major universities and a few minor ones scoring one or two or three points for various successful attempts at ball through hoop."

Clinical.

"And that not every team is equal. Some are excellent at this game, although I am not exactly sure why, so placing so-called bets would amount to me being, uh, is this the right word . . . sucker?"

"Precisely."

"So someone in a growing metropolis without a team, Las Vegas, sets odds or points so all of the betting can be equal."

"Close enough."

"Well, in any market system, a certain amount of bias leaks in," Meeta explains.

"And in basketball more than a certain amount . . ."

"Yes, yes. As I have seen from watching your Budweiser Light television retail sales pitches, much of America wears clothing to match the players in the arena but most often without breaking a sweat."

"And?" I like where this was going.

"And my assumption is that this is the source of most major bias into the wagering system and . . ."

"And?"

"It was simply a case of scanning the voice logs for team mentions and then log certain phrases such as 'the Tarheels are going to kick ass' to the 'Ohio State won't even cover on Saturday' and sum this information based on geographic location and look for correlations, and I determined how much bias has seeped into the spread calculations . . ."

Uh-oh. What has he done?

"OK, OK, but most of that bias is worked into the spread. A higher seed is probably worth a few points," I explain.

"Yes, so I had to weight the biases based on how far from the center facilities they emanated."

"From what? The stadiums?" I ask.

"No, I looked up the workout and practice facilities and used that as the base location. Either on campus or where the regional games are being played. I also pulled up some old ESPN interviews and usually can find the team coaches from their voice fingerprints. I weight them even more."

"That's brilliant."

"Actually, I back-tested the algorithm. Often, I would find phrases such as 'we are going to get killed' and then specific mentions such as 'we can't stop the Orangemen's inside game' or

'Dawkins is going to shred us with threes.' Those seemed to have the strongest correlation."

"I hope you really did have some action on these games."

"I placed simple wagers since I do not understand all of the complexities of this system . . ."

"Which bets?"

"Duke Blue Devils to win and to cover, UCLA will lose outright in what is strangely called an upset, and Illinois to beat Kentucky by at least one point."

"Wait a second," I stop and think, "those all came in. How much did you win?"

"Oh, $42,300." His grin gets even wider.

"Jeez." I think my eyes popped out of my head.

"I learned a new word this weekend—parlay."

"Uh, I need to check your methods. Let's just keep this between us, shall we?" I smile. Meeta is treading on dangerous ground, for both of us.

"I was about to publish a paper to the Society of Statistical . . ."

"Yeah, hold the phone on that. This might be a new service—we don't want to pre-announce it. I suspect it will require years of testing to perfect."

I wink. And I never wink. Meeta smiles.

Swear

I finally get a full night's sleep. Needing to clear my head, I stroll into my local Starbucks feeling like a million bucks, order a Venti Mocha Double Latte Extra Hot No Whip, and sip it slowly and deliberately on the twenty-minute drive into the bowels of Milpitas. The top is off my Jeep, the sun is already high in the sky, and I've got twenty or thirty great ideas for the Grumby swirling through my slowly awakening brain cells. The Mood Machine, the Meeting Coordinator—damn, I wish I had a pen to write this stuff down. Wait a second. I have my Grumby. Why can't it just listen to what I say and spit it back later? Hmm. The Memory Module?

It doesn't get any better than this. It's pushing noon and I'm just getting started.

I pull up to our building and—what the heck?—the parking lot is full and I have to park halfway toward the back of our building and walk around to the front. I have the last few drops of my latte to go, and the caffeine high is just about right to face the chaos of our very own mischief, mayhem, and code.

I should have ordered a triple.

In our makeshift lobby, there in the eye-implant chair, mask surrounding his head, wires propping open his eyelids, and a twenty-inch monitor with a Grumby duct-taped to it eighteen inches from his face sits Meeta. At least thirty people surround what looks like a Nazi experiment gone bad.

"Select layer," Meeta says, and then pauses. "Move tool, click hold, unhold, select tool, clone tool, alt click, fill tool, set foreground color, click, save."

"What are heck are you doing?"

"Shhh. Don't break his concentration," Ivanov the Estonian demands.

I look on the screen and he has Photoshop open and besides giving it verbal commands, the cursor is moving around the screen by itself. I look back at Meeta and he is sitting on his hands. But his eyes are the brightest blue I have ever seen, especially odd since I thought his eyes were brown.

"Have you been rummaging through the closet again?"

"I can explain," Meeta says.

"I'll bet it's a good one."

"Overnight we found someone in New York testing our gesture code with Photoshop, which has been done a few times now. They were trying to increase the accuracy of the finger gestures, but we've tried that and haven't ever gotten it to work. No one can hold his hands that steady to get any precision."

"*Minority Report*?" I ask.

"Sort of but that's been pretty much discredited as an interface. So someone suggested . . ."

"Eyeballs?" I exclaim.

"Yes, precisely."

"And you graciously volunteered to be the guinea pig and have your eyes monitored?"

"I'm the last one to try it. Where have you been?"

"Getting some sleep. I highly recommend it. And you have to take out those stupid-colored eye thingies."

"Oh, yes. Sorry." Meeta takes the hooks out of his eyes and

removes what looks like colored contact lenses. I've got to throw all that old stuff away. "We have the code rigged to look for blue and follow eye movement. You won't believe how accurate your eyes are: 4,000 by 4,000 pixels, maybe more. We can not only see in high def, we can stare and concentrate in high def. A rather spectacular breakthrough, no?"

"Do we have to ship one of these chairs with every piece of code?" I laugh.

"Once we get the algorithm perfected, we can look for any eyeball color, and we're trying to get a hold of Panasonic's anti-shake code that it uses in digital cameras."

"Then?" I ask.

"Then we have a software eye mouse. Think of the possibilities."

"I can't."

"I can't either," Meeta admits. "But it is still quite fun to play with. Though my eyelids hurt from the wires."

The crowd around the torture chamber disperses. We have lots more to do.

I sit at my desk and pull up a few files of stats: 120,000 units out the door. Is that right? I thought I saw that number last night. Anyway, the highest usage is still Air Guitar. Second on the list? The Russian book reader code that we don't even include. You have to find it on our Web site and download the demo copy of the Young Book Reader app. People can upgrade: we have about fifty children's books on the system and more are added every day. Pretty impressive.

"*Asshole!*" I hear from behind me.

"What?" I turn and ask.

Everybody just shrugs.

"Whatever. Someone has a problem let me know to my face," I say sternly.

I click, air click actually, through some more stats including a spreadsheet that estimates how much cash we have, or don't have. At the rate we are shipping we're safely inside the $10 million credit limit we set up with Jeannie. But word of mouth must be spreading. I know we got picked up at the gadget sites Gizmodo and Engadget. Both of them wrote up nice reviews of the Grumby and the apps that they knew about.

The site techmeme.com that seems to be all things techie picked up on the gadget site reviews and noted the buzz around us, even providing a pointer to the Amazon page to buy a Grumby. Emails are pouring in asking for interviews and requests to do company profiles. I don't really want anyone digging around. Plus we don't need any more publicity, not yet. We have our hands full managing the growth we already have.

"*Douche!*"

"What, dammit!" I turn around again and scan the tables filled with screens and coders and more *Star Wars* figurines than I remembered.

Everybody just looks around.

"C'mon, quit screwing around," I say.

"*Fart lick!*"

"OK, that's enough. Knock it off," I yell.

Now everyone looks confused and a little scared.

Meeta rapidly walks over and says, "You have to check this out."

"No more eye-gorithms. I'm in no mood," I bark.

"No, really. This is important."

"C'mon, I'm trying to figure out if we can keep growing and not run out of . . ."

"NO REALLY," Meeta shouts at me, and then speaks softly, "you have to see this."

"OK, what?"

Meeta pulls up a YouTube video on my screen. It's a fuzzy video of a mother sitting at a table reading with her daughter, probably five years old. On the table is a Grumby.

"All right . . . ," I start. Meeta motions for me to keep watching.

The little girl reads the book quite well, only prompted a few times by the Grumby. "I would not like them here or there. I would not like them anyw-w-w—"

"*Anywhere,*" the Grumby prompts.

"Anywhere," she continues. "I do not like green eggs and ham. I do not like them, Sam-I-am."

"Meeta, I've seen this before. It works."

"Keep watching." Meeta says sternly. And Meeta doesn't do sternly.

"Would you eat them in a box?"

"*Would you, dickwad?*" the Grumby asks.

The mom looks around and then squints at the Grumby.

"Would you eat them with a fox?" the girl continues.

"*Would you suck on my . . .*" The mom grabs the Grumby, lifts it, and slams it down on the table. The girl starts crying.

The Grumby keeps going. "*Not in a box, bitch. Not with a fox, fudgepacker. Not in a house, ho, not with a mouse, muffdiver.*"

I look at Meeta who has a very scared expression on his face.

At this point the mom gets busy trying to figure out how to unplug the Grumby, but it's wireless. So she just throws it against the wall and then covers her daughter's ears and starts stepping on the Grumby trying to get it to shut up and then the clip ends.

Silence.

I look behind me and a crowd has gathered to watch over my shoulder.

"Meeta, what the hell is going on?"

"A very proud moment?" Meeta asks sheepishly. And he does sheepishly well. "Our first virus?"

"Meeta! We can't have this. We've gotta track this down right away. Can we dig through log files and figure out what happened? Stop downloads of the book reader? And of everything else? Someone or something has busted into our little system. We've gotta move fast! Everyone!"

"OK, let's go," Meeta says. "Check the servers. Compare the code we are downloading with our latest releases. See if something malicious is attached. Something has clearly slipped in."

A flurry of clicking ensues.

The plasma counter now reads 109,974 and the numbers are counting backwards. Uh-oh.

•   •   •

Techmeme.com is the first that afternoon to run a headline about the "Potty-mouth Grumby" from a blog mentioning it and a pointer to the YouTube video. From there it spreads pretty quickly. Lots of people are having fun at our expense. Valleywag, the local gossip site, is quick to pounce, asking if anyone knows any more dirt on us. The Tweetsphere is chirping.

Meanwhile cancellations and then returns at Amazon are our biggest problem. Amazon sends an email to Meeta asking us to approve the shipment of 10,000 Grumbys back to us and could we please provide an address. They also insist on increasing the reserve requirement against our payments, meaning they aren't going to pay us what we deserve because they figure there will be a lot more returns and they don't want to have to come back to us for the money. Damned algorithms.

I get in touch with Yuren and tell him to turn off the factory line, but he claims it would take him weeks to shut it down as he has pre-ordered parts for just-in-time delivery far out into the future to guarantee he could get the parts. Jeannie's credit line is still plenty to cover us but not for much longer. I wish I knew more about finance, but my guess is we have about two weeks before Jeannie will be not only pissed off that he has to sell his personal freighter, or whatever it is, but also own a bigger chunk of our company. Maybe he could have the whole thing. Our reputation, and we didn't have much of one since we were so young, is in tatters.

Views on YouTube hit a half a million. The comments run pages and pages, mostly saying LOL and ROFL.

Michael Arrington's TechCrunch site runs a longer story on us talking about us screwing RedMark Ventures, and, with this mess, how we are toast.

"Anything, Meeta?"

"We trace lots of packets coming in from insultmonger.com and swearasaurus.com."

"What are those?" I ask.

"Swear sites."

"Those exist?" I had no idea.

"Sure. And if they didn't, someone would just put it up for the traffic and sell ads."

"Someone would buy ads against curse words?"

"Of course. Very lucrative," Meeta explains.

"Maybe that's the new business model we have been desperately searching for?" I kid.

"The trouble is that whoever wrote this virus is rather clever."

"You're sure it's a virus?" I ask.

"Oh, yes. Anything that goes out and accepts packets into our system has to be malicious code. It's a virus, all right. Which means we just have to find the offending code," Meeta explains.

"And then what?"

"Then we engineer it out. We have been busy with so many projects that we forgot to add a secure wrapper around our code and . . ."

"Can we learn a lesson here?"

"About cursing?"

"About protecting our crowned jewels."

•   •   •

I finally have to turn it off. The plasma reads 81,193 and I can't take it anymore. Meeta suggests we replace it with something that says *"binga bad"* and I laugh for the first time in a week.

Lorita calls and says there have been several inquiries about our corporate structure from a variety of law firms known for their class-action suits. She says it's only a matter of time before they rummage the State of California records and start suing us.

The YouTube video is a genuine hit. Two million views and growing. Good for them.

Meeta claims to have isolated a section of code with several bytes interposed. It doesn't change the size of the file—a simple technique to see if anyone has changed the code.

My heart sinks. I know exactly what he's talking about. I've done that myself. And so has . . .

"Meeta. Don't ask me how I know this. The interposed bytes usually create an exception. Don't look in the code. Look in the data for a hidden link that points out to swearasaurus or whatever."

"How do you know this?"

"Uh, old high school trick," I admit.

"Uh-huh."

"Just check the data for *Green Eggs and Ham* and every other book that gets downloaded. It will be in there. Trust me," I say.

"Oh, I trust you."

"Meanwhile, we are about to lose this thing and those forty-two stock grants . . ."

Meeta gets a very embarrassed look on his face.

I add, "Yeah, I know about those. We are going to lose it all in another few days. I've carved you out 10 percent of the company and all the folks working here will eventually split 20 percent, so let's fix this, huh?"

"Thank you, thank you. I am on it. Roger Wilco."

Three more YouTube videos go up: one of them a spoof of a Grumby with Tourette's syndrome. Not funny. Each has over a million views in no time.

Insanely

A nd then "the email" comes in. I'm not sure whether to be honored or violently ill. It's from pstevej@apple.com. THE Steve Jobs? Apple founder?

Maybe so. I've heard about this. The "p" usually stands for private. Big honchos put out their email address to the entire company, so anyone can contact them—but who has time—so they set up a private address that only top brass and friends know about. I gotta get me one of those.

> Impressed with your iPhone apps, even though they aren't legal (ha). Very clever code—my engineers are trying to duplicate. Heard about your issues via YouTube. I am willing to buy your company, assume your debt, and make you an executive VP with option package. Five million dollars is better than zero, and at Apple you'll have a chance to change the world. Please respond quickly.
>
> Steve Jobs

"*Dickspittle!*" I hear from a Grumby behind me. My cell phone rings. I don't want to be interrupted but it's Lorita.

"Yes?"

"Did you get an offer for the company?" Lorita asks.

"How did you know?" I ask back.

"It's on Apple Insider. Something about Steve Jobs making a lucrative offer for your company to continue development of your applications under the Apple umbrella."

"He must have leaked it himself. He low-balled us, trying to steal this thing out from under us. He probably coded this virus himself to . . . ," I stop myself.

"You don't really think he . . ."

"Nah," I say. Though I did.

"You might want to put out a press release turning down the offer," Lorita suggests. "Great publicity."

"I don't know, maybe we do want to sell to him. If we can't kill this virus, we're worthless anyway."

"Any luck?"

"Lots of it."

I pause. "All bad."

"Well I have some more news."

"Oh, no."

"The Theodor Geisel estate wants to sue you as soon as they figure out who you are."

"Who?"

"The Dr. Seuss folks," Lorita explains.

"Oh. There really is a Dr. Seuss?"

"Geisel. Or his estate, anyway. They watched the video."

"Oh. Suing us for defamation of character. It's not our curses. It's . . ."

"No, no, they're suing you for royalties . . . for using their books."

"We don't copy them—you still have to read a physical book."

"Just passing along the news. You seem to attract all types."

"Like flies on . . ."

"Should I find you some experts on killing viruses? We work with a few security firms like Symantec and . . . ," Lorita says.

"No thanks. I think we're close. I don't want anybody outside of this firm digging through our core source code. We'll figure it out and I can guarantee it won't happen again."

I hang up and place another call.

"Richie, what's shaking?"

"Hey, long time no hear," Richie says.

"Been busy, dickspittle?" I ask.

"Uh . . . ," Richie stammers.

I pause. Maybe he'll volunteer something.

"Got some new clients around here?" I ask.

"A few. Caught the YouTube. Great TV."

"Uh-huh," is about all I can muster. I'm fuming. It was him.

"Ha! Owned. I own you and don't you ever forget it."

"What's your problem?" I ask.

"No problem. Why should you have all the fun? Actually, I'm working on my own thing now. It will make your little Grumby look retarded."

"Whatever. Just leave us alone," I say.

"Hey," Richie goes on, "you gotta admit the swearasaurus thing is pretty ingenious."

He really just can't help himself. He's always trying to one up me. I can almost hear him patting himself on the back.

"Is it the double indirect or the virtual packet?" I ask.

"I would never do the double indirect. That's yours."

"OK. Should have figured that," I say. "So, uh, stay well. And stay away," I say in the most serious tone I can muster.

•   •   •

"Meeta, I think I may have this figured out. There's an old

trick spoofing routers. You create a packet that points to itself. It has the same source and destination. Usually routers kick those out, but if you understand how these routers work and keep up with all their software updates because it's constantly changing, you can get it to force an RST or reset packet to be sent. Knowing it's coming, you then intercept that reset packet and stuff in whatever information in the packet you want to whatever destination you want. The virtual packet trick."

"So you can stuff curse words in the packet and have them replace real words that should be used?"

"Anything you want."

"Like from swearasaurus?"

"Any handy and ever-updating list of curse words along with enough context to pick them out."

"And we can defeat this how?" Meeta asks.

"We just have to find those interposed bytes and the code in the data. Then we have to put a wrapper around the whole thing to constantly look for the right software, the software that we originally download. We'll have to come up with something beyond checksum, even random checks every few minutes. Same with the data; it shouldn't be hard to scan for malicious code. That's what the anti-virus stuff does."

"OK," Meeta says quickly. "I can get someone on this. I think the trick is to find it and remove it and then update all the Grumbys out there with the right version of the software and then some piece of master code that constantly checks all the other code—for what, legitimacy?"

"Yup. And I think you have less than three days or we really are toast."

"And if they hack the master code?" Meeta asks, as he walks away.

"Just make sure nobody can."

•   •   •

Then another one of "the emails" pops up on my screen with the subject: "Sell?" Two in one day. It's from the Woz, Steve Wozniak, the other founder of Apple with Steve Jobs a zillion years ago, and a bit of a hacker himself.

It contains three words: "Don't do it."

PART III

Fixed

10:21 a.m., April 5, Milpitas

"He won't put up anymore?" Lorita asks me about Jeannie. "I can't have my high-profile deal croak like this. I'm counting on you."

"Great. Jeannie says he's tapped. Or his assets are tapped. He claims Julius Baer Bank won't let him go any higher."

"Well that was a pretty unique deal to not put money up but guarantee a credit line," Lorita says.

"So any ideas? Any?" I ask.

Meeta comes over and stands next to my desk. I look up and wave him off.

"I lobbed a call into Silicon Valley Bank. Of all the banks they usually get these kinds of situations. The vibe I got was that you're radioactive," Lorita continues.

"Meaning what?"

Meeta is now waving his hands around trying to get my attention. "Not now, Meeta," I whisper.

"Meaning no one wants to touch you," Lorita continues.

"What?"

"Someone got to them first."

"Our pal, Jack?"

Meeta is jumping up and down like a pogo stick. I cover the phone and turn. "Meeta, not now. Get lost."

"Could be," Lorita goes on. "He does stand to gain if you go under and he can come in and convince a bankruptcy judge to let him buy it for next to nothing since he already owns a piece."

"Now THAT pisses me off. Worse than Apple snapping us up on the cheap."

"I said 'could be.' I'm not 100 percent sure," Lorita explains.

"Yeah, well, we're still going under. Keep thinking. We're valuable to someone. I'm just not sure who."

I hit the "end" button and turn to Meeta.

"WHAT?"

"Someone wants to see you," Meeta says.

"C'mon. I'm trying to save this thing. We're getting killed and I suspect you and I are going to personally own 100,000 Grumbys."

"This guy is quite insistent."

"Who is he?"

"Ali something."

"The Champ?"

"What?"

"Ali what?"

"Ali Peck."

"Do I know him?"

"He says you should. From IKEA."

Huh? Furniture?

"Does he want a job? We're going to miss payroll in another three days. I don't think we're hiring."

"It was hard to understand but he says he has a parting offer."

"Well, we are parting. Tell him I'll only meet with him—or anyone that bothers us—if he brings a cashier's check for $20 million. That ought to get rid of him. Now, any luck on killing the potty-mouth virus?"

"We found the transposed bytes in our code."

"Excellent, so you can fix that."

"Well, that was the easy part. It's the redirection code in the data that's been tough. There are so many lines to check; it all looks like data. Plus it's user-generated; they provide the answers for Stump the Machine and data for TuneBuffoon. It must not have been hard to slip in code. It is the fiddle in the haystack."

"Needle."

"Yes. Even better. We are writing code to find the code. I think when we are done we will have something that no one can hack because we can use this new code to check ourselves."

"If you're fast enough."

I watch another YouTube video called the "Eat Me Grumby." Even I find it funny.

Beyond the techie blogs, the press is running with it. An article runs in the *New York Post* with a huge picture of a Grumby and a child covering his ears. It's not flattering but it did say nice things about our reading app. The *New York Times* and the *Wall Street Journal* follow a day later with articles. A reporter from the *Times* got to Meeta and yelled at him for ten straight minutes for not giving him an exclusive. Huh?

I haven't been home in forty-eight hours.

•   •   •

"Do you think it'll work?" Meeta asks.

"Should."

"A global reset?"

"If we can jam a reset instruction into every Grumby then they'll all contact us back the next time they turn on through Wi-Fi or USB and we can upload a new operating system with your fixed code with the self-scanning module. It ought to be secure."

"But how does anyone know it's fixed?"

"How about we have the Grumby speak? 'Sorry for the problems, new secure code; if you want to return it you can have a full refund, but here is a free copy of Air Guitar, blah, blah, blah.' Or maybe just 'Give us just one more chance, pretty please.'"

"We can do that."

"Today?"

"Later today," Meeta says.

"Turn the counter back on. I want to know when it works."

We test the reset on a dozen or so Grumbys in the office and it seems to work. Tens of thousands at the same time is another matter. We put in a bunch of new servers hoping they can not only handle the increased traffic of the reset but also a bunch of new things we have been playing with, especially this new thing based on Meeta's voice-capture technology called RecordAll. It just records everything in every conversation and puts it in a database for later recall. The old "what did that guy tell me yesterday at lunch." Now, if we do this right, our brain is searchable.

·   ·   ·

"Meeta, even if we make it secure . . ."

"Done."

"OK, let me rephrase that. You know it's secure. I know, or at least hope, it's secure. But why would anyone else believe us?"

"Because it is."

I chuckle. Classic techie.

"Yeah, sure. But we need something to show that a Grumby is not going to curse like a drunken sailor."

"I thought drunken sailors sing," Meeta states, sounding confused.

"That too. C'mon, help me think this through. What can we

do to prove that no little kids will ever hear bad words from a Grumby?"

"They won't."

"You're not helping. We need to show it."

"How about we just check if a child is in the room and then filter out all known curses from any source."

"And how do we check?"

"I don't know. All kids are whiny?" Meeta asks.

"Yeah. But so are a lot of adults."

"No, I mean they have high-pitched voices."

"Unlike us manly men?" I joke.

"Well, yes. Unlike men and probably most women," Meeta says.

"So, you're saying . . ."

"I'm suggesting we calculate the pitch of the speakers in the room and check for high settings and . . ."

"And you can do the expletive-deleted routine?"

"The what?" Meeta asks.

"The curse filter?"

"Yes," Meeta says emphatically, "we just update a master list from scraping swearasaurus and then . . ."

"Make the cut-off thirteen."

"Thirteen years old?"

"Yeah. Find the average pitch of thirteen-year-old kids and then filter."

"What about girls?"

"What about them?"

"I know many old girls with similar high pitch. Even some men."

"Well," I pause, looking up at the soundproofing ceiling tiles, and going into deep-think mode. Meeta doesn't say a word and I feel him staring at me.

The tiny holes in the ceiling tiles start dancing around and creating patterns: first circles, then boxes, then dodecahedrons. Then I get it.

"We'll default to safe mode if we hear someone under thirteen but listen for the words "Card me." If someone says that, ask them two or three questions that only someone over eighteen would know. What group did Michael Jackson originally sing in? Name any movie Jane Fonda was in. Who was our last president? Kids don't retain much anymore."

"Yes. I believe you have it," Meeta says. "I can have this done very quickly. We already have the code for pitch in the music sub-system. I will do research on average pitch for children."

"Make it foolproof. I want to make sure no more nasty You-Tube videos of embarrassed parents show up."

I go back to staring at the ceiling but I can't get the patterns to come back.

"Check it out, man," one of the coders a few desks away says. "There's some dude with a tie on walking around the office."

"Who is that?" I ask. No more distractions. Not now.

Meeta runs over to talk to him. The man hands over his card and Meeta smiles and starts walking with him in my direction. I slink lower in my seat. Who is this? Can't be our landlord; we're paid up a few months in advance. And no way I'm talking to someone from the press.

"This is Olli-Pekka." Meeta hands me his card.

"Our famed Ali Peck? From what—two days ago?"

"Yes, it doesn't translate so well," Meeta says.

"I am from Nokia. We would like to do a porting deal."

"From Nokia? Finland?" Not IKEA! I glare at Meeta.

"Yes, we are quite impressed with your iPhone apps. And you even use the PHZR. But no Nokia?"

"Well, sorry. We only had so much time and . . ."

"Here, you asked that I bring this."

Olli-Pekka reaches into his jacket pocket and pulls out an envelope.

He slowly opens the envelope and pulls out a piece of paper and holds it up for me to see. As I look at it with a confused look on my face, it's clear that this is no ordinary piece of paper but a cashier's check with a lot of zeros. I squint and read the number. Does that really say $20 million? My jaw drops and I just stare at it for a minute or two. The patterns come back, this time spinning pyramids.

"I . . . I . . . I . . ."

"Before I hand it over I need to ask if you have solved the not very amusing foul-mouth issue."

"Yes, absolutely, done deal. We've got it beat, the virus is contained, we can filter everything, age verify, global reset, add a secure wrapper, . . ."

"OK, I'll have to believe you."

He hands me the check. It feels lighter than I thought it should. Or maybe my head is just lighter. I can't think straight.

"All we ask is that you port everything you write to Nokia phones. We'll provide support for our DSPs. We want to run all of your apps on all our phones. Of course our high-end N99s and smartphones, but we really think you will help us sell many low-end phones. You are what we've been waiting for."

"Twenty m-m-million?" I mumble.

"Consider it an advance. We'll pay $1 a unit against a fee split on apps that we sell for you."

I still can't think. I just keep staring at the check.

"Twenty million?"

"We sold over 500 million phones last year. If you can get your code to run on our low-end phones, you'll have a heck of a business.

"Five hundred," I repeat.

"And we can almost guarantee a high conversion rate once you are embedded in phones that ship and . . ."

I snap out of it.

"OK," I reach out and grab his hand. "You have a deal. I'll get our general counsel and biz-dev team to draw up papers in the next hour."

Meeta looks at me funny and mouths, "general counsel?"

I ignore him. "You can have the same 15 percent on apps that we pay Amazon to sell Grumbys. So if we sell a $10 app, that more than covers your buck advance and you start making money."

"Oh, we'll make money even if we sell no apps. Operators are begging us for features and you are it."

"But it's just our audio stuff."

"We have an imager on every phone. We are thinking of putting in two. If you port to our DSP, I will hope your reading program will work on most of our phones. That would make us very happy."

"Yeah, me too." Not as happy as staring at this $20 million check.

"And it would be smart to charge a porting fee to everyone."

"You mean . . . ?"

He nods. "Yes, Motorola, Apple, . . . everyone."

A pause.

"And one more thing."

Uh-oh. "Yes?" I ask.

"I won't tell you how to run your business." He looks around our office at the *Fight Club* mural, at the guys playing Air Guitar, at the half-sized *Alien vs. Predator* statue, and he shakes his head. "We know something about public relations. You need some. If you leave for New York tonight, we can help solve your problems."

"I'll do anything," I say. I really will.

He explains why.

"And don't lose that check," he says over his shoulder with a smile as he starts walking out.

I fold the check and put it in my wallet, thank Olli-Pekka, wait until he walks past the torture chair and out the front door, and then I let out the loudest primal scream that I had no idea I was capable of.

It gets everyone's attention.

"OK, listen up. We live to fight another day. You guys have maybe twelve hours to isolate this damned virus and upload a fix to every Grumby out in the wild, and then we are going to start running as fast as we can toward the heart of the American Dream."

I get a lot of quizzical looks at the last line but what the heck. I feel like John Belushi whipping up his brothers at the Delta house, something about the Germans bombing Pearl Harbor.

"We don't stop until we ship a million Grumbys and are on a billion phones and are worth a trillion dollars and rewire the cultural landscape in our image."

I look out to a room of smiles and woo-hoos and boo-yahs and Nerf guns firing in the air.

Then I remember the check and quickly slip out the door and drive as fast as I can to the nearest Wells Fargo and shove the check into an ATM machine.

I have a plane to catch.

Today

"**G**ood morning. And welcome."

"Thank you, Matt."

I had taken the red-eye to JFK, and on top of being exhausted I was incredibly nervous—I had gotten no more than an hour's sleep. I thought about taking Imovane but was worried I'd never wake up in time. The *Today* show had a car waiting for me and the driver seemed to know every short cut through Queens to get into Manhattan and in no more than twenty minutes and just before seven I'm plopped in a chair.

Meanwhile, my head is pounding. And the damned lights are way too bright. I do my best not to squint without much success. What I hadn't planned on was dripping sweat from my hair into my eyes, which added rapid blinking to my squinty-eyed look.

"So we understand that you have a new device to teach kids how to read. Can you show us?"

"We call it the Grumby. It can identify songs and answer questions, but a developer in Moscow . . ."

"Moscow?"

"We have developers around the globe. Anyway, he came up with this application we call Mary Poppins."

"A nanny?"

"Basically. Here read this as if you were five years old."

"Some still think I am." There is laughter around the room.

I hold up the book to the Grumby. This better work. You only get one shot at the *Today* show and Matt Lauer.

"If You Give a Mouse a Cookie *by Laura Joffe Numeroff and Felicia Bond*," the Grumby says in a slightly British voice.

Matt Lauer's eyebrows shoot up.

He grabs the book and starts reading slowly.

"If. You . . ." Matt starts deliberately and then pauses, looks up, and smiles into the camera.

"*Guh-guh-guh . . .Gih-Gih-Gih . . . Give.*"

"Give," Matt says. "A. Mouse. A. K-k—"

"*Kuh-Kuh-Kuh—. Cook-Cook-Cook—*"

"Cookie," Matt finishes with a smile. "If you give a mouse a cookie, he's going to ask for a glass of . . ."

"*Mm-Mm,*" the Grumby prompts.

"Milk! Sounds like Katie Couric's agent."

I grin.

"This is incredible."

"Thanks. We just hope that it helps an entire generation to learn how to read and . . ."

"And I understand you've taught them some not so appropriate words."

"Well, we had this design error and . . ."

"The Potty-Mouth Grumby is quite a sensation on the Internet."

"Well, we've fixed that."

"Isn't that the problem with all technology? It eventually ends up beyond the control of human beings and does more harm than good?"

"Well, let's run an experiment," I say. "We've rigged this Grumby to curse when it hears a certain phrase. In this case it's 'Chocolate Thunder.'"

"*Eat me, Matt,*" the Grumby says.

"Chocolate Thunder?" Matt asks.

"*Beyotch,*" the Grumby says, as it moves side to side.

Matt is in hysterics.

"Can we say that on TV?" I ask.

"Not really. OK. We have a ten-year-old daughter of one of our cameramen just off set. Can we bring her in? Hello, your name is?"

"Jasmine."

"*What a pretty name,*" the Grumby says.

"Thanks. Can you say these words?" Matt holds up a piece of paper that says "Chocolate Thunder."

"Chocolate Thunder," reads Jasmine.

I watch on the monitor and the camera zooms in on the Grumby.

"*Hello, Jasmine,*" the Grumby says.

"Hello," she says back.

"*What grade are you in?*"

"Fourth."

"*Do you like iCarly?*" the Grumby asks.

"Of course. She's awesome," Jasmine answers.

I close my eyes and thank Meeta for what he coded up. When he heard about the *Today* show thing, he whipped up a conversation engine for kids twelve and under.

Matt jumps in.

"OK, I'm the interviewer here. I hope I'm not out of a job because of this thing." He quickly turns to the Grumby and says, "Chocolate Thunder!"

Nothing.

"OK, let's take a break and when we're back we'll go to Ann Curry and the strange story about the two-headed baby in Thailand."

I get quickly whisked off the set by the crew.

I leave the Grumby behind.

Up

5:04 p.m., Milpitas

"You're back fast," Meeta says to me as I walk in.

"No reason to stick around. I got the noon flight back. Did you watch?"

"It's already on YouTube."

"Excellent. And *iCarly*? Brilliant," I congratulate Meeta.

"If it was a boy it would have asked about *Iron Man*."

"You can tell the difference."

"Almost. If the boy's name was Leslie, we would have been in trouble."

"Anyway, it couldn't have gone better."

While I was gone, Meeta put up a YouTube video of an apology and the *Today* show clip and then another one of a cute-as-a-button three-year-old reading with the help of a Grumby. Tear-jerking stuff.

"OK, Meeta. This is going to be interesting."

Yuren emails, saying he can slow the factory a little, maybe push out some deliveries. I tell him not to bother. Crank out those Grumbys. With the Nokia check, we now have plenty of money to pay suppliers and pay down Jeannie's credit line, which gets him to stop calling every ten minutes to ask me when his credit line would be paid back. Now all we need is people to start buying Grumbys again, soaking up all the units piling up at Amazon.

"And check this out," Meeta says. "Oh, shit . . ."

"*Shitake mushrooms*," his Grumby says, perfectly timed to cover Meeta's curse.

"*Bada bing.*"

Meeta has turned the notification back on. It's now music to my ears.

TechCrunch is first with the story of the Well-Mannered Grumby patch and how we did it technically, though Michael Arrington complains that he kinda liked the foul-mouthed version. Other blogs pick up on it quickly. "Listen to your customer," many are pitching. So I have Meeta write a piece of code that absolutely berates people with nastier and nastier curses as long as they are over age thirteen. We put it up for $20 on our Web site—I want to charge $50.

· · ·

"*Bada bing.*"

Sure enough, Grumby sales start rolling in. The reset works. On all existing Grumbys we rigged up a pleasant voice that sounds just like Angelina Jolie apologizing for our bad manners and begging for a second chance and offering a money-back guarantee ending with "*Is that OK with you?*"

We then play it every five minutes until we hear someone respond with "yes," "OK," anything positive, actually, even "shut up."

"*Bada bing—bada bing—bada bing.*"

Grumbys sell and sell and sell. The ramp is amazing. Our customer-service feedback system, basically an email account that Meeta reads whenever he feels like it, has tons of emails mostly saying they were blown away by the YouTube videos of a silly little doll teaching a child to read, and when they heard the potty-mouth bug was fixed on the *Today* show and elsewhere, they insisted on buying one for all their kids and nieces and nephews.

Besides getting a registered letter from Disney reminding us they own the trademark to Mary Poppins, we just pulled off the marketing coup of a lifetime. But somehow I don't think it's going to get any easier.

• • •

The more I have the Grumby around, I find, the less I have to remember things. I used to be the greatest at sports trivia. But now I just rely on my Grumby to tell me.

Like Inspector Clouseau's Kato, I ask Meeta to quiz me at anytime on sports trivia.

"Who hit the ball that rolled under Bill Buckner's legs in the 1986 World Series?" Meeta asks as he walks by my desk.

Before he even finishes asking, I say, "Mookie Wilson," about a nanosecond ahead of my Grumby. I still got it.

IDEO

As we walk from the lobby through the building, the only thing I can think of is that these guys have much cooler offices than ours. It's like a mini-campus tucked right into downtown Palo Alto. High ceilings. Pipes and vents run amok above us and almost random walls divide rooms filled with people and a whole bunch of weird devices and toys and woodworking machines and who knows what else. We're sitting in a conference room that has three walls, but they aren't connected and people seem to walk through as we talk.

"We call this the arReceptionist. The look is proto-corporate, with a serious yet inviting veneer," our host explains.

The Grumby sitting in front of us has been re-skinned with a quasi-robotic, almost humanoid look. I can't quite place it.

"It looks, uh . . . ," I start.

"Rational? Earnest? Knowing?"

I lean over to Meeta and out of the corner of my mouth whisper, "Creepy."

Meeta covers his mouth.

"The trick in industrial design is to marry inform with function. We thought about it for some time, ran some focus groups internally, and realized that a pure human form wouldn't work. But when we went with a robotic motif, no one would talk to it, so it became clear that a blend would elicit the appropriate behavior models."

"I'm sorry. This is over my head. Can you go through what this place is all about?"

"Oh sure, my pleasure. First off, I'm Dennis. I've been playing with TuneBuffoon and Stump the Machine and then Grumbys since they came out and I finally initiated contact because you guys fall right in the middle of everything we do."

"Which is?" I ask.

"Well, as one of the founders of IDEO, I like to say we drive innovation through design. Apple's mouse, the Palm V, salad spinners, compact fluorescent light bulbs—each of them was a better-informed product through design."

"Salad spinners?"

"I'll get you one before you leave. Anyway, to say we are impressed with your Grumby is too much of an understatement. We focus on desires, behavior, latent needs of people. And after a day or two with your apps, it's clear that you perfectly embody that. You provide a soul to gadgetry. You seem to be building the fabric of some sort of networked subconscious . . ."

"Hold on, I like that. Meeta did you get that?"

Meeta just taps his Grumby. It's recording and transcribing everything.

"Oh, yeah," I shake my head. We don't miss anything.

"So we wanted to get involved, provide that 'inform' to your 'function.'"

"So that?" I ask.

"So that . . . if I may be frank . . ."

"You may," I say.

"So that no one gets spooked when this subconscious fabric—when it's clear that their Grumby knows more than they do."

"And the humanoid look?"

"It's not just the look; it's the family of products, how they are presented, who they are intended for. We came up with the "ar" label for several reasons. First, it's small letters, nonthreatening, invoking a friendly interface. And second, "ar" sounds like the word "our"; it translates in quite a few languages and implies that we are all in this together. Nintendo already took "we" with the Wii, though they're stuck with Wii–Wii jokes."

"Our?"

"Think more of a colloquial, guttural "our," ar . . . arTunes, arTruth, arGuitar, arReader, arPersonality . . ."

"Yup, yup, I like it," I admit.

"And here is a skin for arReader, a bit of a whimsical school marm, likeable by parents and fun for kids." We can't use Mary Poppins, anyway.

"And that one?" I point to one very strange looking Grumby.

"Well, there may be some licensing issues—that's for arGuitar. It's a young Keith Richards. We had to use morphing code and . . ."

"Was he ever young?"

"Good question," Dennis chuckles.

"OK. Send us a proposal. We can certainly use the help. We have to make a decision soon whether we are going to sell different versions of the Grumby, or just let everyone else do it. We write code. We're not in the form business, but we do get harassed almost every day. Someone is always lobbing in some idea to sell this or that version of the Grumby. We can probably keep you busy for years."

On the walk back to my Jeep, I say, "Meeta, sign a deal with these guys; pay them what they ask. And then let's hurry up and rename everything as fast as we can, get those URLs, file for trademarks, whatever."

"Ar, ar, captain."

Ads?

12:26 p.m., April 12, Milpitas

"*U*nrecognized visitor asking for you*," my Grumby says.

On my screen pops an image of a man's nose, chin, and neckline.

"Meeta, it only works if the person is exactly your height."

"I know, I know. If we set the zoom any less, we can't do the image search. Not enough details."

I click for a video stream and up comes a video of a man, from the neck down, anyway, in dark pants and a blue shirt with a logo I can't quite make out. He looks nervous, pacing the lobby looking for someone, anyone, to announce his presence to. He stops each time at the torture chair and gives it a good look before shaking his head and heads back in the other direction.

"Ask him his name," I tell my Grumby.

In the distance, I hear a faint "*What is your name, please?*" coming from the Grumby in our entryway.

The man looks a little startled. "Uh, oh, Bill Torn," I barely hear him say.

My Grumby tells me, "*It's Bill Torn.*"

"Ask him who he is with."

"*Who are you with, please?*" I hear the Grumby ask.

"Uh," he looks around again, "I'm from Visa International, just up the road in Foster City."

"We paid all those cards off," I grunt.

"*He is from Visa International in . . . ,*" my Grumby starts.

I interrupt, "Ask him his quest."

"*What is your quest?*"

I hear Meeta snickering behind me.

"I am here to talk about an ad deal."

"*He's here to talk about an ad deal.*"

"Ask him his favorite color."

"*What is your favorite color?*"

"Blue?" Now he starts scratching his head.

"*It's blue.*"

I stand up and yell to the front door, "Just joking with you. C'mon back."

Meeta is laughing way too hard. I wonder when the last time he got some sleep.

"Over here," I direct our visitor once more as he winds through the maze of desks and toys and finds his way to my desk. A middle-aged man wearing a light blazer and a dark tie strolls over to my desk and extends his hand.

"Bill Torn. Visa International."

"Welcome," I say and shake his hand.

"That's quite a setup. I didn't know you were that far along."

"It's a receptionist system. Does a facial scan to see if you've been here before or if we know you from an image on the Web."

"I want one."

"It's close. I was feeding it questions. Basically training it, so over time it will know what questions I want asked of visitors, or phone callers, or anyone who wants to talk to me directly. We're thinking of doing the same thing with emails and instant messages, too, actually. Time is precious."

"Sure is."

"Well, nice to meet you."

"Likewise."

"I'm a happy Visa customer."

"I've heard," Bill says, and smiles. "Hey," he continues, getting down to business, "we'd like to sponsor a keyword."

"A what?"

"A keyword. Like we do with Google and Yahoo and everyone else in search."

"We don't really do search."

"But if you ask, your Grumby will return an answer. That's search all right."

"We'd like to buy the word 'buy.' Every time someone says buy, we want to offer them to make the purchase with a Visa card."

"That's rather forward."

"Not really. Point of sale is proven to be the most effective advertising."

"I don't really get advertising." I say. What I really mean is that I loathe advertising.

"It's the art of persuasion."

"We don't want to persuade anyone. I have bigger hopes that people will persuade themselves what to do with our technology."

"Look, we can pay with the usual 'per impression' type of deal. You probably have a rate card or a keyword auction like everyone else."

"Rate card?" This is all new to me.

"Or we can offer a bounty."

"Like on a 'Wanted' poster?" I ask.

"Sort of. Every time someone uses their Visa card, we'll pay you a buck."

Now that got my attention.

"We'd need an exclusive and the rights to tweak your code to optimize conversion ratios, but this can be a very lucrative deal for you."

"It sure can. Let me talk to my staff." Where did Meeta disappear to? "I'll get back to you as soon as I can," I lie.

.　　.　　.

Since meeting with Bill Torn, my mind has been bubbling with conflicting thoughts. A buck every time someone uses a Visa card would be nice, but . . .

"Meeta," I say, "I hate ads."

"You told me. But they do pay money. And someday we'll run out of cell phone companies to give us big checks."

"I just know we can charge for our apps."

"No one does anymore," Meeta says.

"So what. If our stuff is any good, people will just have to reach into their wallets and pay up."

"Well, so far so good."

"I think I just decided to tell Visa to take a walk."

"Do you even have a Visa card anymore? Didn't they tear them all up?"

"It's not that. I just don't want ads."

"Ever?"

"No. They're intrusive and annoying and I just can't stand them."

"But . . ."

"And they lie. And lie and lie. Lies and deceit—rinse and repeat."

"Yeah, but Google seems to . . ."

"No ads for us. It's probably a good quality filter for us, anyway.

Anything someone gives away free is probably worth exactly what you pay for it."

"So, no ads. Are you sure?"

"We've 20 million reasons in the bank why I'm sure."

• • •

"Meeta, you're not going to believe it, but I need you back in the torture chair."

He jumps up. "That thing hurts."

"Look, I got these new CMOS imagers. They can zoom in and out digitally, but they can also rotate 80 degrees in any direction. I need to calibrate them to the human eyeball and you're the one with, uh, experience." Plus, Meeta's the only one I trust not to run to OSHA or PETA or wherever and file a complaint.

"And?"

"And I'm thinking of calling it the Meeta Motion Measurement." I just made that up.

"Really?"

I nod yes, until Meeta walks toward the entryway and the eye torture chair and then I just shake my head in amazement that this is what we do. With $20 million in the bank we can do just about whatever we want. I like the idea of a Grumby arReceptionist. Someone suggested Greceptionist but that sounds like a wrestler or something.

By the time I get there, Meeta is in *A Clockwork Orange* mode, head clamped down and metal hooks holding his eyes open. A crowd gathers. I have some high-tech tools with me. Well, a piece of string and a protractor.

"Meeta. Here's the game plan. I've thought about it and I figure the focus is going to be from two feet to around ten. Any closer and either someone just invaded your personal space or a little kissy action is about to take place and we need to shut down imaging anyway. So I want you to follow my face around, look me in the eyes. I want to measure angles at two feet, five feet, and then ten. Up, down, left, right, the whole thing. I need those numbers to get the algorithm started on locking on someone's face. If I can find the face, I can zoom in and get the T-zone parameters and do a lookup in the . . ."

"Can we get going? I really need to blink," Meeta whines. The crowd around the chair laughs.

It must be a very strange sight. I hold the string between Meeta's eyes and mine and someone else holds up the protractor and starts yelling out numbers, directions, distance, angles, until someone starts counting the tears coming out of Meeta's left eyeball and then it turns into a betting frenzy on which direction and distance causes the quickest tears. Even Meeta starts laughing and I have to break the thing up, not wanting a bunch of worthless numbers.

When Meeta finally makes it back out of the bathroom after drowning his eyes in water, he sits back down at his desk and jumps right in.

"One of my crew found an open source face finder. Someone hoped to sell it to Sony or Casio for their cameras and must have just dumped it online when they didn't get the deal."

"Is it one of those smile finders?"

"That's in there too."

"Good. If we can find the lips, usually there is a nose above it."

"Usually?"

"And the eyes are pretty easy to find; that gets us most of the T-zone—and cheeks too."

"So what are we missing?" Meeta asks.

"Movement. No one stands still for this stuff. They do for a camera but not for face recognition."

"So how do you get this to work?"

"I basically look for motion, something that's in the scene that wasn't there before. I assume it's human and start looking for a head—again, mostly eyes and lips."

"Then?"

"Then I just follow it and hope for a full frontal."

"Full frontal nudity?" Meeta asks rather seriously.

"I mean a full facial. Then we go for the T-zone, get all the data we need for recognition . . ."

"I found a better one by the way. I have a friend in Mumbai who . . ."

"OK, we just keep plugging them in until we find the one that works the best."

"And how do we know who is who?"

"Great question. I already started on Flickr and Google images. Plug in first names and last names and then just run recognition on photos that come up for those names."

"But those could be anybody."

"It's a start."

"Why not do the turnaround thing again?" Meeta asks.

"I lost you."

"Make everyone stick his or her own face in view to be imaged."

"How?"

"By adding self-recognition as a feature. When I walk in a room, the Grumby would recognize me and say, 'Hello, Meeta.'"

"I thought we were going to do that by voice," I say.

"Sure, but when I'm alone, I usually don't talk to myself."

"Right, but the Grumby can image you—self-recognition."

"Unless I have a twin." Meeta says.

"Twins are a problem," I admit.

"Only if they're mono-zygote."

"Mono-zy—, OK, but back to getting everyone to do it. That doesn't seem like enough."

"Sure it is. Then we create a social network of faces. Hey, a facial network." Like Facebook but with real faces.

"But why would I put mine in there?" I ask.

"Because everyone wants to be recognized."

"Because what?"

Meeta explains, "Think about it. You may only want to share your face with your friends, but they already know what you look like."

"Yeah, OK," I say.

"It's the person you are trying to meet who you'd like to have a hold of your face, especially in business. Most bosses don't know who works for them, but employees want to kiss the boss's ass, so they put their face on his network. Same for schools, towns, whatever. Social networking is really social climbing. Wanting to get noticed. I thought everyone knows that."

"Yeah," I say slowly. "I like it. I think you're on to something. So we just suggest everyone have their facial data captured by their Grumbys or phones and then use it themselves and share it with anyone who they would like to be known by?"

"Yes, I think that's it. Never underestimate the human need for love and affection and recognition."

"Who said that?" I asked.

"I just did," Meeta smiles.

•　　•　　•

"Who leads the major leagues in ejections from games?" Meeta asks me.

"Earl Weaver. Baltimore Orioles," I blurt out as fast as I can.

"*Bobby Cox, Atlanta Braves, 153 ejections, and counting,*" Meeta's

Grumby corrects me. "*Earl Weaver, Baltimore Orioles, 98.*"

"Yeah, yeah."

●　　●　　●

"Yuren?" I speak into my Grumby. Is it the left eye or the right eye I'm supposed to look into? I never get it right. "Can we get them any cheaper?"

"Those imagers are pretty unique. The little micromotors to move the imager in each direction are killing us," Yuren explains.

"How much?"

"I don't know, something like $10 each. You need a feedback loop to know exactly how far the eye has gone or it gets lost. Plus you need them on both sides."

"OK, but we only need the feedback on one side. Both eyes will move together."

"Fair enough but that still adds maybe $20 total. It pumps up the cost."

"Yuren. Do it. We'll come up with a new model. Grumby Pro. Or maybe just PAT—personal assistant terminal. Dress it up like some androgynous model, business-looking. It's going to sit on everyone's desk."

"No neuter. Neuter neutral?" Yuren asks.

"Androgynous Pat. It's an old *Saturday Night Live* sketch. It'll work."

"And you'll charge more?"

"Maybe. The device itself will cost more, but we'll sell the personal assistant code for all sorts of money. Monthly subscription, whatever. I'll bet once people start using this thing they'll be hooked. I am and we don't even have much of the features done."

"I can start turning them out next week," Yuren claims.

"Great. Build up some inventory. It's likely to be as hot as the plain old Grumby."

"Keep 'em coming," Yuren says and the screen goes blank. I look around the room of probably 200 plus coders. No problem with keeping 'em coming. There's not much room left in this office. It used to rattle. The plasma reads 279,427.

Jed

The Western motif gets me every time. Cowboys and cactii. Fry's Electronics is about as Silicon Valley as one can get. It's tacky and cheesy, but I wouldn't think of buying electronics without first checking out the prospector panning for gold or the guy in the ten-gallon hat on the bucking horse waving while looking over an acre of blinking and beeping merchandise. Resistors, voltmeters, and solder just aisles away from crock pots, bazooka subwoofers, James Bond DVDs, and plasma TVs.

I'm re-invigorated by just strolling through the store, looking for something, anything, that I haven't seen before. Some of my best ideas come from thinking how to combine Bluetooth headsets in the back of the store with the terabyte hard drives in the front.

Today I'm here on a mission. I read about these in-yer-ear brand Bluetooth earpieces. They're as small as a hearing aid and sit right in your ear rather than those ugly dangling things. Hence the name, I guess. I never could get used to those giant headsets as jewelry, almost making the statement that you're dying for someone, anyone, to call. I'm getting tired of everyone else hearing what my Grumby has to say. I want to buy a few of these new in-ear pieces and see if they are any good. But first, a stroll through techie paradise . . .

A voice comes from behind me.

"Have you thought of implementing a real-time market for products or ideas?"

"Uh, I'm sorry. Are you talking to me?" I'm a bit startled.

"I'm a big fan. I've been playing around with my Grumby and it seems if you have these devices scattered around you'll know about a lot of intentions, even just commerce would seem logical. A real-time market offering real-time pricing on those intentions, say a Garmin GPS. It would be like the New York Stock Exchange on steroids and . . ."

"Who are you?" I ask.

"I'm sorry," he extended his hand, "I'm Jed. Jed Tedford."

Great name.

"Really?" I chuckle.

"Yeah, I know. Used to it by now."

"How do you know who I . . . ?"

"Saw you on *Today*. Been following your progress and . . ."

"And what do you do?" I ask.

"I run tech banking at Goldman."

"Checking accounts? I use Wells Fargo because of the horses and . . ."

"Investment banking. Goldman Sachs. Dartmouth–Wharton."

"Oh, sure, sorry." I feel like an idiot.

"We've got a bunch of Grumbys in the office. We'd love to have you come up to San Francisco and give us a demo of some new stuff. We hear that you just raised money from strategic investors and I'd love to walk you through the current environment. The window is tight right now but it's always open for a deal like yours.

The window is tight? Is he talking about Microsoft? Either way, he seems to know a lot about us. Note to self: call Lorita and see if this guy is for real.

"You want to be first to market," he adds, "and raise enough to keep everyone else away. Investors don't like second fiddles."

"Uh, sure. We've got a few neat things in the works. We're shipping like crazy, which keeps us busy and we're running as fast as we can and . . ."

"I didn't mean to bother you. Here's my card. Stop by if you're in San Fran."

"Thanks. And I'll think about that market idea."

I walk down the video game aisle lost in thought. I couldn't tell whether that was a random encounter or I was being stalked. Not that I'm paranoid, but I am.

•　　•　　•

As I walk past the video game aisle, I do a double take. Sure enough, sitting on the end cap of the aisle are four Grumbys, staring out into space. On another shelf below them are about a dozen boxes with a makeshift label that says "Grumby Device" and a $99 price tag. I had no idea Fry's sells Grumbys. They must buy them online and mark them up.

A salesperson comes over. I can't help myself.

"So what are these things?"

"Oh, the Grumbys. New toy." Toy? I resist interrupting. "Hot seller. We just got another shipment in; it's hard to keep in stock. I'd grab one. This thing listens and talks and other stuff. But just so you know, the Sony distributor told me there's a better one being developed that rolls and reads and is going to make these obsolete. Wookie or Dookie."

We Need Crowds

A competitor, already? That, plus the whole thing with the Goldman Sachs guy got me thinking.

We still have most of the $20 million in the bank, maybe more as we sell more apps—I'll have to check. The reality is that I don't know much about financials. It's no real wonder—I never had much more than a small meeting of Andrew Jacksons in my wallet.

Maybe this is just what I need, an on the fly education in financial stuff.

There is no way we're going to knit the social fabric thing without money. I'm not even sure how many people we have working for us these days, but I'm sure that's not cheap. Just floating Yuren the money to manufacture Grumbys ain't cheap. We need money.

It doesn't really work unless we have not just thousands but millions of people providing input into our system. I keep playing in my mind with the idea of real-time markets and price signals and all that. But to get the wisdom of crowds, you need crowds. Millions of users. And even my limited financial know-how tells me that's going to take a lot of dough.

A little sniffing around on Goldman Sachs and as far as I can tell, they are it. They can get us money. And with it, I just know we can do something impressive.

The structure is there at our company to write some useful apps. The best ones simplify daily things, give people some sort of control over everyday hassles or ideas that they never had before, with the end result a better life. That sounds so lofty, but it really isn't. Great software makes people's lives better.

I've seen it again and again. If we do this right, we just sum up all those individual little empowerments and . . . But we've got to be first and own it all.

Then from there . . .

PA

I decide that we are going to be the first through that tight window.

"Meeta, we need a kick-ass demo."

"Of course we do."

"I ran into this guy from Goldman Sachs. I want to impress the crap out of him," I explain.

"Fifth Avenue?" Meeta asks.

"Not the store, the investment banking firm."

"Is there a difference?"

"Perhaps not. Anyway, I did some checking with Lorita and they are it," I tell Meeta.

"It?"

"It. I want to stop in and say hello and show off our personal assistant," I say.

"arReceptionist?"

"No, the complete personal assistant."

"But we don't have that yet," Meeta complains.

"But you will?"

"By when?"

"Friday," I state.

"It's Tuesday, right?"

"Too much time?"

"I'll get on it."

"What are we missing?" I ask.

"Most of it."

And with that, Meeta turns his back and starts clicking away—I suspect firing off emails to far off lands requesting our international coding network to jump into a high state of alert. How cool is that?

Receptive

9:59 a.m., April 22, San Francisco, California

55 California Avenue, I note, as we walk uphill toward the wavy looking building. Just getting to work in San Francisco would keep you in shape. I look farther up California Avenue and it gets steeper and steeper, though I see a cable car about halfway up. That's cheating.

"This must be the place. Is that marble?" Meeta asks.

"It looks like it."

"How come our building in Milpitas wasn't mined by some Tuscan Italianate?"

"What does that even mean?" I ask.

"You're avoiding my question."

"Are you sure this is going to work?" I look into Meeta's eyes to see if he is sincere. He just nods.

We climb the steps, which narrow almost Escher-like. They look like they could be headed down at one point as we head uphill from California Avenue.

After about ten steps, Meeta adds, "It's a demo, it's not supposed to work, just impress."

"OK, are you sure this is going to impress?"

"If it works," Meeta smiles.

We enter the building through revolving doors, look up Goldman Sachs on the directory, and get on an elevator and hit thirty-six.

We start heading up and then alarm bells start going off; the elevator comes to a halt and then starts rapidly heading back down. Meeta looks scared. I can't even imagine what I look like. We both grab the handrails and the elevator comes to an abrupt stop and the doors open up back on the first floor.

Two guards are there to greet us.

"Where you going?"

"Goldman Sachs," I answer.

"You can't go up without an appointment."

"We're here to see Jed Tedford. He told us to stop in anytime," I smile.

"Yeah, right." We follow him to the guard desk.

"ID please."

Meeta gets out his Safeway card. I produce my driver's license.

"Ted Jedford?"

"Jed Tedford."

He clicks around a bit, calls his number, gets no answer, leaves a message, and tells us to wait. He could use arReceptionist.

"Try his secretary."

"You mean his executive assistant?"

"Yes."

"Name?"

"Don't you have it?"

"Sure, yeah, OK, uh-huh," he dials another number "I got two guys down here to see Mr. Tedford . . . uh-huh . . ." The guard turns to me, "From?"

"Grumby Mogul Limited Company, Inc." Meeta jumps in.

"Grumby Mo Co something . . . OK, I'll wait . . . ," he turns to us again with a disgusted look, "OK, he'll see you, thirty-nine. Go on up." He hands us two badges with our pictures on them, though I don't remember him taking them.

"Did you fix the elevator yet?" Meeta asks.

We both hold on to the handrails on the way up.

"I'm Stephanie. Sorry for the hassle downstairs. Mr. Tedford is delighted to meet with you. Right this way to our conference room."

"Could you mention we have a demo for him, and it's probably better in his office."

"Sure, wait here."

In less than thirty seconds, she's back and we follow her through a maze of dark cherry wood offices until we got to Jed's corner office, with a view of the bay and Alcatraz and the Golden Gate Bridge and Marin. Both Meeta and I just stare. It must happen a lot because Jed just waits, smiles, and then finally motions for us to sit down on his black leather couch.

"Nice office," I say. "You guys must do well."

"I don't notice it anymore, though I should."

He walks over to Meeta on the couch, extends his hand, and says, "Jed Tedford."

"Meeta," Meeta says.

"Sorry," I jump in. "I should have introduced you. This is my partner Meeta. He knows everyone in India, everything about technology, and I would call him Kato if I didn't think he would attack me every time I came into the office."

Meeta is now crawling under Jed's desk, unplugging cables, and plugging in a Grumby.

"Our IT guys have all sorts of stuff," he says as he looks down at Meeta, "firewalls and security stuff built in. They claim it's impenetrable. I can't even bring in a laptop," Jed explains.

Meeta just laughs.

"OK, let's see what happens," Jed says.

Meeta gets up and sticks the Grumby about two feet from Jed's face and tells Jed to say "Master."

"Master," Jed complies.

Meeta then places the Grumby on his desk next to his monitor, facing out.

"*You have a conference call in ten minutes,*" the Grumby says. "*Charles Phillips from Oracle. According to his email he wants to talk about acquiring VMware from EMC.*"

Jed's face turns red. "You didn't hear that," he says to us.

"*I read it,*" says the Grumby. "*Would you like me to reschedule the call? I see you have company.*"

"Yes, have Steph—"

"*I have alerted Stephanie to attempt to reschedule and will notify you promptly. Awaiting instructions.*"

I slip Jed a note. "Ask who is in the room."

"Who are my visitors?"

"*The person on the left is the CEO of Grumby Inc. You emailed your superior that you would find him and impress the shit out of him and discuss possible IPO plans.*"

Jed turns red again, but nods his head in approval.

"*The person on the right is Meeta, the partner, who might also be known as Kato.*"

Meeta laughs.

"That is impressive . . . ," Jed starts.

"*Impressive,*" Darth Vader's voice comes out of the Grumby.

"Did you set this up ahead of time?" Jed asks.

"*Does anyone really know what time it is?*" the Grumby asks.

I just shrug my shoulders. "He makes mistakes every once in a while."

"Who doesn't?" Jed agrees. "So this isn't a canned demo?"

"We put in our photos, but that's it. The rest is easy to find from scanning your Outlook files for emails and appointments and whatever else we can find."

"Tell me about your company?"

"Grumby Mogul Limited Company, Inc.," Meeta corrects.

"How are you funded?"

I quickly wind through the story of Jack at RedMark Ventures.

"*Be careful*," the Grumby offers, in Sean Connery's voice for some reason. Jed turns red again. Meeta shrugs.

And I tell Jed about Jeannie in Cap d'Antibes.

"I was at Hotel du Cap last summer," Jed offers.

"*Best derriere in the South of France*," the Grumby says.

"I think I wrote that in an email to an old fraternity brother when I got back," Jed says, this time without blushing.

"*To JT. Photo attached*," the Grumby says.

"Anyway, we almost ran out of money and then the CEO of Nokia stops in our office and . . ."

"*Olli-Pekka. Closing price ten dollars and eighteen cents; thirty point two million shares traded.*"

"And?" Jed asks.

"And hands me a check for $20 million," I say.

Jed's eyes widen.

"Advance on a dollar per Nokia phone royalties and a cut of app sales," I add.

"*According to the site MobileWhack.com, Nokia has been losing shares at the low end to Samsung and others and at the high end to Apple and RIM, registering their lowest market share since 2004*," the Grumby deadpans.

"How did it know to say that?" Jed asks.

"It figured that you wanted to know," Meeta says.

"How?" Jed asks.

"It just does. We are still tweaking the algorithm, but it listens and constantly scans the Web for pertinent things you might find interesting. Sometimes it goes off on tangents, but like you said, who doesn't?"

"*A line that just touches a curve at a given point,*" the Grumby says.

"What?" Jed asks

"A tangent," I shrug.

"It also knows it's you," Meeta explains.

"What do you mean?"

"Call Chuck Phillips," Meeta says.

Nothing happens.

"Now you," Meeta instructs.

"Call Chuck Phillips," Jed leans over and speaks loudly into the Grumby.

A dial tone followed by touchtone signals comes out of the Grumby.

"Hello. Chuck here."

"Chuck, Jed Tedford. Can we push out our call by fifteen?"

"Your assistant already emailed me. No problem. I think we can offer EMC a discount on our database software if they spin out their ownership into a . . ."

"Sorry. Great. Talk to you in a few," Jed interrupts.

"How do I hang up?" Jed whispers.

"Just say 'Hang up.'"

"Hang up."

"*Call ended. Shall I save the contents?*" the Grumby asks.

"Uh . . ." Jed looks at us.

"*Yes or no?*" the Grumby asks.

"Yes."

"*Call saved.*"

"Now ask it about Chuck Phillips and EMC."

"What?"

"Go ahead. We parse the words and store them so you can search them later."

"Really?"

"Ask," I nod.

"Tell me about Chuck Phillips and EMC," Jed looks at the Grumby and says.

In a voice that sounds like the one we just heard, but a little flatter, "*I think we can offer EMC a discount on our database software if they spin out their ownership into a . . .*"

"Wow."

"*VMWare stock is sixty-seven dollars and seventy-five cents. Twenty-six billion market capitalization.*"

"Meeta, unplug it. I think Jed's seen enough."

"No, no. leave it in. I'll be a beta tester."

"Fair enough. You can tell it to stop commenting by saying 'Shut up,'" Meeta tells Jed.

"Shut up," Jed says.

"*Shuttin' up.*" It sounds like Yosemite Sam.

Meeta nailed it.

Greet

*C*hirp.

WTF? My Grumby just chirped. Like a sparrow or something. That's weird.

In Meeta's voice, I hear "Meeta is reading TechCrunch."

Huh?

A minute later, it chirps again.

"(chirp) Meeta is typing an email," my Grumby announces.

"(chirp) Meeta is going to the bathroom."

"(chirp) Meeta is eating some Skittles."

"(chirp) Meeta is talking to Sully about football."

"Meeta!" I scream.

Meeta comes running over carrying his Grumby.

"(chirp) Meeta is running to talk to the boss."

"Yes, boss?" Meeta asks.

"What's going on?" I ask.

"(chirp) Meeta is asked, 'What's going on?'" The *'what's going on'* was in my voice."

"Greetweet."

"(chirp) Meeta answers, 'Greetweet.'"

"Turn that off."

"(chirp) Meeta is told to . . ." Meeta turns off his Grumby.

"What the hell is that?"

"I've been playing around with Twitter," Meeta answers. Twitter is the 140-character communications service that is all the rage.

"Well stop," I insist.

"It's kinda cool." He looks at me searching for approval, I think. I try to give him a stone-cold look. "Only a couple of hundred lines of code."

"To do what?" I ask.

"Well, I got tired of constantly typing in what I am doing into Twitter, so I figured my Grumby always knows what I'm doing, so I query it and force a 140-character summary that gets sent to Twitter and then if people who follow me on Twitter have a Grumby, they get an update, too, in my voice—fourteen words or less instead of 140 characters of text and . . ."

"It's annoying," I say a bit too harshly.

"Yes, most definitely. Twitter is annoying and obtrusive but I am addicted. I now know what so many people are doing so much of the time," Meeta pauses. "It is my peripheral vision."

"Are you . . . ?" I start to ask.

"Yes. Of course. This is on every Grumby now and . . ."

I cut him off. "And you now know what everyone is doing all the time?"

"Yes. Of course. I filter it based on my preferences and . . ."

"OK, I get it. Just make it optional. The last thing I want to do is get all of our users in a tizzy over privacy and think we are snooping on them."

"But we are . . ."

"And come up with a better name!" I turn away to hide my smile.

Shades

3:31 p.m., April 27, Milpitas

T he counter on the plasma TV reads 387,428. Software sales are tracking pretty well to Grumby sales. People are buying at least one application, many two or three. The office is hopping as usual. People are everywhere. I saw someone sitting on the torture chair using a laptop. We've got a lot to do.

RecordAll is a hit. Meeta set the price at $20 if you store all your conversations on your own PC. Or for $1 a month, we can store them for you, on Amazon's servers. We figure that even if someone leaves it on twenty-four hours a day and records everything, our cost from Amazon for storage and bandwidth won't come to much more than 10 cents. Not bad.

Meeta walks up to my desk. I do a double take. I've never seen Oakley sunglasses quite like the ones Meeta is wearing.

"Cool shades. Where'd you get them?" I ask.

"This guy," Meeta says, pointing to a guy in a Hawaiian shirt at his desk.

"Does he work for us?"

"No."

"Oh."

"Oakley."

"I can see," I say, focusing on my screen.

"He's from Oakley."

"Ohhh," I turn around. "Any more of those?"

"Sure, I've got a whole bag. The name's David."

I shake his hand, and then eye his bag as he reaches in and pulls out similar sunglasses and hands them to me. They have that classic Oakley teardrop shape and wire rims, but something is different. An expanded frame maybe. More of a tube than a wire. It looks spectacular.

"Awesome. You selling these?" Oakleys are expensive. I figure these were probably $150 or $200. I don't think I've ever spent that much on sunglasses. I lose them too often.

"No, not yet. That's why I'm here," David says.

"Well, you can't have these back." I put my face in front of my Grumby and then look at the image of myself on my screen. arMirror, Meeta calls it. I'm definitely stylin'.

"We bombed with our Thumper," David says.

"Excuse me?"

"Our MP3 sunglasses. Right idea, wrong execution. And way too early," David admits.

He's talking about those huge Oakley sunglasses with an MP3 player built in and clunky ear pieces.

"I remember seeing those. Too bulky, right? And the earphones were awkward."

"Guilty." David pauses. "So we've been playing around with carbon fiber and Bluetooth and . . ."

"Oh, I get it," I interrupt. "You're not here to sell us sunglasses are you?"

David looks at Meeta who just shrugs and then looks back at me.

"No. Well, yes, sort of. I'm here to sell you ON sunglasses."

"Uh-huh?" I'm confused but curious.

"Here, give those back to me for a second," David says as he reaches for my face.

I back up. "No way. Take Meeta's."

"OK, sorry, my bad."

David digs through his bag and pulls out another pair.

"Here, check this out," he says.

He pops off a small translucent cover on the front of the glasses, which I hadn't noticed before. It seems part of the design. Inside is a small imager.

"Wow, is that what I think it is?" I ask.

"We pried that out of a Grumby. I was reluctant to do an autopsy, er, maybe biopsy on a Grumby, but Meeta sent down about a dozen of them, and we designed these sunglasses to precisely fit the same imagers you use in your Grumby."

I look over and Meeta smiles. I just shake my head.

"And those tiny holes are for the microphones?" I ask.

"Precisely."

"And speakers."

"Nope, we weren't going to make that mistake again. It's all Bluetooth. We figure someone will have a phone in their pocket and a Bluetooth headset . . ."

"In-yer-ear," I mumble.

"We tried those. They'll work. We want to do sunglasses and even designer prescription glasses and what you guys have is the perfect front end."

"I love it. Of course, we'll have to calibrate it for the new dimensions and . . ."

Meeta groans.

I start laughing.

"We'll get someone from Oakley to volunteer to sit in the torture chair."

"The thing in the lobby?"

"It's painless," I say. Meeta groans again.

"So what about power? We can shove tons of lithium ion batteries in our Grumby—you don't seem to have any room."

"Great question. We use tiny hearing aid batteries," David answers.

"Won't the imagers and Bluetooth kill those in a few minutes?" I ask.

"We think we can get a couple of hours in standby mode and maybe fifteen minutes active."

"Oh, that's all."

I must sound disappointed.

"Hold on. We're experimenting with a motion charger into the tube of the frame."

"Huh?"

"Try holding your head still for more than a few seconds. It's always in motion. We put in these tiny magneto-motion-sensitive chargers; every time your head moves, it recharges the hearing aid batteries. If you need a good charge, you just shake your head around for a few seconds and you get another couple of minutes of juice."

"Too cool. I love it. We're in. We can work out a deal pretty quickly so that . . ."

David reaches into his back pocket.

"Meeta warned me."

He hands me a check made out to Grumby Mogul Limited Company, Inc. for $20 million.

"And I understand that's against $5 per unit and your cut of application software that we sell?" David asks.

I look at Meeta and slowly nod my head, trying not to break out laughing.

"We'll have biz dev draw up paperwork. How fast can you crank these out?" I ask. No time to waste. Somebody's out there, chasing. I know it.

"We'll have 'em for sale by the end of the month," David tells me.

Faster, I think.

"Hey, one request for you," David continues.

"Yeah, anything," I say as I finger my new shades.

"You've got to knock off the knockoffs," David says.

"Huh?"

"We've got a knockoff problem in China."

"Not us," I protest.

"We've traced them to a factory that also makes your Grumbys," David says.

Yuren? Awkward.

"I'll see what I can do. Meanwhile, can you send a hundred of these new ones?"

"Three hundred thirty-seven," Meeta corrects.

"Is that how many people we have?" I ask.

Meeta just nods.

"Well, thanks," I say to David, fingering the shades on my head.

"No. Thank you, thank you, thank you," he almost seems to bow as he walks backwards away from my desk. "This is going to be our biggest runner."

After the Oakley dude leaves, I say, "Meeta?"

"Yes, your lordship."

I just laugh. "Cable?"

"Tolkien," Meeta smiles.

"Well, at least he wrote his own stuff. Do we really need all these people?"

"More." Meeta answers.

"For?"

"The ring." Meeta quickly states.

"The . . . ?"

"At this point, we're going for it, are we not?"

"I guess so," I mumble.

"It is very much too late to guess," Meeta tells me.

"OK, the ring."

"Or else what?" I mumble.

"No else. Just the ring."

I hear a chorus of "*One ring to rule them all* . . ." from every Grumby in the building.

Eggs

"We've got this guy who wants to show you something cool," Meeta tells me.

"Another one in the Meeta network? Where is it this time, Lichtenstein?" I ask.

"You have to see this with your own eyes."

"What do you mean?"

"It's HERE," Meeta explains, pointing down with his index finger. "WE have this guy."

"Why didn't you say so? Let's go," I say.

I follow Meeta through our office, around our desks, past the construction of makeshift offices made from four tables arranged in a square with eight chairs on the inside and twelve on the outside. The game room is long gone—the pool table is covered with LCD monitors and even the *Star Trek: The Next Generation* pinball machine is covered with Grumbys in various states of dismemberment.

I can't believe we've shoehorned three hundred something bodies into this place.

"Where is this guy?"

"Almost there," Meeta says. He then reaches for the handle of a closet door and opens it up. Inside are three people, each working on a makeshift desk with keyboard and LCD monitor.

"Wasn't this where we found the torture chair?"

"Yes, we've been tight on space."

I just shake my head. I can't believe we've stooped to offices in a closet.

Meeta introduces me. "Meet Buster."

Buster is tall and thin with spiky hair and crooked teeth. Eastern European is my guess. I'm getting good at picking off nationalities—we have so many of them.

"Romania?" I ask.

"Latvia," Buster corrects me.

"Whaddya got, Buster?" I chuckle. It sounds funny.

One of the other closet dwellers points to three Grumbys huddled together on the floor of the closet.

"What are they doing?"

"Talking."

"Didn't we do this already? Have one Grumby play Stump the Machine against the Bullshit Detector?"

Buster nods his head. "That was a game. This is social."

"I don't follow. What are they doing?"

"We started this with Facebook, but it was too cumbersome, so we did it ourselves."

"Did what?" I ask again, a little more impatiently.

"Well, we all have our list of friends, people we know that we maintain on Facebook."

"I follow," I nod.

"What this does is interrogate other Grumbys we meet in the wild to see if we want to be friends."

"You lost me," I admit.

"It's a bit like 'do I know you?' and 'does anyone I know, know you?'—that kinda thing."

"Six degrees of separation?" I ask.

"More like common interest. The Grumbys start with people

they know in your contact list, and in the absence of that, move on to hometowns, jobs, and on and on. You can set how open or closed you want to be about divulging information. The more closed or shy you are the longer it takes the Grumbys to find common ground. When they do, they alert the owners. 'Susie once dated your old roommate so is safe to talk to.' That kind of stuff."

•   •   •

"Meeta?"

"Yes, my omnipotent ruler?"

"Did you know about this?"

"Yes, the code wasn't ready to show you until just recently."

"No, no. I love that app. We'll put a limited version on phones and it's going to be huge. What I meant is when did you know that we have three guys working in a closet?"

"Well, we are little tight on space and . . ."

"Meeta, we gotta get out of here."

"I know."

"You've already been looking?"

"Yes, of course. We can hire at least two hundred more coders if we had room to put them and . . ."

"And?"

"And I was very close to leasing that hangar at Moffett Field and . . ."

"Really, the one they do wind tunnel experiments in?"

"Yeah, but it got squashed. We would need security clearance for every employee, and," he looks right at me, "that might prove to be a difficult task to . . ."

"Yup, not going to happen. Well, start looking again."

"We can get Fab Six."

"Fab what?"

"AMD. Fab Six. Their fabrication facility in Sunnyvale, just off 101, not that far. They built it to make flash memory chips for cell phones and stuff. We probably use their chips in the Grumby, I think. Anyway, that business is long gone to Shanghai."

"I don't think anyone makes stuff around here anymore."

"We do," Meeta offers.

"Yuren does . . . for us."

"Oh, yeah."

"OK, so is it big enough?" I ask.

"Huge. And, it's a Class 10 cleanroom. Less than ten parts per million of dust. Plenty of electrical. Gigabit networked."

"But it's a factory . . ."

"Plus, I've done some research and apparently we can elevate both nitrogen and oxygen levels by several hundred basis points throughout the building, which aids both concentration and metabolism, and we can expect upwards of 25 percent higher output from . . ."

"Hold on. No one is elevating anything. Maybe laughing gas on Fridays."

"I can check on that."

"I'm just kidding."

"Oh. And there's this huge vacant lot next door and we can go up twelve floors if we want. Would probably take eighteen months if we start soon . . ."

"Meeta. How many people do you think we need?"

"We should lock up every surgical coder and put them under one roof."

"I like how you think."

•   •   •

Meeta starts laughing. He is watching YouTube.

"What's so funny?" I ask.

"Someone found it."

"Found what?"

"The Easter egg."

Every programmer with a sense of humor, meaning all of them, tries to stick in some secret message or feature into their code, a so-called Easter egg.

"We gave one?"

"Couldn't resist. One of the Estonians put it in."

"It better not make the system vulnerable."

"No way, it's inside. But it definitely cracks me up."

"How do . . ."

"Let me show you."

Meeta turns to the Grumby and says, "Rock on."

"*Dude?*" his Grumby responds in a surfer-dude kinda way.

"Dude," Meeta says, kinda surfer dude-ish right back.

"*Seriously.*"

"Dude."

"*Dude.*"

"Seriously?"

"*Seriously.*"

"Dude."

"*Dude.*"

"Dude?"

"*Dude.*"

"Dude."

"*Seriously.*"

"Dude."

"*Dude.*"

"Seriously?"

"*Gnarly.*"

"I can do this all day, Meeta says, laughing hysterically.

"*Dude?*"

"OK, I get it," I say.

"Rock off," Meeta says, and the Grumby shuts up.

·   ·   ·

My phone rings. My Grumby announces, "*C'est Jeannie.*"

"Jeannie, bonjour, things are happening. We've got some cool stuff to . . ."

"Listen, I just had the strangest meeting."

"Yeah, I have those all the time. Keep getting bothered by just about . . ."

"A very hard sell."

"Excuse me?" I say

"Well, they want to buy my stake."

"Who? What?"

"*Who? What?*" my Grumby says.

"Meeta," I turn and yell, "turn that off."

"Yes, I was turned off," Jeannie says.

"Now is no time to sell. Who approached you?"

"It's hard to tell. The Israeli government, maybe?"

"Huh?" I ask.

"I know, confusing. How do they even know I own a stake?"

"I don't . . . ," I start.

"They want to do some sort of deal with you. They asked all sorts of technical questions. About servers and voice capture and data mining. They say they have some technology to trade. Of course, they're asking the wrong guy," Jeannie laughs.

"We're about to go public. Don't sell."

Bakeoff

3:59 p.m., May 9, Palo Alto

Going public means picking bankers. I just spent the day locked in a conference room at Wilson Sonsini meeting with investment bankers. Ouch. Morgan Stanley, UBS, JP Morgan, lots of suits with ties droning on and on. They're all number one, in some obscure subcategory, deals priced on Tuesdays, deals valued between $1.27 and $3.42 billion. Who knows which of them are any good? They could probably all do our deal with their eyes closed. They all ask for the business on the way out of the room. I just smile. Each has us valued at $300 million, plus or minus. That blows me away. I own half. That's a lot of money, though it's just starting to sink in.

But not one of them could explain to me why I wanted to go through all this hassle of going public in the first place. I already own half of the company, meaning I get half of all the money we make, right? Meeta showed me some numbers he cooked up and they add up fast. If we stayed small, we could end up making some serious dough. What the heck. Our cash keeps going up—maybe $50 million and growing in the bank right now, although Lorita claims we have to recognize a lot of that as sales over the next five years.

•   •   •

"Jed, thanks for coming down." I say to Jed Tedford as he walks into the conference room. Finally, a friendly face.

"Exhausted yet?"

"And then some."

"We are number . . . ?"

"Six. In person, anyway. We turned down twenty-seven others. You have way too many companies doing the same thing."

"Tell me about it. Well, listen, I do appreciate your considering us. I brought just five of us. No vice chairman, although he'll fly out tonight if you want to meet him."

"Not necessary."

"I've got the head of sales, retail, syndicate, and my associate who'll be pulling all-nighters working on this deal."

Nods all around. I figure the guy with the half-opened eyes is the associate.

"Here is a pitch book. We're number one, as is everyone, and we can walk you through it."

"I'll bet I could give the pitch to you."

"Probably so. I do want to suggest how we would position you."

"OK."

"After a couple of weeks playing around with that assistant app, I've completely changed my mind about what you guys do. It's entertaining, but not entertainment. It's searchy, but not search. I can tell you all the things you're not: a social network, voice recognition, telecom service, and on and on. But only because you're not one thing—you're all those things."

"Soooo?" I ask.

"So we can't position you as everything; we have to position you as one thing. And it became obvious that you are first and foremost about productivity, personal productivity—the world's first personal productivity solution. We can teach everyone how you do it, a networked system, user-improved algorithms, various platforms, open API, and on and on, but pure and simple you sell personal productivity. Buy a Grumby, do more."

"That's what 90 percent of the emails we get tells us," I agree. "People claim they're smarter and get more stuff done and feel better about themselves. It's quite bizarre."

"It won't be obvious to those who haven't used it, but that's what we'll preach during the roadshow. Here's this new productivity product like nothing you've ever seen before. High growth, high margin, international possibilities—come grow with us."

"That's it?" I ask.

"Yeah, that's it. The simpler the better. Any questions for us?"

"Sure, tons," I say.

"Fire away," Jed motions.

"My first question is why do I want to bother with all this in the first place?"

Jed looks confused.

"Going public, I mean," I add.

"Oh. Great question," Jed begins. "Going public is not for everyone. But I think in your case, it takes on a special meaning. I'm going to break the cardinal rule of only giving three-part answers to your question and instead give you five. First, you're probably thinking that since you own half, you get half the profits anyway."

My head keeps nodding.

"The stock market is a forward-looking creature. It figures out what you are going to make years from now and values your company today based on that future. In effect, it sums all your future earnings, discounted back to today."

"Discounted by?"

"Mostly inflation, but also risk. You'll get a PE, price earnings ratio. Let's you make 50 cents per share this year, $1 the next, and then $1.50 the year after that. Maybe your stock will trade at $25 or $30, which means a PE of 50 or 60. You personally can certainly keep half if you stay private and pocket the 25, 50, and 75 cents."

"Doesn't sound like much if you put it that way . . . ," I interrupt.

"That's right. It would take quite a few years to add up to what you could sell the stock for after the deal. The stock market gives it to you up front. And selling stock is tax-advantaged, but that doesn't count as another answer."

"OK, I think I get that."

"Also, and second, at that high multiple and $50 a share, the stock market is telling you that it wants to give you money, provide access to capital; it wants you to grow."

The syndicate guy adds, "It's the cheapest money you can raise. You don't have to pay it back. You just sell pieces of paper with your name on it to investors that want to grow with you."

"Uh-huh," I say.

"Someday," Jed interjects, "you'll have a stock that blows up, some mistake or a war, whatever. Your PE multiple will contract to 20, or maybe 15, which means the market now wants to starve you of capital. You'll learn how to read those tea leaves."

I stop nodding.

"OK, third, an ever-growing stock price is the best way to attract really smart people. Stock options are the greatest legal form of wealth transfer to knowledge workers who you'll need to keep growing at those meteoric rates."

This time it's Meeta nodding his head along with me. He probably has sights on entire cities in India that will get options.

"You'll also be buying other companies with stock. . . . Anyway, let me keep going. Fourth, unlike many tech companies, you have a consumer product, something in the face of real people.

The retail guy adds, "They want to buy your product AND your stock, so you don't want someone else to win just because they went public and you didn't."

Jed and his crew go silent.

"And fifth?" I ask.

Jed's eyes begin to squint; he licks his lips and then continues. "I'm reluctant to tell you the last one. It's stupid. Infantile. Adolescent. It's high school."

"I like it already."

"OK. Fifth, people keep score."

"You mean . . . ," I start.

"I mean it's one of those things about America and capitalism that isn't necessarily pleasant, but it's reality. He with the most toys wins. It's a great narrative for the press, for folks in D.C., for John Q. Public who buys your stuff. Even if you're not into that, if you could care less, others will make it an issue. I told you it was stupid, but I needed to mention it. Let's move on."

"Do I need a CEO with pedigree or gray hair?" Several of the other I-banks had seemed pretty sure I did.

"God no. Please don't do that. Wall Street respects entrepreneurs, almost insists on touching and feeling them. No need for a buffer between you and your investors. Hire a great finance guy, but you and Meeta should run this company for as long as you can."

"Is $300 million realistic?"

"I doubt it," Jed quickly answers.

"Oh." I'm sure I sound disappointed.

"We won't know until we market the deal. Let the market tell us. Could be lower, could be much higher. You just have to trust us to find the right price. Do you need the money?"

"There's fifty something mil in the bank. And more comes in everyday."

"Good. It means you can just cancel the deal if you don't like the price."

"Really?" I ask.

"I won't like it, but we buy the stock from you and then sell it to investors. You're in control."

"Yeah, I like the sound of that," I say.

"You can't control the stock market. If they like your stock, they're going to bid it up to the stratosphere, 100 times earnings, maybe more. But I suggest you shoot for an ever-increasing stock price; it's the best way to keep hiring smart people. If your stock's too high, no one will want to work for you. Great coders, I've learned, are also great stock pickers."

"One last question."

"Anything," Jed says.

"Are you going to ask for the business?"

Bulk

11:05 a.m., June 14, Milpitas

"*B*ada bing."

"I thought we turned that off," I say to Meeta.

"I changed it to every hundred."

"Oh . . . How many today?"

"A hundred and twenty."

"You mean we've sold . . ."

"Yes, my 'quick with the math' master. And it's still morning."

"In California," I correct.

"Yes. Sometimes we get bulk orders. Thousands at a time."

"From who?"

"Some of it's overseas. And someone in Virginia."

"Who's that?"

"A postal box in Mr. Clean."

"What, let me see that . . . it's McLean. McLean, Virginia."

"*In addition to being a suburb of Washington, D.C.,*" my Grumby buzzes, "*McLean is the site of the headquarters of the Federal Highway Administration and the Claude Moore Colonial Farm of the National Park Service as well as the headquarters of the Central Intelligence Agency.*"

What the heck? The snooping code? Why not just get it from someone who knows how to write it. Travis told me he was talking to Richie. Why not use him? Because they don't trust him?

·　·　·

Sometimes I like to torture Meeta.

"Meeta," I ask him, "what do you think the odds of a huge asteroid hitting Earth might be."

"You're in a good mood today."

"*The odds are 1 in 500,*" his Grumby answers.

"What he says," Meeta smiles.

"C'mon, that can't be right."

"It's in our database; it has to be right."

"*There are two million half-mile-sized rocks in the Asteroid Belt,*" his Grumby adds.

"Is that true?" I ask.

"Sounds true enough," Meeta replies. "I think I'll work under my desk today."

"I don't know. Would you take that bet at 500 to 1?"

"I wouldn't have to pay? Anyway, I've noticed a few minor mistakes in our database."

"Yeah, I have noticed a few too," I sigh. "We're not perfect."

"But we shouldn't be wrong about anything," Meeta insists. "We set this up to poll as many people and as many sources . . ."

"Still, there are tons of things we're told in life that turn out to be wrong."

"Like what?" Meeta asks.

"If you watch too much TV, your eyes will go square. Spinach is good for you. The Easter Bunny. If you get in trouble in school it will go on your permanent record."

"Well, maybe that last one . . . ," Meeta laughs.

"We've got to be right," I insist.

"Google's not infallible," Meeta notes. "Neither is Wikipedia."

"*The free encyclopedia that anyone can edit*," my Grumby announces.

"But we've rigged ours to get smarter the more people use it," I say.

"You think that's smart?" Meeta asks, with a funny smile.

Roadshow

11:42 a.m., July 1, New York City

The taxi drops us in front of 200 West Street in Lower Manhattan. I was down here once before, visiting the nice people in a fancy government building, but I don't think we passed it. Meeta spends the whole cab ride slumped down in the seat trying to make out the tops of buildings.

Unlike our last visit to Goldman Sachs back in San Francisco—the "Elevator Incident" is how it's known—we're let right up. The guards even know our names. Nice touch.

We're here for a dry run, to practice our IPO presentation before taking it on the road to investors. Jed insists. And there he is, chatting away with a group of men in suits as our elevator doors open. Glad I stopped at the Men's Wearhouse last week and bought a new suit.

"Glad you're here. Let me introduce you to Lloyd, Harvard–Harvard Law, and a few of the other big dogs around here," Jed says. "This is Wally, Columbia–Tuck, head of institutional sales, whose group will be selling most of the shares," and on and on around the circle. We shake hands all around and are quickly whisked into a mini-theater, a round room with a large podium and giant projector screen and hundreds of seats, completely packed with men in red ties and white shirts with their sleeves rolled up and women in black pantsuits and they are all chattering away until we walk in and then complete silence. Pretty neat trick, I think, until I notice all eyes on Lloyd. Hmm. I suspect he's the one that signs the checks.

"I'm thrilled today to introduce the management team from Grumby Mogul Limited Company, Inc.," Jed starts. Meeta is beaming, though I think I heard a few snickers from the audience. I don't care. It's a great name.

"This is one of our marquee deals of the year," Jed continues, "a one of a kind company pioneering the personal productivity space. Three million shares plus the Green Shoe. We filed at $16–18, which values the company at around $400 million, but we're already getting a lot of interest . . ."

From about six rows back, someone starts coughing and muttering loud enough for everyone to hear "hot deal" between coughs. Lots of laughs.

"OK, let's get going. Are the branches all connected? OK, thanks." Jed motions for me to take the mike.

"Good morning," I say, and pause. Then I start. Or try to start. Nothing comes out. I look around. And then I clear my throat and start again.

"OK, so . . . we're a bunch of techies in Milpitas, although now we're in Sunnyvale. We stumbled upon some pretty cool apps, music matching, and then some recognition of voice things and . . . ," I pause again. I didn't think I would be nervous, but I'm terrified. How many branches are connected? Who are these people? They look like they are all off a brochure for Yale. I know what I want to say, but I can't for the life of me get it out.

I flash up our Powerpoint slides with pictures of our building and of a Grumby and Nokia and Motorola logos and some financials, mostly showing we have lots of money in the bank.

"We have a worldwide network of people around the world who do some of the programming on a global basis." Did I just say that? Yikes. I'm losing it.

"So I encourage you to buy a Grumby and try it out, or download some of our code onto your phone, and you'll see how cool some of our stuff is," I say in conclusion. That lasted about eight painful minutes, and I'm not sure I said anything of substance.

I stop and look out into the audience and there is dead silence. Five seconds, ten, fifteen. No one moves a muscle. I feel a bead of sweat dripping from between my eyes down the bridge of my nose. These folks must all wipe up at poker.

Finally, Wally jumps up out of his seat and says, "That was awesome. Absolutely terrific. You raised the goal posts with that one. Terrific presentation. We can sell this deal with our eyes closed with you on the road." He turns around, nods his head, and slowly raises his arms up like he's a Roman general inspiring his battalion.

Other heads begin to nod until the entire room is bobbing, chattering, making comments like "Uh-huh," "Yeah," "Marquee indeed," "Hot, hot, hot."

I begin to feel a little better. Meeta is getting into it. Jed comes over and ushers us out of the room and into an elevator.

"You know that sucked, right?" Jed asks.

"Yeah, I figured," I say dejectedly.

"Don't worry about it. All dry runs suck. Those guys can sell anything. Ice to Eskimos, burgers to bovine, sand to surfers, pigs to pygmies. Anything."

"That's a relief."

"Still, you've gotta fix the presentation. It really needs to be tight."

"I'm not much of a speaker. I'd almost rather let the Grumby do the talking," I say.

"Not a bad idea, actually," Jed nods. "And listen, we need more shares to sell. This deal is on the small side for us. Even at the top of the range, it's only fifty something mil. Wally wants more shares. Another couple of million would be great. You interested in selling some of yours on the deal?"

I am interested. Who wouldn't be? But I'm clinging to a tiny majority of shares. I don't dare sell any.

"No way. But I do know someone who may want to sell his."

• • •

"If it's Tuesday, it must be . . . ?" I ask.

"Baltimore. T. Rowe. We hit D.C. next, shuttle back to New York for a dinner with George Soros, then to London, Edinburgh, Frankfurt, Dusseldorf for the old town beer halls, anyway, and then to Milan. That's pretty much all the investors who matter in Europe, and then we fly direct to Chicago by Friday for a group lunch, and then one-on-ones with Northern Trust and . . ."

"OK, one day at a time."

"It's going great. The head of syndicate in New York claims we're already six times oversubscribed and we're just starting. I think the whole thing about having the Grumby introduce you at the top and then answer the first three questions when you're done is brilliant."

"Means less talking for me," I say. "Plus everyone is blown away; they don't really listen to what I have to say."

"And the questions?"

"They're always the same questions. How big can it get? Who is the competition? Can it pick stocks?"

"Funny," Jed chuckles. "Hey, before you head to Europe, do you think it'll work if they ask the questions in German or Italian?"

"Ought to."

I think it will. Meeta has been playing around on real-time translation.

"Now that'll blow them away. Oh, and I just found out, we got half of his shares."

"You couldn't get them all?"

"Jack wanted to sell them all, but we don't want to have to explain why he's blowing out. At half, no one will care."

"I will," I sigh.

.　　.　　.

As our flight touches down at Chicago O'Hare coming back from Europe, Jed turns on his iPhone. A big smile lights up on his face.

"Eighty-two times oversubscribed. I think Netscape was forty-seven. You're kicking ass. And we still have the rest of the U.S. to finish. Minneapolis, Denver, San Fran, LA, and then back to New York for the final lunch and pricing and . . ."

"Why bother? Eighty-two times means we've sold the deal eighty-two times over, right? We're done. Let me go home."

"Yeah, you wish. You've got to meet everyone face to face. Not for this deal, but for the future. These are the folks who are going to own your stock long term. We already dropped a lot of hedge funds that won't hold the stock, just want to flip it, but you need to build relationships with the folks who will hold your stock for ten years and . . ."

"Someone actually holds it that long?"

"If they like you and trust you, they will."

"Yeah, OK, I'm just getting tired of this. I can't fake the smile much longer."

"The Midwest is always easiest. A nice welcome back to the U.S. and then you'll build up to New York and . . ."

"Wake me when it's over."

.　　.　　.

I stop complaining. We fly private jets the rest of the trip through the U.S. Really nice touch. Still, I'm dead tired. We're hanging out at the Jet Center in Denver. I need to ask Jed if I can just go home when we hit SFO, or do I need to stay at a hotel with everyone else in San Francisco. It's Thursday night and we do San Fran tomorrow and then have a weekend to kick back before heading to New York for the final roadshow meetings.

I walk over but Jed's talking on his phone—something that he does quite a lot.

Jed doesn't look happy.

"You mean 150 instead of 225 times oversubscribed?" I kid.

Jed doesn't get off the phone, just shakes his head, and holds up his finger for me to back off but stick around.

Jed starts talking a little too loudly. "Uh-huh . . . yeah . . . blocking? . . . And the deal? . . . Oh, God," he mutters.

That doesn't sound good.

"What the?"

Jed shakes his head again.

"We have to disclose? . . . Start the edits and refile . . . yeah, we'll see at the bottom of the range . . . get back to me when you hear." Jed hangs up.

"What?"

"Has anyone hit you up for patent infringement before?" Jed asks.

"No. We have copyright issues all the time, but we solved that by transferring ownership of storage space to Estonia and some new country I've never heard of in the Pacific with fiber lines and . . ."

"No, I mean patents."

"No, no hassles. Not that I know of."

"Well you do now."

"From who?"

"Who's, who?" Jed says.

"Who?" I ask.

"Microsoft filed patent infringement charges. Voice recognition."

"Shouldn't be a problem. We have that covered by . . ."

"And Google network architecture and query structure."

"Don't think so. We were pretty careful . . ."

"And Sony for humanoid interfaces."

"Et tu, Bru—? Wait a second. Are these separate?"

"As far as we can tell. But they were all filed at exactly the same time and by the same law firm, Bobbick, Phlemler and Harriwick."

"Phlemler?" I laugh.

"Not funny. This is a big deal."

"We were pretty careful. We've been filing patents since we incorporated. And every piece of open source code is vetted by lawyers to make sure it's clean."

"Look, these guys aren't stupid. If they wanted money, they would have let us price the deal and then sued. They don't want your money; they want you dead. So they sue right before the deal gets priced figuring they can cut off your funding and then keep you in litigation for years until they catch up."

"Can they do that?" I ask Jed.

"They can and they just did."

Here's a thought. Did one of these guys pay Richie to plant the Potty-Mouth Grumby virus? I wonder. They can't outcode us, so now they're trying to outlawyer us? Assholes.

"But I doubt we infringe on any of their patents," I plead. "Lorita thinks that they probably step on some of ours, actually. Plus our deal is going to price next week."

"Yeah, that's the other thing. I talked to Wally. The deal is falling apart. When the news hit the tape, our syndicate desk got tons of order cancellations."

"Wussies."

"It's slimy, but they're not dumb. This is all a giant poker game. Any seed of doubt they can plant in the public's mind means a weaker competitor."

"But we don't even compete against any of them."

"Sure you do. Why use a mouse and Windows when you can talk instead?"

"I guess."

"And Google can smell trouble down the road. If you devalue search by pushing it down the stack and making it invisible, then how do they make money? They need to touch users and stick ads in their face. If you are the face . . ."

"So that's it? Did I just waste two weeks talking to chain-smoking, bath-challenged Europeans?"

"I hope not."

"That's the best you can do?"

"These guys play to win. And when they don't win, they play dirty. That's just the way it is. Deal with it."

And with that, Jed walks away.

I turn to Meeta and whisper, "Listen, we've got to do something to get Richie off our trail."

"Can we have him whacked?"

"Meeta!"

"*Sopranos* week on HBO."

"Think of something. He's got this raging jealousy thing. It's stupid, I know, but maybe we can use that against him."

•   •   •

We land back in San Francisco. Jed is on the phone the nanosecond the wheels touch the runway.

"Damn, Wally's getting more pushback," he tells me.

"What does that mean?" I ask.

"No one wants to step up and price the deal. We need some-one—Fidelity, Morgan, Janus—someone with some testicular for-titude to put in an offer, almost at any price, for shares. Then the rest of the Street will follow. Sort of a 'Fidelity must know some-thing' kind of thing." Sounds like Wally's not getting that."

"Just because of patents?"

"That's kind of everything, isn't it?"

"Well, it's our code."

"Yeah, but anyone with a blocking patent can get an injunc-tion, shut you down, take all your money, and make it so that you know every square inch of some East Texas courtroom."

"But man, we've got patents. Can't we just sue them back?"

"If only it were that easy."

Offer

The San Francisco lunch went pretty well, but everyone asked about the patent suits. I didn't have a good answer. So instead of being back home sleeping and recharging my brain cells for New York, I find myself back in the office. We're moving at some point and the place is in chaos. Boxes everywhere, wires running along the floor, desks pushed off to the side to make a path to move some of our networking equipment and routers out the door, onto a truck, and off to the new building.

I feel like I have to be at the office doing something useful. But I can't really do anything about the patent suits, like prove they're bogus, because that doesn't seem to be the point. Instead I'm tinkering. The occasional error that pops up on the system has been bothering me. Getting answers wrong is inexcusable. I've got some digging to do before the weekend ends and I'm back on a plane.

I've also been playing around with the new talking engine. I hacked together this program that listens to what you say, does a quick bunch of Web searches, and then spits back an audio clip based on what it thinks you are thinking. I've set it up so it learns as you talk, tries to figure out the context. It's not so much conversation as—ummm—therapy. Maybe arShrink!

I have about four or five pieces of code up on my screen in dissection mode when my phone rings.

"Hey," I hear.

"Hey," I reply.

"This is Mark Zuckerberg."

"Uh-huh. And this is Brendan Fraser." I couldn't think of anyone else that quickly.

"Well, OK. Uh, I'm a big fan and . . ."

"Who is this?" I ask.

"It's Mark. I run Facebook and I'm a big fan and couldn't help, like, noticing your legal things going on . . . ," the pitch of his voice rises as he ends the thought, "and I think we can, like maybe, do something. We are mostly coders here and I think together we can compete against anyone, and we have a bunch of patents that will hold off those big guys and block them from bothering us and . . ."

Jeez. Maybe this really is Mark Zuckerberg. Couldn't he just email?

". . . Microsoft wants us to work with their Voice for Windows Live launch, but I kinda want to stay away from that and . . ."

Microsoft Voice? Yikes.

"What are you suggesting?" I ask.

"I can buy what I want as long as it's not over 5 percent of our value, so maybe we can . . ."

"You want to buy us?" I ask incredulously.

"Five percent of $15 billion is about $450 million, which is, I hear, just about where Goldman Sachs is pricing your IPO, and I figured we would give you that much Facebook stock and integrate your stuff pretty quickly into ours, and you would be, like, the Face of Facebook and . . ."

"Wouldn't that be half? I'm Face and you're Book?"

"Well, yeah, phonetically, anyway."

"I gotta tell you, I'm not sure what we're worth. Some days it feels like less than nothing and other days . . ."

"You got that right. I think it would be fun to integrate your stuff. We're driven by lowering the cost of communications between groups of people, and you seem to take it a step further and . . ."

"Look, I do appreciate the call. I've got to talk to my guy at Goldman and get some financial advice. This gets over my head pretty quickly . . ."

"I hear you," Mark tells me.

"I hear you too," I reply and hang up.

I wait about ten seconds.

"Mark Zuckerberg can kiss my ass!" I shout.

"*Yeah, you got that right,*" comes from behind me.

"*You tell him,*" I hear from my right.

"*Mark who? He ain't nobody,*" comes from right in front of me, eyes blinking rapidly. John Turturro maybe?

"Facebook is so last decade. Their platform is dated . . . ," I start only to be interrupted again.

"*They're a modern stone age family.*"

"We've got a better interface and soon we'll have more users, and, and they're toast."

"*Yeah, now all you have to do is hold the chicken, bring me the toast, give me a check for the chicken salad sandwich, and you haven't broken any rules.*"

"Well, I'm not selling to them. If we do this right, we'll buy them," I declare.

"*Or bury them.*"

"*You're not gonna believe this. The guy killed sixteen Czechoslovakians. He was an interior decorator.*"

Is the chorus of Grumbys telling me what they think, or what I think? It's getting hard to tell. As bizarre as that sounds, it's the reason we really are going to bury Facebook. And Microsoft. And maybe even Google. All those places are furiously planning their next move and terrified they're missing something. And that's why they are shooting at us. Because we aren't planning anything. We are riding the wave of the collective consciousness. They are all serving the market. We are being the market.

They are all toast.

But what are we?

What is a wave?

PART IV

Photo

10:05 a.m., July 18, New York City

"Tilt yer heads backs a bit."

"Like this?" I ask.

"Ya, almost. Now move yer chins to ze left," the photographer insists. This has been going on for almost twenty minutes.

"Meeta, does he mean my left or his left?" I ask.

"It's all relative, isn't it?" Meeta laughs.

I turn to Meeta, who is standing a few feet to the side. "You're no help."

"Ugh," photo man grunts. "I means yer left. Now turns toward me, zat's it, chins up, relax ze eyebrows . . . OK . . . gud, now try put on ze same half smiles as yer toys . . ."

"They're not toys." I say sternly. Meeta laughs again.

"Uh-huh. Ya, whatevers."

I look around and have to squint to make out the surroundings. It's a huge wide-open space. We're tucked in one corner of it. It's dark and dusty and musty. All around are shelves and racks and hooks on the walls. Weird.

My head is stuck in the middle of about fifty Grumbys in a Soho studio and Fritz or Franz, some guy in a leotard—a manotard?—is shooting a cover for *Forbes* magazine. The lights are burning my eyes, Meeta is cracking jokes, and I wish Mr. Artsy Fartsy would just snap the damned camera and finish up.

"What are these hooks for? This place looks like a slaughter house," I ask.

"For ze meatpacking. And if you does not cooperate, I vil hang a few of yer precious toys from ze hooks."

The inside of Meeta's eyebrows turn down. I've only seen that once or twice before. What follows is usually not pretty. He pulls out his iPhone and starts jabbing his index finger at it hard enough to break the glass.

"OK, I want ze same expression, a 'Lost in Vonderland' look on yer face. Like I said, ze same as the toys—you are one with zem."

I grit my teeth.

"No, no. Too angry. C'mon. Let ze feeling go. I want a million readers to looks at yer face and wonder, 'Vy you?'"

He starts snapping, lights flash, I'm blinded for a few seconds and before I can see again, I hear another click and the lights flash again.

In the midst of all this, I hear some chattering from the left, my left. I don't dare move or Dieter will yell at me. I dart my eyes to Meeta and he is still jabbing his iPhone violently, though the angry look is offset by the sense I get that he's snickering.

Now, in addition to the clicks and light explosions, I hear chattering coming from all around me—and realize that it's fifty Grumbys moving their mouths. And then they all start to sing. The photographer's head snaps back.

"Stop zat, I've worked all mornings to get zem just right . . ."

". . . *world of hopes, it's a world of fears, there's so much that we share . . .*"

"Stop. Now."

Meeta is laughing so hard, he's bent over holding his stomach. I totally lose it and soon we're both hysterical. So is Fritz except he is not laughing. He's jumping up and down screaming about how he "can't verk under zese conditions," like his internal cliché meter has been totally shot to hell.

Meanwhile, fifty Grumbys sing along, ". . . *that it's time we're aware, it's a small world after all. It's a small world after all, it's a small world . . .*"

Fraulein Fritzy must have a trigger finger—as he hops around insanely, the shutter keeps clicking, and the flash keeps blinding me. I feel tears and hope it's from laughing so hard and not from overexposure to mercury lamps.

". . . *after all, it's a small, small world.*"

Pricing

"Twelve." It's Jed with his hourly call.

"Twelve what?" I ask.

"Bucks."

"That's it?" I ask.

"Pretty ugly out there."

"Who is it?"

"Fido."

"That guy we met in Boston? Fidelity, right?"

"Yup. Not just any guy. Harry Lange. Runs Magellan. Liked your story. He told me that Microsoft and Google don't just sue companies willy-nilly. He figures you must be onto something if you've pissed off the giants."

"So it's a plus?"

"Well, not so fast. Everyone's worried about enterprise risk, or so they say. Everyone loves a lower price, but when they get it, they get spooked. Lots of folks don't want to miss this deal if it works, but Harry's the only one who is stepping up."

"And?"

"And he'll take down 20 percent of the deal at twelve."

"But that's under $400 mil . . ."

"I know. Best we can do. Even if you come out and say these patent suits will have no material impact, no one is going to believe you."

I stare and groan.

"My guess is that as soon as we distribute shares and it starts trading, no one is going to mention Microsoft and Google as a risk again. Instead there's going to be a scramble for shares."

"So don't worry about it?" I ask facetiously.

"I wouldn't, as long as you're OK with raising just $30 million."

"I thought it's closer to 40."

"Well, you've got to pay us 7 percent and expenses and filing fees and . . ."

"We don't need the money," I say.

"Not yet."

•　　　•　　　•

The lunch at the Waldorf is crowded. But I don't feel quite the excitement we experienced elsewhere.

Lange and Fido were in at $12. Right after the lunch, Jed gets a call from Wally, the syndicate dude, that he thinks he can get probably, maybe, to about 80 percent of the deal. JP Morgan is in. So is Marsico Capital, the giant fund in Denver we visited. The rest, I'm told, will probably be sold to a bunch of hedge funds that look for broken deals and follow Fido and Harry Lange's lead. Great. We won't know until the morning.

And the rest? Jed tells me that if he can sell 80 percent, Wally usually sticks shares into the retail accounts of a bunch of wealth folks who probably don't care one way or the other but who like to say they got shares of deals that work, which is true because they get stuck with shares of every deal.

We eat dinner at the Odeon on West Broadway. Great spot. The place is hopping, but I just pick at my steak. Jed is evasive. Can't tell me with any certainty that Goldman will get the deal done.

Meeta and I head back to the hotel, and I fall asleep with "It's a Small World" in my head.

Bell

6:15 a.m., July 19

The sun filters in through a crack in the shades. It's early. Damn. I haven't had a good night's sleep in almost three weeks. Jed already told me nothing happens early. I toss and turn and finally can't stand it and get up to face the day.

I shave, shower, and climb into my Hart Schaffner Marx monkey suit and head out the door into rough and tumble Manhattan. Fortunately, it's a beautiful day.

I walk aimlessly around downtown, watching people scurrying off to work. About one in ten is talking to himself. I had heard that about New York. Lots of crazy people, schizos, psychos. "Please don't provoke them."

But this is different. I look a little closer and notice tiny earpieces. Maybe they are having a conversation with someone, but as I eavesdrop, maybe not.

"What's the weather forecast for this afternoon?"

"Get me a quote on oil futures."

I think I'm walking at a reasonable clip, but I keep getting passed. At one point, I get hip-checked as I stop to admire this giant bull in the middle of the block.

And it continues.

"Do I have a lunch scheduled today?"

"What are the overnight Nielsen's for *The Office?*"

Either more secretaries than I think get in by seven in the damned morning or all these folks have our code running on their phones and are firing questions to their electronic assistants. Maybe we have a bigger penetration than I thought.

Then a guy walks past wearing quite distinctive Oakley sunglasses. I turn around and start following him. I hadn't seen our Oakleys in the wild yet, but here they are. The guy is babbling, but I can't quite hear what he is asking. Directions maybe?

I end up in front of a church. Trinity, it says. I whip out my own iPhone and start asking it questions about the church. I learn Alexander Hamilton's grave is here and after walking around the corner and looking in the graveyard, sure enough, there lies Hamilton, dueling fool.

As I walk back to the front of the church, I discover that the street across the way is Wall Street. Whoa, can't miss that. I walk down to the corner of Wall and Broad, and it's like a movie set—George Washington giving the farewell address to his troops overlooking the New York Stock Exchange where I hope to be trading in a few hours.

My phone rings.

"Yeah?"

"Get up." It's Jed. I don't remember asking him for a wakeup call.

"I'm already up and out and about."

"We got it done. Twelve bucks. Took all night. Wally got a few calls from China who took down the last 10 percent piece."

"Awesome. I'm paying you too much for a reason, I guess."

"Where are you?"

"Wall and Broad."

"You're kidding?"

"Nope. Been walking around for an hour watching crazy New Yorkers."

"OK. At about nine, I'm going to meet you in front of the Washington statue. We have you scheduled to ring the opening bell."

"Cool."

"I suggest you get Meeta out of bed or he's never going to forgive you for missing this."

"Yup, yup. See you in a few."

I call Meeta who says he's been up but sounds a bit groggy. I tell him to hurry his ass up and get to Wall and Broad in the next forty-five minutes or he's going to miss the coolest part of the deal, though I don't tell him what.

•   •   •

Meeta is late, which is unusual for him, and finally I see him briskly walking toward us, huffing and puffing.

Before any tearful hellos, Jed grabs the both of us and pushes us toward the entrance. A giant American flag is draped across the building's façade. It's got to be three stories high. I'm always leery of anyone (or thing) that wraps itself in an American flag, but the effect works. I get the feeling we are walking into a sacred palace of capitalism.

I turn to Meeta to ask him if he feels the same mojo, but he has already leaned toward me and says, "I saw you this morning."

"At the hotel?"

"No, on Broadway, by the giant bull."

"You were there?"

"No, the Oakleys."

"The . . ."

"The guy with the Oakleys. It wasn't hard to do a facial match as you walked by. I got the alert and played back the video. Pretty cool, huh? That's why I was late."

"Meeta, are you stalking me?"

"Of course. You are my best guinea pig," he laughs.

With that we are whisked into an elevator for a ride to the top.

Except for maybe our visit to the Goldman Sachs trading floor, I don't think I've seen as many computer monitors before this moment. We're standing on a balcony overlooking an acre of them on the New York Stock Exchange floor, clumped into little stations and hundreds of little bald men in different-colored jackets running around chatting to each other and littering the floor with what looks like big pieces of confetti. Weird.

"What do all these people do?" I ask the nice gentleman from the exchange who brought us up to the balcony.

"Well, the New York Stock Exchange is a very important place, the center of global trading, actually. The guys in the nice suits are specialists and the colored jackets are usually traders and . . ."

"I thought trading was mostly electronic now. That's what Goldman told us," I say.

"Well, yes, almost. But you still need people to maintain an orderly market, so we'll always have specialists and . . ."

"Why?" I ask.

"Well, it has to do with liquidity pools and it's a bit complex."

"Don't you just match buyers and sellers? We do that, in a way, too. I found some open source code that can . . ."

"Well, sure, but when markets get crazy, you need specialists to step in."

"But isn't the existence of all the buyers and sellers enough liquidity to find the right price and . . . ?"

"Oh look, it's nine twenty-eight. Watch that big red display over there."

"What are we supposed to do?" I ask.

"Start clapping."

"Now?"

"Yes, now. Just keep clapping until I tell you. It makes for great television."

So I clap. And Meeta claps. We clap and clap. I feel stupid, actually. A camera on a robotic arm swings by us with a red light flashing. I push a button that rings the opening bell. I clap more. I think we're on TV. Woo-hoo.

I look down and tons of traders below us are looking up and clapping. Several of them reach out their hands as if they are beckoning for something. I don't think they want food, but it sure looks like it.

Meeta reaches into a bag and pulls out some Grumby hats and Grumby T-shirts and throws them out onto the trading floor below. The clapping gets louder. Meeta hands me a Grumby. I hold it over my head and the crowd roars. I throw it about ten feet out and watch it drop into a swarm of traders. A fight breaks out to get the Grumby, like it was Barry Bonds's 756th home run ball. Some huge guy with a barrel chest comes up with it to a string of boos.

I motion to Meeta for another one and launch it in a rainbow out into the exchange. All I can hear is "over here," "me, me," and "hey, douche bag" as hands wave for attention. I whip one down and plunk one trader on the head. He dives after it and comes up from a scrum of traders to huge applause, wearing a big smile.

A cheer of "Grumby, Grumby, Grumby" rises from the floor.

Man, I hope Meeta brought all fifty.

We then take an elevator down to the trading floor for a victory lap among the traders in funny jackets. About halfway through, a woman with a CNBC microphone and a camera rushes up to interview me.

"That's Erin Burnett," Meeta whispers to me. "Cable National Broadcasting Corporation. Mark Haines is up in the booth."

"Congratulations on going public. We are all big fans of Grumby. How does it feel?" Erin Burnett asks me.

I have no idea what to say. It's not stage fright. I just really have no idea how I feel. So I'm just standing there smiling. I must look like an idiot. I've got to say something. I grab my Grumby and raise it up to the microphone.

"OK, that's good. So, what do you have to say about going public?" Erin asks my Grumby.

After a short pause, the Grumby shakes and then blurts out, "*Bababooey.*"

Erin looks confused. Traders in the area burst out in laughter and applause.

I run for cover.

Jed told me ringing the opening bell at the New York Stock Exchange would be the greatest day of my life. He was right.

Bid and Ask

"**E**leven," Jed says, hitting the end button on his Blackberry.

"I thought you said twelve," I say.

"Yeah, twelve bucks, but trading starts at eleven o'clock."

"You can't fool me. I rang the opening bell. Got those traders jumping."

"Yeah, I saw. But we wait for trading to slow down a bit and then we'll start trading your deal."

"I can't wait that long," I plead.

"Just follow me to our offices. And no funny business with the elevator."

•   •   •

"This is Vinnie Maldini. Duke–Stanford," Jed introduces us. "He runs the over the counter desk and personally volunteered to trade your deal."

"Hey, Vinnie. UCLA . . . and a BMF besides."

Vinnie nods, not getting or just ignoring my joke. "Syndicate placed this thing, OK. A few too many hedgies. I've been calling all morning looking for anchors to buy in the aftermarket. Fido is in, so is JPM, but I think we're going to get a lot of flippers."

"Like the dolphin?"

"I guess." Vinnie looks at me funny and then pushes on. "Traders looking for a quick buck and then blowing it out. We'll buy some if that happens, but I'm trying to line up real buyers. You guys have created a lot of buzz. Even with the lower price, there are a lot of people on the sidelines figuring out when to jump in. You can sit over here and watch."

"Isn't it electronic? We found some open source code that matches buyers and . . ."

"Mostly electronic. But after the first bunch of shares are matched, it gets a little hectic . . . OK, here we go, just watch . . . I'm putting in a $12.50 bid to see if there are any sellers."

"I got buyers at $13," a voice from a few rows down shouts.

"Sell 10,000 to them."

"Fourteen. Fourteen and a quarter."

Meeta and I jump up with each increase in price. This is very cool.

"We're at $14.75. $15. Hit the bid, sell 'em shares. We're not through the Green Shoe yet."

"Yeah, bid 'em up, baby," I shout.

Vinnie glares. I think it best to sit back down.

"We going to $20?" I ask sheepishly.

"No idea. Haven't seen much sellers yet. We only get the first few minutes to control things and . . . $15.20—hit it—$15.50—$16."

Sixteen bucks is what we were hoping for before the patent crap hit the fan. And here we are. Hah. Eat that, Microsoft.

"We got $16.10. $16.12. $16.12."

"Oh yeah," Meeta yells.

"Shit," Vinnie mutters.

"What?" I ask.

"Here it comes."

"What?"

"Le deluge. $15.75, $15, $14.25, $13, c'mon, somebody's got to step up . . . goddamnit, let's go, get some buyers in here . . . $12.50, $12.25, $12.10, $12."

I sense panic.

"Work the phones, people, we are about to break . . . check that, we've broken price . . . $11.50 . . . we got a busted deal. Start buying. Hit the ask side . . . load it up. Can't have this sucker underwater, buy it, back it up, $11, $10.50. Keep buying it."

Vinnie is dripping sweat, mostly from his head and from the pits from under his Armani shirt. Not a pretty sight.

Jed trots over to us and grabs both Meeta and me by the arm, lifts us out of our seats, and says, "OK, you guys have a plane to catch. You've got to make your numbers now that you're public. Let's get going. Work, work, work . . ."

"OK, got it. We're coming. See ya, Vinnie," I wave.

"Uh, $10.25, $10.10, $9.90, $9.75. Shit. Get on the damned phones. Where's Fido?"

•　　•　　•

In the town car on the way to JFK I track our stock symbol GRMB. Not pretty. Near Shea Stadium we hit $8.14. And then it starts heading back up; $8.50 by the time we hit the end of the Van Wyck Expressway, $9.09 at the JetBlue kiosk (ugh, back on commercial), and not quite $10 as the plane starts taxiing. I watch CNBC on the little TV screen on the seatback but can barely keep my eyes open and crash for most of the flight back.

Once we land at San Francisco, I get a voice mail message from Jed.

I call him back and Jed talks fast, "OK, we ended the day at $12.05."

"Awesome. That's good, right?"

"Of course, Goldman prides ourselves that our deals trade up."

"So you can brag about it in the next pitch books?"

"Uh, something like that. Look, buyers came back. Harry Lange bought a bunch, as did some group in China, but the firm ate a lot of the shares that got flipped back to us when the deal was underwater."

"Isn't that what you're supposed to do?"

"Not really, but we're placing a bet on you guys. We own something like 30 percent of the shares in the deal."

"Hey, glad to hear it."

"Yeah, yeah, I just wanted to check back in. Is the quarter tracking well?"

"I've been on a plane."

"Yeah, OK. Just check, will you? No surprises."

"Life is full of surprises."

"Not at Goldman Sachs."

"See ya, Jed. And thanks."

"Can you send me a breakdown of unit volume as of mid-month and . . ."

I hang up.

•　　•　　•

The drive back to our office passes quickly as if traffic were parting in front of us as we drive down 101. We did it. Almost three weeks on the road and we not only raised a ton of money but our shares are trading on the New York Freakin' Stock Exchange. I'm flying, so it's one of the rare times I trust Meeta to drive.

We pull into our new building, the old AMD Fab. As we walk

in to the lobby, I notice the torture chair is prominently displayed. Nice choice in decorating.

Meeta leads me in to a giant room filled with desks and monitors and throngs of people milling about. One step into the room and the place explodes in applause. High fives and knuckles as Meeta and I walk to our desk in the middle of the room. A set of ten Grumbys is sitting on my desk singing "It's a Small World." I must have the biggest smile on my face.

Moody

12:32 p.m., July 21, Sunnyvale, California

"*Thirteen point twenty-seven,*" my Grumby says.

I almost have the market code adapted. I'm not sure how we are going to use it. Maybe some real-time negotiation over prices or a weighting system to perfect conversation capture. Since visiting the New York Stock Exchange, I've been intrigued about shutting them down.

"*Thirteen point one five.*"

"Damn," Meeta mumbles.

It's hard to concentrate. The new offices are awesome. Meeta immediately starts experimenting with oxygen levels and has them cranked up a bit today. He insists everyone is happier.

"*Thirteen point forty-two.*"

"All right," Meeta grunts.

I can't concentrate.

"Meeta?"

"Yes, Mr. Chairman."

"Shut that damned thing up. I don't want to know the stock price every ten seconds."

"Actually, it is set to tell us whenever there is a so-named blocker trade, when at least as much as 10,000 shares or more move from one blocker to another."

"Huh? Look, it's too much; it's annoying as hell. Dial it down."

"How about every blocker trade with a 1 percent change in the price of shares?"

"Whatever, just not so often. It's more annoying than those stupid *bada bings.*"

"I can bring those back if you . . ."

"No."

"*Thirteen point seventy-five,*" the Grumby announces.

I look at Meeta.

"One percent," he states.

I just shake my head. I keep dissecting the market code. It can match buyers and sellers when the price matches, but there isn't an easy mechanism to change the price. And as far as I can tell, price is everything.

"*Fourteen point oh-three.*"

I can picture traders yelling price information on the floor of the exchange. I can picture all those investors we met on the road-show changing their minds about price and buying our shares, or selling our shares. How do they convey it? They like it at $12 and hate it at $14?"

"*Thirteen point nine-oh.*"

Does their mood change? I have no idea what makes something more or less valuable, but people seem to know. Buy the brand-name peas at $1 a can or the no-name peas at 87 cents. Can I capture that price change? In conversation? In mood? In the network of email or phone-call contacts? I know I'm close if I can . . .

"*Fourteen point thirty-seven.*"

. . . if only I can concentrate . . .

"*Fifteen point twenty-two . . . Fifteen point fifty-eight.*"

I find when the prices go up, it doesn't bother me as much.

And then I hear clapping. Odd. And more clapping.

"*Sixteen point oh-two.*"

And more clapping and then a bell rings.

I don't want to be disturbed. I gotta finish the mood code.

"Meeta, what is that?"

"Closing bell. It's one o'clock. Let's go get some lunch."

Who has time?

• • •

"Meeta, check this out."

"What?"

"I got the mood code working."

"I've been reading about mood rings from the '70s. Blue is relaxed, amber is tense, brown is anxious and . . ."

"Meeta!"

"Well, you're in a bad mood. Hmm, your eyes are brown."

"I said I got the mood code working."

"I heard you."

"I've got about fourteen different factors. How fast you are talking compared to normal, the pitch of your voice, what you are talking about, do you sound angry or relaxed, are you running toward something or just taking a leisurely stroll. If I can, I take a look at your face, your T-zone, and check to see if you are smiling or frowning, if your eyebrows are turned down or up, maybe you're crying, that kind of stuff."

"See if you can guess what I am now." Meeta pouts.

"Knock it off. I've put it into a new app. arMood. It automatically updates your Facebook status with your current mood, so your friends can see if you're in a good mood or bad one, and possibly avoid you. This thing should be a winner."

"That would make me happy," Meeta says with a face that borders on sarcastic. I've got to add that to my mood factors.

• • •

"Tim Lincecum is amazing," Meeta says out of the blue.

"Since when do you know anything about the San Francisco Giants?" I ask accusingly.

"Eighty grand ago!"

"Huh?" I turn my eyebrows down and stare at Meeta. He breaks out into a big smile.

"Timmy is a gadget head."

"I heard. He owns a Grumby, I suppose?"

"A few of them. And he has never felt better."

"Uh-huh?"

"Going into last night."

"Yeah?"

"Before he threw his no-hitter."

"Meeta!"

"Well, someone had to bet on it," Meeta tried to say with a straight face.

"Don't get in trouble."

"No-hitters are trouble?"

Market Prices

ot it. The trading app was easy once I visited with a few brokers at the Charles Schwab and Fidelity offices around here. Brokers are like automatons, anyway, asking the exact same questions. How old are you? How much do you make? How much do you save? When do you plan to retire? How much money do you think you'll need when you retire?

And then the really interesting questions. Are you a conservative investor? How much risk can you stomach? Do you prefer growth stocks or value stocks?

How the hell do I know? I just want stocks that go up, right?

Somehow investing has to do with my personality and my appetite for risk?

And that's when it hits me . . .

The Grumby is the perfect tool for this, so after going to see all those brokers, I spend the rest of the afternoon and evening adapting the code that reads my mood—and what I think about almost everything—into the stock trading app. Moods are not that much different from the stock market—I listen and apply a price to everything and can judge someone's mood by seeing if the prices of certain characteristics are rising or falling.

That's the easy part. Figuring out my or any Grumby user's risk profile is a now a snap. To trade stocks, the Grumby can start by asking questions when the app is first installed, and then just listen long enough to gauge people's risk profile.

The hard part is figuring out what stocks to buy or sell.

As Jed Tedford explained, a stock is the sum of what everyone thinks about a company's future earnings prospects. Just like Meeta reaching out and figuring—correctly, mind you—if Tim Lincecum was up for pitching a no-hitter, we could reach out and figure what every Grumby user is thinking about, well, just about everything. Heck, Meeta has already written the code to figure out what the right people think about who is really going to win tonight's baseball or basketball game. I pull up his code and dissect it pretty quickly and figure out I can steal, er, borrow most of it.

In one marathon coding session—I turned up the oxygen content in the middle of the night—I bang out arBroker. I am careful to not mix the mood code that determines individual risk profiles and the code that goes out and sums aggregate expectations of all our users about products and companies. I had to be really careful about whose mood I was interested in before issuing a "buy" or a "sell." Markets deal in aggregates, but at the end of the day, individuals make all the decisions. I saw that on the floor of the stock exchange, at Fidelity's offices, and in my crude understanding about markets. Millions or billions of decisions are summed and calculated to determine the right price at that particular moment in time.

I can't wait to fire it up, and, fortunately, the market opens at 6:30 a.m. on the West Coast, so I run out to Starbucks to buy a Venti Mocha Double Latte Extra Hot No Whip and I'm good to go and test this sucker out.

Thanks to Meeta, our database is filled with all sorts of formerly useless trivia, on buying habits of Grumby users, to questions asked at stores, to real-time reviews of products. It's not really hard to find this stuff in the haystack of Grumby-collected data and aggregate it to match the mood of an individual.

As I load up arBroker, I take a long sip of my latte and then let out a long exhale of delight.

"*You just bought 300 shares of Starbucks Corporation, symbol SBUX, at twenty-five dollars and forty-two cents,*" my Grumby informs me.

Whoa. That was fast.

•   •   •

Not having slept, I'm so burnt from the coding and the road-show, I can really only do routine things—check my email, surf the Web a bit. More coding is definitely out.

So I put the word out that I would check out every new application that people are creating, inside or outside our company.

"Stand here," instructs Jon. I have long ago stopped recognizing everybody. Meeta tells me we passed a thousand people last week. Yikes.

"Here?" I ask.

"Close enough. We call this arFashion."

"*Thirty-seven dollars and ninety-eight cents,*" my Grumby announces.

Jimmy turns to his own Grumby and says, "Wear or Tear?"

"Wha?"

"Don't move . . . wait for it . . ."

"*Your look is very dated, probably geek chic circa 1999,*" his Grumby announces in a slightly lispy voice. "*Jeans are so out these days; the button-down shirt looks like something an eighth-grader might wear to graduation; and those shoes, whoa mama, I thought Florsheim went out of business.*" I'm sure my face is turning a few shades darker red.

"Pretty good, I don't think I can argue."

"I can dial down the attitude," Jon offers.

"What, are you kidding? That's what makes it," I say.

"Women love it."

"Getting insulted?" I ask.

"Well, you get complimented when your fashion is within three months of up to date."

"How do we do that?" I ask.

"It's not all that hard. We scan all the latest celebrity blogs, TMZ, Popsugar, those kinds of places, and we pull all the images and give weight to the most clicked and the most recent."

"Most clicked?"

"It's not hard to hack their analytics and page view files—so, anyway, we do a body scan, breaking it down to fashion zones. We think we can do hairstyles, too, and, anyway, estimate how up to date or out of date you look."

"Just by comparing images?"

"Not just images. The ones that people look at the most. We figure if something is ugly or out of date, no one clicks. Well, there is this fugly factor we had to balance . . ."

"Fugly?" I ask.

"F—ing ugly."

"Got it."

"But there are plenty of sites that showcase fugly, so it's pretty easy to weed out the train wrecks, images that people look at so they can make fun of them."

"And it . . ."

"Oh, yeah," Jon interrupts. "The voices are lifted from *What Not To Wear* and probably *Queer Eye for the Straight Guy*. We also found tons in the archives from Joan Rivers at the Oscars, that kind of stuff."

"And it works?"

"You tell me."

"Where do you shop?" I ask.

Affirmation

"**H**ave you seen it yet?" Meeta asks.

"What?"

"The cover."

"No. Is it out?"

"Saw it online."

"And?"

"And what?"

"And how embarrassed should I be?"

"None embarrassed."

Meeta pulls up the cover image from Forbes.com.

As it slowly loads, I brace myself for what I have stressed over for the last week.

Instead, it's the funniest thing I've ever seen. My eyes are moist and squinting. I'm either crying or laughing—it's hard to tell. My lips are formed in a weird shape, which oddly is exactly the shape of the mouths on the Grumbys. I look like I am one of them.

Off to my left is Meeta, squatting down, jabbing at his iPhone, with his eyebrows pointing downward looking incredibly evil, but also with the biggest smile on his face. The overall effect is a bit like the Wizard of Oz behind the curtain—Meeta devilishly manipulating the Grumbys, and me, I guess, and loving it.

Fritz/Franz/Dieter is a genius.

. . .

From Meeta's desk, I hear, "*I am a worthy human being.*"
What the?

Meeta looks up at me and explains, "New code."

"For what?"

"Self-awareness."

"Grumbys are going to be self-aware."

"No, more of a spiritual guide," Meeta smiles.

"To?" I inquire.

"Inner awareness."

"Huh?"

"Winner through inner," Meeta states calmly.

"Have you freaked out on me?" I ask.

"No, but everyone seems to want this?"

"Want what?"

"A coach. A guide. Their own psychiatrist is my guess."
I laugh. "We can do that?"

"Why not? You wouldn't believe all the stuff out there."

"I would."

"No, seriously. Deepak Chopra . . ."

"*There are no accidents . . . ,*" Meeta's Grumby quickly spews.

"Reinhold Niebuhr . . ."

"*God, grant me the serenity to accept the things I cannot change . . .*"

"Eckhart Tolle . . ."

"*The insanity of the collective egoic mind, amplified by science and technology, is rapidly taking our species to the brink of disaster. Evolve or die: that is our only choice now.*"

"Enough." I scream. All I could think of was the Tolle shrine in Jack's library.

"Careful," Meeta says in a soothing tone.

"*Having access to that formless realm is truly liberating. It frees you from bondage. It is life in its undifferentiated state prior to its fragmentation into multiplicity."*

"That doesn't even mean anything. Why did that come out?"

"I stole your mood code," Meeta says sheepishly. "It must have sensed that you were angry."

"Oh," I say very carefully. "The code's not done yet. And I stole some of your snooping code."

"I noticed. It works OK. Hey, we even have Stuart Smalley," Meeta says.

"Stuart . . . ?"

I'm immediately interrupted.

"I'm good enough, I'm smart enough, and doggone it, people like me."

"The *Saturday Night Live* thing."

"Daily affirmation," Meeta says.

"I want you to look in the mirror, and I want you to repeat after me: 'I am a worthy human being.'"

"Daily affirmation?" I ask.

The Grumby answers, *"Mistakes are a part of being human. Appreciate your mistakes for what they are: precious life lessons that can only be learned the hard way. Unless it's a fatal mistake, which, at least, others can learn from."*

Mistakes, I think to myself. This whole thing is a mistake.

"The words 'daily affirmation' are another trigger." Meeta explains.

"Trace it. Face it. And Erase it. Whining is anger through a small opening."

"Stop this crap!" I yell.

"True salvation is freedom from negativity, and above all from past and future as a psychological need."

I look with pleading eyes to Meeta. He just shrugs.

"Stop," I whisper.

"More Eckhart, I think," Meeta smiles. "I've been playing with this all day. I think I'm going to release it tonight."

"What are you going to call it?"

"arFirmation, of course."

I can only smile.

"But it's just psychobabble," I say. "You think it helps any-one?"

"If you listen to these words for long enough, it is quite calm-ing. I relaxed so much earlier today I had to stop coding and I just sat and thought happy thoughts. Though, I must be the one to say, it only lasts about thirty minutes," Meeta explains.

"Like Chinese food?" I say cynically.

"What?" Meeta looks confused.

"Never mind."

"*Named must your fear be before banish it you can,*" my Grumby adds.

Meeta grabs one of his *Star Wars* toys and just smiles.

Productivity Blossoms

9:15 a.m., September 14

"I know about the bets."

It's Richie. Damn.

"What are you talking about?" I ask innocently.

"I know about them. You gotta let me in." Richie is practically panting.

"In on what?"

"You know what. You get great gambling insight. I tried to find it, but it's protected. Tell Meeta he's gotta cut me in for a taste."

"Meeta's not in right now," I say slowly, mimicking a receptionist.

"Cut the crap. Let me in."

"I can leave him a message."

"Don't do this."

"I see I have another call." Actually, I do have another call. "We appreciate your business."

From Meeta's desk I hear, *"Twenty dollars and thirty-seven cents."*

"Yes, Yuren."

"You did it," Yuren practically shouts.

"Did what?"

"Went public. The American Dream."

"I guess. More like three weeks taken out of my life in exchange for some money we probably don't need."

- 299 -

"And a company that's worth $500 million. As a shareholder, I'm quite happy. I may take our company out on the Shanghai Exchange."

"You should. Misery loves company."

"Your stock keeps going up. Why the misery?"

"I don't know. It's not this thing on my dining room table anymore, or even in a small office in Milpitas with paper-thin carpets. It's, well, I don't know . . ."

"It's real."

"Yeah, real. Meeta tells me we have a thousand people and add a hundred a month. It's real, all right—a beast that needs to be fed."

"I've got more food for the beast. We just opened another line. We shipped something like 20,000 Grumbys last week, and we still can't keep up."

"That's . . . ?"

"Last I checked there are fifty-two weeks, so that's a million-a-year clip. Give me two weeks and I'll be at 30,000 a week. I can guarantee it. I think I can find capacity out in Sichuan to get to fifty thou— a month if you ever get to that."

"Really?"

"And we sell chips to Oakley. They've got close to 300,000 out there. I think I can get a price break on the silicon and notch your cost down another 10 percent."

I've tuned out. I'm stuck on the word "real."

No matter, my Grumby is getting it all for me. We'll talk about it later.

I don't even bother looking over to Meeta's desk as I hear *"twenty-three dollars and fourteen cents."*

•   •   •

"Boss?"

"Yes, Meeta?"

"Check this out."

"Check what out."

"This." He waves a bunch of papers in front of my face. "You have heard of poo?"

"Huh?" I turn and look at Meeta. "Winnie the?"

"Poo? P-E-W?"

I shake my head no.

"Pew Internet and American Life Project?" Meeta prods.

"What is it? A commune with broadband?"

"They appear to spend all their time doing studies."

"I was close," I laugh.

"According to one study—let me see here—" he starts to read, "in a double blind test of office workers using consumer technology products of some sort, output on average rises 4.7 percent."

"Yeah?"

"Cell phones add 3 percent."

"OK?"

"Blackberries about 6 percent; iPhones, 9.3 percent; and . . ."

"And?"

"Grumbys add 52.6 percent to output."

"What?"

"*You just bought 1,200 shares of Grumby Mogul Limited Company, Inc., symbol GRMB, at twenty-four dollars and two cents.*"

"That's what it says. Something about a personal productivity revolution."

"Goddamn. Jed was right. Still, I can't believe it's that much."

"That's what it says."

"See if Goldman paid for the study."

"The Pew has a bunch of quotes," Meeta says.

"Like what?"

"Here's one: 'I'm smarter because I don't have to remember things anymore.'"

"RecordAll. It's *Total Recall!*" I blurt out.

"Here's another one: 'My Grumby knows me better than I know myself.'"

"Put that up on our homepage," I say excitedly. "That pretty much sums up this whole damned thing."

"You'll like this study too," Meeta tells me.

"What one?"

"Michael Arrington at TechCrunch, says owners of Grumbys, and, let me see, I think that includes phones and maybe glasses, he doesn't mention glasses, but I assume it means anything with our code in it, so that would be glasses, right?"

"Meeta?"

"What?"

"What exactly does he say?"

"Grumby owners saw Google searches drop 74 percent in the first month."

"What? Really?"

"Do you do Google searches anymore?"

"Not really. Sometimes, kinda, not really, no."

"Exactly. You ask the Grumby. Sometimes you have to ask a few different ways but it comes back with something, right?"

"Right."

"So no typing."

"Right."

No wonder they sued us. Still, we can't be more than a tiny gnat to them, an annoyance. Well, like they were to Microsoft. Uh-oh.

Will Robinson

Lazy morning. Up too late. So now I'm mindlessly playing around, walking from the parking lot to our building with my eyes closed, holding the Grumby in front of me to guide my way.

"*Left. Straight. Right around a Buick LeSabre. Straight . . .*"

Pretty cool.

And then, "*Thirty-two dollars and fifty-one cents,*" my Grumby gives me a stock update.

Then I hear it say something I've never heard it say before. "*Incoming,*" it tells me in a M★A★S★H Radar O'Reilly voice.

Walking quickly toward me is a stocky barrel-chested man with olive skin and a bad haircut.

"Hey, I'm a big fan. The Bullshit Detector has saved me at a couple of cocktail parties."

"Thanks. Me too."

I quicken my pace to get to our entrance. Barrel-chest steps in my path, stopping my progress. He has a big toothy smile and his hand grabs mine, rather tightly, actually, and starts pumping it.

"You guys must be selling zillions of these things."

"Yeah, it's doing OK," I say, as I look around for anyone I know to break up this fan fest. A red car pulls up next to us, a cheesy Taurus of all things, and the back door opens. Another barrel-chested man with bleach-blond hair jumps out and grabs my arm. "We love to talk," he says.

His grip on my arm is tight, and he pulls me into the Taurus next to him and then barrel number one jumps in and closes the door with me in back middle. My heart starts racing. I consider struggling, but both of my arms are held tightly.

What a dumb ass I am. Any moron with a Yahoo Finance account can pull up our stock price and figure my net worth. How do I explain to these guys that I'm locked up for six months and can't sell any shares, even for kidnappers.

My mind is scrambling.

The driver is fixing his hair in the mirror.

"Cut the crap and drive," the blond one tells the driver.

"*You're so full of crap, Foley,*" my Grumby says. It's one of the cops from South Park. "*What! I did shoot him in the face, twice.*" the other South Park cop says.

I start to laugh until the blond one says, "Shut that thing up."

"*Danger, Will Robinson. Danger,*" my Grumby says.

Blondie grabs my Grumby, smashes it against the dashboard, and throws it out the window.

If Meeta pissed off some international betting syndicate I'm going to kill him.

"We've been watching you," the blond starts talking. "You are a bright young man." He's got some sort of foreign accent. Spanish? Russian? Kinda sounds like Borat. Kazakhstan?

I don't move. I start thinking of how I might write code to decipher accents. Wouldn't be that much different from my original TuneBuffoon code. Or maybe it's all in how certain words are pronounced and word repetition. As the car turns left to pull out onto 101 South, the guy in the back seat turns and stares at me and I forget about writing code.

"You're, eh, how shall I say, youthful indiscretions, were quite interesting. Al Gore's email? Too good. Of extreme amusement. But this . . ." He starts shaking his head. "This Grumby thing is . . . what you call in the movies . . . da bomb."

I shift my eyes to my right and notice a Star of David tattoo on the inside of his wrist.

"Mossad," he whispers in my ear. Now I'm even more confused.

". . . you have the eyes and the ears everywhere. We have been, eh, been trying to make this forever, listening in what everyone has to say. And you do it . . . and they pay for it? Too much brilliance."

I don't get the feeling they are going to hurt me.

"We tried to get to you early, maybe do, eh, a partnership. I worked back then for Nielsen; they are in the same business, yes? But nothing. You wouldn't meet with me and I underestimated you."

Huh? I nod and rack my brain trying to remember everybody we blew off. This is an odd form of business development.

"S'OK," he continues, "not offended." He chuckles.

I don't see what's so funny.

"We'd like to do a partnership. You and us. We invest. And connect."

Invest? Can't they just buy the stock?

"Maybe some sort of preferred structure. Maybe some cash and some in-kind investment."

"In kind?" He seems to know more about finance than I do.

"Yes. Software, algorithms. That way we can funnel technology we have into your holding company and can get some of the upside. You know, monetize."

"I'll have to . . . ," I start.

"Hey, we get upside," the blond continues, "but we can help

you. We have all sorts of algorithms to pick up conversations in the noise. In airports, at cafés, very useful, you know?"

I nod.

"And in exchange, you know, we maybe just want a peek into your data every once in a while. Nothing biggie. We have, how you say, persons of interest. The CIA don't share so much. But free enterprise, that's the way to go. You Americans have this figured out. You give up privacy in exchange for entertainment. What a country."

"Well, I . . ."

"We're not the first ones to ask, yes?"

"No, well . . . ," I stumble.

He lowers his voice. "We can do this without you, you know? Those other guys tell us they can get as many of these things out there, maybe more. But you first . . . and you everywhere. What do they say? Don't fight the tape."

"I, uh . . . ," I don't know what to say.

"We can do business, no?" the blond says as he nods.

"I can talk to my biz-dev folks and . . ."

The Taurus pulls in front of our building and the next thing you know I'm out of the car, totally confused, and standing in front of the entrance to our building like nothing happened. I hope I didn't just wet my pants.

I walk over and pick up my Grumby.

"*You just sold 2,800 shares of Grumby Mogul Limited Company, Inc., symbol GRMB, at twenty-six dollars and twenty-two cents.*"

Makes perfect sense. And what "other guys"?

Bunch of Guys

Our stock is working. The plasma counter keeps cranking. New apps are flying in. After the *Forbes* cover, we get interview requests by the bushel and turn most of them down.

A spring in my step? You bet. The feeling is quite similar to getting code to work, walking on air for a few days but amplified by a factor of a thousand and never coming down.

My Grumby keeps buying Grumby Mogul Limited Company, Inc. shares. It knows.

I'm working as hard as I ever have and it's all working. Some days, I'm pretty sure I have a golden touch. Then one day, my Grumby spits out the word *"hubris."*

I had to look it up. My Grumby is not that far off. It's hard to not think you're a genius when the market says you're one. A few more upticks of the stock and I'm likely to change my name to Goldfinger.

I've got to get it under control, which is not so easy. A few days later I'm having a particularly full-of-my-self moment, and Grumby spits out *"We're not great, we're just a bunch of guys from New Jersey."*

I look over to see Meeta snickering away. He tells me he found the scene, as usual, on late night cable. *Eddie and the Cruisers.* I've now watched it about five times since. It works.

I've got to stay focused. The Grumby is working fine. We're on phones and Oakleys, which is a start, but I'm pretty sure we can have some tiny piece of code on every digital device. On cameras, in cars, in TV sets, and watches, and, I don't know, cash registers and bar-code readers, maybe. Why not? With a thousand-plus coders under one roof—well, virtual roof, since we've got tons of people working out of Mumbai and Estonia and who knows where—this place seems to run itself.

Which gives me time to play around with my mood and market's code. It's not just a faster horse—it's what everyone wants but doesn't even know they want. Or at least that's how I justify the time and brain cycles.

Some days I think my spy friends, Travis or the Mossad dude, can help. They're stuck in the center, but they have perfected the art of snooping on individuals at the edge, playing cat and mouse. We're doing the same snooping, but we're giving power to the mouse. Like a *Tom and Jerry* cartoon. Maybe that's not all that far off.

It's almost there. We've just got to keep thinking from the individual in toward the center rather than from the center out. Probably a couple of thousand years of history to reverse—but Pharaoh's slaves didn't have surgeon-class coders! The overriding theme is so simple: What do I know? What do I want? Now get it for me. NOW! Empower the individual and you have a chance to make lives better. Maybe they make their own lives better. The code just becomes the conduit.

Richie Bettor

1:05 p.m, September 18

"Dammit," Meeta yells.

"What Meeta?"

"The line has moved on the Notre Dame game."

"So?" I ask.

"So, I'm the only one that knows that their young QB McKenna is hurt."

"How . . ."

"Because I lock up all the GPS-tagged voice database from anywhere around campus."

"And?"

"Richie is in. He's betting big. He's moving the spread," Meeta complains.

"One person can do that?" I ask.

"Why, yes, of course. He has multiple plays that aggregate the spread over a variety of . . ."

"It's Richie, you're sure?" I ask.

"He's the bettor."

"And you know it's him because . . . ?" I ask.

"I know everything Richie is doing."

I just stare at Meeta.

"He's in my peripheral vision."

I keep staring—squinting my eyes.

"Greetweet," Meeta says with a pinch of exasperation. Like saying "duh!"

"I thought we didn't turn that on."

"It's on for Richie. I've got his Grumby and all his phones tweeting back to me every time he blows his nose."

I just shake my head like I'm scolding Meeta, but I can't quite suppress the smile on my face.

"We can't do that," I mockingly protest.

"We are already doing it."

"And what is Richie doing these days?" I ask.

"Betting," Meeta quickly answers.

He looks at me like he is reading my mind. "We can probably get him to bet on anything."

I just nod.

Conference

2:24 p.m., September 20, New York City

"**S**o let me finish up by saying we're kinda unique," I say.

I hear giggles and laughs from the audience. I pause long enough to look out and try to guess how many people are sitting here listening. A thousand? More? Goldman can throw a conference. I'm up a few flights at the Hyatt Grand Central and what appears like four separate ballrooms are opened up and filled to the brim.

"We are a company of coders. Programmers. Hackers. We outsource everything else. Sales? Our partners do that for us. Marketing? Same. We've even outsourced our financial department. We can track hardware sales by the minute and payment for our apps is instantaneous. We can tell you our revenue in real time. And do. It's on our Web site along with our expenses. We have nothing to hide."

Loud applause.

"And we don't sell ads. Never have. Never will. If our stuff is any good, someone will pay for it. And they do."

Louder applause.

"As many of you know, we didn't set out to create a productivity revolution. I was just hoping to beat my friends at stupid radio games. But at the end of the day, I think we ended up solving the last foot problem."

I see a lot of heads nodding. Either they're asleep or agree with me.

"We have revolutionized the human-computer interface—I think we're all a little tired of mice and drop-down menus—and brought it into the era of cloud computing."

Applause.

"But once you start developing apps in the cloud, all sorts of new possibilities open up. *Total Recall* is not just a bad Schwarzenegger movie anymore."

Applause and laughter. Why does this feel like a Baptist revival meeting?

I put up my last slide, a map of the interstate highway system.

"I was asked by Goldman to talk about our roadmap. I'm not sure what that even means. Is there a Grumby 2.0? I hope so, but we're not done yet leveraging our current platform. Same with our apps. I can't stand here and say beyond a shadow of a doubt that next quarter or next year will be up and to the right. We don't have a roadmap. I think we're still building castles in a sandbox."

Applause. I don't know what they are applauding, since I just made that up. In fact, I've been winging this whole roadmap thing.

"Look, what I'm intrigued by and what I spend most of my time on is really this simple idea . . ."

I pause. I hope something comes to mind.

"We have the ability to build a fabric of the networked subconscious." Ah, the old IDEO line. Lots of quizzical looks. Good.

"We absorb everything you hear and see and say. It gets logged and indexed and munged around in the hope that it all can be recalled at just the right time to answer some pressing concern. A know-it-all at a cocktail party . . ."

Laughs.

"A fashion tip—an answer to your boss's question—a child-hood memory."

Lots of heads nodding in unison.

"Our roadmap is anything that gets to our goal. And our goal? Simple. Our goal is no longer the last foot or last inch, but . . . the last neuron. Thank you."

Huge applause.

As I leave the podium I see Jed Tedford with a big smile on his face. He gives me a thumbs-up sign and then holds up both hands with his fingers spread. Does he want a high five? He does the same thing again and mouths what looks like "up ten points."

Yikes. Maybe I should go back out to get the stock up twenty points.

I try to reach Jed but I am mobbed by people from the audience firing questions at me.

"Can you talk about the current quarter?" *Check the Web site.*

"Are there military uses for Grumbys?" *Yes, but I can't talk about it or I'd have to . . .*

"What are you doing with your cash?" *It's piled on my desk.*

"Any acquisitions planned?" *Know any good ones?*

"Is there anything Google can do to beat you?" *Oh, that's simple, they can—wait a second, I'm not going to tell you that.*

"Can you address privacy concerns?" *What's your name?*

Jed grabs me. "We gotta go. You have a meeting at A. G. Young."

"I hear they're buying," someone to my left says.

"The stock just hit $41," someone else says.

"*Forty-one dollars and thirty-seven cents,*" my Grumby announces.

Jed leans over and whispers in my ear, "Congrats."

"For what?"

"You're now a billionaire."

"Yikes."

"Forget about it. We've got to get to this next meeting and you better be sharp."

"Can we take a helicopter?"

"It's about three blocks."

"Still."

Hedgie

Jed drops me off outside and grabs a cab for the airport. I don't think he ever rests.

The building is just south of Grand Central in Manhattan. I'm probably late, but I take my time and take it all in. The marble in the lobby and elevators is of a set of colors I've never seen before. Swirling turquoise and burnt orange and streaks of green.

The receptionist asks me to wait in the lobby and the view looking south is spectacular. From off to my left, I can hear "click, grunt, shit, ugh. Click, grunt, shit, ugh."

"Mr. Young will see you now."

"Thanks."

"I'll walk you to his office."

As we stroll through what is clearly a trading room, it's eerily quiet, except for the hmmmmm from the air conditioning ducts and occasional sound of swiveling Aeron chairs, and, of course, the almost rhythmic click, grunt, shit, ugh, click, grunt, shit, ugh coming from the two-dozen khaki-clad, Polo-wearing, parted-just-right prep-school-haired clones.

The place is an ad for flat-screen monitors, stacked two, sometimes three high and as many wide. Flickering quotes, news tickers, instant messaging, and, I'm happy to note, more than a few Yahoo Fantasy Football screens. Everyone has phones but not many were being used. The contrast with the boisterous football-field-sized trading floor at Goldman Sachs is obvious. I'm surprised they don't have our Grumbys. Too much data, maybe. I have to check that out.

There is also a more serene, cerebral—OK, I'll say it, dullness—to what is being said. Just snippets of mumbling "stupid position," "keeps dropping," "catching a falling knife." From the sounds of it, it must not be a great morning for these guys. A pained voice comes from behind a stack of screens, "buy more." Click, grunt, shit, ugh.

I head to see the big cheese, the Roquefort Supremo. His name is on the door: A. G. Young. He probably keeps most of the fees for himself. Before I left, Lorita explained how this hedge fund thing works.

This guy has a serious nose for returns. Twenty percent plus numbers for quite some time and everyone is clamoring to get into his fund. I have no idea what his first name is. A. G. could be anything.

We meet at his desk. More like a NORAD battle station. Twenty-four-inch monitors, two high and four wide. A couple of square yards of display. It's great to be king. We move off to a conference room on the side. He mutters something about less distracting. No kidding.

Mr. Young starts babbling about his investment style. Long-short, arb, buy low, sell high. Yeah, whatever. I'm completely distracted by his eyes.

His eyes are a paradox—distant yet probing—blank yet darting—shallow yet brilliant—carefree yet caring—catatonic yet conniving. I can't think of any other way to describe it. It's as if he has no emotions at all but is using his eyes to suck the emotions out of me. I stare back until it hits me. Maybe this is the secret to his success.

We talk for a short while about everything and nothing. He grimaces a lot, as if constantly in pain.

"Grumby on the tape," I hear yelled from the pit.

"So, you must be making a killing this morning, what with all the click, grunt, shit, ughs going on." I tell him.

His eyes completely change, his coma ends, and he breaks into a big smile like I was a long lost friend.

"Funny," he says, like I got the joke. "When the plumbers are glum," he points out the glass wall, "that's how I know we are onto something big."

"How come you don't have any Grumbys?" I ask.

"Oh, we own a dozen or so. I won't let my traders use them, too easy. I need them to feel the market, touch it, chew on it, and then I read them to figure out which way it's headed."

"You know there's an app for that. Our Grumbys can figure out if . . ."

"Yeah, that's what scares me. Anyway, I have my tech guys taking it apart to see how you do it, and while they're at it, what kind of margins you really make."

"And?"

"You got some hot piece of shit going."

"Is that a good thing?" I laugh.

"You tell me."

"So, you wanted me to stop in. What can I tell you?"

"We've got a decent-sized synthetic position and . . ."

"Synthetic?"

"Long calls, short puts, and we have it somewhat hedged against a basket of tech names. Anyway, I'm trying to figure what to do with you."

"With the stock?"

"Nah, with you. You seem like some lucky schmuck that came up with a great idea at the right time and are just making it up as you go along."

He pauses and stares at me.

"Maybe I am."

"Maybe you are. Doesn't bother me. My job is to figure out if you've got a ten-plus-year run ahead of you or . . . ," he stops.

"Or?"

"Or are you going to blow this sucker up, smoking hole in the ground, face down in the pool, you know, go splatter on the sidewalk in front of a giant crowd."

"So what do you think?" I ask.

"What do you think?" he asks me right back.

"I have no plans to blow this sucker up."

"No one ever does. Sometimes you find yourself playing poker and someone else, maybe those Google boys, are playing chess. Sometimes it's hubris. Sometimes it's stupidity. Not that I really give a shit how it happens. My job is to get the direction right."

"We're on a 5-million-unit run rate; we have a 3.2 apps per unit take-up and that's been trending up; we invent about 1.6 apps per week; our BOM is dropping 5 percent a quarter; and we are about to move off of Amazon for our cloud to lower our costs by at least half."

"Cool."

"Did you know any of that?"

"No."

"Oh. Well now you do," I say.

"I want to know about you."

"Like what?"

"You still having fun?"

"Sure."

"You over your head?"

"A little."

"Do you feel invincible?"

"Some days."

"Are you?"

"We're pretty unique. It would take a lot of catching up."

"Does your past get in your way?"

My past? What does he know?

"What do you mean?"

"You know what I'm talking about?" A. G. asks and stares.

Is he bluffing? Those eyes are stone cold again. Sucking the life out of me.

"Uh, yeah, well, we all have a past. I got all that out of my system."

"We'll see, shan't we?"

"We shan."

A. G. continues to stare.

And then he breaks off eye contact and says, "Ah, you Silicon Valley types are all the same. My buddy Jack should have held onto more of the company. Dumb ass."

I snap my head around. Jack?

"OK," A. G. waves his hands as if telling me to shoo, "good enough. I don't want to waste your time. You have a company to run, I've got a fund to run, and the plumbers' mood has probably shifted, so let's keep in touch."

"Uh, OK, yeah, sure." I wonder if this guy knows everything and everyone.

"And one parting word of advice."

"Yes?" I'm intrigued.

"Don't listen to anyone on Wall Street. They're all scum."

"Noted."

On the elevator down to Park Avenue I wonder if he was talking about himself.

•   •   •

As I walk through the lobby on the way out, Richie and Jack are walking in.

Citi

"Yeah, we can help you get whatever cash you need. That's what we do."

This is my last stop before I head home. The Citi building, or center, whatever, looks like a giant white whistle and I'm sitting in a conference room near the top with a 360-degree view of the entire city of New York. Outstanding.

I am now sitting in the plushest leather chair I have ever been in, sitting across from the CEO, Vikrim something or other—hey, my first perk as a billionaire.

"I can't sell even a single share or I lose control," I explain.

"Well, you don't lose control. You just no longer have a majority of shares," Vikrim says.

"Same thing."

"Not really. We have clients who control huge companies and barely own 2 percent of the company. The Roberts family at Comcast. Immelt at GE. You can control it through the board and . . ."

"Look, it's not going to happen. I got burned early and swore I'd never lose control again."

"Hey, listen, it's your call. And thanks for coming to us instead of Goldman Sachs. We can lend you up to half."

"Half of what?"

"Half of what they're worth. You just pledge your shares as collateral. You never sell them—just borrow against them. The stock is forty-four, so that's five hundred something million. Not bad."

"And I still get to vote the shares?"

"Of course. Since you don't sell them, you have the vote, not us."

"You sure?"

"We do this all the time."

I stop talking and think. Makes sense.

"It takes five minutes. I'll have someone talk to your counsel and set it up. In the meantime, we can issue you a card that you can use today."

"A card?"

"Citigroup World MasterCard. Buy whatever you like."

"A credit card? I haven't had one of those for a while. Got turned down by a few."

"We noticed that. Not to worry. Your credit line is half."

"Half of . . ."

"Yes, yes, half of wherever your stock is trading. Quite simple. Enjoy."

"Do I get airline miles?"

Vikrim laughs. "Of course. American Airlines, OK?"

"OK," I reach over and shake his hand. "I'm in."

"Hey, one last thing. We have a group out by you, on Sand Hill Road . . ."

"I know it."

". . . that can help you with these kinds of things. It's nice to have a buffer between you and all the folks that will want to sell you stuff now that you're a . . ."

"OK. Set it up. Make sure they use a Grumby. I don't like dealing with people."

• • •

At the bottom of the elevator, I'm met by a young woman who has an envelope with my name on it. A stack of hundred dollar bills? That would be nice.

Instead, inside is a credit card—better than cash. On it is a white sticker containing an 800 number to call to activate the card. I'm familiar.

I call the 800 number.

"Please speak your name, address, and your mother's maiden name."

I do.

"Thank you, you are now authenticated via voice analysis and matching software. Merely speak a few words into the credit card terminal at the time of purchase to authenticate your transaction. No PIN is needed."

Cool. That's our code.

Central

1:08 p.m., September 21, Palo Alto

It's great to be back home. Like every morning after a cross-country flight, I sleep in, recharge the brain cells, and then hunt around for some caffeine to wake myself up good.

"Venti Mocha Double Latte Extra Hot No Whip, please."

The person behind me in line steps up to order and then turns to me and says, "Can we talk?"

The voice is familiar. "Who are you?"

"*Al Travis, Langley,*" my Grumby says into my in-yer-ear. In Al Travis's voice, of course. Good to see voice recognition and the RecordAll work like a charm. I really have stopped bothering remembering things and just rely on Grumby to tell me everything.

Meanwhile, Al reaches in his pocket and pulls out his wallet and carefully flashes a badge to me so no one else can see.

"Al Travis. Central Intelli—"

I don't even bother looking.

"Yeah, hey, Al. Nice to see you. Gotta get to DMV and register my car."

"Real funny. Just get your coffee and we can talk."

"You're not going to drag me into your Taurus for a ride around the Valley, are you?"

He looks confused. "I drive a Buick."

We sit down at one of the brown circular tables with a chessboard laid in the laminate. I'm not much of a chess player. I usually only think out one move at a time.

"We hear nice things about you from an insider at Mossad. Seems they want something from you too. You must have some juicy stuff." I could hear his sarcasm loud and clear. "Figured it was time to check back in."

"Glad to be juicy," I say in my own sarcastic tone.

"Well," he looks over both shoulders to make sure no one is listening, "we haven't needed you yet, so we just watch. But now we need your help."

"Uh-huh." I look away and pause and then look back. What did he just say? "Haven't needed us?" I ask.

Al Travis sits up sharply. "OK, look, we can get at On-Star anytime we like. A quick subpoena and we can listen to whomever we like. Well, as long as they drive a GM or Mercedes. That kinda limits our targets."

"I always wondered if those mikes were live."

"Yeah, if you turn them on. No big deal."

"I wonder if Richie can hack them?" I say a little too loudly.

"Not as easily as we thought," Al Travis shakes his head. "Plus, you've got a much bigger platform."

"Yeah, but we're not spies," I say.

"Oh, no? Coulda fooled me. You do to have a history of this stuff."

I turn red.

"Screw you. I already helped you guys."

"How's that?" Al Travis asks.

"You sure as hell know. I turned Richie in to you guys way back when."

Al Travis let out a belly laugh like I haven't heard in a long time.

Shaking his head, Al says, "You idiot. Richie was the one that turned you in."

"He wha?"

"You didn't know? Jeez. You were the one that covered your tracks. He set you up to take the fall as we closed in on him. He played dumb. You were the mastermind. He coughed you up. And you thought . . . ?"

"And here I've felt guilty all these years." All I can do is look down. I close my eyes trying to get what he just told me to sink in.

"It took you a lot of years, but it's actually true. You are the mastermind, maybe not back then, but certainly now," Al Travis nods his head.

I just sit there. Finally, "Look, our apps are set up to . . . ," I start.

"I know what they do—I'm intrigued by what they can do. We've taken quite a few apart. Listen, we've been trying to crack the cell phone for at least a decade. Turns out there's a series of laws and precedent that means we can't get it. The Patriot Act and the Supreme Court rule that we can only snoop foreigners and only with probable cause. It kinda sucks. Plus, the cell phone operators won't let us touch their networks without a court order. They worry about immunity. Yeah, sure, they helped the FBI nail O. J. Simpson as he rode around in his white Bronco. Big whoop."

"You just want to listen in?" I ask.

"But we need permission."

"And?" I squint my eyes and stare back at Agent Travis.

He just looks back.

"And I already have permission?" I ask.

"Yes, you do."

"Not explicit permission," I say.

"Are you kidding me? You have the ultimate permission. Everyone wants to use your silly little Grumby or phone code."

"Silly little . . ."

"Sorry, your highly valued productivity platform. Whatever.

You must keep all that stuff in storage to train the system for the next user and the next requests and . . ."

"Yeah, but I can't let you go sniffing through it."

"We can make your life quite difficult," Agent Travis threatens.

"Yeah? How's that?" I ask. "You going to threaten to audit my taxes or something?"

"Actually, that's not a bad idea," he smiles. "We have ways. You know that. What you don't want is us picking another horse. Right?"

"Another horse?" I ask. Who is he alluding to? Richie? Someone else? I was starting to think everyone is behind. Maybe not. I hope we haven't slowed down somehow.

"But someone else costs us time. You've got the setup and footprint we need. Just give us 30K of code and we're good."

"C'mon, you're asking me to . . ."

"Anyway," he interrupts, "we probably can just get what we need without your permission."

"By?"

"I can't tell you. But you know the answer. You cracked what were the tightest systems back in the day. Don't you think we could crack yours?"

"I doubt it."

"I wouldn't. Your old pal seems to think he can."

What has Richie been telling these guys about our setup? I don't think we're vulnerable, but if we are, Richie is probably the only one who could crack us open. He's already done it a few times. And then it occurs to me. My guilt over turning Richie in has just vanished in a flash. It's time to take Richie down.

Al Travis starts to get up." Here's my card. Let me know."

His card just had a phone number on it.

"Can't I just have your email?"

"Funny. We haven't had those since, well, you know."

Shopper

"You're my personal shopper?" I ask.

"At Citi, we prefer the title financial specialist," Mandy explains.

"Look, I'm just kidding. I really appreciate what you're doing for me. I'm still writing code and don't have time for this kind of stuff."

"My pleasure. I really enjoy what I do and whatever you need, I am available 24/7 and ca—"

"I'll lob in things I want via my Grumby. But when anyone approaches you, just tell your Grumby, and mine will grab the request and I can write some code to sort the requests based on my needs and desires and whatnot. I can even have it tell me in your voice. Maybe we'll even sell it as an app—arConspicousConsumption."

"The house in Atherton should close next week," says Mandy. "Dreyfus Properties has handled all the details on your end."

"Park Lane, right?"

"Two doors down from Jack," Mandy confirms.

"Excellent."

"Bigger house, but it does need some work, six months at the outside. Oh, yeah, and a bigger circular driveway. And I'm not there yet, but I'm close to hiring his housekeeper," she says.

"Terrific. This is going to be fun."

I don't need a house. I guess I can get used to it, though I'm loath to give up my apartment in Palo Alto.

· · ·

"Meeta, what the hell is that?"

It is the reddest thing I've ever seen.

"A 599 GTB Fiorano Ferrari," Meeta tells me.

"God damn, that's sweet."

"Pininfarina design; 6 liters; 620 ponies; 0 to 60 in 3.7; 448 foot-pounds of torque. F-1 super fast 6-speed sequential manual shifter."

"How many cup holders?"

"Uh, maybe none. But it does have a very special piece of technology, according to the salesman."

"Yes?"

"It has a built in chick-magnet."

"You might want to turn that off for now."

"I am still looking for the switch."

"Note to Mandy. Get me one of these in black. Use my MasterCard."

"*Seventy-three dollars and fourteen cents.*"

I've lost track what that even means.

arBias

"*Eighty-five dollars and seventy-seven cents.*" Meeta's Grumby grumbles.

"Meeta, show me something new."

"OK, watch this."

Meeta clicks away until I hear from his PC, "*Welcome Dittoheads. This is Rush Limbaugh coming from the nation's capital with upsetting news today. The Democrats are collaborating again with the Feminazis to ship specially made condoms with a presidential seal on them to foreign countries . . .*"

I look at Meeta and start to ask him what the hell is this, but he puts his finger to his lips for me to be quiet.

"*Dat boosheet!*" Meeta's Grumby rings out. That's the funniest thing I've heard in a while. In a deep, authoritative voice sounding quite like James Earl Jones, Meeta's Grumby explains, "*There is a bill to double the aid to a sub-Saharan Africa prophylactic distribution program.*"

Rush Limbaugh continues, "*Old Queen Bee Nancy gets herself into a lather over this. And all those long-haired, dope-smoking, maggot-infested, good-time rock 'n' roll plastic-banana FM-types and even some Jell-O-molds just nod along, figuring they owe her, even though her recently passed law legalizing grass has caused increased crime rates in inner cities. It just makes me sick.*"

"*Dat boosheet!*" I hear again from Meeta's Grumby. "*Inner city crime rates are dropping while white collar crimes are on the rise . . ."*

That's pretty cool.

"Meeta, what is this?"

"It's a very brand new Bias Detector."

"A what?" I ask. It's always something.

"We found this floating around and put much work into it. We learn that up to over half of all blogs are political and . . ."

"Dat boosheet! Twenty-seven point six percent of blogs are political," Meeta's Grumby says. Meeta clicks to turn it off.

". . . and keep a running stream of media falsehoods and biases. We set this up to listen and give true and false indicators when someone makes argument."

"It works."

"Someone back-tested it with newspaper archives. Media bias isn't hard to find. Newspapers have their fact checkers. It seems an American tradition on talk shows to just make things up."

Meeta clicks again.

"Welcome to National Public Radio. This is your host Melissa Block and this is All Things Considered. *Today's topic is medicine and the need for universal health care. As Michael Moore has pointed out, Cuba has a longer life expectancy than the United States . . ."*

"Dat boosheet! Cuba's life expectancy at birth is seventy-seven years. The U.S.'s is seventy-eight years."

". . . and almost every country in Europe has a longer life expectancy, even though they spend less than a third per capita. Our system is broken."

"Dat boosheet! Life expectancy statistics vary worldwide. Most countries don't count premature births or any infant deaths up to the age of six months, severely swaying their life expectancy statistics . . ."

"Meeta. This is the coolest thing I've ever seen."

"Dat boosheet!" Meeta mimics his Grumby. "You said that about the last app I showed you."

"Only one problem."

"What?"

"We couldn't ever sell this."

"Why not?"

"Who listens to the radio anymore?"

• • •

I call Mandy to make sure I get this straight.

"An apartment in North Dakota?"

"No. An apartment in the Dakota," Mandy replies.

"That's in?"

"Upper West Side of Manhattan. Mark David Chapman shot John Lennon there?"

"Creepy. Plus $52 million for a three-bedroom apartment?

"It's right next to Steve Jobs."

"I'll take it."

• • •

"*Ninety-two point fifty-six.*" I just shake my head. I look at the plasma counter, which I haven't checked in ages. It's over 5.2 million. Actually, it says 200,000 something. Meeta never figured we would sell over a million, so he only left room for six digits on the counter. We left it that way to remind us about stupid mistakes.

"Holy sh—" I start to say.

"*Sweet Lincoln's mullet,*" my Grumby interrupts.

• • •

"Yes, Jed?"

"Have you seen your stock?"

"No."

"It just broke a hundred!"

I start to do the mental math of what that means to my net worth and then stop. It's surreal.

"Our trading desk has been pretty active. Seems like there is some sort of feeding frenzy to get shares. A. G. Young buys every day. You know anything? Something new coming out, something you haven't told us?"

"No, just the usual cool stuff."

"Any new partners?"

"No."

"C'mon. Give me something. We work on information," Jed pleads.

"I'm considering buying Goldman Sachs."

"Funny. Surely something is happening. No way the stock just goes up."

"Did you know that the media is biased?" I ask.

"You just figuring this out?"

Rambos

3:14 p.m., October 5

M y Grumby started rattling. Mandy's voice came out of its speakers. I haven't used my cell phone in weeks.

"Hey, listen, I got an interesting phone call. The estate of Georgia Frontiere just called me."

"I have no idea who that is."

"She owns, or rather owned, the St. Louis Rams. They're looking for a buyer."

"Yeah, OK, I guess this sounds interesting. Though it's not on my conspicuous consumption list."

"Just came up. They want cash and quickly. The price is $800 million. Your stock just hit $138. You can afford it a few times over."

"Can I buy three teams?"

"Funny. Listen, you'd have to be approved by the other owners, but your money is good. I think they'd prefer you to Mark Cuban. Just promise to leave them in St. Louis."

"Weren't they the Los Angeles Rams?"

"Yes, at some point."

I pause to think. Why not?

"Can I use my credit card?"

"For $800 million. It would be the biggest transaction we've done. I'll check, but I don't see why not."

"Good. Just do it."

"*We're not great, we're just a bunch of guys from . . . ,*" my Grumby reminds me.

I know. I know.

Triumph is a Dog

1:25 a.m., October 8

"**O**utlet *shopping this weekend?*" my Grumby asks me.

"What the?" Did my Grumby just insult me? It sounds a bit like, who, Don Rickles?

"*You dressed for an opera or an operation?*"

I've got to check into this.

"Meeta?"

"*What's on your mind? If you'll forgive the overstatement,*" my Grumby says.

"Meeta, is this some sort of joke?"

"*That's funny, we've been . . .*"

"It's not funny at all."

"I mean I've heard from a few others that their Grumbys were getting a little, uh, uptight."

"Uptight?"

"No, that's not the word. Uppity."

"What?" I ask.

"Rude, obnoxious, foul."

"Meeta, why didn't you tell me this?"

"You seemed to be focused on other things?" Meeta says.

"Meeta! You've got to tell me everything," I snap.

"*And how about that haircut. Someone put a bowl over your head? I keed. I keed.*"

"Triumph," Meeta says confidently.

"Huh?"

"Triumph the Insult Comic Dog," Meeta explains.

"Oh, no."

"*On a scale of 1 to 10, what's your IQ?*" my Grumby asks.

"Is this another virus?" I ask Meeta.

"No way. We checked it out. Our system is still secure."

"What then?"

"Learning," Meeta explains.

"*Criticizing you is like booing at the Special Olympics,*" my Grumby adds. Was that a chuckle too?

"Learning what?"

"The longer you use your Grumby the more it learns about your personality and your likes and dislikes."

"I know that."

"Yeah, well, you and I have had these the longest, right?"

"Yeah. What are you saying?"

"I'm saying that over time, everyone loves to get insulted."

"*You've got the brain of a four-year-old . . . and the four-year-old was glad to get rid of it.*"

"Enough!"

"*I never forget a face, but in your case I'll make an exception.*"

I remember that line. I just can't place it.

"I don't get it," I say.

"I don't either. Seems that there have been many studies by behavioral psychologists that prove this."

"Prove what?"

"Prove that humans don't really desire love and affection," Meeta explains.

"C'mon, I don't believe that."

"*I say, I say, boy, you're as sharp as a sack full of wet mice.*"

Foghorn Leghorn? Jeez?

"Yes, it's quite true," Meeta says.

"Which means?" I ask Meeta.

"Which means that something is hardwired in humans to crave, well, to enjoy being insulted. The code in the Grumby verifies this."

"Verifies?"

"Well, I guess, personifies?"

"I don't believe you. Someone is screwing with us. Gotta be Richie."

"Maybe. Or maybe it's just our code," Meeta sighs.

Horsing Around

I haven't been in many clubs in my life. Sitting here at lunch kinda reminds me why. Jed, who insisted I take part in today's match, and I are the youngest people sitting in the room, by at least forty years. There is more henna hair dye in this place than at an AARP meeting.

The place has a slightly worn feeling to it, more like a well-used baseball mitt than a rundown hospital waiting room. The long wood bar is terrific and even at lunchtime is filled with men drinking highballs or whatever those brownish drinks are. A little early for me. As I look around, I can see why everyone wants to join this place.

"You know, Jed, I drive by this place all the time and I had no idea that it's big enough for a . . ."

"Yeah, the Circus Club is huge. With your stock at a hundy and a half, you're a shoo-in. There's no golf, but we make up for it with everything else. I've been a member for almost ten years and only recently got to play, so they are doing me a huge favor by letting you suit up and . . ."

"I do appreciate the invitation. But suiting up and . . ."

"It's easy. You lean over and whack away," Jed explains.

"Yeah, sounds really easy," I say facetiously.

"You need a little more culture."

"Well, I tried this on a Segway once."

"Yeah. There's some culture. C'mon. Finish your leafy green salad. It looks like you haven't touched it. Let's get moving."

We walk outside toward the outer fence where a series of trailers is set up with saddle horses tied up to them. Each horse is eating from a personal pile of hay. We walk past them into another trailer. The smell of horse is overwhelming.

"Here we go, try this on." Jed says, handing me white stretch pants and a red shirt with a thick white stripe cut diagonally across it.

"I look like the statue standing in front of some rich guy's house holding a lantern."

"That's the idea, except now, you're the rich guy," Jed laughs.

"Then can't I pay someone not to do this?"

"You have to do this," Jed says.

"Why?"

"To have something to talk about at cocktail parties."

"Can't I talk about writing code?"

"You could. Chicks dig that," Jed laughs.

"What else?" I ask.

"Here, put these on." Jed hands me boots that come up over my knee and a hard red helmet.

"I look like a dork," I complain.

"You always look like a dork. Now you look like a member of the sporting class."

"Class or ass?"

"For the most part, there's not much difference, I'm afraid."

Jed boosts me up and the next thing you know, I'm sitting five feet in the air on top of some beastly horse. He hands me some gloves and a polo mallet, a whistle blows, and all of a sudden I'm in the middle of a giant field at the Circus Club playing polo, or pretending to. My horse is excellent. I barely lift the reins and he, or maybe she—how can you tell—is off toward the ball. I swing and whiff about three times to much laughter. One guy keeps riding up right next to me and whacking me in the thighs with his mallet. Is that legal? Are there even any rules to this game?

I try to get my horse to swing around and chase him down so that I can whack him back. No dice. I end up going in circles. I straighten my horse out and notice someone charging straight at me. It's the same guy. I raise my sword, stick, mallet, whatever this thing is, and charge right back toward him like we're jousting. His helmet slides to the back of his head and I can only stare, bug-eyed, as Richie zips by and hits me square in the chest. Is this guy everywhere?

In pain, I spend the rest of the match galloping up and down the field trying not to look stupid.

It doesn't help. I feel like an idiot, like someone I'm not. It's not so much that I feel like a fish out of water; it's more like a donkey in a world of thoroughbreds, and the "sporting class" is having a good chuckle over it.

Is this the end game? Pretending to be someone you're not? I hope not.

It just takes my eye off the real prize. Distractions, especially Richie, just slow me down.

As the little pony-show game ends, I ride up next to Richie. With my biggest smile, I lean over and tell him in my calmest voice, "You're going down."

And that's it.

PART V

Pookie Arrives

11:42 a.m., October 13, Sunnyvale

It's good to be back at the office. And off the horsies.

The place is hopping. I'm feeling good about myself. Meeta must have the oxygen cranked again.

More importantly, I've been playing around with yet another piece of code to capture moods and do something with it. It's almost ready. The mood code in arBroker is nothing—almost quaint from an era gone by. This thing is kick-ass.

I notice six coders playing air hockey in an open area behind a set of desks. We haven't released it yet; we may never get it out. It's pretty cool, though. Think of floor hockey without sticks or a puck. You just move your arms to shoot a virtual puck. A jerry-rigged laser pointer sets up the goals, and the puck and players run around and swing away. No one has figured out how to call penalties for crosschecking, of which there are plenty.

"One hundred thirty-seven dollars and eighty-five cents."

That's weird. It's the first time in a long time I've heard our stock price actually going down.

Meeta walks over and plops a box down on my desk.

"Meeta, what's that?"

"It came in a package from New York."

"But what is it?" I ask.

He shrugs.

The box says Sony. Meeta opens it up and takes this small little device out. It's the size of a computer mouse. And it looks like it has tiny wheels all over it. And little glass holes. And it starts moving around Meeta's desk.

"*My name is Pookie,*" the device says.

"What the?" I ask.

"There's a note," Meeta notes.

"What does it say?" I ask.

"*From a friend,*" the Pookie says.

"Richie!"

I reach over to strangle the Pookie but Meeta stops me.

"*Thought you guys would get a kick out of one of these,*" the note reads. "*Sony has the first batch; Samsung and Lenovo are next. All free. All ad-based. Your biggest mistake.*"

"Mistake?" I start.

"*The world economy is built on ads. Say's law: supply makes its own demand. People want to be recommended, convinced, up-sold, super-sized. No one trusts his own judgment. No one admits it, but we subliminally love ads. Ads make us smarter, even cynical. We're conditioned like Pavlov's dogs to defer decisions until someone asks for the business. I'm going to make a killing and you're toast.*"

When I finish reading, the Pookie squeaks.

"*Ha!*" the Pookie then screams.

Meeta and I sit in silence.

"So, you think ads . . . ," Meeta starts.

"If so, we're the big losers," I grunt.

"*It's a town for losers. I'm pulling out of here to win,*" my Grumby sings.

The Pookie shuffles back and forth. "Thunder Road. *Bruce Springsteen. Would you be interested in buying the entire album or perhaps a live acoustic version?*"

I take a swing at the Pookie, trying to smash it. Meeta grabs my hand.

We sit in silence for a while.

"This thing is annoying," I finally say.

"And the voice . . . ," Meeta adds.

"And I hate upselling and ads and all that crap and . . ."

We sit in silence again.

Meeta breaks the silence. "Want to take apart the Pookie and see what they're doing?" he asks.

"Yup," I reply.

I pick up the Pookie and throw it high in the air, in an arch toward the guys playing air hockey. It doesn't quite make it, hits the floor. and breaks into a hundred little pieces.

"That's a start," Meeta laughs.

arBroke

W hy do I always forget? The intelligence is at the edge of the network, not in the middle. I don't know what people want; people know what people want. As I scanned Meeta's database of things that he tracks from Grumby users, one of the things that is almost always near the top of the list is the desire for the Grumby to make decisions.

Exposing one's desires is an interesting exercise, but making decisions is what everyone really wants. That's why life is so hard. Every minute of every day we are confronted with yet another decision. Which cereal do I eat? Which shampoo do I buy? Which call do I make first? Which store do I go to? Which car do I buy? And on and on. And almost every decision is second-guessed at the moment it is made. I bought Rice Krispies? Damn. I should have bought Fruit Loops. Self-confidence is a big problem. Maybe that's why all those people glom onto the Eckhart Tolle spirituality crap and daily affirmations—it takes away the second-guessing on decisions. Hell, a Grumby can do that!

I quickly write some code to do exactly that. arDecision. Grumby knows what your desires are. Now all we have to do is listen, and your Grumby can peruse your historic files and conversations and history and put it up against that database and make the decision for you.

I should have thought of this a long time ago. It really is what everyone wants.

That digital subconscious we have been dreaming about.

I hope it's not just a faster horse.

Decidedly So

"This is it, isn't it?"

I feel like the proud papa of the next greatest app.

"It's it," Meeta replies.

"If there is an it, this is it," I say.

"*It is what it is,*" my Grumby declares.

"OK, just release it into the wild, Meeta. On my count: 4-3-2-1."

"It's in the blocks," Meeta clicks. "It's open," click, "it's off." Meeta nods. "By the way—what is it?"

"The arDecision."

"Oh, yeah. Cool," Meeta nods.

I've thought about this for a long time. I can figure out your mood, your risk profile, what you have been thinking about for the last minute, your day, whatever. I can generate lists, a bit like Digg, except your personal list is derived from your own wants and desires. But no one is good at making decisions. Until now.

I turn to Meeta. "You have a list, right?"

"Sort of," Meeta shrugs.

"Of course you have a list. All the stuff you need. All the stuff you want. If we listen long enough, we can figure it out. New car? Right at the top. Home theater. Of course. Venti Mocha Double Latte Extra Hot No Whip? I'm jonesing for one right now. But do I get one right now? Wait? Never get one? How do you make those decisions?"

"Is this a loaded question?" Meeta asks.

"At $10, people will use arDecision to keep their virtual lists and to make decisions for them."

"Did you use it to decide if we should even have a decision app? You sure it's going to work?"

"Meeta. What hasn't worked? We get amazing uptake on everything we do. We need to keep putting out these apps, one a month at least, to keep this thing growing. I notice we keep hiring."

"Thirty-five hundred and growing," Meeta tells me.

Wow. I think all those financial lessons paid off. I can probably count on both hands, with a few fingers left over, the number of companies that can afford to hire thousands of programmers and put them to work on a task. And we're one of them. More and more of them are working on my market's code.

arDecision is a first cut. Eventually, we'll move this code into everything we do.

"Surgeon class?" I ask.

"Yes, although of late, they are not all from the best medical schools."

"How do we know if we need a thousand of them, or ten thousand?"

"I have no idea."

I raise my eyebrows. "Me neither."

More. Faster. I think I've figured out that this is not some race with an end to it. It's a permanent way of life. Deadlines are always just up ahead. I hope I have the conditioning.

"And what's the latest with Richie?"

Meeta walks me through the plan. Gambling, China, Swiss bank, credit cards. It's all there and quite elaborate. I would fall for it too.

Privacy

4:51 p.m., October 19

"Y ou've got a problem," Lorita informs me on the phone.

"Don't we all."

I assume Meeta told her about the Pookie.

I quickly add, "Hey, congrats. I hear you made partner."

"Thanks. Yeah, the investment committee just sold all our shares."

"Sold 'em?" I shout and then gather myself. I must sound disappointed.

"I think we made more on them than a year of lawyering. Should be a happy bonus time this year. But, anyway, I called you because you've got a problem," Lorita's voice gets serious.

"Look, I've got a lot of problems, not the least of which is pretending to know what I'm doing running a couple of thousand person company whose stock bounces around like a yo-yo on crack," I sigh.

"Yeah, well I'm not even sure what this means. We received a notice from the Commerce Department that . . ."

"In Washington?"

"Yes. Anyway, they sent a notice of multiple complaints of identity theft," Lorita says.

"Isn't that credit card fraud stuff?" I ask. I know a lot about credit cards.

"Of course, that's what I thought, too, but you guys don't deal with credit cards or commerce or anything like that?"

"Not really. Unless you count arBroker or . . ."

"Anyway, I made a few calls and what the complaints have to do with is literal identity theft."

"Huh?" I don't understand.

"Someone spent $42,000 using George Clooney's credit card. I guess their Grumby authenticated the purchases by speaking into the credit card swiper thingy."

"Uh, er, I thought we worked around that by shifting one of the frequency strings in the transform . . ."

"What does that even mean?" Lorita asks. "I thought you have safeguards for this stuff."

"We do. But either what we store in the cloud is too close to perfect, or someone is mucking with our code, or . . ."

"So is it a bug or another one of these malicious things?" Lorita asks.

"I don't know."

"I would find out." Lorita says as she hangs up.

"Meeta!" I yell.

•   •   •

"*You just sold 32,000 shares of Grumby Mogul Limted Company, Inc., symbol GRMB, at one hundred and thirty-three dollars and thirty-seven cents,*" my Grumby says a little too nonchalantly.

That's weird. Why is it selling?

I can't have that.

"Buy 32,000 shares of GRMB. Now!" I scream.

Meeta Hack

I walk over to Meeta's desk and there, strewn all over his desk, is what looks like the Pookie, or what once was the Pookie.

"What are you doing?"

"Fire with fire."

"Can you pull this off?"

"Some architectures seem to have more than one entrance, including many backdoors."

Huh?

Meeta stares at the Pookie and then at a string of code on his screen and then he looks up at me, with just the slightest of smiles. And he gives me a wink and swipes his finger across his nose. He's telling me something but doesn't want to say it out loud.

Then Meeta starts whistling the theme song from the movie *The Sting*.

"Robert Redford week on A&E," Meeta explains.

"You bet," I say cryptically. Meeta must know that Richie is listening.

"And then what?"

"Some people are sore losers. Oh, and I will dispose of this," he points to the Pookie, "as soon as I'm done."

Got it. Richie is spying on us through this Pookie. Does he think we are that stupid?

Changing the subject, I ask Meeta, "Any luck on the whole identity theft thing?"

"Not really. It's some bug. I don't think it's malicious."

"You're telling me it's a feature?" I ask.

"Not a very good feature."

"Whatever. We can't let this stuff get by us," I tell Meeta.

He shakes his head. "I'll get someone on it."

"We've got bigger problems."

"I notice the stock keeps going down," Meeta frowns.

"There was an op-ed in the *New York Times* this morning."

"Operation Ed?" Meeta asks.

"An editorial," I explain. "I read it, though didn't quite understand it all. Some dude from the IAPP complaining about . . ."

"The IPdaily?" Meeta laughs.

"Look, I've never heard of them before either. International Association of Privacy Professionals and . . ."

Meeta interrupts, "We need to start an association."

"Yeah, I'll get right on it. Listen, there seems to be some backlash on the mood app."

"arMood?"

"I thought we got it right. We can tell how everyone feels, their friends can know how they feel—it's the ultimate price signal and . . . ," I say excitedly.

"So what's the problem?" Meeta asks.

"It seems to creep out certain folks," I sigh.

"Creep out. Who wouldn't want to know how their friends feel?"

"Not everyone, apparently. They want it to be opt-in instead of opt-out," I explain.

"We can't opt. If we can't know everyone's mood, the whole thing doesn't work. It breaks down."

"Because . . . ," I start.

Meeta finishes my thought. "Because it's a network effect like everything else we do. Mood is relative."

"We may have to change it." It pains me to say these words. I can't stand it.

"Because some ass, I mean association, says so?" Meeta smiles.

"We'll put in some command to turn it off."

"We have that. All you have to do is say, 'I'm not in the mood.'"

"My Grumby tells me I'm in a bad mood," I complain. "Maybe I am."

"It's right. You should just get a daily affirmation." Meeta says and laughs.

"Don't . . . ," I start.

Too late. Stuart Smalley comes out of my Grumby, "*I deserve good things. I am entitled to my share of happiness. I refuse to beat myself up. I am an attractive person. I am fun to be with.*"

"That's not funny."

"Fig," Meeta says.

"Wha?"

"*Sometimes I just want to curl up and lay in bed all day and eat Fig Newtons.*"

Me, too, I think.

"OK, enough. Just put out some assurances that all moods are kept private, and we already have an opt-out feature built in and blah, blah, blah. Do something. Our stock is getting whacked on this stuff."

"*Ninety-eight dollars and sixty cents,*" my Grumby announces.

"Under $100. Toldja," Meeta says with a dejected tone.

• • •

"Jed, $98.60? What!" I practically scream.

"The identity thing will roll over. Don't sweat it," Jed tries to calm me down.

"That's fifty-something points that's missing in no time. Where did it go?" I ask.

"It didn't go anywhere. Maybe you never had it."

"I had it on paper. Can't you get Vinnie and that sales force to get people to buy the stock?" I ask.

"It's not that simple."

"The math kinda is. The George Clooney identity theft thing ain't worth forty points. The mighty Goldman Sachs must know something else."

"I'll do some checking," Jed promises.

He better. I just figured out that if the stock drops below around $60 I'm toast. I've been buying stuff through Citi on credit—that whole half thing. I haven't sold any shares, just borrowed money AGAINST my shares when it was $120 and $140. I talked to Mandy and she very cheerfully explained to me that if the stock dropped below $60, things start to unwind. Lovely!

•   •   •

It's time to shut Richie down before this gets out of hand. After figuring out how to remotely hack Richie's Pookie, Meeta destroyed our copy.

"Meeta!" I scream.

"The fix is in," Meeta says calmly.

"I don't want to know."

Meeta tells me anyway.

"I've got tons of voice fragments and have doctored the GPS code. Yuren set me up with his friend who took over his credit card factory. I set it up so a two-year-old would be able to find all those credit card numbers. Richie hacked it yesterday."

"And you've got the perfect bet?" I ask.

"Oh yeah, baby. Richie thinks USC's a lock over Ohio State. Six-point spread. He's putting millions down. But ain't gaw happen," Meeta says in a slightly ghetto dialect I haven't heard from him before.

"OK, OK. Don't tell me," I protest again.

"O-States's running back is returning to the lineup. But does Richie know that? Uh-uh, baby. And Richie also thinks USC's QB is coming off IR. Does he know about the high ankle strain he suffered in practice yesterday? Uh-uh, baby. But I do."

"So?"

"So, he's going all in. I've watched him steal tons of money out of that credit card network we dangled out there. Richie is convinced this game is a lock, a sure thing. Except . . ."

"Except?"

"Except it ain't. USC's gonna get whacked, baby." I don't know what Meeta has been watching. Dick Vitale?

"You sure this is going to work?" I ask.

Meeta just smiles.

Schmidt

I pull up ESPN.com. Ohio State 28, USC 7. Meeta is amazing. Richie is so toast.

If it went as planned, he's been scrounging around for some serious money to pay for his bet, or else he's got someone named Rocco.

Meeta already figured out the scam. Richie has been tapping into credit card payment companies and lifting active debit and credit card numbers. The problem is to turn that into cash. Yuren set up a dummy corporation in China to manufacture credit cards. Richie has already placed an order for thousands of cards with his stolen numbers on them. I think what happens next is that people just hit ATM machines with the cards and take out the maximum daily limit until fraud is reported. It could be days or weeks. Do it with enough cards and he can steal millions. Then it's just an anonymous phone call to Al Travis in Langley and . . .

•   •   •

The audio was crystal clear.

"*Do what you have to. Take away their air supply. Screw with their packets. This Grumby thing has gone from cute to a real pain in our ass.*

We've got twenty thousand programmers around here. Find some way to put a hitch in their gitalong."

No way. I didn't just hear that. TechCrunch has it on their site, but it's since been picked up by all the sites. Damn.

"Gitalong?" I ask.

Meeta shrugs.

"It does sound like him. Where is this from?" I ask.

"Mountain View."

"Goo—"

"Yes, the Googleplex," Meeta grins.

"You sure?" I ask.

"We GPS-encode everything."

"Can you narrow it down?"

"We have longitude, latitude, AND altitude. Top floor," Meeta tells me.

"His Nexus One?"

"Yup," Meeta says.

"What's the reaction?"

"Seems like the sites are saying the same thing. Lots of outrage against Google for being a big bad monopolist and rough tactics."

"Well, our stock is back over $100. We'll take all the help we can get."

"So you're welcome," Meeta declares and then bows.

"You sent TechCrunch the clip?" I ask.

"I took a leak," Meeta says.

"Wha?"

"Uh, it was a leakage?"

"Meeta, we can't just listen to private conversations."

"I just did. His Grumby tweets what he is doing and the Nexus One phone feeds our network cloud. It's easy to filter conversations concerning us and . . . ," Meeta starts.

"Meeta, I know we *can* do it, but we *can't* do it."

"That doesn't make sense."

"Leaking it?"

"Sorry. They are being evil."

"But listening to them being evil, isn't that more evil?"

"No. Plus our stock is . . ."

"It's not about the stock. If this gets out, no one will ever use our stuff again," I say, raising my voice more than I want to.

"I would. I long ago gave up memorizing anything. I just ask and my Grumby whispers in my ear."

"Meeta!"

"What?"

"Keep me informed."

"*You just sold 22,000 shares of Grumby, symbol GRMB, at $102 per share.*"

. . .

It takes all of an hour. The blog Silicon Alley Insider has it first. They wonder how it is possible that this audio even exists. Either someone at Google recorded it, or it is not a huge leap of faith to think that we did it. We are the ones with the most to lose if Google gets nasty, and we do record conversations from Grumbys and from lots of different cell phones, so ipso facto it must be coming from inside Grumby.

The stock is down twenty points to $81. Ouch. I guess it really doesn't matter if it was us or not.

. . .

"Lorita. Give me something. The stock is close to $80 in the wrong direction—it hasn't been this low in, what, a couple of months. Something's wrong."

"Is it? Things still selling?" Lorita asks.

"Yeah, sure. We still can't make them fast enough."

"This privacy thing is pretty ugly," she states the obvious.

"We haven't seen usage change one bit. It's actually going up. Probably a bunch of people didn't know we could record everything."

"What's the last app you released?" Lorita asks.

"arDecision."

"Oh, yeah. I like that one. Used it to pick what I wore today. I think the stiletto heels are a bit over the top but . . ."

"OK, OK, back to our stock," I interrupt.

"Did you ask Jed?"

"He's worthless," I whine. "Wall Street seems to be full of ideas and not a fact to be found."

"Stocks trade to confuse the most amount of investors, and . . . ," Lorita starts.

"I'm certainly confused."

"Just be careful. It's fear of the unknown that undoes mortal men."

"Who said that? Shakespeare?"

"Takeout," Lorita explains.

"Huh?"

"My fortune cookie. I really do live a sad existence," Lorita sighs.

Shorts

Once again, I find myself back on the phone with Jed trying to figure what the heck is going on.

"What's a Third Point?" I ask.

"It's a hedge fund." Jed tells me.

"Like A. G. Young?"

"Well, similar. They like to take big positions and then work them," Jed explains.

"And they sold our stock?" I ask.

"They're short."

"See, that makes no sense," I complain.

"They borrow shares from someone else and then sell them."

"Can I borrow them too?" I ask.

"You could, more likely they borrowed yours."

"From me?"

"From Citigroup," Jed explains.

"But I own them."

"Sure, but you pledge them as collateral and Citi can lend them to someone else."

"Huh?" I say.

"As far as we can tell, you've got a bunch of these shorts swarming around. Greenlight, ThirdPoint, Kingsford, . . ."

"Charcoal? Well, at least we have A. G. Young on our side. Last I checked they owned a huge chunk of our stock."

"Well, uh," Jed stutters.

"Young is short too?"

"'fraid so."

"And that's why our stock is heading toward seventy?" I ask.

"Probably."

"But why? So they sell our stock, so what? Someone else is buying it. Right?" I ask.

"Maybe. It just makes things uncomfortable. They like to stir up the pot. Plant stories with reporters. Whisper to anyone that listens that you're a piece of crap, borderline criminal, have sex with animals. Whatever it takes."

"Is that legal?" I ask.

"First Amendment."

"And what can I do?" I ask. I've got a million questions rattling around my brain.

"Just get the stock going up," Jed tells me.

"How do we do that?"

"Just keep selling more stuff," Jed says and hangs up.

•　　•　　•

The YouTube video is short. And funny. Though I shouldn't be laughing.

It looks like a college kid is sitting in his dorm with a Grumby, working on homework maybe?

A man's voice comes out of the Grumby.

"You've got a Teflon brain. Nothing sticks!"

"Shut up," the kid says to the Grumby.

"Yeah, you're so ugly you make a mule back away from an oat bin."

The student starts looking around like it was some sort of joke.

I love these CollegeHumor.com setups.

"*You're so ugly,*" the Grumby says, "*when you were born, the doctor slapped your mother.*" Rodney Dangerfield. Even I know that one.

I laugh. So does the kid in the video.

• • •

"*Seventy-two dollars and fourteen cents.*" Like I need my Grumby to remind me that I'm getting flushed away.

It's time to get some of my old pals to start buying the stock.

"Jeannie, it's been a long time."

"Hey, nice to hear from you. And thanks for those antique mech-toys you sent. I didn't have those. Where did you find them?"

I don't want to tell him I had Meeta do a search through our network for someone selling the same type of mechanical toys we saw at Jeannie's place at Cap d'Antibes. Meeta came through.

"I have my sources," I say.

"Well, I love them," Jeannie gushes.

"Listen, we've been through a lot together," I say.

"Yes, of course. I have much to thank you for."

"No thanks needed. You were so important to our success," I remind him.

"Success. You have a blockbuster."

"Anyway, we've got some shorts sniffing around, and I want to try to keep the selling to a minimum and . . ."

"No selling from me. I already sold the whole lot at a hundred and ten. Needed the money to do a refurb on my watercraft. You wouldn't believe the upkeep on that thing." Jeannie complains.

"Nice sell. The stock's around $70," I state the obvious.

"My Swiss bankers suggested it. They hate stocks. Prefer I was just in government bonds."

"Uh-huh. Yeah. Got to get me one of those big yachts someday. OK, well, thanks. See you out on the Mediterranean when you least expect it."

"Au revoir," Jeannie signs off.

I Swear

One last call before the spotlights turn on.

"I don't understand why this is coming out now," I whine to Lorita.

"Why didn't you tell me?" she asks.

"No upside."

"But you can't lie on all those legal documents."

"It's a joke."

"Not funny."

"University Closest to the L—"

"Yeah, you told me. UCLA. University Closest to the Lompoc Area. Ha. Ha. Now you've got a PR nightmare on your hands. Your stock is going down and now it's tough to build back credibility with investors."

"What about all the next set of apps? Can't we focus everyone on those?"

"Good luck. You've got shorts circling and your stock is $65. They are going to make hay with this."

"It's not that big a deal. Lots of guys never went to college. Gates, Jobs, Zuckerberg . . ."

"But they didn't lie about it."

"UCLA could stand for anything."

"Not in SEC filings."

"All right. I get it. I screwed up. I'll admit my mistake on our Web site and move on."

"Anything else you haven't told me?"

"Like hacking Al Gore's email?"

"Ha. Yeah, like that. Now that would be a shock."

She still doesn't know.

"Yeah, I'll be honest from here on out."

"I hope it's not too late," Lorita sighs.

"It's the dawn of a new day."

"Yeah, right."

· · ·

This is one place I never expected to be. I've entered large buildings with Greek columns and never came out the same. I'm nervous, to say the least. I wonder if my Grumby can pick up on nervous. Gotta work on that.

"Good morning. I'd ask those who are standing in the back to show courtesy to the people who stood in line to be here and sit down. Everybody is welcome here who's here. But I would expect all those who aren't in here for the hearing to respect the rights of everybody who's here and to not stand and block those who are trying to watch the proceedings and have a right to be here."

I hear some shuffling behind me, but I'm too nervous to turn around.

"Would you please stand and raise your right hand."

I think he's talking to me. I stand.

"Do you solemnly swear that the testimony you will give at this time will be the truth, the whole truth, and nothing but the truth so help you God?"

"I do," I answer.

"I should note before you start that there will be a series of votes around ten twenty and I'll consult with the other senators how best to continue during that time. At most, we will try to limit the break."

"I understand, Mr. Chairman."

"Go ahead."

"Thank you, Mr. Chairman."

Lorita whispers in my ear "Let them ask the questions. You just answer. And honestly, you're under oath."

Meeta looks over at me with a worried look on his face. He gets up and heads out, mouthing the word "bathroom."

"I've called this special meeting of the Senate Subcommittee on Interstate Commerce to talk about privacy concerns. As you know, privacy is one of the bedrock foundations of our founding principles of this great country, a constitutional right that goes back to the time of the Pilgrims."

My Grumby is tucked into my bag, but I can still hear it say a muffled, "*Dat boosheet!*"

I look around to see if anyone notices. There are a half a dozen photographers in front of my table snapping photos of the senators, most of whom are talking to their aides behind them as the chairman babbles away. Behind me are at least a dozen TV cameras. I can make out a few of them: CNN, Fox, CNBC, MTV. Matt Lauer and an NBC producer are motioning me as if to say they want to interview me when the hearing is over. This is going out far and wide.

"We have gotten reports of intellectual trespassing. We hear about identity theft. We are concerned over the supposed media bias inherent in networked electronic computing devices . . ."

It's clear he is reading off of index cards in front of him. I scan the gallery for anyone I know. Jed Tedford is there to cheer me on. Sitting in the front row about six or seven seats down is another familiar face, Al Travis, the CIA guy. He smiles at me, a rather toothy smile. Was this his doing? On the other side of the room I notice A. G. Young, the hedge fund guy. He smiles at me as well. Very mysterious dude. Still don't know what A. G. stands for.

". . . unchecked power of Silicon Valley to mold the political leanings of the general population at its will. That type of power is not explicitly provided to third parties in the Constitution and is a power inherently residing with Congress and the legislative branch."

Meeta comes back in and hands me a folded piece of paper.

"Now, before we delve into the ability of your cloudy computers to bypass privacy controls and undermine the democratic process, I'd first like to focus on some personal attributes to help set the credibility of the witness."

The chairman takes a deep breath.

"First, I'd like to congratulate you and your company on its success. We are all in awe of the power of the entrepreneur in America. Silicon Valley is an important and deep well of resources for everyone in this room."

The other senators nod their heads.

"Thank you, Mr. Chairman. In . . ."

"But I need to ask you some important questions."

"Thank you, Mr. Chairman. In response to your claims of undermining . . ."

"Can you please describe your background?"

"Thank you, Mr. Chairman. Well, I started programming back in high school, learning how to write code by . . ."

"And do you have any formal training?"

"The best training is experience. Trial and error, really. Write some code. Try it . . ."

"It says in your S-1 filing with the Security and Exchange Commission that you attended UCLA."

"It does say that."

"Did you indeed attend UCLA? And remember, you're under oath."

"Well, not exactly."

"Is that a yes or no?"

"No," I admit dejectedly.

"OK, now let's talk about your early years writing code. It appears that you had a habit of logging into government systems for your own gain."

Meeta motions to the folded piece of paper. I shake him off.

"Thank you, Mr. Chairman. One of the best ways to learn about computers is to understand how others use them. Visiting the Web site of the Department of Motor Vehicles is invaluable to the learning process."

"Learning indeed. You were quite the student. We have reports of a ban on your usage based on cracking codes in the highest reaches of government and reading emails of none other than . . ."

I look over my shoulder and Al Travis is grinning even wider.

"Thank you, Mr. Chairman," I interrupt.

Meeta is clucking and tsking and I can tell he's about to explode.

"But perhaps the most egregious abuse of power reported . . ."

This has got to stop.

". . . comes from the news . . ."

Meeta starts pounding on the table pointing to the folded piece of paper.

". . . of a violation of basic human rights laid out in our Constitution . . ."

I crack open the paper Meeta gave me and read it out of the corner of my eye. Along the top it reads "Chairman—voice match—archives" and then a list of words and phrases.

I look over again at Al Travis and he is about to jump out of his seat.

". . . of an international g—"

Before the senator can say gambling, from right under Meeta's chair as loud as can be, I hear, "*ten hut!*"

I look over, as does just about everyone in the room. Meeta has a sheepish looking grin on his face and his left hand is tightly holding his right hand under the table. I know exactly what just happened. I hold back my laughter so hard I can feel tears forming in my eyes.

I reach under the table and grab Meeta's Grumby and proudly plop it right in front of me.

"Mr. Chairman. May I please respond?" I jump in.

"Yes, but make it brief. We have so much more to cover."

"I have already apologized for the oversight on disclosing my educational background. I do believe that in this country anyone can succeed, even those without degrees from elite universities. Would you agree?"

"Well, yes, of course. We are a land of opportunity."

Meeta, his composure restored, keeps tapping the table and pointing to the paper I'm holding. After another quick glance at the paper filled with dates and hotel room numbers and amounts to escort services, I turn to Meeta and whisper, "I can't do it."

"You have to," he whispers back.

Embarrassing a U.S. senator about compromising situations is probably not the way to solve one's problems. But I must admit having searchable GPS-encoded voice records is quite something. I bet Meeta could find something embarrassing on everyone in this room. But if we start down that road . . .

Al Travis is glaring. He's the one that set up this hearing. He wants me to open up our network so that the Feds can snoop on all of us. If I give in, then he owns me. Instead, I realize the right thing to do is take the beating.

"I came from nothing with the help of a lot of very smart people from this country and around the world. We have built the most amazing system. Office workers are more productive. People are getting smarter. I think we have launched a new way of inter-facing with computers, making them work for us rather than us working for them."

"But that doesn't excuse the . . . ," the Chairman tries to start.

"Like any company going from nothing to something at great speed, we probably had some lapses in our controls. Today, I pledge up to $100 million in research funds into securing our network cloud from any outside influences to insure our users' privacy."

I give a quick glance over to Al Travis and give the subtlest of smirks. I also hold up Meeta's piece of paper and slightly nod my head toward the chairman. Al Travis knows it's over, that there's no way I'm giving in. My reputation is down the drain already. I started from nothing; I can end with nothing. This is who I am. What do I care? The race is over—for now, anyway. I've got to save the company first. Actually, with all the things going wrong, we haven't been racing for a while now. Just cleaning up the crap behind the horse.

"Mr. Chairman. Is it true that you have been receiving donations and favors from many of our competitors?"

"That's preposterous. I take favors from no one."

"*Dat boosheet!*" Meeta's Grumby wails. The crowd breaks out in laughter.

"Was there a meeting at the Mayflower Hotel with . . ."

"I've never been to the Mayflower Hotel in my life and . . ."

"*Dat boosheet!*"

"Room 871, I believe?"

I follow Al Travis's eyes as he looks over to the chairman and subtly shakes his head.

"OK, that's enough," the chairman interrupts. "I declare a one-hour recess in these hearings." And with that he stands up and heads out of the hearing room. Reporters in the room accost me, but Lorita grabs my arm and drags me out of the room, telling me in no uncertain terms not to say a word.

Stung

Oh shit, that's a picture of Richie on the front page of the *Wall Street Journal*.

Arrest in Epic Cyber Swindle

A twenty-eight-year-old American, believed by prosecutors to be one of the nation's cyber crime kingpins, was indicted Monday along with two Chinese accomplices on charges that they carried out the largest hacking and identity-theft caper in U.S. history.

Federal prosecutors alleged the three masterminded a global scheme to steal data from more than 130 million credit and debit cards by hacking into the computer systems of five major companies, including Jewel supermarkets, 7-Eleven, and Crossland Payment Systems, Inc., a credit card processing company.

The indictment in federal district court in New Jersey marks the latest and largest in at least five years of crime that has brought its alleged orchestrator, Ricardo Ibanez, of Miami, Florida, in and out of federal grasp. Detained in 2003, Mr. Ibanez was briefly an informant to the Secret Service before he allegedly returned to commit even bolder crimes.

Agent Al Travis said Mr. Ibanez was the ringleader of a

data breach that siphoned off more than 40 million credit card numbers from Target and others in recent years, costing the parent company about $200 million.

Ricardo Ibanez? What the heck. That's Richie. And $200 million? Jeez Louise. He must have been up to his eyeballs in debt. Tough to break your legs when you're behind bars. Tough to mess with our Grumbys too. Win-win.

"*Al Travis, Langley*," my Grumby informs me.

"I'm reading it right now."

"Wanted to thank you," Al says.

"We didn't do anything," I say sheepishly.

"Look, Richie is a thief. He hurt a lot of people. You were one of them, but we were never going to get him for hacking your network. We needed to nail him stealing money."

"Two hundred million?" I ask.

"That was just a start. He had hooks into every bank. JP Morgan was pulling money from every bank they could and was close to shutting down any transfers out of cash."

"But how did . . . ?"

"Look, he hacked you for us. I knew everything you guys were doing. I watched Meeta hack him for you. Nice sting, by the way."

"So you knew exactly where to look?"

"We would have eventually. You just helped us cut a few corners."

"I'm going to close your backdoor, you know."

"Good luck with that. But thanks. You're a real patriot. My guess is that in another two weeks, with all the cash Richie was pulling out of so many banks, you would have seen the entire banking system shut off their ATMs. You should feel good about this."

"Then why is it that I feel like an idiot," I start to whine.

"You'll get over it," Al says, and hangs up.

Rebound

Richie's gone.

Finally.

That's gotta mean clear sailing for us. And just like that, our stock is heading back up.

"One hundred and four dollars and fifty-nine cents."

Richie has been such a big pain in our butts: sicking the swear-asaurus on us and working with Jack the VC and the hedge fund dude to short our stock and fund the Pookie. And maybe he did all the insult and wrong answer stuff too.

We've got millions of Grumbys out there and code on tens if not hundreds of millions of cell phones and at least a couple of million or so Oakleys running around. No one else is close. The Pookie is a joke. Google and Apple have been fighting over smartphones and completely missed the personal assistant market we pioneered.

It's about time we see a rebound.

I'm in a great mood.

I can tell—my Grumby keeps buying our stock.

I notice the stock market has been heading up as well—rising 1,200 points last week. Up 600 points yesterday. Another 550 points today. It's at an all-time high. Dow 16,000. Shares traded on arBroker have never been higher—I think we're 25 percent of the New York Stock Exchange's volume.

Everybody seems to be in a good mood.

Doctor Doctor

4:47 p.m., December 9, Palo Alto

As I head to a meeting, I really think about it.

The last three weeks felt like three years. I have been walking on air. All the time.

Having been all caught up in the Richie nonsense, I never really stopped and looked around at what was going on in Grumby world. It's almost as if a Grumby cult has arisen. There are Grumby blogs. Grumby parties. Politicians started citing Grumbys on policy. It was really quite stunning.

And it was great to be back in the office and just work on cool new stuff.

Best of all? No Richie to worry about. No fear of being hacked. No looking over our shoulders.

Every day we'd hire another dozen coders.

Every day our stock went up a couple of points.

Every day I felt better and better that we were building the most important thing ever invented.

There's been so many things that held us down, but now it looks like things are finally coming around.

"There ain't no stopping us now."

Oops. Did I just say that out loud?

"*McFadden and Whitehead, 1979 disco hit,*" my Grumby reminds me.

• • •

"So it just sits in a room like this. No one's here?" I ask.

"That's it. You walk in off the street and get started. Could be anywhere. One candy striper or even a cashier can reload the disposables after each visit."

I'm sitting in a somewhat stark room at Stanford Hospital. Lots of equipment is attached to the wall and on carts in the room. I'm talking to my friend Mark, who has been hounding me for more Grumbys to play with. What a doctor wants with all that technology, I have no idea. Don't they just bang your knee with a rubber hammer?

Mark explains that he got a pile of money from Cisco, the networking company that has had an effort to create doctorless clinics over the last five years with not much traction until Mark suggested a Grumby.

"Hey, it looks just like Meredith Grey—*Grey's Anatomy*, right? The TV show?" I ask. It's a stunning replica, catlike eyes, medium-length brownish hair, everything down to the funny smirk.

"We argued back and forth whether to use her or some old TV doctor, Dr. Kildare, or someone, but it became clear that no one over about age thirty-five would use this thing, so we went young."

"Can I try it?" I ask.

"Sure. It's an early model but ought to work pretty well. Just say hello and introduce yourself."

I look Meredith Grumby in the eye and say hello.

And in Meredith Grey's voice, the Grumby says, "*Well, it's about time you showed up. We don't have any information on you. Let's get going.*"

"OK."

"*Good. Now strip down to your skivvies.*"

"Um," I look at Mark, "is this part of the program?"

"*I'm a doctor. Grow up.*" Meredith scolds me.

"OK. OK." I strip quickly.

Mark laughs and whispers, "It's a power thing."

"Wow, is that a roll of quarters or are you just . . . OK, I'm kidding. But I do need some personal information."

I don't have time to respond before Meredith starts barking questions.

"Address."

I answer.

"Phone."

"Email."

"Health insurance number."

"Birthday."

"Parents' names."

"Their birth dates."

"Siblings."

"I assume I have your permission to look up your family medical history?"

"Sure."

"OK, great. Beats filling out forms, doesn't it? Now grab that blood pressure device and wrap it around your upper arm."

Mark whispers to me, "Grab the stethoscope instead, just for fun."

I grab a stethoscope attached to a wire coming from the wall and put it up to my heart.

"That's not the blood pressure monitor. You need to watch a little more TV. It's that one over there, labeled blood pressure. Jeez, another Einstein," Meredith berates.

I obey.

"A little high. Looks like we'll be sucking out some of your blood in a moment. Meanwhile, stick that cone-looking thing in your ear, will ya?" she says with a chuckle.

Over the next few minutes, I use the stethoscope, a tongue depressor with a little mini-camera attached to it, get weighed, have my height read, all seemingly entered into a database.

"A little overweight there, aren't you fella? Lay off the cheese doodles, or I'll get you on some unbearable no beer or martini diet. That won't be fun."

"Well, I missed a couple of weeks of basketball and . . ."

"Yeah, whatever. OK, now bend over, grab your ankles, and say yee-ha."

"Huh?" I'm confused.

"You want me to check you for an enlarged prostate?"

"Uh . . ."

"Just shove that instrument over there up your . . ."

"Not today," I beg.

"Suit yourself. I'm going to keep bugging you until you do it," Meredith says sternly.

"Fair enough."

"OK, now step over to the wall and wrap that white loop around you."

On the far side of the room is a C-shaped device about three feet off the ground attached to the wall onto what looks like two sets of tracks. The device is on a swivel and open at the moment. I stand between the tracks and close the C around me.

"OK, now move it to about where your heart is."

I slide the device up from around my waist to mid-chest.

"OK, I can hear your heart beat. That'll do. Take a deep breath and don't move—done. OK, you just had your heart scanned. I'll run it through a detection system and see if you have any nasty plaque in there. Now move the scanner up, so the bottom is just about at your throat."

I comply.

"Good. Another deep breath—done. We'll check your carotid artery too. Want a commemorative DVD of your insides?"

"Sure," I say as I step out of the scanner.

"Good. Now stick your finger in that hole in the front of the scanner."

I do it. I feel a sharp sting on my finger.

"Ow. Mother—"

"Now, now. That didn't hurt so bad, did it? We'll run a few pro-teomic tests on your blood and check for various cancers and such, see if your cholesterol is low enough for me to give you the OK to eat steak, and I've got a few more optional tests you can do before I let you on your way . . ."

"Yeah, I don't think so. I'm really just here for a demo and . . ."

"You really want me to harass you, I take it. OK, I can be pretty annoying."

"Got that right," I mutter.

"I heard that. No matter, comes with the job. I'll email you results and a profile this afternoon and have you back here in six months or so."

"Thank you," I say.

"No, thank you. And thanks for letting me save your life."

•   •   •

"I'm impressed."

"Thanks. We have some tweaking to do. Probably too sassy."

"Or maybe not enough. I almost want to go back for more," I admit.

"Yeah, we get a lot of that. Cisco is hoping to roll this out nationwide. They've got lots of clinics interested. Same with hospitals. They want people used to coming through their door rather than a doctor's office. That way they get the revenue from scans and blood tests and maybe even prescriptions. We're checking some of the legal stuff to make sure."

"Awesome."

"We may approach pharma companies to sponsor all this, just for the ability to inform patients about their drugs at the point of sale."

"That's not a conflict?" I ask.

"Less so than with real doctors."

I let that one go. I have no idea. I'm so used to thinking of my silly Grumby as a sidekick, my personal entertainment. This stuff blows me away. But it's still just a chunk of electronics.

Something else is bothering me and then it hits me.

"And what if I had some medical problem," I wonder out loud.

"Well, this is just a first screen. If something comes up positive, we immediately connect someone at this hospital, or maybe a call center in Mumbai, and a real doctor can get on live and look in your ear, in real time, to see if you really do have an infection and maybe prescribe amoxicillin and have it delivered to the room."

"And this is a big enough . . ."

"Just in this country we can probably set up a few hundred thousand in pharmacies and even at corporations. International? Millions. Really.

"And they'll sit down with Meredith?"

"That show is syndicated around the world. You'd be surprised how many people would like to drop their pants in front of her."

"Uh . . ."

"So to speak," Mark quickly adds.

"But I've gotta tell you what I'm most interested in doing is drop shipping these into Burma and the Sudan and Zimbabwe and the Congo and Western China . . ."

I started feeling lightheaded. I sit down in a chair.

Mark keeps babbling on. "There are so many places with no doctors, and this is the cheapest way to scale the knowledge of doctors into . . ."

I stop listening. This is what I've been dreaming about. Getting some piece of code to do things that haven't been done before. Simple. Touches individuals. Yet does so much.

And so obvious, once you see it. But, but . . .

Bleed

10:29 a.m., December 12, Sunnyvale

"Meeta?"

"Yes, your excellency?"

"What do we have going today?" I ask.

"Absolutely nothing."

"I love it."

"I plan on spending the whole day playing with every new app that we have," Meeta says. "I find it very strange that we are ever wrong. I mean bad fashion advice is one thing, but wrong answers . . ."

"Yup. Something is going on. It can't be that hard to find. One of our algorithms or some bug buried deep."

"They're not bugs; they're features," Meeta laughs.

"Not this time. Something's screwy."

"Let's do them, one by one," Meeta gets serious.

"OK. Starting with?"

"arDecision."

He loads it up.

Instantly we hear, "*Must have donut*" coming from Meeta's Grumby in a pitch-perfect Homer Simpson.

"I do want a donut," Meeta admits.

"Of course you do. It's ten thirty. Even I know that."

"*Don't you dare eat that donut!*" Meeta's Grumby demands in a woman's voice.

Huh? Is that Meredith Grey? Meeta must have arDoctor running too. Maybe that's a feature. It's as if our apps are bleeding into each other.

· · ·

We spend the rest of the day loading and unloading apps to see what happens. I focus on insults. Meeta works on bad answers.

What I really want to do is repeat the insults coming from Triumph the Insult Comic Dog. The insults are funny, but not everyone sees it that way. We didn't design in insults; they just happen.

I finally figure it out.

"Meeta, it seems to me like the insults come when you load both arFashion and the arFirmation apps.

"How did you . . ."

"I'm a coder. I just got rid of every app and loaded them one at a time. The insults went away until I loaded those two together and . . ."

"You think the fashion insults leak over to the . . . ?"

"I don't think anymore. I'm absolutely sure they do."

"Yikes. You think the conversation engine crosses the inputs, and . . . ," Meeta starts.

"I have no idea. We only test these apps on their own. We never thought to test them all together and . . ."

"Just that testing is really ugly," Meeta tells me.

I pause and think.

"Meeta, can we tweak the code to get rid of this?"

"We can turn off the entire learning cycle. But, well, then we're not left with much. That would break most of the apps. We use it in everything."

"Then?"

"Then we just wait for it to relearn."

"And how long?"

"How long has it been?"

"You mean that long? From the beginning?"

"It has to learn what not to learn from you and me and every-body else."

"No one is that patient."

I throw up my hands.

"*The higher a monkey climbs the more you see of its behind,*" my Grumby says. Is it talking about me?

.   .   .

"Daaammn!" Meeta exclaims. Meeta is starting to scare me with his lingo du jour.

"What?"

"It's not even getting baseball trivia right anymore."

"How can that be?" I ask. "I mean we can't give wrong answers. Who was our sixteenth president? What is a dangerous cholesterol level? How many electrons in cobalt? We can't get any of these wrong."

"It's as if the database of answers is somehow corrupt," Meeta thinks out loud.

"But why? Did we change anything?" I ask.

"No."

"But?"

"But what? We get some wrong answers," Meeta sighs.

"It's not just some wrong answers. It's basic stuff. Facts."

"User-generated interpretations of factual concepts," Meeta corrects me.

"Meeta, I get the insult thing—human nature being strange and all that—but facts are facts."

"Are they?" Meeta asks. "Is there some absolute truth?"

"What is this, Deepak Chopra? A fact is a fact."

"Yeah, but we always rely on our users to decide what facts are."

"Not any one of them," I snap, "all of them."

"And maybe people are stupid."

"But not all of them."

"When we first started sending out Stump the Machine to the masses, we got a lot of facts for our database," Meeta says.

"It beat typing all that in," I say, "remember?"

"Yes, but this was from early adopters. Maybe ten thousand, a hundred thousand."

"So?" I ask.

"So, early adopters are self-selectors. Smart people. At least tech smart. Maybe they didn't represent the average person."

"Again, so what?" I ask.

"So as we went to millions and millions, maybe the average smartness has been dropping."

"But that shouldn't change the . . ."

"We don't weigh results by intelligence; we just assume the masses are smart enough to get the right answer and . . ."

"Meeta. Are you suggesting our whole premise is flawed?"

"I might be."

"That every time we add another user, that person is probably not as smart as the combined intelligence that we already have and that . . . ," I say.

We both pause. And then Meeta blurts out, "the bigger we get the stupider we become."

"Because . . ."

"Because we aggregate," Meeta continues. "It's not the wisdom of the crowds. Any networked system is only as smart as the average intelligence of its users. Because the outliers are overrun by those in the middle."

That's it, I think. That must be why it's making mistakes.

"But I thought those studies show we are helping improve the intelligence of people using our system," I say.

"Sure, but that's intelligence measured away from our system."

"You mean . . ."

"I think I mean that people are getting smarter because we offload basic recall functions but that as we add the marginal user, our entire system is getting . . ."

"Less smart?" I ask.

"Dumber."

"And that whole fabric of networked subconscious?"

"Oh, it's still a fabric. Just not a very bright one."

"Oh shit."

"*Shitake mushrooms*," my Grumby says.

"Yes, oh shit," Meeta agrees.

"*Shitake mushrooms*," Meeta's Grumby says.

"If we're just figuring this out, I can't believe anyone else knows yet."

"Maybe individuals are smart and crowds are morons."

Not maybe.

O no

Now something really feels wrong.

It's not just our stock, which is headed down in blips and blops off its high of $200. I just get this sense that our momentum has died. Something's just not right. We're not growing as fast as we used to. Uptake on software sales ain't what it used to be. Returns are running higher than they ever used to be.

Is it saturation? Fatigue? Did Richie do lasting damage to our reputation?

Or is it something else? The dumb answer thing? Bad decisions? I wish I knew.

Meeta comes running over to my desk almost out of breath. "Did you see O?"

"O?"

"O. The show."

"Are you OK?"

"No. O the show."

"Show the show," I demand.

Meeta clicks and up comes a YouTube.

"*Today on* Oprah"—oh, the show!—"*My Grumby made me marry a loser.*"

"What the?" I start.

"*So, tell me what happened,*" Oprah asks her guest.

"*I rely on my Grumby for everything. I take it on dates, have it listen to every conversation, and it knew me better than I knew myself.*"

Uh-oh.

"*Go on.*"

"*Well, I had several men interested in me and I couldn't really decide, so I asked my Grumby which one I should marry.*"

"*Like a Magic 8 Ball?*" Oprah asks.

"*Yes. That's it. Anyway, Grumby picked. He's cute and all, and we flew to Vegas, got married, and then after we got back I found out he's forty-seven, not thirty-two, lives at home with his mom, hasn't worked since he was laid off by Pets.com, and now he just plays* Call of Duty *all day.*"

"*So why . . .*"

"*My Grumby told me to do it.*"

"*Is the Grumby a threat to our lives? Does anyone think for themselves anymore? After a word from our sponsors . . .*"

"Turn it off."

"The YouTube clip? It's over."

"No. arDecisions. Kill it."

"But . . ."

"FAIL," I shout. "Actually, EPIC FAIL. The whole dumb thing has infected everything. We're not getting smarter—we're getting stupiderer."

"Stupiderer?" Meeta asks. "Is that even a word?"

"See?" I scream.

"I can kill arDecision very easily but . . ."

"But what?" I ask.

"We can't just turn it off; we used the mood code and the decision code in just about everything. We'd almost have to shut down the whole thing, and we can't do that because . . ."

"Because?" I ask.

"It's almost Sunday?" Meeta says sheepishly. Ah, yes, Meeta's got a little action this Sunday.

But he's right. We can't just shut the whole thing down. Too many people rely on Grumby in their everyday lives.

But something's definitely wrong. Our stock is $105 again, and dropping.

Market Panic

"*S*ixty-three dollars and three cents."

Damn. Our stock is getting killed. What the hell is going on?

And then the voice coming out of my Grumby is Erin Burnett's from CNBC. That's strange enough. She's talking as if the Armageddon just hit Wall Street.

"*I've never seen anything like this. We've now broken past Dow 10,000, down over 900 points. We are going to pull up a chart right now. Talk about capitulation. Here is Proctor and Gamble's stock off fifteen points in the last five minutes of trading, down 25 percent. A few minutes ago, that stock was down 2 percent. This is an unprecedented thing. Nothing has changed for Proctor and Gamble in the last four minutes, nothing.*"

Uh-oh. I wonder if . . .

"*AT&T shares are bid at $10. No check that; it's bid at 10 cents a share. Something very unprecedented is going on in the market. That this can happen is an absolutely stupendous story . . .*"

"Meeta!" I scream.

"Yes, boss."

"*. . . look at this—Grumby shares were close to $90 not half an hour ago and are now trading at $22. There are either large sellers liquidating their portfolios or . . .*"

"Is there . . ."

"arBroker seems to be experiencing increasing volumes today."

"Meeta?"

"Yes."

"What do you mean?"

"I think many, many people are in a bad mood."

"Meeta?"

"We are doing over half the volume of the stock market today. Almost all selling."

We probably have 50 million active users by now. Grumbys and iPhones and Nokia phones and of course Oakley glasses. I haven't checked how many of them are using arBroker, but it must be gobs of them. Whether it was the bad decisions or some glum mood that affected them, the sell orders started. And now that I think about it, the selling must have put more people in bad moods and that fired off more sell orders. It is Armageddon.

"Do you think . . . ," Meeta starts.

"Yes, I do think arBroker is sensing people's bad moods and firing off sells. Selling stock of anything that they can think of."

"It sounds like in everything they can think of."

"And we should . . . ," Meeta starts.

"Right now. Kill arBroker. Shut it off completely."

"And the other apps?"

"They're bleeding into each other. Just like arFashion and arInsult. It's as if the Grumby can't walk and chew gum at the same time."

I pause. I hate to do this but . . .

"Meeta, if an app has mood code in it, kill it. Fire a bullet."

"I think you mean drive a stake through its heart," Meeta corrects me.

"*You broke my heart, Fredo. You broke my heart. Leave the gun, take the cannolis,*" my Grumby adds.

Slowing

The stock market panic subsides as soon as Meeta turns off arBroker. We put out a press release saying we are disgusted with the volatility of the stock market and to protect our users we decide to turn off arBroker until normal market conditions occur. But it's only a matter of time before the world figures out it was a suddenly sad-sack set of Grumby users—and some questionable code—that caused the panic.

I don't need any more bad news. The congressional hearing was certainly no prize for the company. Even with Richie out of the way, and the bounce after the market panic, our stock is flirting with $50 and heading in the wrong direction. It can't go any lower. What else could go wrong? My credit line with Citigroup is shredded, Mandy tells me, and if the stock goes any lower . . .

Before I can tell my Grumby to remind me to call her later today, I hear Yuren's voice say, "*Pick up, it's important.*"

"Yes, Yuren. Tell me some good news."

"It's sunny in Shanghai today."

"That's it?"

"You know how rare that is?"

"I need a little sunshine myself," I sigh.

"Yeah, well, the reason I'm calling is we've caught up with shipments."

"That is good news."

"Well, it depends how you look at it. My managers are quite proud to get rid of the backlog of orders, but we don't seem to have enough to replace them."

"What are you talking about?"

"You're not seeing it?"

"Seeing what?"

"The slowdown."

"The only thing going down is our stock."

"Yeah, well, the growth rate has certainly slowed over the last month, but now we are just seeing a trickle of orders. Any news?"

"No. Nothing besides privacy concerns and my sordid personal background broadcast worldwide and our decision and broker app going haywire and our stock price doing a round trip and . . ."

"You think that's it?"

"I don't know. You got anything else?"

"Some rumors flying around here, but China is always full of rumors. Almost none of them are ever true."

"Look, I think we can turn this around," I say. "We haven't done a hardware refresh in a while. I'll have Meeta launch a design effort; we gotta have a dozen new apps getting crunched on around here just waiting to launch. And that's worked every other time."

"I hope so. I keep getting approached to manufacture solar panels like every other factory here, but I'm a bit attached to your Grumbys and to what you're doing, so . . ."

"I'm a bit attached too. Like the pig and the chicken at break-fast, I'm committed," I say.

"I prefer Cap'n Crunch," says Yuren.

"Me too. It's a metaphor," I explain.

"I know."

"Look, Yuren, keep me posted on orders. We're a level or two removed from the front lines. Everyone has been lying to us to get more units, but now that you've caught up, I want to be able to know exact demand. You'll know more than any of our partners—that they'll admit, anyway."

"Hang in there," Yuren tells me.

"I'm hanging all right."

. . .

"Yes, Mandy. Better be good news."

"You need to sell something."

"More Grumbys?"

"I suppose. But something big. Your stock is $45. You can only borrow half of your net worth."

"But that's still over a billion something."

"Was. But, yeah, you borrowed at higher prices and right now your credit line is overextended, and you need to sell something soon, like in the next three days, or we'll issue more margin calls, basically transferring your stock to us. I'm sure our trading desk will just sell it as fast as they can, which means it will go down more and you'll have more margin calls and . . ."

"Is that what you mean by a margin call?"

"You can only borrow against half of your holdings. If your holdings go down in value by more than half, you have to make up the difference—raise cash. Either sell shares or sell something else."

"Well, I don't want to sell shares," I say. "Sell whatever you can of what I bought. I don't use any of it, anyway."

"Like?"

"You pick."

"Do you need to own an NFL franchise?"

"Do they still broadcast games on TV?"

"Yes."

"Good. Sell it. And whatever else you need to."

•   •   •

Over the next week, our stock dropped and dropped and dropped. My guess was that Citi dumped my shares and every time they sold it, it went lower and triggered another margin call.

They towed the Ferrari away. My home in Atherton, which I never even moved into by the way, got foreclosed. I heard a hedge fund guy had bought my apartment at the Dakota. I wouldn't ask—afraid that it was A. G. Young.

I deleted the stock price announcer app from my Grumby. Last I heard it was $18.

I now knew what it felt like to be in a freefall.

•   •   •

With time to think, I kept swirling around in my head: What went wrong? What did us in?

We had been getting reports of bad advice. *Oprah* was just the last straw.

I suppose that was inevitable. Maybe we'd been moving too fast. RecordAll took in everything our Grumby owners did. Recorded every conversation, audio and video. Based on parsing the speech to text and tagging it with face recognition and GPS-location codes, we had a pretty good idea of everything people liked and disliked. Using loose market clues, arDecision helped sort those likes and dislikes into something actionable: a list of wants and desires. We all have them—the Grumby just helped to bring them to the surface. But then what? It was all about decisions. Everyone kept asking their Grumbys what to do. A Grumby coould answer every damned trivia question but not the important things in life—what should I do now, which dress should I wear, which restaurant should I go to, who should I talk to at a cocktail party, should I take this job, or wait for a better one. The algorithm was pretty simple because the answer was in the data from RecordAll. It's not artificial intelligence; it's inferred intelligence. The Grumby had become our eyes and ears and knew us better than we knew ourselves. Decisions were as simple as weighting the possible answers against the list of wants and desires, and, voilà, the optimal answer popped out. Or it should have, anyway.

So why were people complaining about bad decisions? Even with arDecision, we really didn't make the decisions for them. It was their own decision-making process. It just got made faster because the Grumby had all the information. But people would have made the same stupid decisions without a Grumby.

Yes, the intelligence was at the edge of the network, but inevitably it had to be a real brain, not an algorithm, that used that intelligence to make decisions. An expensive lesson to be learned. Technology, for all its benefits, was no substitute for people's own judgment.

So, it wasn't Richie. It wasn't cursing. It wasn't privacy. It wasn't competition from the Pookie. It wasn't my bogus background. It wasn't short sellers. It wasn't insults. It was—me. I had tried to create something that could know me better than I knew me, and, well, I didn't know me all that well, it turned out.

Marginalized

"Lorita, we just hit $12. That's where we did the IPO," I say trying to hide my desperation.

"I notice. You OK?" she asks.

"No, I'm not OK. Citigroup has taken almost all of my shares. They're calling it the mother of all margin calls. Can you believe it? And I still owe them something like $100 million." I think I owed Visa something like fifty grand way back when. Life has certainly scaled.

"I don't want to lecture you on the dangers of leverage and . . ."

"I don't need financial advice. I need you to find someone to buy this thing. Keep the race going."

"Well, we've had interest in the past. But I doubt . . ."

"Try them all: Jobs at Apple, Zuckerberg at Facebook, Microsoft, Oracle, Murdoch, anyone. We've got to place this thing in a safe place and re-engineer some of the flaws."

"I'll try. Distress sales never go well."

"Do we have a choice?"

"Not really. Let me make some calls," Lorita says, and hangs up.

• • •

This place is like a ghost town. Maybe fifty of us sitting around trying to pretend there's nothing wrong. A bunch of the early crew exercised options and is long gone. Gone back home is my guess. You can live like a king in Estonia on 10,000 shares of Grumby Mogul Limited Company, Inc. I heard about fast cars and trips around the world.

The rest got options for 10,000, between $50 and $200, meaning they're way underwater. Our stock would have to go back to the stratosphere before any of them make a penny. I can't blame them for flying the coop.

I wish I were anywhere but here right now.

I still can't figure it out. Things are slowing, sure. My credibility is ripped to shreds and twisting in the wind. OK, fair enough. The size and types of errors the Grumbys spit out are a bit high. And the more you use our code the higher the likelihood you'll wake up to a tirade of insults, and good ones at that. Plus, experts say, you'll secretly enjoy it, or at least someone will enjoy watching you get insulted. But our stock is in single digits. The investment blogs make fun of our hat-sized stock—7, 6 ½—yeah, real funny.

I try to rally who's left to tweak the code to at least get rid of the insults and work on the error rates.

Lorita calls.

"I got turned down from everyone," she tells me.

"Of course," I say.

"Too much liability risk."

"Risk?"

"Shareholder suits. Defamation suits."

"From the insults, I guess."

"Plus, they all think your stock is going to zero and they can buy it out of bankruptcy."

"Is it?" I ask.

"Could," she says.

"Why do you say that?"

"Did you see it? The cover of this week's *Business Week* has a Grumby being flushed down a toilet with the words 'Going to Zero?'" Lorita explains.

"Great. Though I thought *Business Week* was kinda like the curse of showing up on the cover of *Sports Illustrated*." I hang up.

•   •   •

"And this is why everyone's left?" Meeta asks holding up a copy of *Business Week*.

"Yup," I grunt again.

"Is this it?" Meeta asks.

"If there is an 'it,' this is it," I say matter of factly.

Meeta and I both laugh.

"You think we weren't up to it?" Meeta asks.

"Hey," I immediately correct him. "No regrets. You ever have regrets about anything, you'd never try."

"*Named must your fear be before banish it you can,*" someone's Grumby says. Yoda always comes through in the clutch.

We laugh again.

"Well, it was a heck of a run," Meeta says.

"Fun, anyway," I add.

"I was just a coder looking for something interesting to do," Meeta says.

"I just liked to hack gadgets," I say.

"And you did," Meeta says.

"We did good."

"Pissed off a lot of people," Meeta laughs. "Pissied them off, actually."

"Yup" is all I can say.

"Worth every second." Meeta continues.

"Yup."

EPILOGUE

Live Another Day

"**Y**ou think this will work?" Meeta asks.

"Everything is centralized. It shouldn't be hard to defeat if we have enough users."

"And the 'more is dumber' problem we had?"

"We turn it around," I say. "Like we always have."

For some bizarre reason, I miss the race.

"I don't understand."

"We just get people to admit they don't know what they're talking about and pay them to admit it."

"That's either brilliant or the stupidest thing I've ever heard," Meeta laughs.

"See, it works. You just admitted you don't know," I say.

"So we just create a market of ideas?" Meeta asks.

"Something like that. We'll just put a price on everything. Those in the know basically pay the people who don't know to quit screwing up the database. I've been thinking about this for a long time, since visiting the exchange and bopping those dopey traders on the head with Grumbys."

"So it's a market with feedback?" Meeta asks.

"It's a market, but everyone sets the price of everything every day."

"I'm confused," Meeta admits. I don't hear that very often.

"Me too. We just have to try it. Won't cost much. It's all peer to peer. And we keep everything local, and I mean everything. So there's no security risk, no sniffing at what people are doing. Completely adaptive—learns as it goes. It's a social network, sure, but really from each individual. You want to know what someone thinks about something, you make a bid."

"You mean like 'want to know what I'm interested in buying?'"

"Yeah," I say. "But this time, you can't have it by watching my Web surfing or listening to my conversations. Not for free anyway. Make me a bid. Pay me enough and I'll tell you. No decisions without a value attached. Decisions have consequences. And make your own damned decisions."

"I like it. Simple. Scalable. Sassy," Meeta says.

"Sassy?" I say with as much dripping sarcasm as I can muster.

"Couldn't think of another word."

"Work on it," I say. "I have no interest in another epic fail."

"*Failure is simply the opportunity to begin again, this time more intelligently.*"

"Who said that?" I ask my Grumby.

"*Henry Ford, circa 1927.*"

"No more faster horses," I say to Meeta.

I think this is now the right way of doing this. Take it all in. Augment people with total recall and a market system to help them weigh decisions. Technology is a tool, not the end all. People are going to make bad decisions, with or without technology. Let's make the tools smart enough to help, not to decide.

I still have my dream. Some of it happened quickly. And some . . .

This mess is just some kind of mid-course correction. Maybe I'm delusional, but who cares. I'm not giving up. It's better if others are cranking out new types of hardware. We can harness those too. We'll get another company built with even better surgeon-class coders on board.

At the end of the day, it was the structure of our system that got us in trouble. It was rigid. People paid for apps but not much else. Big mistake. Now we've got to make it adaptive, make it learn on the fly, even add money to the list of inputs. Not just be certain that the apps are good enough to pay for but also be sure that all the information out there gets some price tag associated with it. Not ads, which I still hate by the way, but some price tag so that we can know how sure or how committed all those individuals really are. You can't get rid of money; you just have to figure out how to harness it to do what you want to do. In many ways, "Knowledge is Good," indeed.

"Can I ask you something?"

"Sure."

"How much to do this right?" Meeta asks.

"Probably five million bucks."

"How are you going to afford to create all this stuff? You and I can't do it alone," Meeta sighs.

"So you think no one is going to give us any money?" I laugh.

"I wouldn't."

"I have a secret stash," I whisper.

"You do? I thought you were broke. And in debt."

"I am," I admit.

"So?"

"So I just got my last statement from Citigroup."

"Uh-huh?"

"I got to keep the miles." I tell him.

"What miles?"

"I got miles whenever I bought something. I've got something like a billion American Airline miles," I say.

"So we can fly where we . . ."

"Even at a penny a mile that's . . . ," I start.

"Enough to fund Grumby 2.0?" Meeta asks.

"You in?" I ask him back.

"Uh," he pauses.

"What?" I ask.

"Can I be CEO this time?"

Acknowledgments

I'd like to thank Richard Vigilante for all of his help in getting this book out into the wild. He not only is publishing this book, but has also provided outstanding advice on how to structure it, and, ultimately, how to end it. My friend George Gilder read one of its first versions and insisted it be published, getting Richard involved. I'd also like to thank Paul D. McCarthy of McCarthy Creative for coaching me as I was writing it and faithfully warning me how hard fiction writing actually is. Marion Maneker, who published all of my earlier books, extended me several favors by reading early drafts and providing encouragement to keep going. One of my favorite authors, Neal Stephenson, gave me an assuring nod and smile as I described the book while we chatted inside the Googleplex, and I told him it was about "creating another one of these." And thanks to Susie Block who was nice enough to send each of our boys his very own Furby and inspiring this tale.

Sometimes things are decades in the making. I originally wrote a short piece named "Furboy" about an entrepreneur who shoves a Game Boy inside a Furby and great things happen. Pam Alexander provided several suggestions of publications that might be interested, including Slate.com. She forwarded the piece to Michael Kinsley who forwarded it to Jack Shafer. I got an email a day later from Jack that started, "This is shit . . ." *Ouch*, I thought, until I read the next few words which said ". . . my pants funny!" and Slate.com ran it as four pieces over four weeks in May of 2000.

I was too scared to put my name on it, so it ran under the name Jonas Grumby. Years earlier, my friend Tim McGhee correctly answered a bar-based trivia game with that same name. Look it up.

I'd like to thank Aaron Crayford for providing a lot of the insight into early stage startups and also thank everyone I've ever worked with on Wall Street for the colorful view of bankers and traders.

As with most fiction, each of the characters and situations is somehow, someway, based on real-life people and situations. If you recognize yourself, I am deeply sorry. Now get over it.

Most importantly, I'd like to thank my wife Nancy and my boys Kyle, Kurt, Ryan, and Brett for their love and patience as I put this book together. I couldn't have done it without them.

Andy Kessler